PRAISE FOR
# CHILDREN OF THE FLYING CITY

"An arch, omniscient narrative—by turns brutal and sweet—unspools into an ambitious, wide-ranging story of survival and loyalty."
— *PUBLISHERS WEEKLY*

"Perfect for anyone who loves action and mystery
and cliffhanger endings."
— *SLC*

"Sheehan crafts a richly detailed world and uses
multiple points of view to relate the narrative, keeping
the characters central to the high-stakes plot. Following in the
tradition of Kenneth Oppel's *Airborn* and Philip Reeve's *Fever Crumb*,
this fantasy, about close friendships and the power of fighting for
what's right, will hook readers seeking adventure."
— *BOOKLIST*

"Richly imagined and emotionally resonant,
*Children of the Flying City* is a fantasy for young and old alike.
At times evoking the starkness of Cormac McCarthy and the dark,
humanistic fantasy of Stephen King, Sheehan will make your
imagination soar, tear your heart back to the ground, dust you off,
then send you back to the sky with a grin on your face.
This book gave my heart wings."
— *PIERCE BROWN, #1 BESTSELLING AUTHOR OF RED RISING*

"*Children of the Flying City* feels, at once, timeless and
wondrously, gloriously new. Jason Sheehan has crafted
the bones of a great story, the prickling flesh of unforgettable
characters, the gasp of gorgeous language, and he's tucked
a velvety, multi-chambered secret at the book's center."
— *KATIE WILLIAMS, AUTHOR OF TELL THE MACHINE GOODNIGHT*

# CHILDREN OF THE FLYING CITY

## BY JASON SHEEHAN

DUTTON CHILDREN'S BOOKS

**DUTTON CHILDREN'S BOOKS**
An imprint of Penguin Random House LLC, New York

First published in the United States of America by Dutton Children's Books,
an imprint of Penguin Random House LLC, 2022
First paperback edition published 2023

Visit us online at PenguinRandomHouse.com.

THE LIBRARY OF CONGRESS CATALOG IN PUBLICATION DATA IS AVAILABLE

Printed in the United States of America

ISBN 9780593109533

1st Printing

LSCH
Edited by Julie Strauss-Gabel
Design by Anna Booth
Text set in Plantin MT Pro

*For every kid out there who was told by the world
they were nothing special and decided to prove the world wrong*

# CHILDREN OF THE FLYING CITY

# ✦

# ON A DARK NIGHT, YEARS AGO

✦

**THIS THE ONE?** *asks the man in the hood.*

*Yes, says my father.*

*You sure? Don't have any others lying around?*

*This is the one.*

*Just that he seems kind of small . . .*

This is how he imagines it happening. Sometimes, if he's feeling particularly good about himself, or particularly bad, he imagines it in other ways. But mostly, it's like this.

*In the dark, the man looks down at me. Rain drips from his hood. He reaches out as if to touch me, then thinks better of it and pulls his hand back.*

*He's a good boy, says my father. Strong. Smart. He'll serve you well.*

*Says you, says the man.*

*He's my boy, says my father. I know him.*

Sometimes the boy imagines his father as a king in hiding who sent him away for his own safety. Sometimes the boy imagines him a loving man in a bad situation who sent him away for his own good.

In his imagination, the boy gives his father riches. Nobility. A kind heart. Sometimes the benefit of wisdom that he can't yet understand. But he understands a lot, this boy. He knows things and things and things.

*He'll do, says the man.*
   *Yes, says my father.*
   *Your payment, says the man.*

There is the clink of coins changing hands. Depending on how the boy is feeling, sometimes it's many coins. Sometimes few.

*You'll take him now? asks my father.*
   *Yes.*
   *Can I have a minute with him?*

And that is where the boy's imagining stops. Some things, they hurt too bad even for pretending. He doesn't want to think about the last time his father saw him. The last things he might've said. A last touch, in the dark while the boy slept.

He doesn't remember the night, so he has to imagine it. He can remember his father a little. He's pretty sure he has it mostly right, but can't say for sure. It was dark. He was sleeping. He was five years old.

And the boy never saw his father again.

# THE FIRST DAY
# OF SUMMER

✦

## HIGHGATE, THE FLYING CITY

# GO!

**THE BOY SURVIVED,** as boys sometimes do. For years, on and off the streets. He did many things, saw many things, suffered many things. A few of them left scars, and a lot of them made for good stories, but we don't have time for any of those right now.

Because right now it is later. Years. And the boy—twelve now, almost thirteen—squats, fingers gripping the crumbling concrete between his too-small shoes, on the low wall at the edge of a roof six stories up. He's watching the cops scramble up the creaking fire escape and counting down the time until their arrival.

He says, "Ten seconds, Jules," and flexes his toes inside his shoes, ready to run, to jump, to fly if he needs to.

Jules says, "I know."

"And I'm being generous."

"I *know*."

Jules is big and strong and just a little bit older than the boy. They've found the door they need to go through. One they'd scouted the night before and the night before that. On those nights, there was no lock. Now there is. Because that's just the way life works: things only go wrong when it really matters.

Mouse looks past Jules as he pulls at the lock and rams his shoulder into the door. She says the boy's name, and he glances back at her and smiles quickly, as if to tell her not to worry. Not about any little thing ever. He pulls up the scarf he wears over his head, covers his mouth and nose, smothering that smile. But Mouse knows it's still there.

The cops are upset. Yelling up the fire escape at the boy crouched there watching them. They're angry at being made to run and climb and jump. If they make it to the roof, they won't be wagging their fingers and scolding the boy and his friends. The police will break their bones with lead-weighted clubs and then throw their bodies off the roof to smash on the pavement below.

*Slipped while fleeing.* All three of them.

*Tragic.* Of course.

The boy is fine with this. He understands the rules and plays by them, too. He'd been up on the roof by himself before all this. Had brought his wrenches and loosened all the rusted bolts that secured the top of the fire escape to the roof. Two seconds of work and one good shove—that's all it'll take to send the whole thing crashing down. He has the wrench in his hand right now. Has already adjusted the bit so it will fit neatly over the heads of the two bolts.

"Five seconds."

"I know," says Jules. "Mouse, my tools."

Mouse hands him a chunk of rock from the roof, a little stub of twisted rebar sticking out one side. Like a hammer.

Jules weighs it in his hand. He says, "Nice," then lifts it, swings, hits the lock. Hits it again. And again. And on the fourth try it works, but he smashes his finger a little, tears off the nail. It hurts, and he drops the rock hammer and tears spring to his eyes and he wants to stick the finger in his mouth and suck on it, but he doesn't. Because he would never.

The lock is broken. He hits the door with his shoulder and it scrapes open. He calls to the boy, voice sharp and loud with pain.

Mouse goes down the stairs first, leaping an entire flight, the ragged scrap of a shawl she wears billowing out behind her like stone-colored wings. She lands on one foot, one knee, one hand, looks back through dust and darkness.

Jules waits for the boy.

The boy walks.

The first policeman's hand touches the lip of wall around the roof.

The boy asks, "You ready?"

"Course," says Jules.

"Then what are we waiting for?"

"After you."

"No, you first. I insist."

Then they laugh. They both go through the door, push it closed. Jules pulls two wooden wedges out of a pocket and shoves them under the door. Chocks. He hammers them in with the palm of one hand, then kicks each one for good measure.

And then they run, all three of them—down a flight and another flight, feet going *slapslapslapskidslap* on the old steps, hands skimming the loose, rusted railings for balance. They're careful not to trip over the garbage strewn in the stairwell, the mounds of rags and blankets that might be people sleeping.

The closed door and the chocks won't hold the police. Not for very long. But that isn't the point. It isn't meant to *stop* them. The boy and his friends only need a few extra seconds.

Three floors down, they tumble. Laughing. Harder to stop than it is to keep running, and they end up in a pile.

The boy says, "Door," and Jules bangs on it twice with his fist.

It opens a few inches.

Three floors up, someone kicks the other door that Jules had wedged closed . . .

"Wait," says the boy.

. . . and kicks the door again—a huge, booming sound . . .

Jules says, "Gods, they're so slow."

"Grown-ups," Mouse says, and shrugs.

. . . and kicks the door a third time. This time it bangs open, squealing and scraping and hitting the wall with a crash.

The boy says, "Go! Go! Go!"

Jules and Mouse squeeze through the narrow gap. Three floors below the police, the boy waits, taut like a rubber band. Waits, quivering, until he sees the first cop face looking over the rail, down into the stairwell. They lock eyes. The cop shouts cop-ish things down at him.

The boy grins behind his scarf. Ducks through the door and pushes it closed.

Keelan is waiting on the other side. He sneezes. "They see you?"

"Yup."

"Okay, then."

And Keelan is already doing like they'd practiced. He fits the hook into the ring the boy had screwed into the wall days ago. Slips a loop of strong wire around the knob. People are looking at them. It's almost dawn now. The city just waking up. The first policeman hits the door almost as soon as they get it secured, and the boy and Keelan startle back at the sound. But the wire holds. At least for now. The two boys look at each other, wide-eyed, snort with laughter, turn, run.

He and Keelan follow after Jules and Mouse. Down a hallway, mostly empty, past doors, mostly closed. Everything smells of dirty water and old carrots. Like people living too close. Like smoke. Once upon a time, this had been a nice place to live. It isn't anymore.

Mouse and Jules are waiting, crouching by a door all the way at the end of the hallway. Keelan and the boy come at a run, waving them on. Behind them, the sounds of the police struggling with the door, kicking and cursing.

There are places in the world where all that noise would bring the curious to their doors—throwing them open to see what the fuss was about—and there are places where noise like that would make all the doors shut tight. This place is the second kind. So now anyone curious, furious at being woken when it's still dark outside, and everyone already awake anyway is running for their own door. They're twisting locks and smothering breakfast fires, shooing snotty children away, or just turning their faces against the walls and covering their heads with their hands.

The boy can hear pounding footsteps. He crosses the mouth of an interior stairwell just as two panting, red-faced cops reach the lower landing. Keelan is just behind him.

The police point and yell, "Wait!" and "Stoprightthere!"

The boy shouts, "Go! Go!" at Keelan, but digs his own heels in and stops. He slaps Keelan on the back as he goes galumphing past. Then he looks down the staircase at the police. At the end of the hallway, Jules is leaning into the door. He's arguing with someone on the other side. The boy can hear him shout, "We paid!" and wonders if this is going to be a problem.

Probably not. Jules is big for his age. He can be scary.

The cops start up the stairs. They are sweating, gasping for breath. They're not moving fast at all. The boy glances again to the far end of the hallway. The door is open now. He sees Mouse hesitating, watching him. At the other end, he hears the door to the stairs down from the roof crash open.

He raises a hand and waves bye-bye to the police coming up from below. Then he runs.

Mouse goes through the door.

The boy is a second behind her. He can see the cheap lock on the door, the frame splintered where someone tried to close it against Jules's suggestion that it needed to be open *right now*. He hooks a sharp turn, grabbing the frame, and scrambles through. The people who live in the apartment were paid to leave their door unlocked from midnight until dawn. Not a lot, but still. They were *paid*. And now they act like they have no idea what is happening as the boy and Jules and Mouse and Keelan all go scrambling right through their too-small home, pushing past grandmothers and crying babies, knocking things over in their hurry.

In the kitchen, there's a small window. It leads out to the fire escape they'd all just gone up. There's a plank of wood lying on top of the railing, stretching all the way across the narrow alley three stories below and leading to the fire escape on the other side.

They all run for that window. The boy shoos them along. The cops are right behind them, but the hard part comes next.

It's the part where the boy is going to have to die.

Jules goes first out the window, holds the plank. Mouse climbs right up his back and over his shoulders onto the board, runs across it like she's flying in the gray half-light. On the other side, the twins, Tristan and Llyr, are holding their end. They're small, just six or seven years old, and have to lay their whole bodies on it. They bounce like they're on a carnival ride, scream like they're having the time of their lives, but Mouse is across in a flash, hardly seeming to touch the wood.

Keelan goes next. The fastest of the cops are at the apartment door now.

Jules says, "Last chance to change your mind."

The boy shakes his head. He says, "I'll be fine. Go."

So Jules goes. The boy holds the board with his whole weight, trying to keep it from jouncing straight off the fire escape rail. Jules running across it rattles his bones in his skin.

But Jules makes it, jumps off, shows both thumbs to the boy, all his teeth. Everything is going swell. Keelan and Mouse are already lifting the plank, levering it up. Arun and Sig are waiting on the roof to grab the plank, haul it up, use it to lie across the gap between that roof and the next. Then everyone runs.

It's the plan. It's how this is all supposed to go. They'll be long gone before the cops can go down to the street, across to the next building or the next, and then climb all the way back up again to the roof.

But the math was always cruel. No matter how they figured it, one person would always be left behind on the first fire escape— the person who had to hold the plank.

The boy.

He waves to Jules on the other side. Sees the plank being lifted. Jules waves back. And then the boy sees Jules's eyes go wide.

That's how he knows.

The police are right behind him. Right in the window, close enough to grab him.

And so he jumps.

# FALLING

**FALLING THREE STORIES** takes no time at all. It's over before you even know it—particularly if you're the one doing the falling.

Did the boy's whole life flash before his eyes? Hard to say. Hard to say, always, what goes through the minds of boys, isn't it? And anyway, there wasn't very much time.

But this is a story we're telling. We can make it do tricks. We can make the falling go quick as a finger snap or last days and days. A boy like this? He doesn't really have much life to flash anyway. So maybe there was time.

If he *did* remember some things, perhaps he saw not just the rail of the fire escape receding, but himself at five years old, brought here, to the Flying City, by the man who'd taken him from his father and then handed him off to a different man and a different man after that until, finally, he was put to work in a Highgate bakery called Hargrove & Sons for a man who had no sons of his own.

Maybe he saw himself—pale and pasty, thin as sticks in a shirt too big for him and pants cut off raggedly at the ankle—learning how to turn the dough and scrape the pans. How to pop balls of raw dough into his mouth when no one was looking and hold them in his cheek like chaw, then swallow them whole when being hungry yet surrounded by the smells of food all day got to be too much to bear.

It's hard to say. But his life was all he had. And in this moment—this instant between the fire escape and the ground—let's say he remembered many things. Like how, at first, he fought hard to hold on to every recollection of home, parents, sweetness, warmth, but slowly let them go until his dream of the night he'd been taken away was the only thing he recalled. He carried with him the smell of rain, quivering light, strong hands, cold blue eyes in the darkness, not much else. Not even his name. To him now, that night is when his life began.

At six, he escaped from the bakery for the first time—slipping out a high window left open in the summer heat. He carried nothing, knew nothing, had nothing inside him but a bottomless hunger and a hatred for bread, flour, the heat of the ovens, and the man who owned the bakery. He lasted three days before ignorance (and a group of larger boys) caught up with him, and was eventually found lying among the trash on Lethe Road. He'd been hit hard enough that two of his milk teeth lay in a puddle nearby, then stabbed in the belly and left to die.

But he didn't die. He was returned to the bakery, thirty-six stitches holding him together like a broken doll. As soon as his wound had scarred over and stopped itching, he escaped again, was caught again and returned, and escaped again.

If he recalled himself at six, it would be as a wilder creature. Dirty and with ragged nails, his face chalked with flour, eyes burning like coals. Beneath the grime and dust, his hair was black and too long. The other boys were afraid of him, a little, so they would laugh at him and call him names and put spiders in his hair. Sometimes he fought them, and sometimes he won and sometimes he didn't. At night, while the biggest and the strongest of the boys slept on the flour sacks, curled into warm dents in the shapes of their bodies, the boy squatted in a corner of the flour loft, arms wrapped around his knees, staring up at the narrow windows that were now nailed shut.

When the boy was seven, the man who owned the bakery tired of him and passed him to a man who owned a chandlery. And though the boy liked the smell of the shop (beeswax and scorched cotton and spitting oil fires), he escaped anyway, was caught and beaten and moved again.

The next man was a trader in soaps and lye who used the boy like a mule but soon went bankrupt and was forced to sell everything he owned. The next had a factory that made brooms. The one after that cooked tar and one day beat the boy so badly that he would carry the scars for the rest of his life.

That man disappeared shortly after, at night, somewhere in the twenty well-lighted steps between the bar he frequented and his own front door, leaving behind nothing but a smear of blood on the stone and one sticky shoe. It wasn't the boy who did it. That's important to know. But he certainly didn't mourn.

For a time, the boy stayed with a man in the Machinists Quarter called Judocus the Fish, who was impossibly tall and ancient and stringy, with fingers stained permanently black by grease. The Fish collected smallish boys and used them to crawl around in the guts of big machines in need of oiling and adjusting. The Fish knew more about machines than anyone the boy had ever known, and he taught some of it to him, which the boy appreciated. When he fled, he left a note for the Fish on his workbench. *I learnt a lot from you*, it said. *Thank you for not hitting me. I hope you think kindly of me if we ever meet again in different circumstances.*

If he remembered anything, he would remember that note. He'd had to ask one of the older boys in the Fish's workshop how to spell *circumstances*. The rest of it he managed on his own.

Thirteen times, the boy escaped. Thirteen times, until escaping became his vocation. On the streets of Highgate, the Flying City, he learned how to steal and not get caught. How to beg a penny, cut a pocket, roll a drunk, run and run and run. The boy was smart and fast most of the time. Clever when he had to be. Lucky when everything else failed him. For a while, it was enough. Right up until it wasn't.

He would surely remember the day he was picked up by uniformed cops who knew him as a thief and a runaway. They brought him to the crookedest cop house in the Marche, which was the crookedest neighborhood in the entire Flying City. There, they cuffed him to a loop of metal set in the concrete between two other runaways—a boy and a girl—to wait for a truancy cop to pick them up.

The boy was older, but not by much, built thick and with a wild mess of coppery curls on his head. He said his name was Jules Cael—offered it like a gift as soon as the boy was shoved down beside him. Jules said the girl didn't talk, but he knew she was called Dagda.

"I call her Mouse," Jules said. "You know, 'cuz she's small and don't talk."

The boy's best friends. And this was how they'd met. Who wouldn't remember that?

Jules had asked him if he knew how to slip a handcuff. The boy did, of course, but he'd said nothing. There was something about Jules that seemed to suck all the air out of the world anyway. Like all the words worth saying already lived in his mouth.

"I do," Jules said. "Six times I done it." He swelled up and tapped his chest with his knuckles, making his chains rattle. "If I know anything, I know about escaping. Here. Let me show you."

Spit helped, he said. Fresh blood did just fine. But if you were smart, you never ran without a bit of grease smeared somewhere on you. Whale oil smelled bad but worked a treat. Oil jelly was even better. You made a duck of your hand, he explained, tucked up your thumb, greased the way as best you could, and then just wiggled yourself free.

"You try," he said. "'Less you wanna sit and wait for the cops to come back."

The boy slipped free of the handcuffs easily enough. They weren't made for such small hands anyway. And when it was done, Jules applauded, then clapped the boy on the shoulder and turned to run. But the boy lingered.

"What?" Jules asked. "The Mouse, too?"

The girl, Dagda, was watching him. She wore oversized men's trousers, rolled at the ankle, bunched, and belted to fit, and a shapeless smock the color of stone. Her hair was black like the boy's, but longer, tied back with a leather band. Her eyes were green like bottle glass. Her skin pale but knotted with precise, tangled ropes of milk-colored scars that made it look like someone had run a hot wire just beneath it or that something small but hungry had chewed its way through her. The boy had looked at her with his head tilted one way, then with his head tilted the other.

"You wanna come?" he asked her.

The girl said nothing. She looked up at him, sniffing, her unusual eyes darting from the boy to Jules to the boy again.

The boy leaned closer. "He seems okay," he said, meaning Jules. "You wanna come with us?" It was the most words he'd said to someone all at once in longer than he could remember.

If the boy saw his life at all while he fell, he would've seen

Dagda raising her hands to him in answer, her chains clanking. He would've seen the lines on her face and the scars running along the backs of her hands and up into her sleeves when he'd reached for her cuffs on that day years ago. He'd seen witch marks before, but never like this. He'd seen scars from belts and bats and blades and fire, but this wasn't that either.

Spitting into his hand, he'd touched her skin gently around where the iron bit, and blushed furiously when the girl stiffened at his touch like she'd been stung by something. Her eyes were wide and her nose twitched furiously, so the boy looked away and muttered, "Sorry. Sorry. I'm . . . sorry."

The girl never said a word. And even later, in something like safety, when Jules and the boy both pushed back sleeves and pulled up pant legs to show her their own scars and marks of passing through a world that seemed to hate them at every turn, she said nothing.

"You ever seen something like that?" Jules asked the boy, jerking a thumb at the girl.

And the boy shook his head. He scratched thoughtfully at a scab behind one ear. "No. Seen lots of things, but never something like that."

So the boy had asked her.

"Hey," he said. "What's with your face?"

And Dagda the Mouse had lunged and snapped her teeth like she was going to bite him, so he'd squirmed away from her. Then she'd pulled her knees up to her chest and her smock over her knees and her hands into her sleeves, laid her face down into her folded arms and shook like she was crying.

The boys looked at her in fascination. Then in discomfort. Finally, Jules punched the boy in the arm and said, "See? Your problem is you don't know anything about talking to girls."

The two of them laughed out loud for a long time. Eventually, the girl looked up, her eyes dry. She almost smiled.

And after that, they were fierce friends. It happened just like that, the way things never do for grown-ups. Together, the three of them ran and ran. They could go from Haelish's Guns at one end of Front Street to the Angle up near the mail yards without ever touching pavement.

But over and over again, the three of them would find their way back to the loudness and teeming streets of the Marche, because the Marche was a good place for hiding. For being mostly overlooked if you were small enough and quiet enough and fast enough. When they were hungry, they stole. When they were bored, they explored. When they were tired, they curled together in the dark places of the Flying City and held on to each other and waited for dawn.

As he fell, the boy might remember the breaking yards at the very edge of the city where he and his friends found work among the salvagers and the cutting shops, taking apart old ships for rich men who would sell the parts to other rich men who would then use them to build newer, better ships.

In the yards, no one cared where they came from or who'd run away from where. The boy was good with machines, thanks to his time with Judocus the Fish. Excellent with tools. So he would *certainly* remember being ten and eleven and twelve, breathing steam and smudging oil from his eyes, squirming through dead ships dragging a jangling tool bag behind him. He would remember hanging from ropes beside Jules and Dagda while bigger boys cut the metal skin from rusting hulls, peeled it back and let the smaller ones climb inside to find treasures. The plainest, they handed over to the men who employed them for a dipper of water, a bowl of juk with salt and green onion. The best they learned to hide away and sell to those in the Marche who would pay. The boy enjoyed the work, sure. But mostly he did it because the thieving was so good.

If he had time, he would remember all of this. A flicker of images—raw dough, his own blood, the Fish's stained-black fingers, white scars on pale skin, Jules laughing, the blue flame of a cutting torch. The boy at twelve loved no god or grown-up, had never known one who'd done him anything but wrong. Instead, he had his friends and all the great and sweeping joys that came from being a child left alone with nothing governing him but his own quick mind and the limits of what he could get away with.

So maybe he thought about all of this as he fell. Maybe not. Maybe he thought about pies or his shoes or gravity. Maybe there was no time for any of it. But I know one thing for sure.

I know that the boy fell smiling.

Because he knew something that the cops didn't.

# MILO QUICK

**THE BOY JUMPS,** the cops right behind him.

In the air, he rolls, looks at the sky. Spreads his arms and his legs. His heart pounds like a bird's heart must when it flies.

He falls so fast that the uniformed men don't even see it. They only know that he went over the edge, high enough up that the fall would probably kill him. Break his legs, at least. One less filthy little runaway for them to worry about.

Across the alley, Dagda, Jules, and the rest are all lifting the wooden plank up to the roof, hand over hand. The police see them and they yell a little, shake their clubs a little, but you can tell their hearts aren't really in it. Because one of the kids is dead now (or broken, surely), and none of them really want to keep chasing the rest. They don't want to climb out the little window onto the fire escape. They're tired and don't want to run up and down any more stairs. One dead boy? That should be enough.

So groaning and cursing, most of them start to file out of the apartment, shouting at everyone inside to stay out of their way. But one of them lingers, leans out the window and looks down into the alley.

Doesn't see the boy dead.

Doesn't see him crawling away on two broken legs.

Says, "Hey!" and points. "That other one's gone."

Which isn't true at all. The boy is right there. It's just that the cops can't see him, buried like he is in bags upon bags of shredded cloth, stolen bedsheets, old newspaper, a hundred lines' worth of laundry. He'd fallen straight into the pile and the pile had closed over him, just like it was supposed to, and inside it (at the bottom of it, really), the boy is laughing and laughing because he's alive. Because even though he'd practiced this over and over last night—from the first floor, then the second (Tristan and Llyr had each gone twice from the second, just for fun, shrieking the whole way down, smiles so wide they glowed in the dark), then the third, which he'd decided was quite high enough, thank you—every time feels like the first time.

He has both hands clamped over his mouth, but he can't stop. Doesn't want to stop. He could've *died*, but he didn't, so now he laughs just because he still can.

Above him, his friends are already on the opposite roof. Gone. Vanishing into the dark where no one will ever find them, because they know every hole and hiding place in the Marche.

And down below, the boy has disappeared, too. Neat as a magic trick. He's thinking he's safe. That the game is over now. So once he catches his breath, he sits up, claws the dirty, damp bags away from his face, and looks up just to see one more time the distance that he'd fallen from and lived.

The police are all there, looking right at him.

The boy stares back, and for just a second, no one seems to know what's supposed to happen next. The boy hadn't expected this. The police certainly hadn't expected this. So they look at each other silently. Then everyone does everything at once.

The police all start yelling and pushing each other in their hurry to get through the window or down the fire escape. One of them almost falls.

The boy sneezes, his nose full of dust, and then he starts fighting his way through the bags like he's swimming (except that he doesn't actually know how to swim).

And the cops are cursing and the boy is cursing and he can hear boots ringing on metal as he struggles and throws bags out of his way. He's angry because he'd planned for everything, but he hadn't planned for this. And the police are angry, because the boy fooled them (almost) and lived when they expected him to be dead. They're even angrier than they were before.

One of the cops jumps from halfway down, lands in the bags, makes a grab for the boy, misses by an inch. The rest are close behind.

So the boy runs.

Of all the things he's good at, this is the thing he's best at. He's spent years on these streets, always on the run from something or someone who wanted to find him, hurt him, kill him. But the boy knows that if you're quick, they'll never even see you. Never *catch* you. And in addition to all the other things the boy is, he's also very, *very* quick.

So quick that he'd made it his name. He was Quick. Milo Quick.

Milo bolts down the alley, feet pounding wet stone. At the end of it, there are a few stairs, a rusted iron railing, then the street beyond, just beginning to wake.

He jumps the stairs, skids, shoes slipping even as his feet keep pumping. He catches himself with one hand and keeps moving as the police all come rushing after him, strung out in a line, shouting, faces red and furious, reaching but never quite touching him.

The street is wide, smooth, paved with great slabs of stone cracked and broken by time. The boy goes across it, darting in front of two bicycles and slipping beneath a cart loaded with boxes. He pops up on the other side and twists between a knot of men carrying heavy sacks on their shoulders who spin to look where he's going and collide with each other.

Milo is already gone. Three steps, a sharp turn, then he jumps to catch the edge of a windowsill with his fingers. He runs his feet straight up the wall, pulls the rest of himself after, pushes off, grabs a second-story sill, then pushes off again to land on top of a short wall stretching along the edge of a building housing two navy bars, a tooth mechanic, and a place that sells soup.

Behind him, something crashes. More shouting, different languages. There's no time to look back.

He wobbles a little on the wall, ten feet off the ground, but runs along it, fingertips brushing the building beside him, other arm held out for balance. The police are below him now with mouths full of curses. Milo runs on, feeling his own lips skinning back from his teeth in a smile.

At the end of the wall, he jumps, arms making circles in the air. He rolls when he lands, then bounces to his feet. A policeman falls, reaching for him. Another trips. This street is busier, and the boy jinks and dodges, monkeys up a rattling fence and leaps down on the other side. He slips into a squeezeway between two buildings dressed in crumbling white plaster, dead tufts of wire and cable sticking out of them like hairs growing from an old man's ears. The space is so narrow, he has to turn sideways and shuffle.

He's pretty sure now that he's left the police behind, but he doesn't even care about that anymore. He is Milo Quick. He was built to run. So he does it now just for the joy of it. Just because this is his city and he belongs in it like no place else.

All around him, Highgate is waking up. Like a living thing, it yawns and stretches and farts. It groans with the first morning breeze, belching out plumes of coal smoke and oil smoke and wood smoke and steam. This jutting island of stone floating far above the waves of the Clean Sea. This impossible city in the sky. It sprouts cannons like flowers in a window box. At dawn, it shines like every window is afire.

And the Marche is the thudding heart of it, just now stuttering awake. In the pale and pinking light, Milo can hear ten languages in twenty steps. The news vendors crowd every corner and every bridge, all shouting at once, jostling for territory with the coffee sellers, who carry brass tanks on their backs and wear clattering belts of cups. The rag merchants appear from nowhere like ghosts haunting the wet streets. And the junk carts, too, with their jangles and bells, bread and jam, switchblade knives, and good tobacco by the dime weight.

The Marche is crowded and untidy. Its narrow alleys smell of yeast and oranges and sweat, of hot tar and spilled beer, lye, salt, curry, and a hundred other things. Every wall is scabbed with paint and hieroglyphed with graffiti. There are black shadows under high, arching bridges and bright places where the sunlight shatters against brilliant glass. It is damp (always) and loud (always), squeezed on all sides by other, duller neighborhoods: the Machinists Quarter, the fancy houses of Burnhill, Front Street with all its faded amusements. Below it, the dockworks and breaking yards rattle and spit sparks. High above are the aeries where the airships circle and dock. No piece of the Flying City goes unused. There is no inch of it not crowded by two inches of things.

On a roof near Oldedge Market, Milo Quick meets back up with his friends. There's an anchor point there for one of the city's floating aerostat turbines, painted like a storm cloud, detailed with bolts of flaking yellow lightning. On a lip of concrete around it, they have lined up their take from last night. A corroded bolt. A broken piece of wiring guide. A bent nail. A doorknob. Milo is grinning as he walks over, fishes in his pocket, carefully sets a drive end bearing beside all the other things.

Jules asks, "Good night?"

"Good night," says Milo. "We're ready to do it for real next time Emil brings down a load from the cutting shops."

And everyone smiles and jumps up and down and shoves each other. Practice—that's what this had been. A game. Fun because no one died of it. A few days from now, a shipment of parts will come into the yards from one of the shops where Milo has friends. When it does, he'll know about it. They'll steal all the most valuable pieces. Run. If chased, they'll know exactly what to do.

But now it is daytime and everyone has real work to do. Pockets to pick, trouble to cause. Arun and Sig are going home. They're tired after hustling all night in the Blue Lights. Milo sends Keelan to Shippers Alley to have a look at the warehouses and docklines. Tristan and Llyr go to Front Street. Milo, Jules, and Dagda agree to meet around lunch. At the place they normally do. In the meantime, all the treasures of Highgate won't just steal themselves.

Milo waits while everyone else leaves. When they're gone, he picks up the trash they'd taken for practice and throws it at seagulls. He looks up at the aerostat drifting high above, stretches like a cat in the rising sun, and then snakes his way back down into the market where the chop bars and carts sell hot spice-bread with butter; cockles and oysters lifted up from the ships anchored below and sprinkled with vinegar; congee rice with tiny shrimp or crackly bits of salty pork fat and chilies; smoked fish; noodles in fiery red broth; tea by the leaf; tin bowls of spicy peanut butter soup poured over sticky rice balls; eggs boiled in the shell; or chunks of lombok packed onto sticks, dabbed with red curry and charred over a coal grill. His mouth waters. He's hungry in the vague, distracted way that he's always hungry. If you asked him, Milo would tell you that if you could find a nice, dry spot above the Marche's racket, you could almost eat the good smells for breakfast.

Almost.

If you asked him, Milo would tell you that there was nothing finer in the world for starting a day than a sweet coffee and a twist to smoke. Maybe some black bread. A little bit of whitefish, sour with vinegar. It wasn't that he knew, but he *felt* like that was right. If you asked him, he'd tell you that he dreamed of a day when he might sit at a table on Exposition Square like a gentleman in a suit made just for him, with a cup of coffee and a smoke and the day's papers still warm in front of him. That, he thought, would be the life. Evidence of victory over something that he didn't even yet have a word for.

In the meantime, he steals a sweet rice ball from under the cloth of a lady not paying close enough attention to her business and eats it while crouched beside the door of a tower so crowded that men pay to sleep in the stairwells and whole families camp on the landings. He watches the people go in and out. Counts them because he likes counting things. Holds the door open with his foot for a minute between people to get a look at the lock, then moves along when someone throws a rock at him.

Milo Quick is twelve years old. He is a thief, a runaway and a criminal. An orphan. A child of the Flying City. These are his best days. He has friends, a home inside half a ship lashed to the edge of the city by ten thousand strong cables. He is fed more often than he's hungry, dry more often than he's wet, and safe . . .

Well, he's never very safe, but he is quick, and that counts for a lot.

But that is all about to change. So watch close. Don't blink. If you have to pee, do it now. Because if you look away for just a moment, you might miss something important. Everything changes starting now.

And it all begins with an old man and a bird.

# THE OLD MAN
# AND THE BIRD

**ON THE FIRST DAY OF SUMMER** in the Flying City, Milo found a drunk man passed out between two rain barrels in an alley, went through his pockets without waking him, and cut the wallet out of his pants pocket with a hook-bladed knife he kept for just such work. The wallet was empty, so he took the man's hat instead and stashed it where he knew he could find it again, then lifted a nice pen from a different man walking along the street, pretending to yawn and bump into him, apologizing loudly but never slowing down.

He took a fork from a table selling dozens of them, snatched a jacket lined with silk from a tailor's stall, stole a pickled egg from a bowl and ate the whole thing in two bites. The jacket was too big for him, but he wore it anyway, flapping his arms and laughing, the sleeves hanging down over his fingers.

He went down to the docklines to count Armada ships and see what was coming and going. On the roof of a warehouse, he took off his shoes and splashed his feet in a puddle, then lay back and watched the airships twist above him. He knew the names of every model he saw, what their sails did and what each rope was for. Then he put his shoes back on and climbed down onto the streets, decided it was too hot to wear the jacket anyway, so offered it to Sabeen the Machine, a coffee seller with one regular leg and one scraping metal clockwork one. It fit Sabeen perfectly, and they bargained hard, Milo finally agreeing to two free coffees a day (white, with sweet cream) for him and all his friends, for one week, starting immediately.

It was a good deal. Milo held the cup in both hands. He drank standing still, watching the people around him and wondering what each of them had in their pockets. When he was finished, he handed the cup back to Sabeen and went and sat on the crumbling relic of a wall near the top of the shallow bowl that contained Oldedge Market and watched an old man box a carrier bird.

This was not normal. Carrier birds were big but not mean. As far as Milo knew, they didn't eat anything except trash. They were scavengers (rather like Milo was)—picky about their territory, but not aggressive.

And men, of course, do not normally pick fights with birds. Men hit other men. Sometimes they hit boys, too, when the boy isn't fast enough to duck or smart enough to stay clear when a man's blood is up or he has the stink of rotgut on him. That was just wisdom. Something Milo'd paid to learn.

But men didn't fight birds, not in Highgate or anywhere else. And they certainly did not do so formally—standing with fists raised and loudly challenging those birds to battle over ownership of piles of trash.

This man, though, was doing precisely that. He'd been sorting through a pile of garbage mounded up against the ancient wall close to where Milo was sitting. He'd been kicking at the pile and pulling it slowly apart when the carrier bird had arrived, stalked up beside him, and begun scattering the inedible pieces of trash with its big beak.

The bird, standing on its long, skinny legs, came up to the old man's shoulder. Obviously it believed there was something tasty buried somewhere in the mound of windblown garbage, or possibly it was just bored and amusing itself in one of the few ways available to birds that didn't involve flying. And the old man, upon seeing the bird, had addressed it politely and asked it, please, to go looking for its lunch somewhere else.

In answer, the bird had shuffled its big webbed feet and grumpily moved to a different part of the same pile.

So the man had asked again. He'd spoken a bit louder, but still with what the boy would've said was an overabundance of graciousness. He would've said that because both *overabundance* and *graciousness* were good, big words and Milo loved good, big words. He collected them like shiny pebbles and kept them, just waiting for opportunities to use them.

"Lord Bird," said the man to the bird, "there's hardly lunch enough here for one of us, let alone both. As I was here first, I claim this pile in the name of the kingdom of man and ask that you vacate most expediently this sovereign territory."

This, Milo thought, was a man who also loved good, big words. The boy liked him immediately.

The bird, though, wasn't so sure. It looked at the man, cocked its head to one side and made a gurgling kind of *squark* that made the pouch that dangled beneath its long beak jiggle.

So then the old man stood up very straight. He raised one hand, pointed in the direction of nothing in particular and said, "Go, Bird. Now."

And the bird twisted its head around on its long neck, reached out quite boldly, and pecked the old man right on the hand. Then went back to placidly snapping at the garbage.

The old man's head was fringed with a cloud of white hair, his lip adorned with an impressively curled white mustache. He wore

sandals, a loose pair of white pants, and some sort of sheet, knotted into a shirt that left his arms bare. He fell comfortably into a
boxer's stance with his fists raised and a sharp smile beneath his
whiskers.

"So it's to be war, then," said the old man, bouncing on his toes
and looking out through the bars of his arms. "That suits me quite
fine, Lord Bird."

Fascinated, the boy watched as the carrier bird turned to look
at the old man like it understood every word perfectly. It had a
look on its bird face like maybe this whole thing had been some
sort of terrible mistake, but Milo was delighted. This was the most
interesting thing he'd seen in a very long time.

And then the old man turned, looked Milo straight in the eyes,
and said, "You're my witness to this gross interspecies provoca-
tion, young sir. Remember what you see here, and don't let it be
said that Semyon Beli did not attempt all in his power to bring this
watershed moment to a peaceful and equitable conclusion before
resorting to violence."

Taking advantage of this moment of distraction, the carrier
bird snaked out its head and pecked the old man hard on the arm.

There was blood. The fleshy pouch beneath the bird's beak
flapped. The feathers on its neck fluffed out in rage. And the
old man, without even so much as a glance at the wound freshly
opened on his forearm, answered with a quick left-hand jab (which
the bird ducked easily) and an even quicker right cross (which hit
it right in the beak).

The bird reared back, startled. It spread its wings, shook its
head, opened its beak, squawked loudly, and peppered the old
man with pecks.

But the man ducked and weaved. He stuck his head out and
squawked right back at the bird, doing an impressive imitation,

then jabbed it again in the beak. He shouted, "For man and sovereignty!" and threw a flurry of quick, open-hand slaps in the direction of the bird's eyes.

It was like a man boxing a snake—the bird's head always moving, the old man's hands quick and accurate. But neither would yield the ground or surrender. Milo smiled a giant toothy smile and squeezed his hands together between his knees. He wished his friends could be here to see, because really, who would believe him when he told the story later?

And that was when, from behind him, he heard a rough voice say his name.

# MILO AND MORIC SHAW

**"MILO,"** said the voice. "Been looking for you."

Without thinking, the boy raised a hand. Just one, as if to say *Not now, I'm busy*. As if to say *Don't ruin this*.

It was a strangely grown-up gesture. But in his own head, Milo Quick was a very different thing from the small, skinny, and scarred creature that wore his skin. This boy-creature never so big on the outside as he felt inside. This un-beloved creature with its dirty shirt and dark hair, ragged, chewed nails, and too-small shoes.

True, a wise boy would not have been so dismissive. A wise boy might've at least turned at the sound of his own name. But Milo was enraptured (another good, big word) by the old man and the bird. And as he watched, the man struck the carrier bird again. The bird squawked and fell back a step. The tide appeared to be turning.

Which was when Milo felt a heavy hand crash down on his shoulder like unexpected bad weather. Felt it *squeeze*, thumb digging into the meat of him. Like the bird, Milo suddenly regretted his rash, dismissive actions and his self-importance. He understood that he had misjudged the situation and that he would pay for it.

Milo winced, but didn't turn away. "Shaw," he said. "Didn't see you there."

Moric Shaw. Thin, sharp, made all of hard, bad angles. He had rotten teeth and greasy hair, always pulled back and tied with a scrap of purple ribbon. Milo could smell him, even at a distance. Soupy, like old milk and mushrooms.

The hand on his shoulder squeezed tighter, but Milo didn't twist away and he didn't cry out. He knew Shaw and knew that would only make it worse, so he swallowed the pain and counted long seconds in his head, waiting for Shaw to grow bored and let go (which he did), then step around him, plant himself directly in front of Milo and look him in the face.

He said, "The King needs to see you."

"Busy," said Milo, leaning so he could see around Shaw. And when the slap came, there seemed almost no malice in it. Boredom, thuggery, awful strength—all of those. But it was a book-keeper's slap. A settling of accounts.

"Now," said Shaw.

"Must be important," said Milo, blinking up at the older boy, seeing nothing but impatience in his otherwise-dull eyes. Nothing but anger in the hard, tight line of his mouth. "The King sent his most trusted errand boy."

"Don't be smart," Shaw said.

*If I was smart, I wouldn't have gotten hit,* thought Milo.

His cheek was red and hot where Shaw had slapped him, stinging in a precise outline of the bigger boy's flat, hard hand. He pushed at his teeth with his tongue, checking for looseness. He asked, "The King say what he wanted?"

But Shaw did not like questions. He mistrusted them and greeted this one with a look of confusion, tilting his head to one side, lank hair flopping, and then said, "You," as though that was such an obvious answer that he'd briefly suspected trickery. "Let's go."

And Milo said, "Okay." He stood up, deliberately turned his back on Shaw and dragged a hand quickly across his eyes. It came away wet. He sniffed hard and then turned back. "We'd better hurry," he said. "The King deserves an overabundance of our graciousness."

Then Milo shoved his hands into his pockets and took off at a fast walk. The old man held the bird now by the neck with one hand, and as the boy passed by, he offered both of them, the man and the bird, an almost-imperious nod with no words attached.

Shaw wondered what that was all about, but said nothing. He had to scurry to keep up with Milo and not lose sight of him as the boy melted into the crowds of people filling Oldedge Market.

# SEMYON BELI

**THE OLD MAN AND THE BIRD** both watched the boy go past. Then they looked at each other.

Semyon Beli was Casseri, from a dusty, hot land far from the Flying City. He had been many things in his long and interesting life. The son of a rich man and then the son of a poor man. A soldier three times over, and once on both sides of the same war. A merchant, a cook, a crook, and a sailor. Now he was something else, because that's just the way of the world. Things happen. Often, they are not the things we expect, and they leave us in places we never intended to be.

Now Semyon Beli was a kidnapper. Or would be, soon enough.

"That's the boy," he said to the bird. "I'm sure of it. I must tell the Captain."

"*Squaark,*" said the bird, and tried to poke the old man in the eye.

# MILO

**IT DIDN'T TAKE MILO LONG** to start running. He put the old man and the bird behind him. He put Moric Shaw behind him. He put all his worries and his hunger and his burning cheek behind him. He ran because he was Quick and nothing could catch him that he didn't want to catch him.

So he snaked through the crowds in Oldedge Market the way that only a small boy who knows his way can—darting among the tents and tables of the charm sellers, junk merchants, chandlers, sandlers and panhandlers, the metalsmiths and freelance mechanics, the hawkers selling fruits, vegetables, tacks, teapots, brooms, bullets, and everything else under the sun. His feet pounded stone, scraped curbs, shushed through the tough patches of salt grass that sprouted here and there.

And then like the man, like the bird, like Shaw, Milo put Oldedge behind him, too. On the Lower Cross Bridge, he dodged fleets of bicycles and clanking, smoky putt-putts, knots of soldiers, and carts piled with furniture, suitcases, and machine parts. The crumbling gray concrete of the Upper Cross stretched above him, its pillars like the legs of giants standing in a line, graffiti twining all the way up them. Bursting into dazzling summer sunlight, he turned onto the Street of Doors. He put out a hand, flat like a wing, and felt the tops of boxed flowers brush his palm as he ran.

He hesitated at a corner where traffic was tangled by a gun the size of a rowhouse making its passage from the Machinists Quarter to the shield wall that ringed the city. Its carriage was too wide and long to negotiate the turn toward Front Street, and a crowd had gathered to jeer the truckmen and machine drovers. Everything smelled of salt air and smoke. Above him, the aerostats sang and gulls flapped. When Milo looked up, he could see an airship flying the orange-and-yellow flags of Valonde keeping station in the shifting winds, men hanging like ripe fruit from its lines.

The boy cut down an alley that opened at the far end to fresher air and wind coming up off the sea. Milo lingered a moment, long enough to hear the flat, slapping footsteps of Moric Shaw coming up behind him, then took a deep breath, turned right onto Airy Way, which was the street of the sailmakers, and ran for blocks and blocks under the fluttering canopy of a hundred different cloths, all freshly dyed, stretching from building to building, hung high across the road to dry, and dripping a hundred-colored rain down onto anyone who passed beneath.

# SHAW

**MORIC SHAW** was no stranger to dancing through the Marche. Though not as artful as Milo, or as quick, Shaw had been born there. He'd survived longer than Milo had.

He had size, if not finesse. Focus, not cleverness. Anger rather than joy. He wasn't the sharpest nail, but he had a good memory. Moric Shaw could recall every stone and street corner in the Marche that'd been decorated with his blood. He remembered every spot where he'd stood and refused to move when bigger, stronger boys told him he ought to. And there's something brave and valiant in that. Don't think that there isn't. That Shaw entered our story as a rotten-toothed bully doesn't mean that bullying was the full measure of him.

Oh, it's the measure of *most* of him, sure. But not all. Shaw was strong. Loyal. Persistent. He was a survivor in a place where survival was guaranteed to no one, and least of all to abandoned children. And that's not nothing.

But where Milo looked at the Marche and saw opportunity, Shaw's world was a map of violence suffered and violence offered, his passage through it marked with bloodred pins.

Today, though, he bulled his way down streets he'd known all his life as an errand boy to the King of the Marche, just like Milo'd said. He had his orders. He meant to follow them. And even though he burned with rage in the moments when he saw Milo dawdling, arms crossed, tapping his foot or examining his fingernails until Shaw drew near enough for him to rabbit off once more, he never got close enough to hit Milo again.

Which was what Shaw really wanted to do. So very, *very* badly.

# SANDMAN

**WATCH CAREFULLY NOW.** Don't blink or sneeze.

Milo was close to where he needed to be. Close to the court of the Total King. And he was focused enough on his destination before him, and Moric Shaw behind, that he did not notice the truancy cop, Ennis Arghdal, sitting on a step across Airy Way, one knee cocked, smiling a wolf's smile and eating a cup of brightly colored shave ice with a metal spoon.

Ennis Arghdal haunts this story end to end. Already, he's been in it two, three, maybe four times, lurking in darkness and around corners. Have you noticed him yet? It's okay if you didn't. That's how it's supposed to be, because Ennis Arghdal is a man who is very good at going unnoticed.

But now you've spied him and now you'll know what to look for.

Officer Arghdal was tall and thin and strong as spring steel. He wore sailor's glasses with blue lenses and a long coat no matter the weather. He was, among other things, a truant officer—responsible for finding, catching, and disposing of those errant and unwanted boys and girls of the Flying City who felt that a life free on Highgate's streets was preferable to a childhood of duty and industry spent locked in a caster's shop or chained to a stamping press, crying and learning a valuable trade.

His was a profession of order. Of putting things in their proper places. And so he gathered up the children, put each of them where they belonged like pegs in holes, and collected his pay. He drank no fewer than ten cups of coffee every day. He knew the names of every street and (it sometimes seemed) *every person* in the Flying City. He'd killed runaway boys and girls in the course of his duties, and though he would claim to have no idea how many, he knew the number like he knew his own name.

In the places where runaways gathered, Ennis Arghdal was called the Sandman because he was the one who put children to sleep. Ask a hundred people and ninety-nine of them would say that Officer Arghdal was entirely mad—that he had no home, ate truant children for supper, slept in ditches when he slept at all, was part dog, part ghost, part hunting bird. But the hundredth? The hundredth would simply laugh and say that it was better not to talk about Ennis Arghdal at all, because you never knew when he might be right behind you, listening.

On this day, Officer Arghdal watched Milo Quick burst out of the alley onto Airy Way and then turn toward the docks. He watched the lummox, Moric Shaw, pounding after him but deduced (correctly) that Quick was leading and Shaw following rather than, say, Quick running and Shaw chasing, which might've been something he would've needed to concern himself with.

It was the first day of summer, Officer Arghdal told himself. And though he knew that both of these scurrying creatures were shirkers, runaways, and junior members of the criminal element that plagued his glorious city, boys should be allowed the opportunity to be boys.

Up to a point.

Many years ago, Officer Arghdal had been tasked with keeping an extra-special eye on Milo Quick—on this one boy in a city full of boys. He'd been called to a big house on Apollo Avenue by men who had no reasonable cause to be talking to someone like him. Who, on any normal day, would cross the street just to *avoid* talking to someone like him.

But he'd gone because he was curious to know what these fancy men could possibly want (and because he'd been hoping that they might offer him supper), and as it turned out, what they'd wanted was Milo Quick.

This had all happened a long time ago. Eight years, by the Sandman's count. Nearly. The men who'd offered him the job had flattered him. With their mouths full of wine and nervous laughter, they'd told him that no one in the city of Highgate had a more fearsome reputation than Ennis Arghdal. That among the lost children who littered the dark corners of the Flying City no monster was more feared than the Sandman.

But Ennis (who, it should be noted, did not like being called Sandman and did not like people who didn't know him at all behaving as if they did) said nothing. He'd just nodded and looked around at the room he stood in, cluttered with things that he had no names for. Treasures, doubtless. Valuable beyond coin, though none of it looked like supper.

When, eventually, the rich old men got down to business and offered Officer Arghdal a sum of money, to be paid monthly, that was greater than he was paid in a year for his work as a truancy cop, the Sandman had smiled. His eyes had widened behind his blue glasses. All of this to find a boy? To watch him? To keep him safe?

Ennis had asked them to double it.

Which they did. And then he'd told them he would need his expenses covered, and they'd agreed. He'd told them that his expenses would not be inconsequential, and they'd said *of course, of course* . . . They'd handed him a fancy pen with which to make his mark on a piece of paper that was pushed across the table to him.

Officer Arghdal had asked them only one question. "Why this boy?"

The rich and powerful men had said a lot of things. They'd claimed the boy was nobody. Just a boy. They'd said it was an experiment they were running. A game. A test. That the boy couldn't matter less and that there were questions this one boy in particular might help them answer. Ennis had assumed they were lying to him about some of that, most of it, maybe all of it, because he assumed everyone lied to him. Usually, he was right.

And so, beside a seal made in the shape of a fist surrounded by a garland of roses, he'd written *Sandman* (because that was the monster these men seemed so intent on hiring) and the date, and in the end, no one had offered him supper or even a snack, which Officer Arghdal had thought was very rude. As he was being ushered out of the house on Apollo Avenue, one of the men had put a hand on his shoulder. "The boy," he'd said. "He must be allowed to be a boy. You understand?"

Ennis had stared at that hand. He did not enjoy being touched in such a way. Or at all. He'd looked up at the man, whose name was Callias Fusco, and then down at the man's hand again. The man removed it slowly and stepped back, like you would back away from a tamed dog that suddenly appeared to be not quite so tame as you'd originally thought.

"You can't just tuck him away somewhere, is what I'm saying. Can't . . . I don't know. Stick him in a basement somewhere and feed him fish heads."

"You think I would do that?" Ennis had asked.

"I think you're considering it."

Ennis had sniffed. "You're wrong."

"He must be allowed to be a boy, Sandman," Callias had said to him. "Remember that. We'll be watching."

All of that was a long time ago, but Ennis Arghdal remembered it. He'd been diligent in his work. He'd found the boy as he'd been asked to. He'd kept Milo Quick alive and watched him grow. He knew everything about the boy, everything he'd ever done or said or thought or considered. And for eight years (nearly), he'd been left mostly alone by the men who'd hired him.

Until a week ago, when Callias Fusco had found him eating breakfast at a fish stand in Oldedge and told him that the boy was no longer useful to them and that their arrangement was done. "We don't need him anymore, Sandman," he'd said. "Do what you do best."

Ennis had pinched some raw fish and rice between his fingers and shoved it into his mouth. "What's that supposed to mean?" he'd asked with his mouth full.

The old man had looked at him like he was stupid. "What you *do*, Sandman," he'd said. "What you're known for. People are going to come here looking for the boy. They can't ever find him."

"So you want me to kill him," Ennis said.

And Callias had looked away, folding his arms across his chest and rocking back on his heels. He had three men with him. Ennis had stared at each one of them while he chewed, then turned back to Callias.

"Eight years," he said. "I've kept the boy alive for you for almost eight years, and now . . ." He picked up his breakfast knife and stabbed the air with it. "Now kill him? That's what you're saying? I just want to be sure I'm understanding you."

"You're the Sandman," Callias repeated. "That's what you do."

And Ennis had exploded out of his chair, going straight for Callias with the knife, knocking over the table, spilling his breakfast everywhere. People had scattered, shouting. Callias's guards had grabbed Ennis and beaten him until he spit blood and Callias told them to stop.

"Enough!" he'd said.

Ennis had lost his blue glasses. There was blood in his hair and in one of his eyes. But he'd laughed at Callias from the ground, and at his guards, too. He'd found his glasses near an overturned table and put them back on, then stood up, grabbed a coffee cup from a different table that hadn't been knocked over, and drank, leaning heavily on a chair. He'd smiled, his teeth all bloody, and then said, "Want to ask me again?"

But Callias Fusco was already leaving. Two of his guards limped after him, carrying the third. There were police officers jogging down the street toward them, slowing when they saw who it was causing the disturbance, then turning sharply away, deciding they could do more good elsewhere.

Ennis had sipped coffee and watched Callias go. And then he'd gone looking for the boy. Found him. Watched him every minute that he could manage. That'd been a week ago.

Now, on the first day of summer, Officer Arghdal scraped his spoon and ate his ice and tinted his tongue and teeth even redder. In the brief instant that he'd clapped eyes on Milo Quick, Ennis had seen all he needed to know. With a glance, he'd weighed and measured the boy. He'd assessed his last dozen meals, the last dozen places he'd slept, the last dozen dreams he'd dreamed. He'd seen that the boy needed new shoes, a hot breakfast and a bath, though not in that order.

He still wasn't sure what to do, but he told himself that didn't matter. Something would come to him when the time was right. A solution would present itself. Ennis knew he was more a father to Milo Quick than Milo Quick's real father had ever been. More a friend than Milo Quick would ever know. And if someone really was coming for this boy, they'd have to come through him first. Which was something that Ennis Arghdal, the terrifying Sandman of Highgate, would make *very* unpleasant for them.

But in the meantime, the boy should still be allowed to be Milo Quick.

Up to a point.

# IN THE COURT
# OF THE TOTAL KING

**MILO MADE IT TO THE DOOR** of the King's Summer Palace ten steps ahead of Shaw. An eternity. And he wasn't even breathing hard.

Now he stood just inside the long, low, dirty, dark, and cluttered hall. It'd been a warehouse once, used for the storage of old cheese, various exotic molds, rat droppings, and a thousand tons of sawdust. Or at least that's what it smelled like.

Shaw stood beside him, picking his nose with formidable concentration.

At the far end of the room sat the King on his scrap-wood throne. He was a handsome boy, tall and mop-haired. His eyes gleamed with a light that might've seemed mischievous or boyish if it came with a kinder face. At seventeen, he was older and a bit taller than those collected below him, but he still had a sour child's heart. He was the kind of boy who'd hurt animals and pull the legs off spiders just because he could. Because he was bigger and smarter than a cat or a cockroach and felt the constant, itching need to remind them of this fact. His name was Cuthbert DeGeorge, but almost everyone knew him as the Total King Forever of the Marche and Everything in It.

From his throne, he surveyed the great minds and heroes of

his kingdom arrayed before him—a small army of filthy, scabby, cruel children all yelling and shoving each other and arguing over whose farts smelled worse. All of the Total King's subjects were fighters and all of them were thieves. All of them were children because the court of the Total King was no place for grown-ups. Grown-ups would probably just make them clean the place or tell them all to brush their teeth and go to bed.

Milo waited. He watched Cuthbert as he shouted for one of the boys lingering closest to his throne to bring him a good rock. He watched as a half-dozen boys all scrambled furiously across the rubble behind the throne, scratching and punching each other, fighting to be the one to deliver the perfect stone to the King.

When it was handed to him, Cuthbert bounced it once or twice in his palm, then rose slightly from his throne and threw it hard at the loudest of the boys arguing in the center of the hall.

The rock struck true, hitting a boy called Arik Joffa squarely in the back and knocking a squeal out of him.

All squabbling ceased. In the court of the Total King, every face turned to look upon the throne where Cuthbert DeGeorge once again lounged, one leg thrown over an arm of his chair as if he had nothing better to do in the world than sit there. He held a gentleman's cane in one hand that he never stopped playing with. It was made of dark wood, lovingly polished, and had a heavy silver head carved in the shape of a pug dog's face. For weeks, the King had wanted an *actual* dog that matched the one on his cane. He'd placed a high bounty on the finding of the perfect dog, and though his troops had scoured the Marche stealing dog after dog, none had yet met the Total King's meticulous standards. He was angry, of course. The upside was that at least they'd all been eating well.

From atop his rotten throne, the Total King Forever of the

Marche and Everything in It met the smoldering stares of his loyal subjects and shouted, "What?" as though daring someone to tell him that it was wrong to throw rocks at people. That the Total King Forever couldn't do anything he pleased, anytime he pleased.

He spread his arms and yelled, "No applause?"

He banged the metal-capped tip of the cane on the rotting boards and bits of ship's coaming that made up the platform on which his throne sat, and shouted, "I didn't say stop!"

Milo saw the hate on the floor like sparks in a dark place. Half-heartedly, and with many over-the-shoulder glances, everyone went back to their roughhousing and smashing, but Milo saw the faces of angry boys and girls who wouldn't mind pulling Cuthbert DeGeorge's legs off, if only someone else was there to hold him down.

When Milo looked back toward the throne, the Total King was watching him. He called Milo's name and Milo went, bowing when he stood in front of the throne because he knew that's what people did when standing before kings, but keeping one eye on Cuthbert, too. Shaw followed him up and went to stand at the right hand of the King where he belonged, facing Milo and looking, Milo thought, as proud of himself as any dumb animal ever did.

The King stared at Milo. He sniffed, shifted in his chair, put both feet on the ground, both hands on his cane, and laid his chin on top of them. "Milo Quick . . ." he said, rolling the name around in his mouth like something sweet. "I need something from you."

Milo opened his mouth to ask what it was, but the Total King raised his eyebrows and said, "Ah-ah-ah, Milo. I wasn't finished. I need something from you, but I also have a favor to offer you. Might be an important favor. Might be nothing at all. The game is, you have to agree to what I'm asking before I grant you this favor. Understand?"

This didn't seem like much of a game to Milo at all, so he asked, "Can I refuse?"

The Total King lifted his head and smacked the metal-capped end of his cane onto the boards. "Milo!" he snapped. "You're not playing right. Of course you can't refuse. I'm the Total King. No one gets to refuse."

Milo said he was sorry.

"Now try again. I have a favor to offer you, but only if you agree to do something for me." The Total King leaned forward just enough to make his chair creak. "Now what do you say?"

"Of course," said Milo. "Whatever you ask."

The Total King smiled and spread his arms wide. "Of *course* you will," he repeated. "Now, that's what I like to hear. Did you hear him, Shaw?" He glanced over at his favorite bully. "He said whatever I ask." And then he bounced to his feet, spread his arms, raised his voice so it could be heard by everyone. "Milo Quick will do *whatever I ask*."

Milo could hear thick, growling laughter from behind him. He could hear high, sour giggling. He could feel the furious boredom and hunger for meanness rising like heat off Cuthbert's followers. He could smell it like something sick in the room.

But Cuthbert greased over the crowd with his eyes. He licked his lips and spun the cane in his hands. "That's smart," he said. "That's what I *like* about Milo. Him and his gang, they're rats. They take a little bit here, a little bit there. They nibble, you know? A hat. A wallet. Never so much that it gets noticed. A smart rat never climbs right up on the table, does he? No. He stays below in the dark and carries off the crumbs. And *that* is what I like about Milo Quick." He poked Milo in the chest with the tip of his cane, leaned forward and looked him right in the eyes. "He is a very smart rat."

"So what is it you want?" Milo asked.

The Total King collapsed back onto his throne and kicked his feet up. "No," he said, grinning. "I want you to say it first."

"Say what?"

"Say that you're a very smart rat."

Laughter again. Milo hunched his shoulders and felt sticks and clumps of wet cloth hitting his back, a rain of sawdust in his hair. He said, "I am," because there was no other answer to that question that wouldn't end with him bloody.

"*Say* it."

Milo took a breath. The sawdust tickled his neck.

"I am a very smart rat."

"That's right," said the Total King. "But you're *my* smart rat, Milo." And then he stood halfway up from his throne, looked out over the floor and yelled, "MINE!"

Immediately, the sticks and garbage stopped. The royal court quieted. And the Total King sat back down and said, "See? No one touches what's mine, Milo. Not never. And what I want from you is the same thing I want when I ask for anything from anybody. I want *more*."

"More of what?"

"Everything."

Milo blinked and the Total King tapped his cane impatiently. "Come on, Milo. I just said how smart you were to everyone. How come you don't get this? It's what a king does. Asks for more. If you're working for me and you're giving me something, I want more of it. If you're bringing me a gift, I want a bigger one. If we're having lunch, I want yours. All of it. And mine, too. *More*. That's how kings work."

That was *not* how kings worked.

"So now, I tell you I want more, what am I talking about?"

"My tithe?" asked Milo.

"Your tithe," agreed the Total King, nodding. "That's why I called for you. It's time to talk about your tithe."

A tithe, in case you don't know, is like a tax. An allowance in reverse. Every week, Milo gave half of everything he stole to the Total King. Half of everything his gang stole. Each week, half of everything all the boys and all the girls on the floor of the Summer Palace stole, and half of what all the gangs that worked the Marche stole was owed to the Total King Forever. And with these halves, the Total King provided for his subjects. He gave them protection, things to smash, doctors when they were hurt, lavish forts like the Summer Palace, and all the dog they could eat.

"You want more?" Milo asked.

"*Much* more," said the King. "Times being what they are, with everyone fighting over every little scrap."

Cuthbert got this way sometimes. Like the thing with the dog, he would make demands and expect everyone to obey. Milo thought about what he and his friends had saved up and tucked away. What they had that was extra. He thought about hats—about the collection of hats they had at home. Hats that he and Jules had stolen, working any one of the dozen games they had for thieving in the streets. How they'd kept the hats like a savings account because, with the labels picked out, they could be sold to any hatter in the Marche for a few dollars, easy.

"We're friends, Milo," the Total King continued. "You bow. You tell me how fearsome I am. And you earn pretty good, too. So I'm just going to keep taking my half, okay? Half of everything. Just like always. Only now, you gotta start bringing in lots more."

Milo thought about how they would sometimes wear the hats to dinner at home, all of them. Everyone in whatever finery they could find—too-large jackets with the sleeves rolled, stolen rings that sparkled but were too cheap for the fences to bother with, necklaces that turned their skin green, crooked eyeglasses and, always, hats. Sometimes they would see how many hats they could wear at the same time before they toppled. Sometimes they would throw them down the hallway to see how far they would fly.

"How much more?" he asked.

The Total King made a show of thinking, then said, "How about twice as much. That's reasonable. And neat, too. And if you can't bring in twice as much, I'll just take everything and we'll be in the same place. That way we can still be friends and things won't be, you know, *difficult* between us. That sounds fair, right?"

Milo scrunched his toes up in his shoes. He chewed at a rough spot on his lip, but said nothing.

"Fair," the King repeated, a piece of his smile sliding away, his charm going cool by a degree, maybe two. "You've already agreed, Milo. You can't take it back. So say it sounds fair."

Milo tried to match the Total King's stare, but couldn't. He hated himself because he could not. Hated Cuthbert DeGeorge and Shaw and the world with the swiftness of paper taking flame. He looked down and felt the tops of his ears go hot. Quietly, he said, "That sounds fair."

The King banged his cane on the boards—two sharp taps. "See? Business over. How easy was that?" He threw himself back in the chair again and stretched like a cat, uncoiling his long limbs. "Gotta understand, it's not just you, Milo. There's a war coming. Haven't you heard? And with the Armada? The blockade? Everyone is getting squeezed."

Milo dug his hands into his pockets and shrugged, because the only thing he wanted to do now was leave. He'd seen the ships out beyond the Flying City same as everyone. Airships and waterships flying strange flags. They'd been arriving since spring had begun feeling like summer and then conspicuously not leaving. People were nervous but not surprised. The Flying City was always at war with something—the wind, the sea, gravity. But for a month or more, everything bad that happened in Highgate had been blamed on the Armada. Broken aerostats, shortages of wood and potatoes, bad weather, traffic, toothaches. All the fault of the Armada.

Some people took it more seriously than others. But Milo liked watching the ships and counting them when there was nothing else to do, because he loved ships and machines of any kind. On the other hand, he was also twelve years old and hungry and bored with talking and sick of standing in the murk of the Summer Palace with sawdust down his collar. He didn't care about wars or armadas or anything else just then. He just wanted to be gone.

"Look at you," Cuthbert continued. "You have five fingers showing on your face. Shaw do that?"

"Yes," said Milo.

"Did you deserve it?"

"I was . . . impertinent."

The King grinned. He twirled his cane. "Impertinent," he said. "Ooh, *impertinent*. That's a good word, Milo. A smart word. Where'd you learn it?"

"Dunno," said Milo.

"Think. I'm interested in what you do when you're not here."

"From a man," lied Milo.

"A man you robbed?"

"No, from a man boxing a bird," he said, which wasn't true at all, but was strange enough to distract anyone from its untruthfulness.

"Boxing a bird?" repeated the King. "That's . . ."

"Saw that, too," said Shaw, nodding. "He was watching some old man fight with a bird over a garbage pile when I found him. When he should've been working."

The Total King looked at Shaw, then at Milo, then at Shaw

again. He turned slowly and poked Shaw with the metal tip of his cane. He asked him if he'd slapped Milo, and Shaw nodded.

"Why?" asked the Total King. "Because he was being impertinent?"

And Shaw said that he didn't know. "He was watching the man and the bird and being a smart-mouth," said Shaw. "That the same thing?"

"Nearly," said the King, grinning wider. "Tell me, which hand did you hit him with?"

"Huh?" asked Shaw.

"Which *hand*," asked the King. "Left hand, right hand?" He held out one, then the other. And Shaw did the same. He stuck out his right hand and said, "This one," then smiled like he'd solved a difficult problem.

And the King lashed out with his stick, twirling it expertly and so fast that it blurred. He brought it down on Shaw's forearm. There was a sound. A flat *crack* like a stick snapping. And for an instant, Milo thought it was the cane that had broken.

But it wasn't.

Shaw dropped to his knees and then fell over sideways. His entire body folded up around his broken arm and he began to howl in shock and pain. Everyone else in the big room froze. Everyone but the King, who, beaming, slowly rose, straightened his cuffs, pretended to blow an imaginary bit of dust off one of his many rings, then stepped down to the stone floor.

"That's what smart buys you, Milo," said the Total King Forever into the sudden vacuum of conversation. His words were punctuated by the tapping of his cane on stone and attended only by the screaming and sobbing of the boy with the broken arm twisting at his feet. "Smart is currency." *Tick.* "Smart is power." *Tick.* "But do you know why you'll never have Shaw's job?"

Milo's skin crawled and his stomach knotted. Shaw had his eyes screwed shut and snot coming out of his nose. His screams faded into snuffling moans as the Total King squatted down beside him and laid a hand gently on his head, smoothing down Shaw's greasy hair while Shaw stared up at him, hurt and bewildered. Milo watched as the Total King Forever petted his prized bully and shushed him, told him everything would be all right. He watched as the King reached out and wiped a tear off Shaw's cheek with the heel of his hand, then looked back at Milo.

"Because he slapped you and you did nothing about it," the King said. "Cruelty. Viciousness. Those have power, too. That's why Shaw is Shaw and you are you."

Milo swallowed hard. He felt sick. "And why you are you," he croaked.

The King nodded. He called for help, and two dozen boys came scurrying. He ordered them to take Shaw to the doctor, and then even more punched and kicked at each other to be the ones given the honor of carrying the King's right-hand man.

And Cuthbert DeGeorge, Total King Forever of the Marche and Everything in It, brushed his hands together and scrubbed his palms on the soft patchwork leather of his pants. He stood and looked around at all the action and motion and nodded as though this, finally, had been a good day's work.

"He's going to want to kill you when he's feeling better," the King said to Milo, gazing out over his court and kingdom. "I'm curious to see how you rise to the occasion."

Milo was afraid to move. The air was thick, syrupy, hot with violence.

"Oh, I owe you a favor," said the King. "You did your part, now it's my turn. Give and take. A healthy relationship."

Milo tried not to look afraid. He tried to swallow, but it felt like there was a stone in his throat he couldn't choke down. He looked at the boys and girls lifting Shaw and carrying him toward the door.

"Someone's been looking for you," said the Total King. "Man and a woman. They came here, asking about you. Where they could find you. Walked right in, through my guards. Two days ago."

Milo tried to focus but his eyes were drawn to the scuffle of children with Shaw at their center. He asked, "Who were they?" but his tongue felt thick as a sausage.

The Total King shrugged. "Dunno. Just stupid old grown-ups. One was called Captain. Wore a coat. Looked salty. The other was a woman with one eye."

"What did they want?"

Cuthbert smiled and pointed with the dog's head on his cane. "You," he said. "They had so many questions. *Do you know Milo Quick? Where can we find Milo Quick?* On and on like that. It was so boring."

Milo watched Shaw go out the door, then looked back at the Total King. "Did you tell them where to find me?"

And Cuthbert DeGeorge said, "Of course not," a little too sharply. He laughed a little too loudly and looked away a little too quickly.

"Of course not," he repeated. "You're my friend, Milo. Protected. Subject of the Total King Forever."

Milo said thank you. The Total King nodded.

"One thing though?" Cuthbert said.

"Yeah."

The Total King leaned forward. "They didn't call you Milo Quick."

# MILO QUICK

**WATCH.**

Milo Quick goes still as a stone. He doesn't breathe. His hands and feet are blocks of ice.

"I'm smart, too, see?" says the Total King. "I figured out who they were talking about. Couldn't have been no one else but you. They told me a story—"

But before Cuthbert can say another word, Milo Quick is gone. He has turned his back on the Total King Forever and walked stiffly toward the door. It happens like *that*. Quick as you can blink.

The Total King calls after him, but the boy doesn't stop. He walks with his shoulders hunched, waiting for the blow, the rock. The King calls his name—"*Milo!*"—but Milo is at the door. He's walking through it. Obviously, there are things happening here that we don't understand yet, but that's okay. That's how it's supposed to be. That's just how stories work sometimes.

At the other end of the room, Cuthbert is standing beside his rattletrap throne, face incandescent with rage. He screams, "Know why I threw the rock, Milo?" but Milo doesn't answer. Doesn't even look back.

"Because I can!"

Loud as it is, the Total King's voice rings small and shrill in the huge room. All around him, the remaining boys and girls are watching. They hang back, just out of range of the next rock, but they stare hungrily at the Total King like they want to bite him. To tear him to pieces with their teeth.

# THE CAPTAIN AND THE
# ONE-EYED WOMAN

**NOW,** we all know that the Total King was lying, right? You and I, we *know* that. It's one of the great things about stories. Sometimes we get to know things that the people in them don't. Sometimes we're going to know about things that happened in the past or might happen in the future. Stories are just magic like that.

And right now, one of the things we know for sure is that the Total King was lying to Milo about what happened when the salty man in the long coat and the one-eyed woman came to visit him.

What *actually* happened was this:

The man (who was only called the Captain) and the woman (who hadn't yet been called anything at all) had walked straight into the Total King's Summer Palace two days earlier. The Captain was smiling, because the Captain was almost always smiling. The woman was not.

They did not obey the rules of the Total King's court. They didn't bow or announce themselves, ask permission or wait their turn. Cuthbert had immediately called for his guards to teach the two adults some manners, but by the time the man and woman were halfway across the floor, Cuthbert had about half as many guards as he'd had before they'd come in. And the whole time, the Captain and the one-eyed woman didn't say a word.

Cuthbert's subjects were scattering. Running in every direction like the place was on fire. So the Total King quickly decided that some diplomacy was in order. He stood up from his throne, ordered his guards back, and politely invited the man and the woman into his private chambers—a small, dirty, cluttered room behind his throne that, if possible, smelled even worse than the Summer Palace's main hall.

Once they were safely behind closed doors, the Total King asked them what they wanted, and the man—the Captain—told him a story that'd surprised him. A story about Milo Quick, even though they hadn't called him Milo Quick. Cuthbert didn't believe it was true, but that didn't matter. They said that Milo was very important to them (which didn't make sense because Milo Quick wasn't really important to anyone), and then they offered Cuthbert a certain amount of money for more information. As much as he could give about the boy they weren't calling Milo Quick.

Cuthbert, of course, had asked for more. Like a king does. Which was when the one-eyed woman had leaned in close like she was going to whisper something to him, and then had punched him in the chest so hard that Cuthbert thought his heart had stopped. After that, she'd dragged him out of his chair and onto the floor, where she sat on his chest and held the point of a knife to the delicate skin just below his right eye.

In that moment, the Total King badly regretted locking the door to his chambers. But he was also glad of it, because if any of his boys had seen him this way? That would've been the end of him. He told himself that the trick now was to get out of this alive and with no visible wounds, because after the man and the woman were gone, he could tell any story he liked about what had happened. No one would know any different.

So Cuthbert DeGeorge, Total King Forever of the Marche and Everything in It, told the Captain and the one-eyed woman everything he knew about the boy who called himself Milo Quick. He answered every question they put to him, and then told them even more.

And when he was done, the Captain took the King's hand, shook it warmly and told him he'd been a great help. He said that if Cuthbert wanted to throw them out in front of everybody, that would be fine.

So Cuthbert had, cursing and spitting and making a lot of noise about them never setting foot in his kingdom again. He thought he did a very convincing job of it.

But what he didn't notice was that everyone in the Summer Palace was watching the Captain and the one-eyed woman, not him. And he didn't notice that the whole time he was stomping and shouting and acting like he was throwing them out, he had a line of blood running down his cheek from the prick of the woman's knife under his eye. A single bloody tear.

But see? Now we know about that, too. We know everything we need to.

Because stories are just magic like that sometimes.

# MILO, JULES, AND DAGDA ON THE STREETS OF THE MARCHE

**JULES AND DAGDA SAT IN THE SUN** by the old wall that bordered Oldedge Market and waited for Milo.

It was the same wall where, earlier, Milo had watched the man box a carrier bird. The same wall upon which they'd all sat, scrambled, and played for years, in whose shadows and dust they'd met a thousand times before. Just Milo, Jules, and Dagda together—lounging, anxious, furious, and bored all at the same time. When they were younger, they'd bring things for each other—food mostly, little things they thought the others might like—and it'd become a habit, comforting in its repetition. Like getting coffee from Sabeen in the morning or watching the windup toys made by Sanel the Toymaker at his stall in the market in the afternoon.

"Does it make you nervous when he's late?" Jules asked.

And Dagda said no, it didn't, as she skipped a little ways along the top of the wall with her eyes closed and her hands held out to either side, then stopped, spun precisely on one foot and walked back. "Besides, I know he's on his way."

Which was true. He was. And even though he'd been there first (before receiving his summons to see the Total King), now, arriving a second time, he was late. Last to arrive.

And worse, he'd brought nothing with him. Dagda had saved him half an apple (gone brownish now, but still sweet) and Jules had brought him a sticky rice ball wrapped in a large green leaf. But Milo had nothing to share except news (all of it bad), which was rude, so he began by apologizing, saying, "Sorry. I wasn't . . . I wasn't thinking."

Dagda hummed something with her eyes closed and said it was okay, then walked along the curve of the wall and back again. Jules bit his rice ball in half and offered the remains to Milo, saying "Punishment," with his mouth full, and then smiling with his teeth full of rice and laughing, which made Milo laugh and punch Jules, who then tried to knock the other half of the rice ball out of Milo's hand, and the whole thing turned into a wrestling match that only ended when Milo shoved the entire other half of the rice ball into his own mouth and chewed furiously, saying, "See? See? It's gone now. Too late!"

No one passing through that corner of Oldedge Market paid the boys any mind, and Dagda just shook her head and tried to stay out of their way.

Eventually, they stopped. Dusted themselves off. And then Milo told Jules and Dagda what had happened with the Total King—what he was demanding and what he was threatening. He told them about the rock and about Shaw. The broken arm. The flat, sickening crack of the bone.

He didn't tell them what the King had said to him after *He's going to want to kill you when he's feeling better.* Because, to be honest, Milo was trying very hard not to think about that himself. And he didn't tell them about the man called Captain and the woman with one eye, either—how there might be two people walking the

streets of the Flying City right now who maybe knew him by another name. His *real* name, which he'd never told to anyone, not
even Jules, because the boy who'd had that name was gone. Lost.
Dead (or mostly dead). And Milo Quick was just Milo Quick.

The boy thought he was doing this to protect his friends. The
less they knew, he figured, the less they'd worry. He believed that
Shaw was his problem (at least for now). And though the three of
them shared everything and talked about everything, all the time,
they didn't talk about where they'd come from. Or what they'd
been before they were what they were now.

Still, Milo's secrets were heavy. They lay in his stomach like
a rich meal that he'd eaten too much of, and it sometimes took
all of his concentration just to keep them from spewing out.
And as things would turn out over the next days and weeks and
months and years, this—this moment right here and the decision
to keep to himself what the Total King had told him—was the
worst choice Milo Quick would ever make. He didn't understand
it then. *Couldn't* understand it any more than we can know the
person we'll be when we get to tomorrow, or what we'll see there.
But that's the thing about choices. We never know the bad ones
until we make them. And once we make them, there's no going
back. All that's left are the consequences.

But for the moment, Dagda took the news about Cuthbert and
their tithe silently, looking out toward a low bank of clouds fluffing
on the horizon. Jules was in his customary rage.

"What I'm saying is, this ain't fair! Or even possible, is it? We
already give Bert half—"

And Milo said, "Well . . ." and tipped his head a little to one
side, meaning that really, what was the point in them all being
criminals if they didn't cheat a little (or a lot) already? He took
the small, hook-bladed knife from behind his belt buckle and used

it to carve a moon of sweetness from the brown half apple that Dagda had given him. He had no appetite, but he pushed the slice between his lips anyway, forced his teeth to chew.

"Okay, so we're already *supposed* to give up half. And now he wants our other half, too? Which, even if we quit skimming and tucking away our best things, still wouldn't make up for a whole 'nother half again of our tithe. That about right?"

Milo nodded.

"So what are we supposed to do then?"

"We could sell the hats," Milo said. "Enough there to satisfy Cuthbert for a couple weeks."

"No," Jules said, crossing his arms. "I like the hats."

Dagda ran along the wall and jumped over Milo where he sat. The boys, if they'd been paying attention, might've been impressed, but Dagda knew they were just boys. They could only pay attention to one thing at a time.

"We could work harder," Milo said.

"Won't matter."

"You saying we couldn't work any harder if we wanted to?"

Dagda was wearing pink shoes. Milo only noticed once she landed, grit scraping under the bright white soles. He had no idea where she'd found them. Or stolen them. He had no idea that Dagda's feet hurt all the time now. They talked about everything, all the time. Except certain things.

"I'm saying that there ain't much point in us being outlaws, is there, if we spend all day and all night working at it."

Milo snorted out a laugh, pushed another piece of apple into his mouth, then slapped Jules on the shoulder and told him it was all going to be fine. He said, "Cuthbert's just worried, is all," and tried not to think about the sound of Shaw's arm breaking. "About the Armada, all the soldiers around." He tried not to think

about the way he'd frozen in place when the Total King had said
his other name. "He'll probably forget about it sooner or later. He
might've forgotten about it already. But in case he doesn't, I have
a plan."

"You always say you have a plan," Jules huffed.

"Know why that is?" Milo asked.

"Because he always has a plan," said Dagda, bouncing down
off the wall to sit on the other side of Jules. Milo pointed at her
with his knife and nodded, grinning.

"You heard her."

Because all of this was just some grand adventure anyway,
wasn't it? A great game with no parents and no rules and no bed-
times. Because even in that moment Milo truly believed that all
he had to do was keep thinking one step ahead and no bad thing
would ever touch them.

He said, "Can you two gather everyone up for work tonight?"
They'd meet again two hours after dark. Up in the aeries. "At that
place," Milo said. "Where we do the stuff."

"The first place or the second place?" Jules asked.

Milo made a face. "The second place, Jules. No one goes to
the first place anymore."

Dagda asked, "At the top or the bottom?"

"The bottom."

"Really?"

"Yup," said Milo. And despite the sour taste in his mouth and
the tightness in his stomach that never seemed to go away, he
smiled at his friends. "Tonight we're gonna rob the mails."

# DAGDA

**DAGDA REMINDED MILO** to eat some lunch, then slipped off to the east, toward Front Street, where Tristan and Llyr would be, playing Where's My Mommy for the tourists.

She walked beside the old wall that marked the outer boundary of Oldedge Market, letting her fingers drag along the crumbling white stone.

She could remember when these walls were whole, true, strong, and tall, bordering a sloped bowl where concerts and plays were held. The walls had open arches, crawling with ivy and climbing flowers. In the heat of summer, in the dusk, the smells of jasmine and finger limes filled the air. Lightning bugs would cluster in the arches and along the grasses that ringed the walls.

In those days, they would light the transfer cables stretching down from the aerostats with tiny bulbs that would blink on and off, making it look like it was raining drops of light. Music would fill the air, and out beyond the edges of the city, the solar gliders would catch the last rays of the sinking sun as they looped and arced in toward their docking stations.

She'd always wanted to try one of the solar gliders, but she'd been too young and too fragile. Too valuable, her father had said. He'd always been afraid of something going wrong. Right up until everything did.

When the wall curved in a direction she didn't want to go, Dagda ducked her head, pulled her arms in tight to her sides, and slipped into the maze of crowded streets and alleys that bordered the market. She wanted so badly to feel the sun on her skin, but instead balled her hands into fists and held her sleeves over her knuckles to hide her scars. She pulled up the back of her shawl like a hood and buried her face up to her nose in the part wrapped around her neck, smelling smoke and breath and dust like memory in the loose fabric. She made herself small. Just another forgettable girl, making her way a little too quickly, a little too nimbly, out to the bright and wind-beaten blocks at the very edge of the Flying City.

Dagda didn't see the old man watching her. Maybe because she had her head down or maybe because her mind was on other things. He had a white mustache, wore a shirt made of a twisted white sheet, and had a long, bloody scratch down one arm. He stood casually, smiling, smoking a short, stumpy pipe and talking with a short, stumpy man.

The old man is Semyon Beli, of course. The man who boxed the carrier bird. We've met him before. The other one, though? Him, we haven't seen yet.

His name is Reyn Farrago and he's a ship's engineer. He's solid as a packed box, lumpy with muscle, dressed in a stained and patched boiler suit with his sleeves rolled to the elbows and a dirty string around his neck hung with compression screws. The skin of his arms is loud with tattoos.

Still, Dagda slid right past without noticing anything more than the sweet, sticky smell of Semyon's pipe smoke. The two men, though, took very careful stock of her.

"The girl?" asked Semyon Beli.

The engineer nodded, scratching the side of his face with nails showing black half-moons of grease. "If that's what you want to call her, then sure. That's the girl."

Semyon Beli stroked the curl of his long mustache and said, "Remarkable."

Reyn shuffled his heavy feet and looked up at Semyon. "We should tell the Captain."

"Hmm," Semyon hmm'd. "No, *you* should tell the Captain, I think. I, on the other hand, should follow her a bit and see where she goes."

"But what about the others?"

"The others don't matter right now," Semyon said. He started to walk backward away from Reyn. "Go and find the Captain," he said. "Tell him we've found the girl." He shooed at the engineer with his hands. "I'm sure he has his eye on the boy by now, so I'll remain with the girl and see where she leads us. A wonderful plan!"

"But I don't know where the boy *is*," said Reyn, and Semyon Beli threw his hands out wide and smiled beneath the curl of his mustache, his teeth yellow and stained. "He's just a boy, my friend. Think like a boy and you will surely find yourself and him in the very same place!"

# JULES

**JULES WATCHED MOUSE GO,** drifting away along the curve of the wall. When she was gone, he looked at Milo and asked, "You okay?"

"Course," said Milo. "Just . . . Yeah. I'm fine."

There was no one in the world that Milo Quick trusted more than Jules Cael. For years, they'd been best friends, partners in everything they'd done. They'd slept most nights an arm's reach away from each other. Shared meals. Fought battles side by side. They loved each other, though neither would ever say it out loud, and had promised once, a long time ago, with spit and swears, to never leave the other. Not for gold or girls or even death.

But even though Milo wanted to tell Jules the truth, he didn't. Couldn't. So he swallowed his secrets. And when they threatened to come right back up, he closed his teeth and let the words tick silently against the backs of them. To anyone else, it looked like a smile.

"Okay," said Jules. "But really, the mail?"

"Sometimes we get lucky," Milo said.

"Sometimes," Jules agreed. Then he added, "It's dangerous."

"More than riding the pistons down the rope line?" Milo asked. Because they'd done that when they were younger—waiting for the large pistons to be lifted from the engines of ships they were breaking and hung from a line that stretched from the engine compartments to the ground so they could be slid all the way down. The bravest or stupidest among the children working in the yards would leap onto them once they were hung and ride them the whole distance. Jules had been the bravest and stupidest more times than Milo could count. "And there was no treasure at the end of those rides," he finished.

"Fun, though," Jules said.

"Sure," said Milo. "Wouldn't be much point otherwise."

Jules nodded. He was quiet for a minute, then asked, "You really think there's gonna be a war?"

Milo shrugged. "There's always about to be a war, isn't there? Everybody always says so. But there never seems to actually be one."

"Just saying, what if there is?"

"More pickings for us, right? Smashed places. Walls broken down." Milo had no idea. He'd never seen a war before. But he tried to sound confident. "Means good thieving."

Jules made fists, released them. "All them ships, though? And the men on 'em?"

"It's a grown-up problem. It's got nothing to do with us."

"Yeah. I guess."

Milo looked at Jules, who stared off past the edge of the city and scratched at the side of his nose. "You thinking about something, Jules?" he asked.

"No," said Jules, then, "Maybe." Then, "Look, I was just thinking that if there *is* a war, or some kind of trouble . . . I don't know."

And there were a hundred ways Jules could've ended that sentence. And though he said none of them, Milo must've heard all of them, all at the same time. *If there is, I'm going to leave this place. If there is, I'm going to go. If there is, it isn't safe for any of us here, so I'm going to find the first ride I can and leave here forever.* The possibilities must've rung like a bell in the boy's head, because they left Milo temporarily stunned and speechless.

"Anyway," Jules said, "I was just thinking." He chuckled. "Ain't always what I'm best at, is it?"

He hopped down off the wall.

"I'm gonna go find Keelan," he said. "Should be down around the Alley, looking at stuff."

"Okay," said Milo.

"Okay."

Jules didn't look at Milo. And Milo didn't look at him. "See you up there, then? Tonight."

"Okay."

And Jules took off at a fast walk, his head down, the back of his neck hot, and something aching in his chest. He went south toward Shippers Alley, where he knew Keelan would be, counting the things coming and going from the ships docked below. Writing down numbers in notebooks. Amounts of this, lacks of that. Pictures of gulls and pumpjacks and broken generators.

Milo'd said to gather everyone up, so that was what Jules was going to do. He cut through the breaking yards and went right down to the very edge of the Flying City where the dead ships hung like caught whales from the stones. He followed roads that had no names—just ever-shifting paths through the towering piles of scrap metal and copper sheeting and old mattresses and propeller blades—then turned onto an unmarked factory street that everyone in the Marche called Casting Row.

He slipped down it with his eyes on the toes of his shoes and his hands shoved deep in his pockets, weaving through the men and boys who stood before the glowing doors of the liners' shops and metalworking lines that blew sparks like a dragon farting. His feet crunched ash and slag. The bang of hammers and clatter of chain drives was like a heavy curtain of noise that he had to push through, and the pounding heat from a hundred small furnaces and smelting pots sucked the breath from his lungs.

All the way at the end of the street was the slag yard and the shoebox stacks of low, cramped rooms where those who worked on Casting Row all lived—the luckiest of them under actual roofs and behind actual doors. There was a high fence and rattling gates, but only when Jules got close did he look up, slow his steps. He counted doors in his head (three in from the corner, second level up) until he reached one gate in particular, and when he passed by it, he let his fingers trail over the lock. It was new since last time he'd been this way.

Jules nodded. He stopped and looked up at the top of the fence. He leaned forward just a little, as if meaning to peek through some gap between the tin sheeting and plastic, but then didn't. The lock was enough. It was what had been promised to him. He started walking again and didn't look back.

Of all the places Jules Cael had ever escaped from, the house on Casting Row had been the worst. He'd still had blood on his hands when the Sandman, Ennis Arghdal, had caught him and made a deal with him. It was a long time ago, but the only part of their arrangement he'd cared about until he'd met Milo was that his mother would be safe there without him. That someone would look out for her. It wasn't something that he and the Sandman talked about. They didn't have to. The new lock was proof that Ennis was still keeping his part of the bargain. Milo being alive was proof that Jules was keeping his.

Because Milo wasn't the only one with secrets he couldn't tell.

# MILO

**MILO SAT,** slowly shredding the green leaf in which his rice had been wrapped into tiny bits of sticky green confetti. He stared at his feet. At the toes of his too-small shoes dangling a few inches above the ground. There were things he needed to do, but he was doing none of them. Not yet.

Instead, the boy was thinking. Plotting. Planning, perhaps. Hard to know. Maybe he was imagining elephants or counting on his fingers and toes. But probably not.

Probably he was thinking about Jules and what he'd meant when he'd said he was thinking of what he'd do if there was a war. Join up? Find a ship that would have him and sail away forever? It wasn't like Milo didn't understand. The Flying City seemed like it was getting smaller and smaller every day. And how long could they all keep getting by on stolen hats and rice balls anyway? So probably he was thinking that Jules had smelled the same thoughts on him. The same unspoken dreams. The same betrayal.

Probably he was thinking about what the Total King had said to him. Who wouldn't be? Probably he was thinking about two visitors to the Flying City who, somehow, knew his real name.

Honestly, none of us can really know what the boy was thinking just then, only that he had many things on his mind. Some of them might've been elephants. Some of them undoubtedly were not. Lost in the market's morning crowds, overlooked, invisible, he tore his leaf and kicked his feet and thought his thoughts. All we can know is that he sat until he didn't anymore. Until his head snapped up and he looked off toward the edge of the city, over both his shoulders, and then up in the direction of the aeries.

All we can know is that he had things to do. That one moment he was there and the next he was gone. The boy could do that. Like fat in a pan, he could melt into nothing. Like the steam of breath on a cold day. You had to watch him closely to see the change, the moment of transition.

Not far away, a salty-looking man in a deck jacket and an airship captain's hat watched the boy go. Just like Cuthbert DeGeorge had promised, Milo Quick had come to his filthy little clubhouse when called, and the man had followed him all the way back to Oldedge Market. He'd been watching him for quite some time, as a matter of fact. On and off ever since his conversation with the child who claimed to be king of all this rust and garbage. So the Captain knew exactly how quick Milo could be.

Blink and you could lose him completely.

# SHIPPERS ALLEY

**HUSH NOW.** Listen.

Jules put the clang and rattle of Casting Row behind him, but now he could hear something else. It started like the wind combing through the transmission lines on a blowy day. A buzzing hum that came from no place. It started like the sound of the waves when you can't yet see the ocean.

Watch and you can see him falter, his steps growing unsure as he listens. For a minute, Jules wondered if something had gone wrong with his ears, but with every step he took, the sound changed. Grew larger. Louder. It became the sound of rolling thunder in the dark. Of something huge and monstrous shouting into a storm.

Jules wasn't afraid, because Jules was fearless (mostly). But the hugeness of the noise was enough to make his heart pound. He scrambled up a stack of wooden pallets, leapt and reached for the hanging rung of a metal ladder bolted to the side of a storehouse. He climbed and the sound grew louder. He ran across one roof, jumped to a second, and the noise gained weight. It grew corners and sharp edges. He could hear raised voices. Shouting. Stomping feet and rattling iron. When he came to the edge of the second roof, he scrambled up onto the chest-high wall that ran around its edge and stood there, taking a deep breath.

Shippers Alley was below him, a broad lane normally choked with trucks and carts, piles of cargo, and the crews of the ships moored above and below. Precarious docks stretched out into the nothingness past the edge of the city, the cargo rails snaked above, and the sweeping arms of massive cranes that brought up loads from the water-going ships anchored below. In the past weeks, the Alley had been quieter than usual with fewer and fewer ships able to pass through the ring of the Armada unmolested. There'd been shortages of everything but rumors.

But today there were *hundreds* of people. Maybe thousands. There were pull-carts piled with luggage and wagons with people hanging from the sides, beating their way through the crowd with sticks. There were lamps and clocks and bags and furniture and entire trucks abandoned like islands in a sea of people that stretched back for two blocks. And all of them were shouting. All of them were waving their hands in the air. All of them were pressing forward, toward the edge of the city.

And somewhere down there in the mess of it all was Keelan.

# TRISTAN AND LLYR
# ON FRONT STREET

**DAGDA FOUND THE TWINS,** Tristan and Llyr, huddled with their backs against the Front Street battlements. They'd positioned themselves between the Statham Confectionery and a brightly dressed harlequin man trying to sell stale popcorn balls from a cart. It was a place that smelled better than anywhere else in the entire Flying City—like hot sugar, warm butter, caramel, and corn all together.

Front Street ran block after block along the edge of the Flying City. Visitors to Highgate always loved the view, the snapping flags, the brick archways of clamoring arcades and the smells of food and beer and frying things. They would come here to hold hands and stroll, marveling at the impossibility of the place as they walked along the battlements with nothing between them and the long drop down to the sea below but a low, toothed stone wall and the squat, round towers of the coastal artillery. The air cabs loaded and let off on Front Street. Or had once. At night, it lit itself up like a carnival and offered different pleasures. But no one born to the stone and wonderment of the Flying City ever went there. Not unless they were coming to swindle, sandbag, or fleece those who didn't know enough to stay well away.

Tristan and Llyr were slapping each other and haggling over

the split of a single sticky popcorn ball. They were still dressed in their stolen fancy clothes. Their eyes were red and raw from pretending to cry. They stopped fighting as soon as Dagda approached, though. They grinned at her and offered melting fistfuls of popcorn, but she shook her head.

"The man gave us this," said Tristan.

"No one was buying," said Llyr.

"You're supposed to be working," Dagda said. Because they were supposed to be begging coins off the tourists, pretending to be rich children lost or abandoned here in the only part of the Flying City where such a child might last more than five minutes before disappearing.

"No people," said Tristan.

"All vanished," said Llyr.

"Look around," said Tristan.

And Dagda did, looking up and down the reach of Front Street and seeing plenty of buskers, hawkers, cabbies, soldiers, and food sellers, too, but only a very few people who didn't spend every day working here. The harlequin man had no customers at all, and it looked like it'd been so long since he'd seen one that he'd forgotten what they looked like. He just stood there, sucking on his teeth and staring out toward the sea.

"That's odd," she said. "Where is everyone?"

But Tristan and Llyr had lost interest in the conversation and gone back to slapping each other and pulling each other's hair. Dagda asked them whether the popcorn ball was their breakfast or their lunch. Tristan said one, Llyr said the other. She asked them whether they'd eaten anything all day *not* held together with melted sugar, and Tristan said, "Seagull!" and Llyr laughed and showed her teeth. "See the feathers?"

Dagda shook her head. She said, "Time to go home anyway.

Hopefully you can put all that energy to good use, because we're working tonight."

The harlequin man sneezed hard enough that the bells hanging from the drooping points of his hat jingled. He sighed and wiped his nose on the sleeve of his bright patchwork coat.

Dagda said, "Let's go now." She told the twins to follow her. To stay close. And then she glanced one more time up and down Front Street at all the quiet and lack.

# SEMYON BELI

**SEMYON BELI** had been following the girl for blocks and blocks, all the way to this abandoned place with its winking lights, good smells and emptiness. When he passed by them, neither the two little ones nor the girl paid him any mind. He was just another old man walking Front Street, taking in the sea air and the spectacular views.

And Semyon Beli gave not the slightest sign that he'd noticed them either, even though he most certainly had.

He simply walked on, humming a little tune to himself, until he reached what he thought was an advantageous bit of wall between two artillery positions, climbed up onto it, sat down and let his feet dangle over the edge of the world.

He gave his attention then to the broad sweep of ocean and sky—and to the lines of Armada ships floating casually on the water or twisting in the air, just out of range of the Flying City's prodigious and abundant guns.

Semyon knew things that Milo and his friends did not. He knew, for example, one hundred and nine different knots that sailors tied. He knew how to find his position on the sea in a storm. He knew how to swear and bargain reasonably well in eleven different languages. And he knew that very soon this city was going to be uninhabitable—that those ships, sent from halfway around the world by powerful, angry, frightened men, had come here to burn Highgate to the ground.

It'd been a miracle that the Captain had brought them in at all—high and silent five nights ago, running the Armada's blockade lines in their little airship, the *Halcyon*. They'd floated like a leaf on the wind, carefully threading a blind spot through the night patrols that Semyon had discovered after nearly a week of watching. The *Halcyon*'s attack motors had already been unusable, her cordage more knot and splice than cable, every handkerchief aboard strung to catch any whisper of wind.

The drop into gun range of the Highgate coastal artillery had been like a suicide barely averted. Every light on them, swooping gunboats on their tail. And the Captain in the pilot's box, laughing the whole way.

But he'd been right in choosing his approach. He'd said that no one shoots at the mailman. Not when he's arriving, anyhow. So they'd hung those little blue-and-white-checked flags that Semyon had stolen—the colors of the Transit Post, international airmail—from the bowsprit and the aerials and the foresail stays. And that'd saved them, most likely. Those flags, careful planning, inspired piloting, and a spoonful of luck.

Maybe two spoonfuls, all things considered.

Once the Highgate defenders had seen the *Halcyon*'s borrowed colors snapping in the wind, they'd cleared a slip for her to land, blared the emergency sirens, and leveled their big guns and lights at the pursuing Armada gunboats. The Highgate skirmishers had spilled wind, hauled up and closed ranks behind them, chasing off the *Halcyon*'s pursuers with deck guns and harsh language. For weeks upon weeks, the Armada's blockade had harassed any ship coming or going from the Flying City, cutting it off by sea and air, determined to make sure nothing arrived and doubly determined that nothing—not a stick, not a breath, not a man or woman, boy or girl—left. So when the *Halcyon* had run the blockade? Gods, they'd *cheered* the Captain from the docks. Pounded his back like a conquering hero when he'd docked the ship and stepped over the rail.

And those men in the aeries, they all knew how bad things were going to get, and how soon. The artillerymen were sleeping by their guns. They'd already greased the carriage of every carronade and boarding gun and painted the decking on the emergency slips red, the better to hide spilled blood.

If Semyon Beli closed his eyes, he could too easily imagine the Flying City afire, so he did not do that. Instead he tried to fix it in his mind the way it was here and now—lovely, bright, and sweet, sparkling in the summer sun. If they were lucky, if the Captain was fast and clever, he might never have to see it any other way. He could not save the city (because some things are just not possible, not even for Semyon Beli), but he *could* be gone before the worst happened.

But not yet. For now, he just watched the Armada ships. More were arriving every day, from all quarters of the compass. And none were coming for the view. From a pocket he took a collapsible telescope and glassed over the ships he could see, saying their names silently to himself, his lips barely moving. He repeated each one three times—the better to remember them once he was back aboard the *Halcyon* and in front of his charts. Because they were going to have to leave this place soon.

And leaving, Semyon knew, was going to be *much* harder than getting here had been.

# JULES AND KEELAN
# ON SHIPPERS ALLEY

**DOWN ON THE ALLEY** the crowds were so thick that Jules couldn't see the ground. From above, it was just a surging ocean of people all shoving and shouting, dragging luggage, gripping children, waving papers in the air. At the front, people were jammed right against the safety rails around the elevator platforms. A line of men, some of them police, stood on the other side, pushing back. There were armed soldiers on the docks.

Jules finally spotted Keelan on the edge of the mob, pressed up against the brick wall of a sorting house, standing on an overturned cart that'd spilled a load of bags and boxes. He had a long scarf wrapped around his neck and the bottom half of his face, and a heavy coat swallowing the whole of him despite how warm the day was. In his hands, he clutched a thick sheaf of papers covered in notes and numbers. When Jules got close enough, he could see that Keelan was drawing something along one edge of the top page. A crane with the sun shining behind it, its cargo platform packed with frightened people who were just a mass of dark, angry scribbles.

Keelan didn't hear Jules coming. The sound of too many voices, all raised at once, all shouting to be heard over every other voice, must've filled his head like static. So when Jules was suddenly just *there*—dropping down from the roof above onto the cart beside him—Keelan was so startled that he jumped and nearly dropped all his papers in the dirt.

"Jules," he said, then dragged the back of one hand across his nose, seeming to forget that the scarf was there. He pointed to the crowd and said something that Jules couldn't hear. So Jules grabbed him by the shoulder and leaned closer. Even still, Keelan nearly had to shout. "It's been like this all morning," he said. "The crowd just keeps getting bigger."

Jules asked what they were all doing, and Keelan shrugged, sniffed, hugged his coat tighter around himself. He said, "The only things coming up from the boats are guns. The only thing going down is people. More and more of them every hour. I don't know what's happening, do you?"

And Jules said he didn't, which was maybe half true. Then he said it didn't matter anyway, because Keelan needed to gather up his pens and papers and come along.

"We're working tonight!" Jules yelled, but Keelan couldn't really hear him, because just then the crowds surged, stumbling and shouting, as a group of men in uniforms rushed past, shoving people out of their way, and more people—dragging luggage and carrying babies and stacks of boxes—came following behind.

"We have to go!" Jules yelled.

"Where?" yelled Keelan.

"Milo says we're going to rob the mails tonight!"

And Keelan sneezed and said, "Oh. Okay." He shuffled his papers, pulled down his scarf, then pointed at something behind Jules's back. "That man has been following me all day. Is that something I should be worried about?"

# THAT MAN

**THAT MAN** was absolutely something Keelan should've been worried about. Firstly because it was some strange man following him all over the Flying City, and let's be honest, nothing good ever comes of something like that.

But also, this wasn't just any strange man. His name was Vaclav. He was sail master aboard the *Halcyon*—the ship that'd brought the Captain, the one-eyed woman, Reyn Farrago and Semyon Beli to the Flying City. And he was, among other things, enormous.

No. *Enormous.* That word, in this context, means something. If you are very tall, imagine someone taller. And then imagine Vaclav being even bigger than that. And if you're very small, imagine . . . I don't know. Imagine the largest person you can, then add some in every direction. That's how big Vaclav was.

He stood across the Alley from Keelan and Jules like a stone. He was gray like stone. Hard like stone. Unmoving like stone. Big as a mountain and just as cheerful. He stared stonily and didn't care at all that the unusual child with the pens and papers could see him. The Captain hadn't told him to be sly, and sly wasn't something Vaclav was good at being anyway. The Captain had told him to follow, so he'd followed.

This was just where he'd ended up.

# JULES AND KEELAN

**JULES TURNED** and looked at the man Keelan was talking about. He could see Vaclav over the heads of all the people pushing their way into the Alley. He was big (enormous, actually), but standing so still he was almost invisible.

"It's nothing, Keel," Jules said. "Just some man."

"You sure?" asked Keelan. He didn't like the look of the big man. He didn't really like the look of anyone, but this man seemed worse than most. People called him Keelan the Coward because there'd never been a loud noise, a raised voice, or even an angry expression that he hadn't run from. Or wanted to very badly. Even his friends called him Keelan the Coward. Even Milo. It didn't bother him. At least not too much. At least not so much that he'd ever say so out loud. He knew that cowards might get made fun of, but they also got to keep all their blood inside them, and that, to Keelan, seemed like a decent bargain.

"I'm sure," Jules said. "It's nothing. Let's go home. I'll race you."

# VACLAV

**VACLAV WAS STILL WATCHING** the awkward boy when he tucked his pens and papers away, jumped down off whatever he was standing on, and took off running, legs pumping and elbows flapping like a goose scared by its own reflection in the water.

His own son would've been maybe the same size now as this odd child, Vaclav thought, with the same tangle of limbs, all of them too big and going in different directions.

Another boy had come, and he ran, too. Vaclav watched both boys across the river of people between them. Both of them scrambled and slithered against the flow of the crowds trying to make it to the elevators and the ships below. Both ducked and slid through gaps that only children could see, turned a corner, and were gone.

Vaclav knew that boys sometimes ran for no reason. Sometimes they ran just because they hadn't yet become old enough to know to save their running for when it really mattered. The big one seemed to run for the fun of it. But the one he'd been watching (Vaclav had forgotten the child's name already, thinking only of his own son's name) ran like he had reasons.

He ran like it was for his life.

There was no way he was going to be able to find him again in this crowd, Vaclav thought. No way to follow. Which was fine. He didn't want to be here any longer anyway.

So Vaclav turned and walked away from the Alley. It was time to go talk to the Captain. He had to move against the crowd, but for someone his size, that wasn't very difficult at all.

# MILO QUICK AND
# THE CAPTAIN

**LATER,** when he had all the time in the world for thinking about it, Milo Quick would be unable to say exactly what it was that he'd noticed first about Reyn Farrago's wrenches.

Was it the sound they made? The fine, metallic clinking of the dozen box-ended combination wrenches hanging from the man's belt as he slouched through Oldedge? Or the gleam of them, maybe. The way they seemed to say *steal me steal me steal me* every time the summer sun glinted off their polished, chromed beauty.

The boy had been sitting beneath a sun-faded orange-and-white tent in Oldedge, negotiating with Sanel the Toymaker. Sanel sat cross-legged on one side of a blanket the color of an old bruise, feet in rubber sandals, eyes staring, enormous and unblinking behind magnifying lenses. Milo sat on the other side of the blanket, staring back.

Between them, Sanel's toys all ticked and skittered. He made automatons—small, clever little windups that did remarkable things. There was a ticktocking gentleman in a cloth suit who walked and bowed and tipped his hat to anything that crossed in front of him. A dragon that breathed actual licks of fire. A toy girl who would dance in circles, her arms raised, dark hair flowing out behind her.

The houses of Highgate's richest families were filled with

Sanel's toys. But today, Milo was negotiating for something much simpler. He'd already laid down two wallets and a filigreed cigarette case. A capped ink pen with a steel barrel. Clucking his tongue, he'd tossed the top hat he'd stolen earlier into the air and caught it by its brim, rolled his wrist and flipped it up onto his own head, where it promptly fell down over his eyes.

"It's a good one, Sanel," the boy had said, peeking out from beneath the brim to see if Sanel was laughing. "And fresh, too. Still warm from the last head that had it. So what d'you say?"

The toymaker's face had split in a grin. He'd lifted the hat off the boy's head and put it on his own, running one long, delicate finger along the brim to give it a jaunty set.

"Deal?" Milo had asked.

Sanel had nodded. He laid down a ring of cast brass on which perched a silvery spider with six tiny glass pebble eyes and eight jointed legs that could be moved so that it looked like it was clinging to your finger, or ready to leap and bite.

It was a toy. A rich child's party favor. But it was more than that, too, because the boy had plans for it. Because the boy *always* had plans. He'd slipped it onto his finger and held it up to admire it. He'd curled the legs and touched their sharp tips.

"You're perfect," he'd said to the spider. "I'm gonna call you Henry."

One thing Milo knew for sure: *that* was the moment when he'd first noticed the engineer and his clattering wrenches. Reyn had gone slouching by Sanel's tent, the singing wrenches tied to a rope around his waist—so easy to grab and cut and run. He was short, stooped, his arms banded with muscle and crawling with tattoos. He'd loped along almost sideways when he walked, like a crab scuttling.

Milo was standing before he even knew he was standing, eyes stuck to the engineer, dragged by the gravitation of those sparkling wrenches. He'd stepped carefully clear of Sanel's dancing, bowing, clicking toys and drifted smoothly into step behind the shuffling man. The boy was hungry. Everyone was hungry, all the time. And Milo knew that those tools in his hands could feed him and his friends well the next time some rich man came to the yards with a ship that needed breaking.

So watch him now. He stops when the man stops, moves when the man moves. He stays still as a shadow when Reyn suddenly stretches all the way up onto his toes and looks around, muttering, "So where are you, then?" As he waves his hands and says, "Too many people, too many people . . ."

The boy has already drawn his hook-bladed knife. All he has to do is pass close, cut the man's rope belt, grab it and run. In his head, the day goes quiet. His blood hums in him like it is made of bees. He's so focused on the man and his wrenches that he doesn't see the tall man in the long coat who's been standing in the shade, watching Reyn Farrago shuffle back and forth and back and forth across the market for nearly an hour now, tools jangling, waiting for this particular boy to make a move.

This is the Captain. Young, handsome, smiling, tipping his head now and then to ladies who pass him by. Who else could it be? Captain Rodion Klim of the airship *Halcyon*, who'd come all the way to the Flying City to steal Milo like a watch or a wallet. Who'd been watching the boy for days and nights now, sniffing after him like a hound.

*You like fishing, Reyn?* the Captain had asked, paring his fingernails with a pocketknife and running a thumb over them to make sure they were smooth. *Because that's what we're going to do today. We're going fishing. You and me. And you're the bait.*

He'd tied the tools on Reyn personally. With spit and the tail of his shirt, he'd polished every wrench until it glowed.

*The boy won't be able to resist these,* he'd said. *Not if that king of whatever-and-whatever was even close to right about him.*

He'd patted his engineer on both shoulders, yanked the neck of his boiler suit straight, pushed back a lock of Reyn's greasy hair and then shoved him out into traffic.

*So handsome,* he'd said, laughing. *Who could resist you?*

*Now walk.*

An hour of waiting. Nothing compared with how long it'd been getting here. And when he'd spotted the boy making his move, the Captain had peeled himself out of the shade and fallen in step behind him. Months of danger, weeks in the air, days and nights spent searching, and now he walked right behind the boy, his hands in his pockets, an odd little smile on his face. He was almost on Milo's heels, nearly close enough to reach out and touch him.

And the boy, maybe, felt it. It's difficult to say. But at the last moment, Milo slowed his hand. His nose went up like a hunting dog's. He spun the knife in his fingers and held it with the coolness of the blade pressed against the inside of his wrist, then reached out with his empty hand, not sure what he was going to say or do, and tugged on the engineer's sleeve instead. Shuffling along, with his head down and his shoulders hunched, he wasn't much taller than Milo.

"Hey," the boy said.

Which was when the engineer started to shout.

Milo hadn't been expecting that. He stumbled backward when Reyn yelped, and felt someone catch him by the arm and hold it in a tight grip.

"Get your hands off my engineer, boy," said a voice from behind and above him.

And the boy did what boys do. He panicked. He jerked his arm and leaned away to run, his shoes scraping the street. But the hand on his arm was strong and he was spun around, looked up, saw a tall man. Blond hair. Graying leather coat worn open. Milo tried to stamp down on one of the man's feet, but he moved out of the way, so Milo thrashed against him, butting him with his head, then jerking his arm again and trying to squirm free.

The man was not moved. He just twisted himself out of the boy's way, lifted him by his arm, shook him and snapped, "Hey! None of that."

"I'm trying to help you!" Milo yelled.

"Sure you are."

"Behind you!" Milo yelled again.

And the man coughed out a single dry laugh. "You really expect me to fall for that?"

Milo bared his teeth like an animal. He thought (finally) about the knife in his other hand—his *free* hand—and pulled it in tight to his body, ready to cut this man open.

But the man was ready for that, too. He stepped back and lifted the hand he held Milo with, levering Milo up onto his toes. He said, "Drop that knife or you'll never use this arm again, Milo."

And the boy froze, his eyes wide. He looked up at the man again, saw the blond hair curling out from beneath the slouching, brimmed hat of an airship captain. The blue eyes. He was soft-faced, which he tried to cover with the thin scruff of a beard. He had a scar that traced a line back from his cheek, below his eye, and he was missing part of an ear, too.

"You're the Captain," Milo said.

"Captain Rodion Klim," said Captain Rodion Klim. And then he lifted Milo up even higher, until his toes barely touched the street and he had to clamp his mouth shut to keep from crying out. "And you're Milo Quick. Or at least that's the name you're using now. Right, *Milo*?"

His lips twisted when he said Milo's name. His smile souring like milk left out in a glass.

"I've been looking for you for a really long time."

Milo squirmed. The Captain's other hand was already balled into a fist. All around them, people moved to get out of their way.

"You were the one with Bert," Milo said, then shook his head. "With the Total King Forever."

"I was!" said Captain Klim brightly. He leaned a little bit closer. "You know, he wasn't supposed to say anything about that to you. But he's bad people, that kid. He told me *everything* about you, Milo. And my friend hardly had to hurt him at all." He gave Milo's arm a little twist, leaned closer still and looked past Milo, at something beyond him, as he whispered, almost in the boy's ear, "You and I have lots to talk about, Milo. But drop that knife or it's going to become *unpleasant* between us really quickly."

And Milo knew the Captain meant that. He knew it as sure as he knew anything. So he did the hardest thing there was to do. He relaxed. He was afraid and the man's grip on his arm was like iron, hard enough to make his eyes water, but he breathed all the way out, then all the way in again.

"I drop this, it'll be gone before it hits the ground," he said, then slowly brought up his knife hand, flipped the blade around again and made a show of tucking it away behind his belt buckle. Then he showed the Captain his empty hand like it'd been a magic trick. "And I need it."

The Captain relaxed a little. His smile softened a little. "See?" he said. "Now we can talk like friends. No one has to get hurt."

His grip was still tight, but he was no longer twisting the boy's arm, no longer lifting him quite so high. And as soon as Milo had his feet under him, he yelled as loud as he could, "Now, Jules! Get him!"

The Captain twisted around, trying to look behind himself,

expecting to be attacked. And as soon as he turned away, Milo dropped to the ground, pulling with all his weight against the man's grip, and sank his teeth into the first two fingers of the Captain's hand, biting hard enough that he tasted blood and his teeth scraped bone.

The Captain shouted and reflexively pulled his hand away from the boy's mouth. Milo tumbled loose and rolled, scraping his cheek and his knees, but his feet were already moving. He darted off so fast that by the time the Captain blinked, Milo was already gone.

"Boy's getting away, Cap'n," said Reyn.

"I can see that, Reyn. Thank you," said the Captain, looking back over his shoulder again.

"They's no one there, Cap'n."

"I know that, Reyn."

"They never was."

"No. There wasn't."

"He fool't you."

"He did."

And Reyn laughed, bright and sharp and inappropriately loud, even in the crowded market.

The Captain didn't seem to notice. All around him, the Old-edge traffic moved and grumbled and scraped and honked, but the Captain did not budge. From out of his jacket, he took a clean white silk handkerchief and wrapped it around his fingers as he scanned the crowd for Milo but saw no trace of him. Not even a shadow.

"I like that boy," he said. "Now that we've been properly introduced."

He smiled as he squeezed his fingers, smiled while his blood fell like rubies and spattered the stones at his feet.

"I like him, Reyn. I really, really, *really* do."

# DAGDA AT HOME
# IN FORT KICK-ASS

**DAGDA SANG TO HERSELF** under her breath as she herded
Tristan and Llyr down along Front Street toward the breaking
yards. She sang, "Home, home, time to go home," and watched
the twins swirl and scurry among the sparse crowds, sprinting just
to stop short, just to run again, just to chase a bird or stare into
the reflection in a pane of glass. Just to scramble up onto the top of
the shield wall and hop between the stones there, like gray teeth in
a giant's mouth—both of them deathless and fearless and careless
of the fall waiting for them on either side. They were birds, these
children. Had flying in their tiny bones.

She sang, "Time to go, time to go, time to go home," as she
ran behind them, through the cramped and cluttered spaces of the
Marche where it butted up against the breaking yards, down paths
carved between piles of old mattresses or rusted pipes or shattered
mirrors pulled from the bodies of broken ships, scaling scaffolds
built of rotted planks and prayers between homes hammered together from the pieces of things that no one else wanted.

Dagda had to run hard to keep up with the twins. They beat
her to the trick door that led inside the pressure hull, and when she
arrived behind them, they were slapping each other, arguing over
who'd touched it first. They left it to Dagda to decide, and she said,

"You both touched at exactly the same time," which seemed to satisfy them long enough for her to herd them inside, down crooked hallways, past dozens of doors until they reached their own.

The place where Dagda and Milo and Jules and their friends all lived was a run of three rooms in the belly of a dying ship lashed to the edge of the Flying City. Dagda shared one room with Milo and Jules. There was a second room for Keelan to sleep in when he was home, and for Arun and Sig to sleep in all day when they worked all night, and a closet in that room where Tristan and Llyr slept like two small animals curled together in a nest of their own clothes and toys and blankets and things. The third room was the main room, the living-in room, with its steel porthole windows and wood floor curling in the damp. It had furniture that had suffered the kinds of abuses that can only be doled out by eight children left completely on their own—chairs that all wobbled, a table that'd been the backbone of a hundred forts, a couch that sagged and sighed and poked the unwary with loose springs. There was a kitchen with a small oven they used for storing treasure, and a metal sink where they could light fires for cooking.

Once, it'd been a suite of rooms on a beautiful ship, rented out by the richest and most powerful people. Now it hung off the edge of the Flying City—it and dozens like it banding the docks and breaking yards of Highgate like armor, some still being taken apart piece by piece, and others turned now to more interesting purposes. This one was their home. Milo called it Fort Kick-Ass, which made Dagda laugh every time he said it.

Dagda shut the door behind her. She went to check on Arun and Sig, who slept like the dead, sprawled across blankets on opposite sides of a room that had once rented for a child's weight in coin. She'd known rooms like this when they were still new and fancy. She could still remember the way polished wood felt under her hands and the smell of beefsteaks and fried potatoes delivered under silver domes, on automatic carts that rolled silently through carpeted halls. She'd had a dress then that seemed to swirl around her like it was made of gray smoke. It scratched against her legs when she sat, stiffly upright between her father and her laughing mother, drinking iced water and crunching the cubes between her teeth.

When she looked for them, Dagda could see the ghosts of finery everywhere. So mostly she didn't look.

The twins were full of sugar and would not sleep. Would not sit still long enough even for Dagda to wipe the stickiness off them, so she sent them up into the masts instead, to look out for Jules and Keelan and Milo coming home.

They'd gone, happy to do anything that wasn't sleeping, but ten minutes after she'd shooed them out the door, Llyr came banging back into Fort Kick-Ass to tell her that a storm was coming in. Five minutes after that, Tristan was back because he was thirsty and he wanted coffee or water or whiskey.

"You're a boy," Dagda said. "Boys don't drink whiskey."

"What's whiskey and why can't I drink it?"

"You just can't. And there's no coffee."

"Water, then."

"So get it yourself! You know where it is."

Tristan got a drink and went back out the door, and ten minutes after *that*, Llyr was back again to tell Dagda that she'd seen a funny-looking bird. And then Tristan again, wanting a hook and some string. And then both of them together, saying that the clouds all looked like dogs and dragons and that Dagda had to come out and see.

"I don't want to see," she said. "I've seen enough clouds. Go watch for Milo." And after that, she went into the closet they used as a bathroom, stood beside the hole cut into the floor that dropped three hundred feet into nothing, laid down the metal grate that Milo had dragged home one day, made sure the door was locked, took off her clothes and dumped a bucket of water over herself just to rinse off the dust.

She tried to brush her hair, but had to be careful. It'd been coming out in clumps lately, which she'd been hiding in a clear plastic bag she'd found in one of the ship's empty rooms. Her scalp was a mess. There were patches that didn't have any hair left at all, that she had to cover by tying what was left up just right and hoping no one noticed. She was going to have to do something about that soon. But not today.

After she was dry and put back together, her joints powdered with the white talc she got from Sanel in the market, and her hair smoothed and oiled and tied, she went back into the main room and drank three cups of water. Her insides were warm, but it was okay, because if the rain came (as the rain always did), it would make the morning cool. If she could get out early enough. Before the sun. She wondered how long it'd been since she'd last tasted ice. Felt it crack and shatter between her teeth. Felt it cooling her all the way through.

Llyr came through the door. She said Jules and Keelan were coming and that Jules looked angry and that, also, Tristan had hit her for no reason, and also, was there any candy in the house?

"You've had enough sugar," Dagda said.

"Says who?"

"Says me."

"And why do you get to say?"

"Because I'm bigger than you. And I've hidden all the candy and only I know where it is."

"Is it in the can on the top shelf by the orange box?"

"No," said Dagda.

"Fine," said Llyr, and stuck out her tongue and left.

Dagda went and moved the candy from its hiding place in the can on the top shelf by the orange box. And by the time she was done with that, Jules and Keelan were back and the day went on pretty much like every other day ever had.

# SANDMAN

**ENNIS ARGHDAL SAT AT A CAFÉ** on the edge of the breaking yards called the Beautiful Stranger. He came here most days just to sit at a table outside and scowl at things.

From his seat he could also watch the approach through the yards that Milo and his friends used to get home. He'd walked up from Airy Way after Milo had passed him on his way to see Cuthbert DeGeorge and come here. After years of following Milo, he'd gotten to know the boy's haunts and habits pretty well, so he'd taken his time. It was a nice day despite all that was going wrong with it. Even to a man like Ennis, it felt somehow . . . *ungrateful* to waste it.

At the Beautiful Stranger no one will sit near the Sandman. No one will speak to him unless they absolutely, *absolutely* have to. He wore no uniform. Hadn't in years. Just his coat, his blue glasses, a white shirt, pants with suspenders. But people knew exactly what he was. The stories people told about him were terrible and, in some cases, even true. But over the years, he'd become like a ghost. Some fearsome thing with bloody hands and a wolf's head that lived more in the nightmares of a thousand malingering boys and girls than it did on the actual streets of the Flying City. *Be fast and be silent or the Sandman will get you. And when he catches you, he'll kill you.*

None of that was completely true, but none of it was completely a lie either. They called him Sandman for a reason. But was he as bad as the stories about him supposed?

That depends. Monsters are rarely monsters all the way through. And good people are typically not as wholly good as the stories about them would have you believe. Sometimes they are, but not often. The truth usually falls somewhere in between.

Here's a story that's true. Can you remember when Milo was six and he escaped for the first time from the bakery, Hargrove & Sons?

If you'll recall, it didn't go very well for him. He was beaten up, stabbed, and left for dead, but somehow he eventually ended up back at the bakery, safe and more or less sound. It was like magic. The boy claimed no memory of how it'd happened.

Ennis Arghdal was how it had happened. The Sandman had found Milo lying in the gutter, dying, had scooped the unconscious boy up in his arms and carried him all the way to a man he knew who could put most any broken thing back together for a price.

"If you're going to make a habit of this, I'm going to want a raise," Ennis had said to Milo. He'd spoken into the tangle of the boy's hair, his head cradled against the Sandman's shoulder. Milo never even knew he was there.

Here's another. Do you remember the day Milo met Jules and Dagda? They were caught and locked up together on the street outside that cop house in the Marche. But Jules had helped Milo escape. And then Milo had helped Dagda escape. And then the three of them ran off to have adventures and fun and to live like small, dirty kings on the fringes of the Flying City.

But what if I told you they weren't the only runaways chained up there that morning? That of *course* it wasn't just the three of them, because that would be ridiculous, wouldn't it? That the three children who would become the most important parts of this story all just somehow conveniently ended up in the same place at the same time in the perfect situation to become friends for life and blah blah blah?

Nonsense. There were absolutely other children there. Several of them, actually, covered in tears or snot or blood or all three, all handcuffed to loops in the concrete, none of them happy about it. And once they'd been sitting a while, who should come strolling around the corner but Officer Arghdal himself. He'd arranged to have the boy picked up. Jules, he'd put there. The girl had come all on her own.

Ennis was still wearing a truancy cop's uniform then and looked hard as nails. He'd stopped before the chained runaways, smiled, and said how sweet it was that the officers of the Highgate constabulary had done his job for him.

Most of the children wouldn't look at the Sandman. Only Jules (because *of course*, Jules) had raised his hands, rattled his chains and called Officer Arghdal by his first name.

"Bit tight, Ennis," he'd said. "Something I done annoy you?"

Officer Arghdal had whipped around so fast, he'd blurred. Jules was chained between Milo and Dagda, but the Sandman looked only at Milo, who was already dragging at Jules's sleeve with his fingers and whispering, "Don't. Do you know who that is?"

"Course Mr. Cael knows who I am," said the Sandman loudly. "We've met socially." And then he'd looked down at Milo, sneering.

"This one . . ." he'd said, flicking Jules on the ear with a finger hard enough to make Jules cringe, "is trouble. I suggest you listen to absolutely *nothing* that he says."

And then Ennis had left all the children right where they were. He'd gone off whistling and gotten himself lunch. When he came back, Milo, Jules, and Dagda were gone. The remaining runaways had still needed to be dealt with, which he'd done quickly. Three he sent to Polis Square to be branded. One he would sell back to her rich mother later for a bribe. And one—a pale and spiderish boy with too-long arms and too-long legs and two runaway brands on him already, one on the back of his hand, the other burned into his cheek just below his right eye—the Sandman took with him. They'd walked together all the way to the shield wall that ringed the edge of the Flying City, but only one of them came back.

So . . . good man or bad man?

Don't worry. You don't have to decide yet.

Watching was most of what the Sandman did now. And if he did it here, sitting in one of his favorite seats, with the day's papers in front of him, a cup of coffee, a plate of griddled pork and rice flecked with hot chilies, and a smoke bought from a girl who'd sold him two (one for now, one for later), then who was there to tell him he was doing it wrong? Keeping track of Milo Quick had been easy when the boy was six and seven and eight and barely smart enough to bang rocks together. Less so now. But the Sandman had his ways, and after a thousand hours spent sitting at the Beautiful Stranger waiting on the boy and the boy's friends, Ennis had developed a feel for the place. He knew just about everyone who came and went. He'd learned their names, jobs, habits, and tastes. He could feel it when something was off or out of place. It would itch at him until he set it right.

And today, what was bothering Ennis was the woman in the heavy leather deck jacket and eye patch who was pretending not to watch as Dagda and the twins, Tristan and Llyr, came lashing out of the Marche at a run and vanished into the breaking yards.

He'd never seen her here before, this one-eyed woman. She

didn't look like a ship breaker, or smell like the cheap side of the Marche. She was dressed like she crewed aboard one of the airships, but he was sure she wasn't waiting for anyone, because he'd been watching her and she hadn't once looked at the door. She had a coffee in front of her, but it'd gone cold. Ennis couldn't say exactly what was wrong about her. Not yet. But he knew for sure that nothing about her was right.

Of course, we know *exactly* who this is. It's the one-eyed woman who was with the Captain when he visited the Total King Forever, the one Cuthbert told Milo about. Her name is Lalia Ivona Vicario, the Captain's first mate and second-in-command. He'd sent her here to keep a quiet eye on Milo Quick's front door—to watch and see the comings and goings of the boy and his friends. She'd been bored after ten minutes, annoyed after twenty, and furious pretty much since the day she was born.

More to the point, she was trouble. That much, Ennis could tell immediately. He didn't know what kind, exactly, but he knew the shape and taste of it. So he watched her. He sucked at his cigarette and shoveled salt pork and rice and hot chilies into his mouth with a metal spoon. When he smiled, smoke leaked out between his teeth like he'd swallowed a devil, and when he stood, finally, he had to uncoil the length of himself from his chair and stretch the kinks of waiting out of his spine. He'd decided that he needed to meet this woman, so he crossed the patio at the Beautiful Stranger to talk to her.

He said, "Fair winds," to her in a voice lighter and higher than his own. "Buy you a drink for your service?"

And she said, "Not interested, sailor," without even looking at him. "My only service is delivering the mail on time."

"That's a noble enough service," said Ennis. "Without the mails, how would my mother tell me how disappointed she is in me?"

Shockingly, that drew a smile out of Lalia. She bit down hard on it the instant it was born.

"My name's Yoon," said Ennis. "Silvano Yoon. And that offer of a drink still stands. Even if you are only a mailman."

"Only a mailman. That's funny."

She turned, finally, to look at him, and Ennis took her in with a single glance. Brown hair, curly, pulled back tight. Her cheeks and knuckles wind-chapped and burn-scarred. One honey-colored eye as cold and joyless as a doll's. The other hidden behind a black leather patch. "And I'm sorry . . ."

"Silvano," Ennis repeated. "And you are?"

"Ligeia Lindsay," said Lalia Ivona Vicario. "And I'm sorry, Silvano, but I was just leaving."

"The mail won't deliver itself, I suppose."

"If it comforts you to think that's my reason, then sure."

The woman stood then and walked straight off, digging her hands into the high pockets of her jacket, its loose belts clacking. She smelled of machine oil. Her boots were old-fashioned, heelless, strapped high up her shins. Her hair was held back with a locking hose clamp. She went in the direction of the Marche, not the yards. And she hadn't finished her coffee, which was fine, because Ennis sat down at her table and finished it for her.

He knew her now. Not her name (because he knew that had been a lie) and not what she did (because that had been a lie, too), but that she was a liar, which was more important than knowing anything else.

Because why would she bother lying to him unless she knew that he was here watching Milo Quick's front door, too?

Ennis tapped his foot. He sat very still and thought very hard. Callias Fusco had told him that people would be coming to the Flying City looking for the boy. He'd assumed that meant soldiers, men from the Armada. But maybe he'd been wrong. Callias had said they couldn't be allowed to find Milo. And on that one, single point he and Ennis were in complete agreement.

He fetched his lunch from his first table and moved it over to the one vacated by the woman calling herself Ligeia Lindsay, ate it, and drank the last of his own coffee, too. While the afternoon shadows stretched around him, he watched Jules and Keelan the Coward pass by, headed for home. Dagda and the twins were still inside. He knew that the other two, Arun and Sig, were probably asleep. They'd been out all night fast-handing sailors and airship crews in the Blue Lights. A dangerous business, but they did it reasonably well.

The boy did not come home. Which wasn't at all unusual except in the ways it rubbed up against the other things that had happened today: Moric Shaw, the boy's meeting with the King of the Marche, the rest of the children being home already, the one-eyed woman and her lies.

Ennis grunted. He closed one eye and looked out at the world, then sniffed. "Milo," he said. "Milo, Milo, Milo . . ."

Once upon a time, there'd been a man who cooked tar. He beat Milo so badly that the boy still wore the scars. The Sandman had waited for the man one night along a stretch of well-lit road, wearing brass knuckles on his hands, lamplight flaring in the blue lenses of his glasses. He'd killed the man and thrown his body from the edge of the dockyards.

Once upon a time, he'd watched the boy and his stupid friends gathered and laughing around a greasy fire in the yards. The boy had stuck the stubs of two pencils into his upper lip and lurched around like a vampire, and Jules and Dagda and all the others had laughed and laughed. The Sandman had sat back in a shadow, watching through a broken window with a pain in his chest like he'd been stabbed. He'd closed his eyes and smiled at the feeling, but only because he knew no one was looking.

So again, good man or monster? Everyone is a little bit of both, perhaps. They're different things in different lights.

Back at the Beautiful Stranger, Ennis slapped his hands down on the table, said "Gods-damned boy," and stood up quickly. He knew now that he wouldn't be able to sleep until he saw Milo Quick breathing and alive. So he crushed out his cigarette, pinched his glasses tighter on his nose, and went out into the streets looking for him.

# MEANWHILE, BACK AT FORT KICK-ASS . . .

**MILO'S FRIENDS** were also wondering what was keeping him.

"Business," Jules said. He crossed his arms and leaned back on the couch. "You heard what he said about Bert and his new rules. Milo's doing Milo things."

"But he should be back," said Dagda.

"Did he *say* he was coming back?" Jules asked.

And Dagda thought about it and realized that, no, he hadn't. He'd told them to bring everyone else home, but hadn't said what he was going to be doing.

"Milo things," Jules insisted. "He'll be 'round eventually. Stop worrying."

So they all went to sleep. Except Tristan and Llyr, who were put in their room and told to amuse themselves quietly, but immediately snuck out, touched everyone's stuff, drew on the walls, and tore most of the pantry apart looking for where Dagda had hidden the candy.

# LALIA, SEMYON, AND VACLAV

**AFTER A DAY** spent following their various charges all over the Flying City, then home again to the edge of it, they met where they were supposed to meet: outside a shuttered run of closed-up junk shops in the shadow of a long staircase that climbed to one of the city's upper levels.

Vaclav was thoughtful. Semyon was hungry. Lalia, who'd arrived first, was fuming and pacing with her hands balled into tight, hard fists.

"Lalia, dear thing," said Semyon Beli. "Whatever has gotten you into such a state?"

And Lalia told them—about the café and the man there. "He spotted me," she said. "Picked me right out."

"Is it possible he just wanted to buy you a drink, Lalia?" Semyon asked. "Handsome woman like you, it has to happen now and then."

Lalia's fury was like a whip-crack—sharp and sudden. For a moment, she and Semyon did nothing but shout in each other's faces until Vaclav, who was growing bored with all their noise, stopped it by stepping between them and looking down at Lalia.

"The man," he said. "He was who?"

As tall as Lalia was, she'd still have to look up at Vaclav to bite him on the chin. "Don't know," she said. "He was at that stupid café the Captain sent me to. Sitting at another table. Came over and asked me my name."

"This is not so strange," said Vaclav. "This place? Peoples everywhere?"

"No," Lalia said. "This was different."

"How was different?"

"The way he looked at me. The way he walked. I don't know. There was something about him."

"Love at first sight?" asked Semyon.

Lalia leaned around Vaclav and pointed a finger at Semyon Beli. "Wait until we're home again, old man. The minute we make delivery, I will murder you where you stand."

Semyon Beli just smiled. "Like you would be the first one to try."

"Explain him," Vaclav said to Lalia. "The man."

"What?"

Vaclav raised his ponderous hands. He touched his forehead, his nose, his chest. "Explain," he said.

So Lalia described Ennis Arghdal as best she could—the long coat and the blue glasses, what he had done and what he had said. Saying it out loud, it seemed ridiculous that she'd been bothered by this Silvano Yoon. Maybe he was just some man, lonely, stupid, and irritating. There'd been something about him, but it was something she couldn't quite say with words. A feeling more than anything. Like he was the punctuation in a letter that contained nothing but bad news.

"I don't know," said Vaclav when she was done. "He sounds—"

"He sounds like nothing we need to be concerned about," interrupted Semyon Beli, who was thinking only of mint tea and a curry he'd smelled earlier, of gin and lime.

Vaclav looked at Semyon. He'd spent months listening to the old man talk and talk and talk, and he was tired of it. He was tired of so many things—of the ship and these people, of Lalia's bad moods and Semyon's terrible singing and all the Captain's plans. He had a stone's patience, but even a stone will crack eventually, if put under enough pressure.

He looked down at Lalia and asked, "Tell me again why we come for this boy?"

"We were hired," said Lalia.

"Because we're being paid to, my friend!" Semyon barked, talking right over Lalia this time, smiling broadly and spreading his hands. "Because if we were to count it out, we're likely earning more per ounce for carrying this one boy over the water than we'd get running with our holds full of poppies and lead. Who doesn't want to get rich like that?"

Vaclav didn't say anything at all. He missed his own boy. He wasn't sure he wanted to get rich by taking someone else's, but he wasn't sure he *didn't* want to get rich that way, either. Carrying a boy over the water and away from this place? That was almost a favor, he thought.

"We're saving him, Vaclav," Semyon said. "Remember that. The boy might not understand that, but that's what we're doing."

"That's what the Captain *says* we're doing," Lalia interjected.

"And the Captain is correct," said Semyon, folding his arms over his chest. "We are heroes. Rescuing him from this place and those who've kept him here. From a life that isn't any kind of life."

"And the girl?" asked Lalia.

"And maybe the girl, too," agreed Semyon. "Speaking of which, now that we all have our children safely tucked in, perhaps we should go back up and see how the fishing has been for the Captain and Reyn. If he's managed to lay eyes on the boy, it means we're all that much closer to going home, yes? But first, maybe some lunch."

# MILO

**AFTER BITING THE CAPTAIN,** Milo hadn't run far.

He wasn't stupid. He knew how dangerous this was. Men don't just grab boys on the street with good intentions.

But Milo was a boy who'd lived the entire length of his childhood in danger of one kind or another. He'd been hit, stabbed, chased from night until morning. He'd had to hold his breath more than once in fear that it might be his last. So Milo had learned how to run. How to hide. How to fight when he absolutely had to. He'd learned that most things happened for a reason—that motors turn when they're given a spark and sails pull when they catch the wind—and that if you can understand that reason, you're ahead of the game. You might live long enough to learn something new tomorrow.

This man, this Captain, knew his name. His *real* name. He'd said it to the Total King Forever like a secret word and had come all the way to the Flying City just to find him. He had a reason. And even though Captain Klim had grabbed him, and even though Milo still had the coppery taste of the man's blood souring in his mouth, the boy needed to know what that reason was. He needed to know *why*.

So he'd run only far enough to get himself out of sight. And then he'd turned around, tucked himself into a good hiding spot and watched Captain Rodion Klim and his engineer. He'd pulled his scarf up over his face, put his lips close to Henry the Spider curled around his finger, and whispered, "Watch them, Henry. They're a real airship crew. And a captain, too. Let's see where they go."

Only, the airship captain and the engineer didn't go anywhere. Not right away. They just stood, unmoving, in a narrow passage near a stand that sold noodles under a flapping blue plastic tarp. The noodle ladies shouted and shook their ladles at the Captain, but he ignored them. He and Reyn were like two rocks in a stream with the Oldedge crowds flowing around them.

And now the boy was thinking about airships anyway, because the boy loved airships. Dreamed about them. On any day, he could see dozens of them, but mostly at a distance—docked up in the aeries or turning in the sky around the Spire, sails out, beautiful. In the breaking yards, he'd squirmed and crawled through a few, cutting them into pieces, hauling tools in a bag tied to his ankle. With cutters or a torch on his back, he'd scaled their sides to peel them to the ribs, gouge out their insides, salvage copper, steel, motors and brushes, penny nails, electric buttons. He'd cut their sheets and gone out on their poles, pruning them like bushes. He'd looped cables and sailcloth around his body and brought them back to trade them for his supper.

At night, when he should have been sleeping, he sometimes snuck through the cordons, past dozing boys set to guard the wrecks with lengths of pipe or clubs weighted with lead. Feeling his way in the dark, he would scale the insides of the ships (by memory when he had to) and climb out onto their decks to stand at their ruined bridges and imagine himself a pirate. A captain. He would mouth orders, point, crank the winches when they were still there, poke buttons if the command posts hadn't already been dismantled. Until the sun came up, he would be commander of his own phantom armada, facing them into storms or stars, making silent, imaginary war with the dozen other ships decomposing around him. A boy at play.

He'd worked as part of a crew of hundreds of boys and girls taking apart the destroyer called *Berserker Alpha*. She was so big they'd slung hammocks in her hold, and every night Milo'd dreamed about bringing her back to life with his own hands and his own tools, cutting the lines lashing the ship in place and stealing it from the yards—he and Jules and Dagda and all the other boys and girls with their dirty faces and scars. He'd take whoever was willing to call him Captain, come aboard as his crew and aim the ship where Milo wanted it to go. He would rescue all of them, and they would cheer and yell his name. In his dreams, he always went the same way. He took the ship, tore it free from the body of the Flying City and went off in search of his father.

So the boy watched. His eyes were hot, dark points above the line of his scarf, dust on his lashes, the smell of his own breath in his nose. He waited while the Captain pulled a hanky from his pocket and squeezed it to his fingers where Milo'd bitten him. He waited until, finally, something seemed to click in the Captain. Some switch that threw him back into motion. And when Captain Rodion Klim and his engineer finally started walking, Milo followed. It was a game he'd played a thousand times before. He knew every inch of this city. He'd spent his life on these streets. And if he didn't want to be seen, no one was going to see him.

Not even us.

# CAPTAIN KLIM

**"LET'S TAKE A WALK, REYN."**

The Captain started back toward the aeries. He took his time, looked into doorways, bought an orange and ate it. Sometimes he whistled, but most of the time he didn't. The boy was still out there somewhere, watching him. He didn't know how he knew, but he knew. He could *feel* it.

It was in a city far from this one that the Captain had accepted the terms of his deal. He hadn't signed in blood. Ink had done just fine. He hadn't promised anything more than he thought he could deliver, hadn't asked for anything less than he knew he could get.

The people who'd hired him had been desperate. Frantic. There were eleven of them. Five men and six women who'd dressed carefully in the finest clothes they had left. They'd met him in a basement beneath a fish shop called Sea & Fortune, all of them gathered around a long steel table covered with a blue cloth. They'd lit lanterns, laid out tea, biscuits, an open bottle of arak and glasses, which was the minimum amount of hospitality required in that place, and the maximum they could manage.

The custom was that the Captain would refuse all food and drink until the negotiation was finished. He would stand, allow them to speak their piece and ask him plainly for what they wanted.

The Captain would be allowed to ask all the questions he cared to, so long as he stood. So long as he didn't touch whatever food and drink was offered. They would argue over money, details. Then he would decide, yes or no. Either way, they would share food and drink afterward. This was just the way things were done. It was what the Captain had expected.

But it wasn't the way things had happened.

Of the eleven men and women, nine came armed. Three were wounded and trying hard not to show it. One had to be pushed in a chair. It was three hours past midnight when they met—the only time any of the eleven felt safe enough to gather more than two at a time, because the city above them was already tearing itself in half. It was either riot or revolution, depending on which side you asked, but the jagged line that separated one from the other ran through neighborhoods, across roads, split houses and families. One side—the Ministries of Order, of Joy, of Municipal Authority, and of Civic Virtue—had the police, the army, the navy, and all the power. The other side had ideas, a little bit of money, the people, half a bottle of arak, and a table in the basement of a fish shop.

The negotiations should've begun with the eleven offering the Captain a seat at their table and his refusal. It should've begun with flattery—*Captain Klim has a reputation, fastest ship in the sky, always finishes the job, does what needs to be done*—and to be honest, he'd been looking forward to that.

Instead, he was met with the smell of old fish and panic, ten clammy handshakes, half-whispered voices taut as bowstrings and then the last woman—eleventh of eleven—who did not stand, did not shake his hand, did not offer her name, said only, "Now you know everyone and we know you. So sit. Listen. We don't have a lot of time."

Her breath had already had the licorice smell of arak on it.

She was neither armed nor wounded, but had blast scars on her cheek, silver hair, exhaustion written into every line on her face. When the Captain began to refuse (as he was supposed to), she waved a hand at him and said, "No. There's no time for that now. This war is nearly over. The Ministries are powerful. They have broken us almost everywhere. Here, they hunt us in the streets like criminals. But we can no longer hold them, and now their ships are sailing from Port Alpha and Bell Harbor. They've left from Asdon and Particle Bay and the Koerwe Docks. The Armada, you understand?"

The Captain said that he did.

"And you know where they go?"

Again, the Captain said that he did. They were going to Highgate, the Flying City, in the middle of the Clean Sea.

"Good." She looked around the table, then back at the Captain. "Now let me tell you *why*."

Then she'd told Captain Klim a story about a mother and a father, a girl and a boy, magic and starships. It was sad and strange and terrible, and even though the Captain had seen many fantastical things in his relatively short life, he wouldn't have believed a word of it if these eleven women and men weren't risking their lives to tell it to him. And if the other ten of them hadn't tried very hard to stop the woman with the silver hair from speaking. If they hadn't even gone so far as to draw their pistols and threaten her life right there in front of him.

Even still, he only believed maybe half of it. Because to believe all of the story the woman told him that night would've been like taking someone's word for down being up or sand and water being the same thing. It was the kind of story that upended the entire world, and you don't need to know the whole story now (because knowing the whole story now would ruin a really good surprise coming later), but trust me. When the time is right, you'll know it all, too. By the end of *our* story, you'll know more than the Captain knows and Milo knows and the eleven people in the basement of Sea & Fortune know. You'll know the *truth*.

When the woman's story was finished, she'd sighed, looked around the room at the ten furious faces, plus the Captain's, and said, "None of us will live to see the end of this. The Ministries cannot allow it. But the boy has to survive. So here's what we need you to do."

There'd been no negotiating. The woman had explained to the Captain what they required and then asked if he thought he could do it. Captain Klim was a talented smuggler and blockade runner. His ship, the *Halcyon*, was fast and his crew knew their business. But this woman wasn't asking him to fill his hold with rifles and lead. She was asking him to do something terrible. Something wonderful. Something impossible. To race the Ministries' Armada to Highgate, find one boy in a city full of boys, snatch him like a goat from wherever he was and get him out of the Flying City before the Armada found the end of their patience and destroyed it.

And after that, all he had to do was bring the boy back again, all in one piece, while the entire world and one very dangerous, very old monster hunted them across every mile.

"So I'm to be your kidnapper, then?" the Captain had asked.

"Find the boy first," the woman had told him. "See how he lives and what the Armada is likely to do. Then you can decide if that's what you are. Or if maybe it's something a little more noble than that."

So Captain Klim had his orders. A timeline. And this one boy, alive and more-or-less well, was a better paycheck than he or any of his crew had seen in their lifetimes. To snatch him from this place and return him whole (unbroken, in other words, and not just in a sack with all his teeth knocked out; not just cuffed and gagged and hollering; and not just pieces of him, either, but the *whole* boy) meant debts paid and freedom for all of them. Those were the promises he'd bought his crew with. Enough money to erase the past. Certainly enough to make the future brighter. And all for one boy. One stupid runaway orphan boy that no one cared about and no one would miss.

But time was running short now. The Flying City was surrounded. And soon—*very* soon, the Captain thought—the Armada would grow tired of waiting. They would burn the whole city down to get the one thing they'd come here for.

But if the Captain and his crew were quick and if they were clever, they might rescue the boy from all that. The Captain had put it exactly that way to Lalia and Reyn and Vaclav and Semyon— that there were things happening all around this stupid boy that he couldn't possibly understand and that if he wasn't careful, he could die of any one of them.

*We're the good guys*, he'd said. *We're going to save that little brat's life.*

# AT THE LOWER
# CONTROL GATE

**MILO'S GAME CAME TO AN END** when it became clear that the Captain was going all the way up into the aeries. The boy knew he couldn't follow him there.

But that was fine, because the boy had places to be, too. For a minute he sat catching his breath on a rooftop where a skinny cat lay sunning itself in the curve of a dish that some people said had once been used to talk to gods and people in the stars. Above him, a fat little skiff slid by. It had a single gasbag, a boxy hull, and just two glittering wings of sail for maneuvering. It was flying low enough that Milo could see the faces of soldiers pressed against the round windows, none of them all that much older than he was, all of them looking down over the Flying City. One of them even caught Milo's eye.

He grinned and waved, because he was still a boy. He did it without even thinking. Then he rose slowly and slipped away into the dusky afternoon.

Down below, in the press of the mob fighting to get through the Lower Control Gate and up into the aeries, Captain Klim felt the infinitesimal change in pressure created by the lack of Milo Quick's hungry attention. He turned and looked back over his shoulder. He had a sniper's eyes. They could pick out a topmast over the curve of the horizon, a polestar on a cloudy night. He thought, for just a second, that he saw the flutter of movement along the edge of a rooftop.

The Captain said, "Bye, Milo," to no one at all, then turned away. He grabbed his engineer by one shoulder and shoved him forward into the crowd. He said, "Let's go, Reyn," and used the man like a ram, raising his docking papers above his head, shouting as loud as he could, and pushing Reyn through the throng. He didn't understand where all these people hoped to go. There wasn't a ship docked above that would make it away from this place whole.

*Well, maybe one*, he thought. If they were very, very good and very, very lucky, maybe just one.

# JULES CAEL

**MILO DIDN'T COME BACK** to Fort Kick-Ass at all that day. When night came, everyone gathered in the main room, rubbing eyes, yawning, wanting water or coffee, ready to work.

Jules spoke. "Milo said two hours after dark, up in the aeries, by the place where we do that stuff."

"The first place or the second place?" Sig asked.

"The second place," Jules said, making a face. "No one goes to the first place anymore. Don't you know that?"

In the corner, sitting on the defeated remains of the couch with her feet up, Dagda raised a hand to cover a small twist of a smile.

Jules continued. "He said to meet at the bottom. By the doors. Does everyone know where that is?"

Everyone did. Jules felt pretty good about himself. "Okay," he said. "Let's go, then. Quick and quiet. Everyone split up and meet at the place. We can wait for Milo there. If there's trouble, we run to the Haunts and then back here together. Everybody got it?"

Around him, everyone nodded. They all waited expectantly.

"Then let's go," said Jules.

And off they all went, Jules last, closing the door behind him. He didn't like doing any of this without Milo. It felt strange. *Everything* felt strange lately. Like things were happening just outside his sight that he couldn't comprehend. Or like the scenery of his

world—the things he'd known the places of for years and years—
was being moved while he slept. Not moved *much*, but just enough
to be wrong.

He took a deep breath and shook his head. He told himself
that none of this mattered. They had work tonight, and work, at
least, had always made sense to Jules. You work. You take care of
your family. You have a little fun along the way. That's how things
were supposed to go. Jules had never wanted anything more than
that.

Plus, no matter how many things in his world got shifted
around by mysterious powers he didn't understand, Milo was still
Milo. And Jules was pretty sure he knew exactly where Milo was.

# JULES AND THE SANDMAN

**THE SANDMAN HADN'T FOUND MILO.** After the one-eyed woman left the Beautiful Stranger, he'd gone looking through the yards and the Marche but saw only the growing panic of everyone else who was *not* Milo Quick. Fear was spreading like a sickness in the Flying City. He heard raised voices everywhere. The policemen had all abandoned their posts.

When night came, he made his way back to the yards and watched the entrance to the half-a-ship where the boy lived—standing in the gloom and staring at the door as though daring it to try something. After a while, it cracked open, spilling weak yellow light and all of Milo's friends out into the dark. When he saw Jules split from the rest of them and turn in the direction of the docklines, the Sandman followed, rushing to get ahead of him without anyone seeing (because no one *ever* saw the Sandman run), then stopping, leaning back against a stack of iron pipes so it would look like he'd been there all day, just waiting.

When he saw the boy pass him, he called out in a booming voice—"Julius Cael!"—just for the pleasure of watching Jules jump.

Jules heard his name bellowed and swore under his breath as he skidded to a stop. He looked around and saw the shivering animal shadows of other boys and girls skittering off into the dark, making themselves scarce before the Sandman spotted them and called their names, too.

"Don't you run," the Sandman said, pointing a finger as though to pin him in place. "Do not make me chase you."

So Jules, acting his part, stood still and shook his head sorrowfully.

The Sandman, playing his, walked over and grabbed Jules by one ear. Together, they walked to somewhere dark and quiet where no one could see them, and then Jules slapped Ennis's hand away and cursed him.

"That *hurts*, Ennis."

"Toughen up, Cael," he said. "Thought you were the strong one." And then he asked about Milo.

Jules told the Sandman everything he knew: that Milo had been missing most of the day, but they had plans to rob the mails tonight. "We're going up to the place," he said. "You know, at the bottom. Up by the thing."

The Sandman knew exactly what he was talking about.

Jules told him about Cuthbert DeGeorge, how he'd broken Moric Shaw's arm, and about their tithe. That Milo'd said it would all be okay because he had a plan, but that he'd seemed worried.

"He was strange this morning," Jules said.

"Strange how?"

"Dunno. Just strange. Not like himself."

And Ennis said, "Could you be a little *less* clear, Cael? I mean, if you really tried hard. It's not like we're doing anything important here."

"I'd explain it if I could."

"Try using small words."

"Sad," Jules said. "Scared."

"That doesn't sound like Milo."

"Didn't I just say that?"

Ennis shook his head. He felt better knowing the boy had been somewhere, alive and well, within the last few hours. But still . . .

He said, "Listen. There might be some trouble."

"What kind of trouble?"

And Ennis couldn't say, because he didn't know exactly. But he wasn't going to say that to Jules Cael. So he said, "*Trouble* trouble," as if that would clarify things.

And in the full arrogance of youth, Jules shrugged and said, "Think you could be a little *less* clear, Ennis? If you really tried?"

The Sandman growled curses at Jules that no boy—not even Jules—should hear. Jules just grinned and filed them away for later use. "There's always trouble," he said. "Ain't worried."

"This is different trouble than usual. I need you to stay close to Milo."

"Why?"

"Because someone is looking for him. Someone I don't want to find him."

"The Total King?"

"No."

"Cops?"

"No."

"Monsters?" Jules asked, bugging out his eyes and waggling his fingers.

"Shut up. There's . . . *things* happening that you don't understand."

"Why?"

"Because you're a child and you're stupid," Ennis said, snapping out one hand and trying to flick Jules Cael on the ear.

But Jules skipped back out of reach and laughed at Ennis Arghdal. He didn't care about this conversation anymore. "And you're getting old and slow, Sandman!" he said, then turned and banged off like a shot.

# JULES AND MILO

**WANT TO SEE A BOY** do something stupid? Watch Jules Cael.

Once he gets clear of the Sandman—once he makes his way through the mazes of trash and pit fires, the shantytowns of scrap; once he makes it along the curve of the yards as far as he can go, and down into the lamplit and steaming universe of the dockworks—he goes and jumps right off the edge of the world.

He does it because he knows a spot down there among the cargo cranes and catwalks stuck along the knuckled edge of the Flying City where Milo likes to hide. It's a place where, once, he and Milo and Mouse took apart a battleship.

Well, not *just* them. They'd had help from half a thousand others like them. But Milo'd been there to organize the thieving for Cuthbert DeGeorge, and Jules had been there to watch out for Milo, and Mouse had been there doing Mouse things. It'd been fun.

But while they were taking apart *Berserker Alpha* and stealing every single thing that could be stolen, Milo'd found a place he liked to go. A *secret* place far out along the arm of a dockline crane that didn't work anymore. No one who wasn't crazy or suicidal would ever go there, which made it an excellent place for hiding.

So that's where Jules was going. To Milo's secret place. He ran along the curve of the dockline until he got to a yellow-and-black

painted bar at the end of a catwalk. It was hung with safety netting to prevent accidents, but Jules never cared much about safety,
and had a running start besides, so he hopped right up onto the
bar and jumped, launching himself over the netting and out into
darkness and nothingness to fall off the edge of the Flying City.

He didn't fall far, of course. Just a few feet, arms pinwheel-
ing, dropping to a platform below the massive fist of machinery
that used to move the broken crane. Beyond that was the arm of
the crane itself with a narrow walkway running the length of the
crane's pyramid of zigzagging iron bars. Jules had to crouch, hold
on, climb, because the crane stuck out at an angle up into the
sky—sixty feet long and nothing below but air and air and air and
then the sea.

But all the way at the end of it there was a small, flat iron perch
that was once the post of the man who guided the crane operators
over their targets bobbing on the water far below. Milo had no fear
of heights or wind or water, so he would sometimes go there on
nights when he couldn't sleep. "This much wind, nightmares can't
find you," he'd once told Jules, and waggled his fingers in the air.
"They just . . . float away."

Jules hated it. He didn't like heights even a little bit, and liked
the thought of falling from them even less. But he went anyway
because Milo was Milo, and all through the spring, with the gale
winds blowing crosswise and all the weather in the world seeming
to smash itself against the stones of Highgate, Milo'd been coming
here more and more. He said he liked looking at the ships. That
he liked the quiet. So lately, whenever Milo would go missing unexpectedly, this was where Jules would find him—sitting alone
under a blanket of oilskins, with rain and water sluicing off him,
watching the ships of the Armada through a pair of high-powered
binoculars with one broken lens.

Jules was halfway along the crane arm before he spotted Milo on his perch, sitting right at the edge of the iron plate, his feet dangling loose over the edge. He was terrified of startling Milo, so when he called his name, Jules did it quietly. Imagining Milo falling made Jules want to throw up a little. He had to close his eyes and swallow hard and hang on tight to the crossbars with both hands.

But Milo didn't even hear him. Or didn't care. He had the binoculars in his lap and was running his thumb over the cracked glass of the broken lens. Tapping it thoughtfully.

Jules edged closer, said Milo's name a little louder. He was holding so tightly to the bars that his hands hurt.

Finally, Milo turned. He had his scarf wrapped around his head, but when he saw Jules, he pulled down the part covering his face and smiled. It was a fake smile, of course, but it's possible that Jules didn't know that.

Milo said, "Hey, Jules. Am I late already?"

And Jules said, "Not yet. But everyone's headed up to the place. When you didn't come home, I figured you'd be up here counting your boats or whatever."

Milo shrugged. "Too many to count these days." He looked back out toward the sea and sky beyond. "Hey, come here a minute. Before the moon is gone completely. Look at this."

And Jules went because he loved Milo and would never, ever tell anyone how he felt about heights. He did it with his teeth clamped closed and his legs full of jelly where his bones had once been, but as far as anyone else knew, Jules Cael was afraid of nothing. He had to kneel beside Milo, because, even crouching down, the underside of the crane arm was too close.

"Careful of the stuff," Milo said.

In the dark, Jules hadn't even noticed the pile beside Milo. He asked what it was, and Milo said, "Supplies. Rope, a bag, some tools. For tonight. I came here to get the rope." He reached up and knocked his knuckles against the crane, as if that explained anything. "And then I saw this."

He handed the binoculars to Jules, put one hand on his shoulder and tried to point him in the proper direction. But it was dark and the sea was moving, and whatever might have been out there was just so many black blobs bobbing blobbily in a gray nothing.

"The wind chases off the airships," Milo said. He chewed distractedly at one thumbnail while he spoke, kicked his feet out over the drop to the sea. "They have to go up so high you can't see them, or move in loops around the city so wide that they're mostly over the horizon. But the waterships, they can't go anywhere. They're stuck. They have to take their sails down and ride out the weather in place." He spit a chunk of thumbnail down over the edge of the platform. "They're hard to see with bare poles, but once you find them, you won't lose them. They've got their storm anchors down, so they can't move. In storms is the only time you can really *see* the ships. It's the only time that fighting the weather becomes more important than pretending they're not what they are."

Jules said, "I can't really see anything, Milo." He spoke without hardly opening his teeth. Trying to focus through the single lens of the binoculars was making him dizzy. Finally, though, he caught sight of something glowing. A ship with its deck lamps lit. "Oh," he said.

"You see it?" Milo asked. And Jules said that he saw *something*, but wasn't sure if it was the something that Milo wanted him to see.

"If you're seeing anything, it's the only thing out there worth seeing right now. That's the *Achida*. I've seen her before. I don't know what's happening aboard her, but something bad. A fire maybe. They're doing emergency repairs, which is why she's lit up. But look down along her sides. You see those?"

Jules said maybe. That something about the ship didn't look right. Like it was fat somehow. And Milo said that was because hundreds of yards of weather covers had been thrown over the side, making the *Achida* look chubby and blubbery. "She's a siege ship. Carrying forty-four guns, all normally hidden under those rolls of canvas. And they're those cannons that fire up in the air, you know? That fire up and drop shells down on you?" Milo made a whistling sound with his tongue and teeth and swooped a hand up and down.

"Mortars," Jules said, not quite knowing if Milo really didn't know the word or was just trying to make him feel smart.

"Mortars. That's right."

Jules took the binoculars away from his face and had to steady himself against one of the cables as the world and his distance above it all came rushing back at him. He closed his eyes and breathed through his nose. Milo didn't seem to notice at all, which was just fine by Jules. "We should get going, Milo," he said without moving his lips. "Don't want to keep the others waiting."

But again, Milo seemed not to hear him. "What you said this morning got me thinking," he said. "You know, about the war? So I thought I should come out here and look for myself. What do you suppose they're doing out there?"

"I don't suppose much of anything about the Armada," Jules said. "Seems to be all some people talk about, but I don't think they know no better neither. They're just . . . you know. Talking."

Jules handed the binoculars back to Milo, who took them without a word and tucked them inside the oilcloth blanket rolled up beside him.

Jules said, "Down the Alley, when I was getting Keelan, there were big crowds. Angry. All of them yelling at the elevator men and running to crowd up against the cargo lines." He frowned in concentration. "I think they were trying to leave the city, Milo. All of 'em. You think it might be because of the Armada?"

"Might be," said Milo. "Cuthbert said something this morning, too. About the Armada. But I don't know." He kicked his feet over the edge again.

"You worried?" Jules asked.

Milo shrugged. "Are you?"

And Jules huffed. "Course not," he said. "Whatever they're up to out there ain't got nothing to do with us."

Milo twisted around to look at Jules. "This morning it seemed like you were thinking about something. You said that if there really was a war coming . . ."

And Jules knew exactly what Milo was talking about, but for a minute he said nothing. He held tight to the cable beside him and tried not to think about the drop down to the sea. "Milo . . ." he said.

"It's okay."

"No."

"Jules, listen. We're getting bigger, okay? Older. This place . . . I don't know. Something about it feels too small lately."

Which was true. He didn't feel it all the time, but now and then, when Milo moved through the Flying City—in places that he'd known all his life—he felt like it was all growing too close and too tight. Like something was squeezing him. Stopping him from stretching himself to his full height or breathing all the way in. He wanted to explain this to Jules. To see if he was feeling the same thing. To tell him that he understood.

"I'm saying, this place, right now . . . It's just . . ."

The boy had practiced these words. Everything he was going

to say. But now, none of the right ones were coming to him. He closed his eyes and took a breath. "Look, if you want to go? If you have a way—"

And that was when Jules started laughing.

He didn't mean to laugh. And he didn't do it to hurt Milo. But he laughed because sometimes a person just does at the worst possible moment.

Hurt and anger flickered across Milo's face. He asked, "You laughing at me, Jules?"

And Jules covered his mouth with his free hand. He shook his head. "No," he said. "Milo, no."

"Sounds like you are."

"I'm not. Swear. I'm just . . ."

"What?"

"Just laughing."

Milo turned away. He could feel the blush burning in his cheeks, and his head felt full of electricity.

Jules said, "Milo."

Jules said, "I'm sorry."

Jules said, "That wasn't what I was trying to say this morning at all. I'm not going anywhere."

"But why?" Milo asked, wrenching himself back around so fast, Jules was afraid he would fall. So fast that Jules actually reached for him with one hand and held him by the shoulder for a second. Milo looked at Jules's hand and Jules let him go. Then he asked a second time, more quietly, "I mean, really, why, Jules? This place . . . Why would you stay?"

"I dunno," Jules said, then looked away, out toward the sea, then over his shoulder, then down at his own hands. "Never been nowhere else, have I? This is my home. This is where you are."

Then he quickly added, "And Mouse and the kids and Arun and Sig. Everyone. I mean, Sabeen? I'd miss Sabeen. Where else would I get coffee?"

"Literally anywhere else in the entire world."

"Not like his."

Milo nodded. "That's true."

"I know. So I'm not going nowhere that you aren't. We're gonna be robbing the mail and cutting pockets together when we're too old to walk. We're gonna grow up and be pirates, just like you always wanted."

Milo looked away again. "So then what if I leave?"

Jules scoffed and shook his head. "You're not going anywhere neither. You can't. You get seasick."

"I do not."

"How do you know? You've never been on a boat. You *might* get seasick, and then what would happen?"

"Tough to be a pirate who gets seasick."

"So we'll be land pirates," Jules said.

"No such thing as land pirates."

"Then we'll be the first. Clever, right? No one'll see us coming."

"Air pirates," Milo said. "Our own airship. Plunder as far as we can see."

"Air pirates, then. You and me."

"And Mouse?"

"And anyone else who wants to come along," said Jules.

Milo smiled, but it flickered out slowly. His face turned thoughtful. Then he said, "I think there's gonna be trouble, Jules. Everyone is right."

Jules tried not to think about how Ennis had just said the exact same thing to him. So he just shrugged and said, "What trouble?"

"The Armada. I don't know when, but I can tell you this. No one brings forty-four guns to a place without thinking they might need forty-four guns for something."

Jules snorted. "And the whatchacallit down there—"

"The *Achida*. Forty-four mortars."

"Yeah. And they're not the only boat on the water, right? I mean there's gotta be . . ." Jules tried to picture the look of the sea the last time he'd paid it any attention, but couldn't recall when that'd been. "There's gotta be, what? A dozen or more out there?"

"Seventy-one," said Milo. "Near as I've been able to count."

Jules didn't know what to say to that. He couldn't understand what a number as large as that might mean. A dozen boats skulking around on the water getting in people's way and maybe or maybe not carrying a bunch of guns on them seemed like something someone ought to be concerned about. But seventy of them?

Jules said, "That's . . ."

"That's more, yeah. And that's only the ones on the water and only the ones I can see."

"So that's . . ."

"Trouble."

"Yeah." Something cold turned over in Jules's stomach. Something that had nothing to do with the dark or the height or Milo. "So what're we gonna do about it, though?"

"I'm working on that," Milo said.

"You got a plan?"

And Milo's smile came back like a flash in the dark. Jules saw it splitting the shadows of his face—just a few teeth, smirking and confident. "I always have a plan, Jules." Then, "Hey, I've got something for you."

He twisted away then, the boy, and Jules stretched up a little to try to see, but Milo was hunched down, doing something with his hand. Jules heard him swear softly under his breath. Saw him stick one finger in his mouth, take it out and then pull at it until something came free.

"Wet," he said, turning back again. "Sorry." And he stuck out his hand with something glittering in his palm.

Jules leaned close to see what it was and saw a spider. A big one, glistening but not moving. He looked at Milo. "What is it?"

"It's a ring," he said. "A spider ring. I got it from Sanel. For you. Look." Milo poked at it with his fingers, showed Jules how the legs were jointed, sharply tipped, and pointed out the eyes. Then he pushed his hand toward Jules again. "It's for you."

So Jules took the spider ring and slipped it onto his finger, curling the legs around so that it gripped him. He held his hand up so that the metal body and the gleaming joints and glass-chip eyes caught the moonlight, and the spider looked vicious, curled and waiting. Then he curled his non-spider hand into a fist and punched Milo in the arm.

Milo punched him back.

They laughed. Milo asked him if he liked it and Jules said he liked it fine, he guessed. It looked mean. Milo told him that he'd named it Henry, but that it was Jules's now, so he could call it whatever he wanted. Jules allowed that Henry was a pretty good name for a spider, if you weren't terribly creative, and then he asked Milo why.

"Why what?"

"Why'd you get it for me?"

Milo shrugged. "Dunno," he said. "Thought you might like it."

And Jules said that he did, and Milo said he'd better, because it'd been really expensive, and Jules said, again, that he did, and Milo said he'd gotten it because of earlier in the day.

"I felt bad," he said. "Like if you were really leaving? I wanted you to have something to . . . I don't know. To remember me by. To remember all of us, and everything."

Jules laughed again. "And a spider ring is how you make sure your best friend remembers you forever?"

"Yes," said Milo, nodding. "It absolutely is. That is *officially* the gift you give. A spider ring. Don't you know that?"

"I did not know that."

"Well, now you do."

"Well, I guess we're even, then."

"Guess so," said Milo. He pulled his scarf back up over his mouth and his nose, leaving only his eyes showing. "We should get going. You look like you're about to throw up anyway."

"Am not," said Jules.

"Okay," said Milo, laughing, and the two boys stood and began making their way back along the crane toward the city. "Hey, you going to call him Henry still?"

"Yeah, I guess. Henry's not a bad spider name at all."

But really, Jules was thinking, *No, I'm going to call him Milo.*

# MILO AND THE
# TRANSIT POST

**MILO HAD ROBBED THE MAILS** four times before. Three times, he'd gotten rich. Once, he'd almost died.

And you should know before we go any further that robbing the mails was no small or simple task. What it was instead was loud, dangerous, stupid, and impossible. *No one* robbed the mails. Everyone knew that. No one could, even if they wanted to. Even just thinking about it was ridiculous.

This was because in Highgate, the mails all traveled by tube—by a pneumatic pressure system like a giant straw blown into at one end. Or, really, like hundreds of giant straws with hundreds of ends. All of the tubes (from those as big around as a fist to those as big around as a boy crawling) carried bundles and packages and letters and small, delicate, important cargo in sealed canisters. The tubes began in sorting halls high up in the Spire where the airships docked and ended in a hundred other places throughout the Flying City. Anything too big to be carried by the pneumos went by cargo rails that carried thousands of pounds at a time and ran on chain drives and gravity. To get *really* rich, a boy might dream of robbing the cargo rails. But to do that, a boy would have to learn to fly. And Milo hadn't yet figured out how to fly, so had to content himself with smaller things.

Mail came and went through the Flying City from everywhere, bound for everywhere else. Mail, it was often said, was the only legal thing that Highgate did well. The agents of the Transit Post Board (who oversaw the mail) were like iron versions of men, merciless and incorruptible. And the system of delivery they oversaw—the octopus tangle of pneumatic tubes, control cylinders, transshipment caissons, and huge, booming and rattling cargo rails—was so complex and poorly understood that, to most people, it bordered on magic.

But not to Milo Quick.

When he was younger and still figuring out how to make his way on the streets of Highgate, finding something to eat and a safe place to sleep had always been the boy's primary concerns. He had no home, so he roamed high and low, hands in his empty pockets and hungry all the time.

One night, when Milo was maybe nine, he'd wandered up into the High Quarter. He'd gone there because the houses were fancier, the nights were quieter and the garbage (which he picked through for food sometimes) was of a higher quality.

Above him, in the aerie's low cradles, the big airships were docking. When he looked up, he could see lanterns swinging and landing lights blinking. Searchlights stabbed into the night sky, raking across the huge gasbags and towering sails of the airships on approach. Even from this far below, the boy could hear the boom of luffing canvas spilling wind and the groan of the massive, impossible hulls as they were hooked and winched into position.

Milo'd wanted a closer look at the airships, so he'd slunk up High Street in the direction of the Spire and the aeries at its very top, past where the nice homes and shops gave way to a ring of cargo yards and cartage houses, drawn on by the vision of the big ships glowing in the haze of electric light. In a maze of sacks and barrels waiting to be hauled up by provisioners, Milo had found a gap in the chain fence that separated the mail yards from the rest of the city—a hole too small for anything but a boy who hadn't eaten more than garbage or drunk more than rainwater in four days—and Milo slipped through it.

Being in the mail yards was dangerous. Everyone knew that. The men of the Transit Post would chop a boy up and stuff the pieces into a mail tube just for standing on the wrong side of their fence. But Milo, in that moment, wasn't thinking about that. He wanted to see the airships. And he was either too young to be scared or too exhausted to care.

So that night, he got to watch the big ships from as close as he'd ever been. And when he was too tired to keep his eyes open any longer, instead of sneaking back out again, he'd crawled into a gap beneath one of the large mail tubes and slept for hours, sung to sleep by the hiss and rattle of the Transit Post's mail system.

When daylight finally woke him, Milo discovered that he could move around the feet of the towering caissons easily if he was careful, that the guards spent almost all their time watching the gates and the cargo, and didn't pay much attention at all to the forest of tubes and valves and chutes that crowded the mail yard. At night, it was even easier.

Milo spent a week living in the mail yard, never sleeping in the same spot twice. He fed himself by stealing from the shack where the guards mustered every morning to receive their assignments. There was an ice chest there where some of them kept their lunches. At night, there was always a tin pot of coffee set on an electric coil. He would drink it all, then make the guards a fresh pot to thank them for their wonderful inattention.

And then, one night, he found a particularly dense cluster of pneumos at the base of the #9 Dispatching Caisson and discovered that if he squeezed in behind the smallest of them, he came out into an empty space between the tubes and the smooth white stone of the caisson. It wasn't big, but it was big enough. And almost impossible to see. It was like a small clearing in a pneumatic forest, and he could curl there like a fox in the noise and darkness, to sleep perfumed by the smells of machine oil and warm metal.

For a little while, this became his home. He was safe there, protected by a wall of brass and copper, lulled by the regularity of the mails making their transit up and down the system. And it wasn't until his third week living in the pneumatic forest, on a cool, clear, and oddly quiet night when sleep would not come to him, that Milo noticed something about the noise of the mails that *wasn't* regular.

And this was how Milo had found The Bend.

It wasn't much of a noise. Just a little extra bump and hiss. A flat, *thunking* kind of sound that came at the end of a long, downhill slide in one of the bigger tubes. Right where it bent.

Milo being Milo, the sound bothered him. So Milo being Milo, he investigated. And Milo being Milo, he was very, *very* thorough.

He discovered, for example, that the pneumo making the unusual noise was named tube 1176a and that tube 1176a had just a little more lateral bend in it than any other tube footing near it. He discovered that this little extra bit of bend was enough to cause canisters traveling through tube 1176a to hang up at the curve. To pause, in fact, until enough pressure from the system built up behind it to pop it free.

Milo hadn't stolen his first watch yet, so he timed this pause by his resting heartbeat and found that it took fourteen beats. When, with a rock, he was able to put a small, rounded dent in the tube at its bend, he was able to increase this delay to almost thirty beats.

There was a maintenance hatch twenty feet down from the bend in the pneumo, used for clearing blockages and inspecting the interior of the tube. It wasn't even locked. Because who in their right mind would want to open it? Tube 1176a was big enough around to hold a boy on his hands and knees. The mail canisters that traveled through it weighed nearly thirty pounds each, and they went *fast*. To go inside while the system was live was like crawling into the barrel of a giant's gun.

But with a mail canister stuck in the tube, there was no pressure in front of it. If Milo were to open that hatch, no breach would show on the gauges of those watching in the Transit Post control rooms up in the Spire. No one would know he was there. And then he would have thirty beats of his quiet heart during which to open the hatch, climb inside the tube, crawl twenty feet in the dark, open the canister, grab something and get out again. All before the pressure popped the canister free and sent it on its way.

He tried it for the first time a few nights later. First just opening the hatch, counting, and then closing it again before the canister was pushed free. Then opening the hatch and actually climbing inside the tube.

*Just crawl in a little bit*, he said to himself.

And then he did.

*Just try to touch the mail canister*, he said to himself.

And then he did.

*Just try to open it*, he said to himself.

And then he tried, but something went wrong. About halfway down the tube, he heard the canister make a rattling, scraping sound, and he panicked. He tried to turn around inside the tube, but there wasn't room. He got himself wedged sideways, one shoulder crooked, neck bent. And he knew that at any second the canister would pop free and come right at him. That he would never even see it coming.

In the end, he'd squirmed enough to get himself straightened out, then scrambled backward as fast as he could go. When he got to the hatch, he tumbled out of the hole and landed on his butt. He barely had time to lift the hatch door, slam it into place and close the heavy latch before the mail canister worked its way loose from The Bend and went whooshing down the tube.

After that, Milo lay back beside the mail tube, stared up into the night sky and began to laugh with one hand over his mouth to muffle the sound. Thirty heartbeats wasn't enough time. Milo knew that now. But Milo being Milo, he hadn't been willing to give up. It would take time, some more experimenting, but there were riches to be had from robbing the mails. He just knew it. All he had to do was figure out how.

And for that, he'd need some friends.

# EIGHT CHILDREN

**AT FIRST,** it all went so well.

They met, as planned, in more or less the right place at more or less the right time. Eight children clustered together at the doors of a warehouse full of ship's stores that went mostly unwatched in the night. The doors had a large and impressively heavy lock, but there were also high windows that could be gotten to easily by those willing to stand on each other's shoulders.

Inside the warehouse, it was dark and smelled of the sea. There was a guard, but he slept soundly and never woke, because who would go to the trouble of stealing water or sacks of flour crawling with weevils?

Eight children crouched in the dark, waiting for their eyes to adjust. When they'd been out on the crane arm, Milo and Jules had seen the weather coming in. Black clouds thick enough to swallow the moon. The clouds were close, but had not yet arrived. There was just enough light left in the night to show them the way.

Eight children in a line wound like a snake across the floor of the warehouse. In the far corner was a wall where, long ago, a clever boy had loosened the boards. Had, in fact, pulled every nail (pocketing them for later use) and replaced them with carpenter's tacks hammered flat. The tacks were just enough to hold the boards in place until the clever boy gave the wall a shove, and then out it fell—enough space for eight children to squeeze through, finding themselves suddenly on the other side of the gates and fences that separated the mail and aerie grounds from the rest of Highgate.

"Quick," said Milo, who crouched while he herded his friends along. Over the years he'd learned a lot about tube 1176a. Mostly, he'd learned how to defeat it.

Thirty resting heartbeats was about twenty seconds—a thing he'd learned after getting a watch of his own. And although twenty seconds was not enough time for a boy to open the maintenance hatch, climb in, open the canister, steal whatever was in it, and crawl back out again (backward), it *was* enough time to open the hatch, climb inside the tube, crawl twenty feet and set chocks around the canister, preventing it from moving completely. It was time enough for someone else to set themselves at a position *above* The Bend, to listen for incoming canisters. For someone else to stand with them, watching for guards. For a fourth person to stand below The Bend, also watching for guards. For a fifth and sixth person to be holding the rope attached to the person inside the tube, ready to pull them out backward when the thieving was done or when the canister started to shift. For a seventh person to be holding ropes onto which the chocks had been tied, and to pull them after the robber was safely out of the tube. For an eighth person, then, to slam shut the hatch as soon as the chocks were recovered, sealing the system and allowing the thoroughly burgled mail canister to pass on its way.

It'd taken years, but Milo (being Milo) had found his way to rob the mails.

Eight children moved silently in the dark, in a line, scampering up to the bottom of the #9 Dispatching Caisson, which extended like a smooth white finger to touch the arcs of the airship docks above.

Everything was loud. It was a busy night.

And at first it all went so well.

# AT FIRST . . .

**IT WAS KEELAN'S JOB** to listen above The Bend and to signal when another mail canister was coming. He went as far up the steep slope as he could go and sat with his ear against the warm metal, his arms wrapped around the tube like he was hugging it. He carried a length of pipe with him. As soon as he heard something, he would bang on the casing of tube 1176a as hard as he could and hope that they would hear him below. Dagda went with him to keep an eye out for guards, because when Keelan sat listening, he did it with his eyes closed and his mouth hanging open like a carp's.

Arun watched for guards from below The Bend. Sig and Jules were the pullers. Llyr was the corker (who'd yank the rope attached to the chocks when the time came), and it had been explained to her three different times that she was to wait for Milo's order. That she was to do nothing at all until Milo said "Pull," and then to pull as hard as she could, and to keep pulling as fast as she could until the chocks were out of the hole. She'd saluted and said she'd do her best, but the first time anyone looked back at her, she'd dropped the rope completely and was swatting at a firefly that was trying to land in her hair.

Tristan was the robber. Milo was the closer, who would slam and bar the hatch. They drew no straws and took no turns. This was just the way it was. Keelan had good ears. Arun could put two fingers in his mouth and whistle louder than all the rest of them put together. Sig and Jules were strong. Milo was quick. Tristan was small and fearless and didn't weigh much more than a dog so was easy to pull when the time came. Even with his arms full of stolen parcels and packages, Jules and Sig could have him back to the hole and tumbling out of it in seconds.

They were *long* seconds, though. And Tristan would whoop and laugh the whole time, loud enough to be heard over the hissing and rattling and roaring all around them as he was dragged, tumbling and backward, out of the tube just ahead of the chocks and the scraping whoosh of the mail canister being popped loose time and time again.

Three times before, they'd done this. And each time they'd walked away with so much loot they could barely carry it all. A month's worth of stealing in one night's work.

Tonight, though, was different. On Tristan's first attempt he had nearly two full minutes in the tube before they all heard Keelan banging. Jules and Sig dragged on their ropes. Milo yelled to Llyr, who (fortunately) was paying attention and pulled for all she was worth. And Tristan came spilling out of the hatch, followed by the chocks and the rope and a dozen small letters and packages—most of which ended up being nothing more than correspondences and work orders and bills of various types, though there was also a box of differently sized metal screws and a pair of ladies shoes in green velvet with feathers and heels like stiletto knives.

Milo had slammed the hatch shut and cranked the bar that latched it tight, nearly hitting Tristan in the head in his hurry. The mail canister blew loose with a *whuff* that shook the tube and passed them by while Tristan lay in the dirt beneath the hatch,

still laughing, the letters and packages spread out around him in
a jumble.

The shoes were likely worth something, Milo thought. But beyond that, there was nothing of value to them in this pull.

"Just bad luck," Milo said to Tristan as he got him up out of
the dirt and back onto his feet. "Remember, heavier is better, usually. You ready to go again?"

Tristan nodded like his neck was a spring, then crouched down
to paw through the discarded letters and torn envelopes Milo'd
thrown in the dirt. He grabbed one to show Milo and asked him if
he could keep it. It was an invitation to a birthday party in a pale
yellow envelope with balloons drawn in one corner. Milo asked
why he wanted it and Tristan shrugged. "Dunno. I've never been
asked to a party. Seems so fancy."

"The party?"

"No, just the letter. That's something I'd like to have. Just to,
you know . . . To pretend?"

Tristan went back into the tube four more times. And though,
at the end of it, they had a small pile of plunder, it wasn't nearly
enough.

The best thing he'd gotten was a box with a cloth ribbon that
contained fruit jellies crusted with sugar crystals and honeyed dates
tucked inside little rosettes of tissue paper. So they all took a break
and ate the dates and the candies (which crunched with sugar crystals, the jelly sticking in their teeth), and when they were finished,
they were all sticky, but everyone was happier. Except Milo.

The boy was worried. They needed to get rich from this, and
Milo's stomach was knotted with all the ways they weren't. They
needed enough to keep the Total King happy and themselves safe
and fed, at least for a little while. Until Milo could figure out what
to do next and next and next. He was worried about the Armada

and Jules and Moric Shaw and this feeling he'd been carrying like an ache between his shoulder blades that monsters were watching him whenever his back was turned, that large and terrible things were coming but were just out of his sight. He felt like maybe Tristan wasn't taking the best things. Like maybe he was just grabbing whatever he could reach, and then laughing about it in the dirt. Like maybe he didn't understand how important this was.

And Milo said none of this out loud. He swallowed and swallowed and smiled and slapped Tristan on the shoulder. He said what a good job he'd done, but that it looked like so much fun, now he wanted a turn. Milo would go into the tube himself. Tristan would help Sig with the pulling, and Jules would be in charge of the hatch.

"Just one time," he said to Tristan. "Promise. I used to do this, too, you know. I want to try it again."

So now Milo went into the tube when the time came. And right away, he knew it was a mistake. It seemed smaller than he remembered. Tighter. But he snaked himself forward as fast as he could anyway, holding the chocks in one hand, dragging the ropes behind. It was hot, too dark to see anything, but he crawled until he reached the canister, felt around it for the edges, shoved the chocks into place to hold it, then opened the sliding front and started feeling the packages within.

Bundles of letters. Thin, flat packages that were likely paperwork, and others that were maybe cloth or clothing or something of value swaddled in cotton. He took one, just to see. Deep inside there was a heavy, square box that rattled and sounded like glass bottles clinking together. He wasted precious seconds trying to maneuver it out of the canister.

In his head, Milo was already counting heartbeats, knowing that Keelan would start banging soon, that Sig and Tristan would pull him, that he would have to hold tight to the packages and make sure they came with him. Pressurized air squealed out around the edges of the canister. Milo could smell his own sour, panicked breath and feel the bony wings of his shoulders brushing the sides of the tube, but he had to find something. He had to make this count. He dug both hands deep into the mail and felt around, finding nothing, nothing, and nothing. When he heard the banging—Keelan's signal—he shouted, "No!" as though his small, desperate voice would be enough to stop the mail from coming and one second from following the next. But just then, his fingers finally closed around a hard-sided box. Metal. Maybe a cashbox. Maybe something even better. He clawed it free and tucked it inside his shirt just as he felt the ropes begin to pull him. He slammed the cover of the canister shut and curled himself around the packages he'd taken like he was hugging them all together, his knees pulled in tight, his arms wrapping everything, his eyes squeezed tightly shut.

And he began to slide. He didn't laugh the way Tristan had, because Milo understood mortality. He imagined he felt the tube swelling with pressure behind the blockage of the mail canister, the whole thing quaking and the canister stuck there like a cork in a bottle. A bullet in a gun, waiting to fire. The metal box dug into his ribs as he slid backward. The bottles rattled against each other like chimes. His knees and the crown of his head rubbed against the smooth, polished metal of the tube. Small as he was, Milo was getting too big for this, and he knew it. Too heavy. He should've let Tristan continue. He should've trusted that their luck would change.

Still, he was moving. Sig and Tristan were pulling him. Milo tried to imagine himself light as a feather, smooth as silk. And for a few seconds, that seemed to work.

Until he got to the hatch and couldn't get out. Because, suddenly, with his body wrapped tight around everything he'd stolen, he was too big to fit through the hole.

Panic. A spasm as he struggled, not thinking, flailing, trying to push with his legs and squeeze his body through. He heard Jules shouting his name. Crunching footsteps. He felt hands on him, dragging at him.

"Let it go, Milo!"

Jules's voice. He wondered how much time was left until the canister came and smeared him along the insides of the tube like jelly. He struggled, twisting and thrashing, too terrified to open his eyes and look, until finally, with the pop and crash of shattering glass, the heavy box of bottles fell loose from Milo's arms and Milo followed it out, landing half on it, half in the broken glass, on his head and shoulders, with letters and boxes and everything else raining out around him.

Someone stepped on his stomach. He'd had the wind knocked out of him in the fall and could barely breathe. He tried to crawl clear, but there were hands and feet everywhere. He heard the rattle of the mail canister coming free from The Bend and Jules shouting about the hatch, heard him grunt as he lifted the heavy door, fighting to get to the bar that locked it tight.

But he didn't make it.

The force of the mail canister passing by slammed the door back open, throwing Jules into the air. As it banged back against its hinges, it hit Sig, too. The sound of the mail canister smashing into the lip of the open hatch was like a crack of thunder. Sparks fountained out onto the ground, and Milo felt the pinprick burns of them on his face. He heard Sig scream and, somewhere, someone or something banging on the tube. Milo didn't know if it was the hatch or Keelan or if something else had broken. He was confused, and all he could think about was how badly he'd screwed everything up. How this was all his fault.

And then he heard whistling. Loud, sharp whistling, coming from below them by the fence. It was Arun.

Milo tried to say *Run!* but no sound came out of him.

The whistling continued. Short, sharp blasts of it. The banging stopped. Milo tried to sit up, gasping for air. He'd lost the metal box somewhere and, as it turned out, the wooden one had held bottles of perfume. Dozens of them. And he was lying in a puddle of spilled perfume and broken glass, the stink of it covering him, burning where it got into his cuts and scratches. He couldn't think. He wheezed and tried again to yell *Run!* but it still only came out as a whisper.

Milo forced the air out of his lungs. Sucked in a fresh breath. Then did it again. He saw Llyr crying, still holding the rope attached to the chocks with one hand, her other thumb in her mouth. Tristan was standing near the tube, dancing back and forth from one foot to the other and making a sound like an owl—*whoo, whoo, whoo*. The whistles came again, from farther away now.

Milo closed his eyes. He took one more breath and held it until he saw stars. Then, finally, he shouted, as loudly as he could, just one word.

"RUN!"

# . . . AND THEN LATER, AFTER ALL THE LOUD NOISES AND SCREAMING

**LOOK,** there's something you should know right now.

We've been through a lot together already, haven't we? And not all of it happy, either. As a matter of fact, very little of it has been happy. But that's just life sometimes. It isn't all puppy dogs and moon pies. Anyone who tries to say different is lying to you.

But as difficult as some of this story has been, the rest of it is worse. I'm just warning you. Some of it is scary and some of it is sad and some of it is cruel and some of it is all three of those things at the same time, so it's okay if you want to stop. If you want, you can just believe that Milo and his friends all escape the pneumatic forest with some bumps and bruises and go on to become daring air pirates (just like Milo wanted). You can believe that they all stay friends forever. That they all grow up and grow old together.

That's *not* what happens, but it's okay if you want to believe it. I promise you Milo wouldn't care.

So stop now if you like. Just stop reading and walk away. Your parents would be happier if you did. You might be, too. Because the only thing you'll get from going any further is the truth of what happens to Milo and Dagda and Jules and everyone else. And the truth, although a good thing (maybe the best thing), isn't very often a happy thing.

Later, after all the loud noises and screaming, Milo would think back on his days as a boy, running through the streets of the Flying City. He would think about the taste of raw sourdough, a metal spider ring, the view from Front Street, laughing with Jules, nights spent commanding phantom airships in the breaking yards and Semyon Beli boxing a carrier bird, and he would know that those were his good days. That his fears, his loneliness, his aching, sour hunger were nothing compared with what would come.

The boy still had things to see, of course. Things beyond the reach of his wildest imaginings. There would still be friends and adventures and victories and laughter. But none of it would ever be quite the same. None of it would ever be so pure as those moments when everything was a game and no one who mattered to him ever got hurt.

It would never be the same, because everything in his life up to The Bend was about wanting. And everything after was about loss.

So yes. Stop here if you like. Imagine Milo, Dagda, Jules, Arun, Sig, Tristan, Llyr, and Keelan in any way you'd like to see them.

Or keep reading and find out what *really* comes next.

You've been warned. That's all I'm saying.

# JULES AND MILO

**IT TOOK HIM A SECOND,** but once Milo found his feet, he rushed to check on Jules.

And Jules was fine, except for being a little shaken up. The hatch (which he'd apparently tried to hold closed with nothing but his weight and his stupid boy's strength) had thrown him ten feet, easy. Hard enough that he'd briefly flown. But he was a boy, and boys are sometimes made of nothing more than rubber bands and terrible ideas, so all he had to show for it were some bruises and a new appreciation for the power of the mails.

"You're okay?" Milo asked.

"I think so," said Jules.

But now there were lanterns and loud voices approaching. The scrape and crunch of footsteps on stone. These were the guards—men from the Transit Post—who would be very unhappy to find that Milo and his friends had broken their fancy, complicated toy. Arun's whistles were still shrilling in the dark, but quieter now, moving farther and farther away. Tristan had run and taken Llyr by the hand, dragging her stumblingly along. Keelan and Dagda were gone. But among the metal trunks of the pneumatic forest, Milo crouched in front of Jules, holding his face in his hands, both of them wide-eyed, amazed to be alive.

Sig hadn't been quite so lucky.

He'd been rushing for the hatch, too. He'd seen Milo get stuck, and run to help. He'd been just a step or two behind Jules when Milo had let go of the packages and come tumbling out of the hole. He'd been reaching out when the force of the mail canister and the pneumatic pressure that pushed it along had blown the hatch open like it was spring-loaded. Jules had been thrown, but Sig, it seemed, had tried to catch the door.

And now he sat on the ground near the ruin of pneumatic mail tube 1176a with his left hand cupped against his chest. All around him, the ground was littered with broken glass, packages, shoes, and letters. The mail canister had shattered against the lip of the hole when it hit, and was now stuck there. A fountain of shredded correspondence blew out around the edges of it and swirled like snow, drifting around Sig, who was staining it red with his blood. He'd stopped screaming, but the air that whistled through the broken hatch sounded kind of like screaming, too.

Milo scrambled over to him and said, "Sig, we have to go," but Sig didn't even look at him. Milo crouched down and shook him a little. Took him by the shoulder and asked, "Sig, can you run?"

Sig turned his head with sleepy slowness. He blinked a turtle's blink, looked at Milo and said, "If it keeps snowing like this, I'll never find my other fingers."

He raised his ruined hand then to show Milo, and Milo looked away, burying his chin in his own shoulder. He pushed himself back away from Sig, but Jules caught him by the shirt and wouldn't let him run.

Milo saw the bobbing lights of the lanterns getting closer. He could hear the grumbling of men's voices. He thought quickly about their options and heard Sig say in a tiny whisper, "What am I gonna tell my mom if I can't find my fingers?"

"He's in shock," Jules said.

Milo jerked his shirt out of Jules's fist and said, "I know. We have to go."

Jules looked at Milo. "You're gonna leave him?"

"For now."

Jules glanced over his shoulder at the lights, then back. "We can't *leave* him! He's our friend."

"Just for now, Jules. Come on."

"I can carry him," Jules said, stepping toward where Sig lay.

"No," said Milo, and stepped between them. He pushed Jules back and looked him in the eye. "We have to go."

But Jules planted his feet. He tried to shoulder Milo aside and reach for Sig, who looked up at him, shaking and staring. But Milo pushed him again. He grabbed Jules by the sleeve and kept himself between his best friend and Sig.

"Jules," he said, trying to catch his eye. "Jules! He'll bleed to death if we take him. He will."

And Jules tried to shake Milo off. He said, "Sig, can you walk?" and Sig said nothing at all, so Jules said, "Do you want me to carry you?" and Sig started to cry.

Milo said, "Jules, you have to trust me. I have a plan. But we have to *go*."

Jules swore. Milo dragged at his arm. A flickering knife of greasy yellow light slashed across them, stuttered by the interruptions of a dozen pneumatic tubes. Jules kicked at the dirt and gravel and said, "Sig," his voice plaintive, pleading. "Please get up."

But he was turning away, too, making to run, to follow Milo up the slope, away from the voices and the lights. Away from the blood and the mess and their friend.

# MILO, JULES, AND DAGDA IN THE DARK

**MILO AND JULES RAN,** but they didn't go far.

A hundred steps, maybe. Out of the pneumatic forest, through the mail yard and across the road. There was a ditch there. Tall weeds grew up from it. It smelled like crushed clover and rot. A hundred scrambling, sprinting steps and that was where Milo just stopped, sat down, grabbed a cattail shoot and started rolling it between his thumbs. He could see both the bobbing lamps gathering at The Bend and a part of the steep road that ran between the upper and lower control gates with the guardhouse halfway along. It was a good spot.

Jules almost tripped over him. It was hard enough to see in the dark, and from behind the screen of weeds, Milo was pretty much invisible. He ended up crouched close beside Milo in the dark and sticky heat, waiting, and probably wondering what was supposed to happen next.

The boy had a plan. Or at least the beginnings of one. He'd been thinking about it since the minute everything had gone wrong, and since he felt like everything that'd gone wrong had been his fault, he figured it was his responsibility to fix it.

Which was what he was trying to do. As quickly as he possibly could.

Quietly he asked Jules if he knew how to make a grass whistle and Jules said he didn't know what a grass whistle was, so that pretty much answered that. Then Milo asked Jules if he had anything on him that would burn and Jules said, "Like what? Like, my clothes would burn, wouldn't they?" but Milo had meant something like a match so that, too, was a no.

It wasn't much of a plan. Not *yet*. But the boy was working on it.

Jules eased forward and peeked over the edge of the ditch like it was a trench and the enemy was right on top of them. Milo sat quietly, thinking. Jules looked back over his shoulder and sniffed. He said, "You smell weird."

Milo shushed him.

"I'm just saying . . ."

"Perfume," said Milo, like it should've been obvious.

Jules looked back out at the road, then turned around again. "Why do you smell like perfume?"

"The box," said Milo. "It was full of perfume bottles."

"Really?"

"A *lot* of perfume bottles."

And Jules was about to ask him how many perfume bottles, but Milo shushed him again. And then he was going to ask what they were doing here and why they were waiting in a ditch when Sig was still out there, and why they weren't, you know, *doing something*, but Milo shushed him a third time and said, "Look. Here they come."

The shutters on their lanterns were opened all the way, so the guards walked in a wavering bubble of soft, greasy light. There were a dozen of them, maybe more—now moving out of the pneumatic forest and onto the road.

Milo whispered, "See? I told you," and Jules asked, "See what?" but Milo didn't answer because Milo was only arguing with himself. Jules didn't know that, though, so Jules poked him in the ribs and said it again—"See *what*?"—and Milo said, "Look," and pointed with his cattail shoot. "Sig," he said. "They're carrying him. And I know where they're going."

Jules squinted into the dark and saw one of the guards walking with something thrown over his shoulder that might've been Sig. He got up on the balls of his feet and dug his fingers into the crumbling dirt at the edge of the ditch. "We gonna go get him now?" he asked.

"No," said Milo.

"No?" Jules hissed back "Milo, what are we—"

But just then there was a noise behind them and they both whipped around and Dagda was just *there*—in the ditch like she'd arrived by magic.

"You two are *loud*," she whispered.

"Milo smells weird," Jules said. "But it's okay, because it's only perfume."

She reached out and pulled a sliver of glass out of Milo's hair. "They're taking Sig to the guardhouse," she said.

"I know," said Milo.

"Because he can also read minds now," Jules muttered.

"They're sending for a doctor named Cobby from the Number Seven Caisson. They think the hatch just blew open and Sig was maybe sleeping there or something."

"Good," said Milo.

"Good?" Jules hissed at him.

"Good," said Milo again, glancing sharply at Jules. "I hoped they would pick him up, Jules. I *knew* they would. And I knew they'd bring him to the guardhouse, because I've been in there before and the guardhouse is the only place in the whole mail yard to bring anybody. They're going to want to ask Sig questions. But before they can do that, they're going to have to fix him up, because he looks bad. I don't think he's actually hurt all that bad. Just broken fingers and stuff. But he *looks* bad"—an image of Sig and Sig's hand bubbled up in Milo's head, but he swallowed hard, took a breath, continued—"which is the point. And he's bleeding a lot. So I knew they'd call someone. A doctor or someone who'd know how to tie up his fingers, stitch him, give him medicine . . . I don't know. Whatever a doctor does. And there's gonna be a bunch of men there, too. Guards, all standing around, because when the doctor's done, they're gonna want to know what Sig was doing there, what he knows about The Bend and if anyone else was with him."

"And that's when we burn the house down?" Jules asked.

"And that's when we—" Milo paused. "Wait, what?"

"What?" asked Dagda, looking at Milo.

"With matches!" said Jules.

"No," said Milo.

"Then why—"

"Are you hurt at all, Jules?"

"What? No. I mean, I got a bruise, but . . ."

"Okay. Can you run? Can you shout?"

Jules leaned back a little, puffed up a little, grinned a little. "I can make a ruckus, Milo."

And the boy said okay, turned to Dagda, and asked where Keelan was.

"I told him not to wait for me. Everyone else should be going back to the Haunts."

"You left him alone?"

"If I'd left the two of you alone, I don't want to think about what would've happened."

"Apparently, we would've spent the whole night talking instead of doing a rescue," Jules grumbled.

Milo asked Dagda, "Do you know how to make a grass whistle?"

"Like with your thumbs and a blade of grass? Yes. Of course."

"Can you make it loud?"

"Yes," said Dagda. "Distraction?"

"Yeah," said Milo. "You understand what—"

In the dark, Dagda nodded. "Yes. Sure. Okay. When?"

Milo looked up. Jules would swear he saw him sniff the air. "When the rain comes."

"What about me?" Jules asked.

"Go with Dagda and make all the noise you can."

"*Finally*," said Jules, grinning. "But what about Sig?"

"We're the distraction, Jules," Dagda said. "You and me just have to lead away as many guards as possible, then vanish. Milo will do the rescuing."

"Alone?"

"He's got a plan," said Dagda, and Jules turned and asked Milo if that was true, and the boy smiled and looked Jules right in the eye and lied to him.

"Don't I always?"

Just then, on the road, there appeared a stout, roundish man with a shining, bald head. He was puffing out heavy breaths as he shuffle-jogged along the steep slope in the direction of the guardhouse, his feet slapping on the cracked pavement. He wore a gray Transit Post uniform and carried a cloth bundle in one hand—nothing more than some burlap gathered together and tied with a string.

"Shh," said Milo. "Here comes their doctor. You two should go."

# MILO

**WHILE DAGDA AND JULES** wound their way through the forest of mail tubes, Milo followed the grassy gutter toward the guardhouse. He collected stones along the way, a heavy bolt that lay rusting in the weeds, the bottom half of a broken bottle and a threaded pipe cap.

The boy was trying hard to remember everything he could about the guardhouse. Seeing as he'd been inside it before—had stolen lunches and made coffee there—he knew it as well as anyone did. A single room. One door and three windows, a table, some chairs. He crouched lower and lower as he crept closer and closer. And when he was near enough to hear the voices of the men inside, he got down on his belly and crawled.

In a proper children's story, this would be the point where the young hero pulls out an invisibility cloak conveniently left to him by mysterious relatives or benefactors. It would be when he drinks the old crone's potion that makes him eighty feet tall or slips a magic ring onto his finger that lets him shoot fireballs out of his eyes. The boy loved those stories, because they always seemed to turn out happily in the end. Because there was always a way out of danger, neatly orchestrated by adults and left there like a treat for the clever little children to find.

Milo, though, had been left nothing by his parents except a

name that he held like a secret stone in his mouth. He could not turn invisible or gigantic or shoot anything out of his anything. And the only ring he had was shaped like a metal spider, and he'd given that to Jules.

Milo was only what he was—a small, scared boy with his hands full of nothing but stones and broken glass. His guts were twisted inside him like noodles on a fork and his head was full of doubtful voices, but he crawled in the dirt anyway as thunder rumbled in the distance and blue-white summer lightning flashed in the lowering clouds. On his knees and elbows, he made it all the way to the back wall of the guardhouse and then crouched there, light shining from one of the windows directly above his head. Because he had to see for himself what was happening inside, he inched up and peeked in one corner of the window, then sank back down again feeling even worse.

Sig was there, in a chair, one arm lashed down to a table. The doctor was hunched over him, working, wrapping things, sewing things. A man was holding Sig in the chair by his shoulders. Another gripped his arm at the elbow. Sig had a stick in his mouth, wrapped in wet leather, and he was biting on it and screaming around it like a horse with a bit. His eyes were huge.

Besides the doctor and the two men holding Sig, there were six others. Nine men total. And every one of them (including the doctor) wore a uniform and a leather belt with a bully stick hung on it, lovingly polished and lead-weighted. They could crack a skull, those sticks. Break bones. Shatter teeth. Milo had a cut-purse knife, a rusty bolt, a pipe cap, and half a broken bottle.

But he also had a plan.

Part of a plan.

And he was hoping hard that the rest of it would come to him as he crouched below the window with his back to the wall, waiting and listening to the banging and scraping of chair legs on the wood floor and Sig's muffled howls of pain. Milo closed his eyes and raised his full hands to either side of his head, pressing the soft parts of his wrists over his ears. And he stayed there until, finally, the rain came—just a few, fat drops at first, but then, suddenly, all of it. All the rain in the world, all at once, falling in a torrent.

Milo lowered his hands and pressed his back against the wall. He breathed deeply and listened for the ruckus.

# THE RUCKUS

**WHEN THE FIRST DROPS OF RAIN CAME DOWN,**
Dagda stood up from the ditch, brought her thumbs to her mouth
and blew. The noise that came out sounded like a train whistle
and, to Jules, seemed nearly as loud.

She did it again. And again. Jules looked around and saw
lanterns winking in the dark, their pawing, bright fingers of light
passing through the maze of pneumatics.

Dagda blew her grass whistle again, then looked at Jules and
said, "It's raining, Jules. *Do* something."

So Jules picked up a rock and slammed it as hard as he could
into the side of a cargo rail, making a hollow, ringing sound. He
took a deep breath and shouted at the top of his lungs, "THEY'RE
OVER HERE! THEY'RE OVER HERE! THEY'RE OVER
HERE!"

Then both of them moved, sliding among the pneumos and
through the rain and darkness like shadows. The game was to get
the attention of the Transit Post men and then lead them as far
away from where Milo was as possible. So Dagda screamed. She
blew her grass whistle, darted away, blew it again. Jules followed,
dodging through thick tangles of pneumatic tubes, relief lines,
pressure seals. He found one of the thinnest pneumos, about as
big around as his arm, and swung his rock against it as hard as he

could. Then did it again and again and again, hoping to dent it, to break it, to beat it apart at its welds. And all the while, he was yelling—roaring at the top of his lungs. No words, just rage.

Dagda whistled again, long and shrill.

Jules bellowed swear words into the rain, which had begun to pour down. He yelled, "SHUT DOWN THE LINES! SHUT DOWN THE LINES!" and swung his rock.

Dagda shouted, "Look!" and pointed with both hands, so as not to lose the blade of grass. There were lights bobbing in the watery dark, moving in confused circles, and more voices answering theirs. "Get their attention, Jules!"

So Jules did. He yelled, "OVER HERE! SOMEONE CUT THEM OFF!" and swung the rock again. Surprisingly, the small pneumatic line broke with shocking violence, giving way at a seam and blowing pressurized air with a high, shrieking bellow, like a hundred teakettles all singing at once.

Thunder crashed. The rain bucketed down. Dagda said, "We should start moving them away. They don't really seem to be coming this—"

Which was when the pneumatic tube next to the one Jules had bashed open also blew—an emergency valve meant to deal with pressure overloads, popping open and sending another gust of high-pressure air into the night, its safety wheel spanging off to rattle among the pipes.

Jules didn't know what to do, so he hit it with his rock. It bent but didn't break, so he wiped his dripping hair back out of his face, then hit another one and another one, shouting as loudly as he could with every swing. All around him, he heard the pneumos shake and rattle because *something* was certainly happening, even if he had no idea what. And he didn't really care, either. All of a sudden, he just wanted to break every single thing he saw.

"Come on, Jules!" Dagda yelled. "We have to move."

She tried to whistle, but her hands were wet now and the grass was limp, so she gave up on that, saw a rusting length of pipe on the ground, picked it up and, like Jules, started swinging it at everything she saw, her lips peeling back in a smile as she felt her muscles stretch and the pipe connect and the tremors of impact roll all the way up her arms. Something was spinning up inside her, like the revving of a small, infinitely powerful motor. When she bore down, she could knock a medium-sized pneumatic tube right out of its mounts. She could bend small ones into a twisted U around where her club struck. And it felt *good*, this smashing. This making of her indelible, irreducible mark on a world that had been her enemy for nearly as long as she'd been in it, and that demanded, always, such quiet of her. Such restraint.

But now she smiled. She swung and she smashed. Now, in this moment, she gloried in being as loud and wild and indulgent as possible.

# MILO

**THE MEN IN THE GUARDHOUSE** swarmed out the door like the building was on fire as soon as they heard the noises start up. They grabbed their lanterns and had their hands on their sticks, and Milo could hear them, standing around the open front door, arguing with each other about what could possibly be happening now.

Milo heard Jules's voice, yelling to shut down the lines, and then some kind of popping explosion. Then another. There were shouts and screams and there was more whistling, a loud, metallic banging like something shaking itself to pieces, and finally, it was enough that the men by the door ended their arguing over who ought to go out into the rain and all took off running as a group, holding out their lanterns and shouting into the dark.

Milo waited for them to pass, then circled around the blind side of the guardhouse to peek through another window.

The doctor was still inside. One man was still holding Sig in his chair, though most of the thrashing had stopped. Sig's eyes were open. His chest was heaving. But the doctor appeared to have finished the worst of whatever he'd been doing. He was wrapping Sig's hand now in clean white bandages and bracing his fingers with bits of metal, and tying knots as neat and tidy as any sailor. A third man stood in the doorway, his billy club in hand

and the leather thong wrapped around his wrist, staring out into the pounding rain.

Milo went to the far corner of the guardhouse and threw one of his stones across the road and heard the plonk of it striking metal.

"Over there," said the man at the door. Milo could hear him. "From the other direction."

The guard still inside with Sig said something, but Milo couldn't hear what. He was listening to just one side of the conversation.

"I did too hear something," said the first man again. "Right over there."

Milo threw another stone and it rattled against something. Hard to hear in the rain, but it was enough.

"Okay, that was definitely something. I'm going to go look."

Again, a pause.

"What do you mean you're not coming with me? I'm not going *alone*." Pause. "Shut up." Pause. "You're a coward, Leef. That's what you are. And I should split your skull for you right now. The doctor can hold on to that little rat himself. You're coming with me."

There was no more whistling in the distance, only shouts and screams and the banging of metal on metal. A blue-white flash of lightning briefly lit up the dark, making the tubes and tunnels of the Transit Post look like some nightmare octopus squatting atop the aerodrome Spire of the Flying City, its thousand tentacles sketched in black against a chalk sky. The thunder that followed seemed to shake Milo from the inside.

*Hurry*, Milo thought. *Hurry.*

The man at the guardhouse door swore loudly. Eventually, the other guard appeared, pulling up his collar and saying, "Just hold the boy yourself, Doc. If it's nothing, I'll be right back."

Milo held the broken bottle now. He waited for the two men to stop yelling at each other, then heaved it as far down the road as he could, hearing it smash and tinkle against the wet stones.

"You gonna tell me that was nothing?" said one of them.

"Might've been nothing," said the other.

"Coward," said the first.

"Am not," said the other. And then, "It's really raining out there, isn't it?"

But they went, the two of them. One stomping angrily, shouting into the darkness at whatever imaginary enemies he thought were out there waiting for him, the other slinking behind.

And that was that. Milo held the bolt he'd picked up from the grass in his right hand. In the left, his knife. He was terrified, but ready. He knew what he had to do. So he turned the corner, took a deep breath, and banged his way in through the front door, gasping and swatting the water out of his eyes.

"Help me!" he said breathlessly. "They're coming. They're everywhere. It's so hard to see . . ."

# COBBY THE BUTCHER

**THE DOCTOR SPUN AROUND FAST,** pivoting like a very round ballerina and pawing at the club on his belt. His hands were slick and bloody to the wrists, and he looked green under the eyes and around the jaw, like maybe he'd already spent the few seconds he'd had alone in the one-room guardhouse gasping for air himself and trying hard not to throw up because there was finally no one around to watch him hyperventilate.

"Who . . . ?" said the doctor. "And the . . . what?"

Dr. Bay Cobbett—Cobby to his friends among the agents of the Transit Post—wasn't really much of a doctor. At seventeen, he'd gone to sea as a surgeon's assistant aboard the *Duchess of Lees*, sailing out of Trafficant in the Green Isles. He told people about it all the time: stories of his adventures aboard the *Duchess* that had grown wilder and bolder with every telling, particularly when he drank (which was often). He'd become the unofficial doctor to the night-shift guards in the mail yard because of those stories—a role to which he was remarkably ill-suited because of the one story about his time at sea that he *never* told. The one about how, after serving exactly two days as a surgeon's assistant, young Bay Cobbett had been asked to assist with an operation to remove a six-inch pine splinter from the eye of a midshipman and had simultaneously thrown up and fainted as soon as the man had been laid writhing and screaming on the surgeon's table.

When he woke up, he found that he'd been transferred to the galley, where he proceeded to serve nearly two decades as a butcher, with as much distinction as any butcher could. And although being a surgeon was not entirely unlike being a butcher—he was good with a knife, could work a needle and thread, and understood a fair bit about anatomy, though admittedly mostly pig anatomy—his greatest fear remained being forced to behave like an *actual* doctor while other people were watching.

Milo knew none of this, of course. But he guessed a fair bit from the sick look on the man's face when he'd walked in, and the fact that the instruments that Cobby had laid out on the table beside Sig included a cheese knife and a socket wrench. The boy knew he'd need to talk fast. To not give this frightened man time to wonder why there was now a second person in this guardhouse claiming to be something that they clearly were not.

"They're *everywhere* outside, sir," Milo said. "I don't know. They sent me down from the upper gate. You're Cobby, right? The doctor? They said you had one of them here with you? That him?"

Milo pointed with his knife to Sig, who just sat there, gape-mouthed, staring at him, one arm still lashed down to the table.

"Well . . . yes," said Cobby, clearing his throat and trying to wipe the sweat off his face with his bloody hands. "I'm Bay Cobbett. And, uh, this is . . . Well, I don't really know his name, actually. But he's certainly the boy that Joff and the Number Nine unit brought—"

"Okay," Milo said, interrupting and striding across the small room toward Sig, trying to act taller than he was, and older than he was, and certainly more sure of himself than he was. "Good. Well, we'll have to bring him up to the gate, then. Through the upper gate. They want him up there where it's more secure, sir, but we can't let any of them see, you understand? Here." He pushed right past the doctor and lashed out fast with the knife, getting the hooked blade under the leather strap that held down Sig's arm, parting it like smoke. Milo looked back at the doctor. "Can he walk? What was wrong with him anyway? Here, take this." He flipped the knife around in his hand and offered it to Cobby handle-first because he knew that there was no faster way to get someone to trust you than to hand them a weapon that could be used against you. For his part, Cobby just seemed stunned by all the questions and simply stood there, unmoving, which was just fine by Milo.

"Here!" Milo insisted, and shook the knife at him.

The doctor took it.

"Thanks," Milo said. "Now, what did you say was wrong with him?"

"He, uh . . . Broken fingers," said Cobby, looking at the knife in his hand, poking the hooked beak of it into one fingertip. "Really kind of disgusting, actually. One flayed open, palm to tip. Multiple compound, uh . . ."

"Uh-huh," said Milo, nodding, and lifting Sig as best he could, digging his shoulder into the bigger boy's armpit. "Go ahead, sir. I'm listening." Milo grunted, straining his legs to get upright, and Cobby kept on talking about broken bones and stitches, fractured this and dislocated that. He stopped to swallow hard, and Milo thought, *This is it. This is where it all fails*, but no. Bay Cobbett was just trying very hard not to be sick.

"But he'll live, then?" Milo asked. He was struggling—just too small to get Sig up out of the chair on his own. He felt his legs shaking. The back of his neck was greasy with rain and sweat.

"Of course," Cobby said. "Yeah. Of course he'll live."

The problem was, Sig was older than Milo, heavier, and taller, too. He pushed again with his legs, held Sig around his ribs and tried to lift. Milo wondered how long it was going to be before the guards came back. How long before he just fell down.

"Hey," said the doctor. "Are you . . . ?"

But then Sig got his feet beneath him and tried them out, wobbling unsteadily, but upright. It wasn't much help, but it was just enough.

"There we go," said Milo, smiling, trying not to seem like he was panting from the strain and gritting his teeth against the weight. "He's bigger than they said he was. But he's all put back together now, right, sir? Enough to travel?"

"He's splinted, if that's what you mean. Stitched up as best I could. You know, when I was aboard the *Duchess of Lees*—"

"Lots of blood for a broken finger," Milo interrupted again. "Sure he can be moved? Because they're going to want him, I don't know . . . They're going to want him talking, I guess."

"Of course," said the doctor. "He's in pain, but that's mostly stopped now. You'd be surprised how much blood one can lose before—"

And that was all Milo needed to hear. "Good, then," he said. "Can I get my knife back, sir?"

"Oh, right."

"My thanks, sir. And the door?"

"Yes, of course. Wait, let me just . . ."

The doctor squeezed around Milo and Sig. He went and held open the door for them as they scraped and waddled across the wooden floor. The bandages on Sig's hand were already showing blood soaking through the white cloth. Milo shifted his shoulder, wrapped one arm around Sig's waist, lifted as much as he could and got him moving. One step, then one more. He bunched his hand in the waistband of Sig's pants and tried to lift him. To get just one leg going, then the other. Six steps to cross the room. Four to get through the door. A few more to get clear of the house. Then, what? A thousand to get him to the Haunts? More? He would worry about that later. There was still a good chance he'd be caught before then anyway.

Right now, there was just one step at a time to worry about. Left foot, then right foot. He stopped at the door to gather himself.

"Here," said Cobby. "I should help you with him."

Milo had nothing else to stall with but a rusted bolt. But sometimes that was enough.

"No, sir," he said to the doctor. "But here. Take this." And he handed the bolt to the doctor.

"What's this?"

"Sir? It's a bolt, sir. A threaded bolt."

"And why do I need a threaded bolt?"

"For the door," said Milo.

"The door?"

"Use it to jam the door once we're gone, sir. In case any of them try to, you know, come through this way. Just shove it in underneath there and hope it's enough to hold them off."

"Hold *who* off?"

Milo leaned forward and looked Bay Cobbett straight in the eyes. "*All* of them," he said, then threw his hip into Sig and started away from the door. "Good luck to you."

One step.

Then another.

"Wait," said the doctor, but Milo did not stop. "Don't you want me to come with you? To help you carry—"

"No, sir," said Milo, waving his free hand over his shoulder, not turning around. "Stay dry, sir. There'll be more wounded coming, I think. They'll need doctoring."

The rain poured down, the wet and cold seeming to rouse Sig a little. He moaned and shook himself, almost took a step on his own.

"More?" asked Cobby, wrapping his arms around himself and watching the two boys disappear into the night and the rain. His voice was weak and shaking. "Oh no."

# DAGDA AND JULES

**IN THE DARK,** Dagda and Jules found the back of the warehouse, the loose boards, their escape.

"I can't believe that worked," Jules said as he got down on his knees and pulled the boards loose, his face alight with the joy of smashing and nonsense. "I mean, I just can't believe that worked, you know?"

"Wait," said Dagda.

"What?" said Jules. He crouched in a curtain of rainwater, all of it crashing off the roof of the warehouse and onto his back and shoulders as he froze with his fingers on the boards. He had to shout just to be heard.

Dagda looked back over her shoulder toward the forest of pneumos, the lights of lanterns still bobbing like fireflies in the smear of pouring rain. She thought, *Milo still has to cross that.* And he had to do it with Sig. Maybe carrying Sig. She had no idea how many guards she and Jules had dragged out into the storm with their shouting and smashing and noise. A dozen? Two? All of them wet and angry and looking for something to hit with their sticks. Men—stupid, furious, frightened men who loved violence as a solution because it meant they didn't have to think of any others. She snapped around and looked down at Jules.

"Stay here," she said. "Don't go anywhere. Wait for me or for Milo, okay?"

"No, Dagda," he said. "No."

"Just wait, Jules."

"Where are you going?"

She reached out. Put a hand on him. Leaned close enough to be heard. "Just say you'll wait. For me or for Milo, okay?"

"Mouse, you can't!"

"Just say it!" she yelled at him, her small hand squeezing into a fist, bunching his soaked shirt. And Dagda never yelled. Not ever that Jules could recall. "Just be here!" she said, letting go of his shirt and pushing him a little. "Be waiting."

Jules stood up out of the waterfall of rain. He scrubbed his hands on his face and blew through pursed lips. "Milo said go, make a distraction, then go to the Haunts. Remember?"

Dagda stood her ground. She was soaked to the skin, her hair plastered to her face. "And we will. Just . . . Just wait, okay? I'm not done distracting yet."

"Then I'll come with you."

"No. You have to wait. In case Milo gets back before I do. Just hold this ground, okay? No matter what."

"Why?"

She looked back toward the pneumos, then at Jules again. "Because no one else can."

And Jules couldn't argue with that. He folded his arms and nodded his head and said okay. He'd wait. Dagda smiled at him. Then she reached back, pulled up the hood of her shawl, turned, and slipped off into the night.

# JUST FALL

**"I CAN'T BELIEVE THAT WORKED,"** Sig said.

And Milo almost laughed. They'd fallen a half-dozen times. They were covered in mud and soaked to the skin. He'd thought they wouldn't make it ten steps. Then was sure they wouldn't make it ten more. He didn't know exactly where they were because of the dark and the rain—because they had to keep working their way around knots of shouting guards and the gleam of their lanterns. He was exhausted. But they kept getting up. They kept working their way through the dark.

Milo said, "Me neither. And it hasn't worked yet. Not till we're home."

Which was when they both saw the flash of a light passing across them. When they heard the voices—men's voices, shouting, saying, "Hey, you!" and "Stop right there!"

Milo stopped. The rain roared around him. Sig hung against him like a weight.

"Can you run?" Milo said into Sig's ear.

"No," said Sig.

"Can you collapse where I drop you?"

"Don't let them take me back, Milo. Please. I don't want them to hurt me anymore."

"It's okay. I have a plan. Just fall when I let you go."

"Please, Milo. *Please*."

"Just fall."

# BLOOD AND MUD
# AND BONE AND RAIN

**MILO LOOKED INTO THE LIGHTS** of two lanterns and they dazzled his eyes. They were close, the two men. He'd somehow managed to almost walk right into them without noticing. He was so tired.

But he stopped and he waited for them to come closer. And then he said, very loudly, "I'm so happy you're here. They're everywhere. All over this area. The doctor told me to—"

"Shut up," said one of the men, then jammed the end of his stick straight into Milo's guts.

Milo dropped Sig into a heap on the soaking ground. He folded double with no breath in him and then he fell, too, curled into a ball, tears squeezing from his eyes, hot, burning nausea in his stomach, fighting to breathe.

"Joff!" said the other man. "It's a kid. What are you doing?"

The man with the stick came closer. He towered over Milo. The dark bulk of his body blocked the rain and the clouds and the sky. "Who are you?" he asked.

"The doctor—" Milo tried to wheeze, but his voice was a croak. "The doctor—"

The man raised his club. "Lie to me again and I will start

breaking things. I will knock every tooth out of your mouth, you understand?"

Milo looked up at him. The man was nothing but a furious shadow. His eyes black pits. Rain dripping from his lips and the tips of his ears. In the glow of the lanterns and the forking splash of lightning, the boy saw him slowly lift his club again. He asked, "Who are you?"

Milo gathered himself. He spoke carefully. "Taking . . . him . . . up . . . to . . . gate . . . so . . . ."

The man swung and the pain exploded in Milo like a hundred firecrackers. He cried out.

"Joff!" shouted the other man again. "Stop it!"

The man spun around and pointed at the other guard with his club. "Shut your mouth, Leef. That's an order."

"He's a *boy*! You can't just—"

"I'm getting answers! If he won't stop lying, he gets the stick. That's my deal. He tells me the truth, I won't touch him. Simple."

Milo cried. His face burning in the cold rain. Nothing was broken. He was sure, because it hurt too bad. The stick had hit him in the hip the second time, the meaty part of his backside. A spanking, really, since he'd curled against it at the last instant. But the man, Joff, was going to break him. Would maybe kill him. Milo knew that. He'd do it just because he could. Because Milo was nothing. Only a boy. And once Milo was dead, if the guard wasn't too tired, he would turn on Sig, too.

Again, the shadow loomed over him. Milo curled as tight as he could, waiting. There was nothing else to do now. He dug his fingers into the mud and muck.

"So let's try again," said the man called Joff. "Who are you and what are you doing here?"

*I wish it was yesterday,* Milo thought. *I want another chance.*

"Boy? You want another smack, do you?" The man raised the stick. "Who are you?"

Milo raised an empty hand. "Wait . . ."

And then, out of nowhere, something hit the man like a cannonball, driving him sideways, even the shadow of him gone. Milo blinked.

"What is *that!*" the other guard shouted. He pulled out his own stick, and Milo saw something roll off of Joff, spring to its feet, turn, and throw itself at the second man, Leef.

Milo pushed himself to his hands and knees, panting. A spike of pain shot through his hip. Mud dripped from his hair and his ears as he raised his head and saw Joff's stick lying in front of him, shining darkly in the sideways beam of a dropped lantern. Behind him, Leef and the shadowed figure went tumbling down the slope, grunting and growling like animals. A few feet away, Joff was also lurching up off the ground. He saw the stick, too. Reeling, he reached for it.

But Milo got there first. Crawling, the boy dug his fingers into the mud, picked up the stick and stood.

Joff was trying to do the same, but only made it up on one knee. He had to keep one hand on the ground just to stop from toppling over.

"Boy!" he roared.

And Milo turned, his face a mask, hands slick, wet to his bones. He gripped the lead-weighted bully stick by its leather handle. When he took a step, he limped.

"You want to know who I am?" he shouted.

"Stop right there, boy!"

But Milo did not. He took another dragging step. Then another. He yelled, "My name is Milo Quick!"

And then he swung the stick with everything he had left in him. He closed his eyes. The impact rang his arm like a struck bell. When he opened them again, the man was down on the stones. He saw blood in the glow of the lantern. He turned away.

Below him, he heard the sounds of struggle.

Without thinking, he hurled himself down the hill. Limping and in pain, he aimed himself toward the noise, slipped, fell, got up again. In the dark and rain, he stumbled straight into the other guard, Leef, who was on his knees, swinging his stick around in a panic. He hit Milo across the back without even meaning to, and no harder than a shove, but it was enough to knock Milo back down into the mud again and to send the man scrambling, swinging blindly, his feet tangling with Milo's feet, his free hand reaching out, catching the boy by the leg, pulling him.

Milo kicked. He screamed. He was close enough now to see the terrified look on the man's face, mud and blood in his eyes and streaking his cheeks. He held Milo by the leg and was almost on top of him, fingers clawing at him, holding him. He pulled his arm back, was bringing the stick down.

But then there was the dark form again, rising up, taking the force of the blow. Milo saw sparks. Dark wings seemed to swirl around the man, and the boy heard him howl once, then grunt, then go quiet and fall backward.

Joff's club was still looped around Milo's wrist, and he scraped his fingers around in the mud until he got it back into his hand. He rolled over and clawed his way toward where the man, Leef, had fallen. Milo found him lying like a lump, face to the rain, not moving. And Milo was still enraged, still hurting, still panting, still scared. He screamed at the man and struggled to his feet until he stood over him, and even though this was the one who'd told Joff *not* to hit him—who'd said that Milo was only a boy and there was no reason to hurt him—he raised Joff's stick in both hands. He panted through gritted teeth and gripped the stick so tight his knuckles were white.

The boy meant to swing it. He was almost completely sure that he was going to. But suddenly Dagda was there, standing in front of him. Blocking him. She had to say his name twice before he would even look at her.

"Mouse?" he asked. "What are you doing here?" He still wouldn't lower his arms.

"Milo, we have to go."

"No," the boy said, breathing hard, looking back at the man on the ground. "I have to . . ."

But Dagda ducked her head to put herself between his stare and the mud. She spoke calmly, slowly. "This is finished," she said. "And we really have to go."

Milo looked at Dagda and the anger drained out of him. His arms fell to his sides. The stick tumbled from his numb fingers and hung by its strap from his wrist. He said, "Yeah, okay," and felt sick. Every part of him was starting to hurt. There was something in his throat that he couldn't swallow. But suddenly he straightened up and said, "Wait. Sig."

"Did you get him out?"

"Yeah. He's just up there. I . . . I dropped him. When the man . . ." Milo trailed off. He looked away and hung his head.

Dagda's voice was soft. She asked, "Can you carry him? To the warehouse. Jules is waiting."

Out of the corner of his eye, Milo saw the blue-white arc of a spark. He looked down and saw Dagda's arm, shattered just above the wrist, her hand hanging limp. He saw pumping silver and chromium rods pushed through the skin, still moving, twitching, grinding in broken sockets. Slick-looking fluid spurted from ruptured tubes. Bones like a bird's bones filigreed with black. Char marks, ragged skin, bloodless. Another popping blue spark and the fizzing sound of a shorting connection.

Dagda flipped the wing of her shawl over her arm, hiding it. She reached out with her other hand and lifted Milo's chin until he was looking back up at her, into her glass-green eyes.

"Not now," she said. "Okay?"

Milo stared at her and said nothing. All words had deserted him.

"Get Sig. Take him to Jules. Then come back and find me. I need help. Do you understand?"

Nothing.

"Milo, do you understand? Get Sig. Do it now, before any more guards come."

"And then find you," the boy finally said.

"I'll be right here. Or around here. I'll need your help."

"Okay."

"Please don't tell Jules."

"Okay."

"Or anyone, Milo. Please."

"Okay."

"You'll come back?"

"Okay. Are you . . . ?"

Dagda shook her head. "Not now, okay?"

"Are you *hurt*?" Milo said. "Does it hurt?"

Dagda looked away, sniffing, then looked back, her eyes bright, her cheeks wet with rain. "Not as bad as some things," she said. "Now hurry, please."

And so he did. Because even limping, even scared and hurt and confused and frightened, the boy was still Quick.

# NOT DONE YET

**MILO AND SIG HOBBLED BACK** to the warehouse together. Sig didn't speak. He'd been curled up and shivering at the
top of the rise. Barely conscious. Milo'd had to shake him awake.

Jules was waiting. He asked where Dagda was, and Milo said,
"She's fine. But we're not done yet."

He told Jules to take Sig. To get him to the Haunts, then to
get everyone back home again. "Home," he said. "Behind locked
doors. Safe. You hear me, Jules? Dagda and I will be right behind
you. You're in charge."

He left again without waiting for Jules's answer, limping back
in the thunder and the lightning and the pounding rain. He still
had Joff's stick, and he held tight to it the whole way back. A part
of him hoped he would run across more guards. That there would
be something else for him to hit.

It wasn't the best or smartest part of him, but it was a part.

# MILO AND DAGDA

**MILO FOUND DAGDA** huddled in her shawl, the hood up, dripping. She looked like a stone squatting among stones in the drizzling rain. Nearly invisible in the dark save for the flicker of her eyes, the flash of her white teeth when she smiled.

"You came back."

Which, Milo thought, was a silly thing to say. There was very little in all the world that could've kept him from coming back just then. Lights still bobbed in the dark, but they were fewer now. Farther away. He glanced down at her arm and saw it lying slack in her lap. She'd done something to it. It wasn't sparking anymore. There weren't fluids pumping from it. It just looked . . . dead.

"Stand up," he said.

And she did, so Milo took his knife and slit sideways along the bottom of her shawl—muddy and tattered and soaking wet. He tore a strip free and wrung it out as best he could, twisting and squeezing, then approached her with the two ends, saying, "Uh . . . this is a . . . um."

"What?"

"Sling," he said. "For your . . ." The word *arm* was hard for him to say all of a sudden. He didn't know why.

She helped him. Milo tried very hard not to stare. Not to even *look*. He tried not to think about what he'd seen and not imagine what it might've been, and he tried not to touch her, not any-where, but that was impossible. He yanked his hand back like he'd been burned when he accidentally touched her bare skin.

But together they managed to get the sling tied. The boy had a million questions right at that moment, and every one of them felt equally important, but he asked none of them. Dagda lifted her own arm into the pocket of the cloth. Milo tied it behind her neck, made it tighter when she said so, and helped her arrange the soaking ends of her shawl around it so that it didn't really show. At her request, he cut another strip and secured it around her body, pinning her arm across her belly and chest, and all the while he was tightening it, he was repeating, "Sorry, sorry, sorry," because he didn't know if he was hurting her.

"Can you walk?" he asked her while he was finishing the last knot, standing behind her, his fingers cold and clumsy.

"Of course I can walk."

He found it easier to talk when he was behind her. Not looking at her. "Can you run?"

"I probably can now. A little."

"Does it hurt?" Milo asked. "You don't seem like you're hurt."

"It does, but it's . . . It's different."

And Milo kind of coughed out half a laugh and said, "Yeah," because *different* was an understatement. Because *different* didn't even begin to describe even the tiniest little bit of—

"We have to go see Sanel," she said, interrupting his spiraling thoughts.

"The toymaker?"

"Yes."

"He's not going to be open now, Mouse. You know—"

"Not in the market, Milo." She turned, blinked at him, her face the same face Milo had known for all of the only part of his life that had ever mattered to him. Dagda the Mouse, who had been his friend for as long as he'd had friends. Quiet, gentle, careful Dagda, who used to sit, leaning against his leg on the deck of Fort Kick-Ass and watch the sun go down into the sea, who could run the entire length of the wall at the edge of Front Street, leaping the gaps and laughing all the way, who had just fought two grown, armed men and won. Or was, at least, the one still standing.

"Can we just . . ." she continued, her voice still soft. She was soaking wet, and so was Milo. Rain ran in rivulets down her scarred cheeks—the scars that Milo barely even noticed anymore. That he didn't even think of when he thought of her. "This isn't something I ever wanted to . . ." She bit her lip, focused. "Can we just . . . or, actually, let's just say that I am the same person that I have always been, okay? This is not what you think it is, Milo, and it'll all be easier if we just act like . . ."

"Like nothing has changed?"

"Yes."

And Milo laughed again, for real this time. He said, "Yeah, that's probably not going to happen, Mouse," and then came around in front of her, the sling and strap tied as well as they were going to be. He looked at her, picked up the wet shoulders of her now-shortened shawl and tried to make it lie more naturally. "But Sanel the Toymaker. Okay."

"I know where he lives. I've known Sanel a long time."

"Okay."

"Okay?"

Milo wrapped his arms around himself and nodded. He tried hard to smile at her, but the best he could manage was a small, shy grin, which, all things considered, was still quite a lot. "Okay. You know where he lives. Take us."

# SANEL THE TOYMAKER

**TOGETHER,** Dagda and Milo had escaped the slopes of the pneumatic forest. Dagda wouldn't tell Milo their destination, but just said to keep up, and then led him down into the Quarters through smoky alleys that Milo had never seen before, down tunnels bored smooth and into arched gardens where trees grew fruit like damp jewels. Wherever they went, there always seemed to be a loose fence slat or an unlocked gate. When they saw people, they avoided them, but the Flying City was eerily quiet. Often, the slapping of their feet was the only sound that wasn't rain or the rumbling thunder.

Dagda didn't speak. The only words she would say were *Here* or *This way* or *Wait* or *Now*. Following her, it occurred to the boy that her world was larger, stranger, and somehow very different from his. That they might live in the same place, but she saw it in ways he never could.

When they stopped, it was in front of a tall, narrow house on the high edge of the Machinists Quarter—all straight lines and smoke-smudged whiteness, with cracked and flaking plaster covering bricks and domed roofs that looked silver in the darkness. There was a small dooryard, fenced with simple black posts taller than he was, thin as fingers, and a gate that Dagda unlatched from the inside by reaching between the posts and doing something funny with her good hand. He heard a high whistle, then nothing. The gate clicked open. They walked up to the door.

"He knows we're here," Dagda said. "Go ahead."

He looked around and asked, "Go ahead and what?"

"Knock," said Dagda, giggling. "Have you never seen a door before?"

So Milo knocked. And Sanel the Toymaker came shuffling to the door in his sandals, loose white pants, no shirt. He was an old man, but his skin was like leather. His hair a mess. They'd obviously woken him.

"Oh, Toy . . ." he said when he opened his door and saw Dagda standing there, soaked and dirty and broken. "Oh, oh, Toy. What have you done to yourself now?"

And it was like Milo wasn't even there at all.

# IN THE TOYMAKER'S
# LIBRARY

**SANEL TOOK DAGDA AWAY,** holding her delicately by
one hand. Neither said a word to Milo.

So the boy just stood there, dripping, smearing wet hair out of
his face and squelching in his shoes. He didn't know what else to
do. There were carpets inside—wall to wall and corner to corner—
that were nicer than any carpets he had ever seen before. The walls
were so straight and so white that they made Milo's eyes ache. Past
the entryway where he stood were beautifully worked glass doors.
The doors were left open, but he still felt strange being here. Like
he was seeing some piece of the world he wasn't supposed to see.
And in his own skin, he felt altogether too ugly, too small, too dirty
and wet to even stand there looking at it.

So he waited. He held his hands knotted in front of his body,
then behind, and then shoved them into his pockets. He stifled
a sneeze. He rocked back and forth on his heels. His hip hurt.
His head ached. He was cold and wet and sore all over. He could
hear sounds from deep within the strange house, but couldn't tell
precisely where they were coming from. And although he considered turning around and simply leaving—running back home, to
Fort Kick-Ass and the comforts of familiar things—Milo wasn't
completely sure that he'd ever be able to find his way back here.

And was *absolutely* sure that the door wouldn't open to him a second time.

So once he'd dripped a sizable puddle in the entryway, he slowly, carefully (and fearfully and curiously) stepped through the glass doors and into the hallway beyond.

Nothing terrible happened. It was, after all, just a hallway. There were three doors along it and a white staircase with a banister of dark wood at the end of it. Milo had seen which door Sanel and Dagda had gone through, but he was who he was. He tried the other ones first.

On his right, a heavy set of double doors opened into a dining room with a large table surrounded by a dozen chairs, all of them tented with canvas furred in dust. The walls were bare but showed the ghostly squares and rectangles where, once, pictures had hung. The boy looked in, then stepped back, closing the doors as quietly as he could.

Behind the second door was a library. Milo almost fainted when he saw it—from the smell of the books (rich and dusty and spicy in the heat of the closed room, like cinnamon in his nose) and from the sheer number of them, all gathered together. There were hundreds, maybe thousands, stacked on the floor, left open on every flat surface, organized on deep shelves that lined the walls and rose all the way to the ceiling. More books than he'd ever seen in one place in his life. More books than the boy imagined existed anywhere.

Over a cold fireplace hung a pane of black glass half draped with another sheet of canvas, a low table covered in old plates of half-eaten food, leather chairs that looked more comfortable than they likely were, standing ashtrays with metal feet cast in the shape of leaping fish, and a sideboard covered in glass bottles and decanters holding the remains of liquor in a dozen colors, but the boy barely noticed any of this. Everything in the room could've been made of candy and he still would have seen only the walls of books, climbing skyward.

Milo stepped inside the library the way some men enter church—with a reverence born of equal parts wonder and terror. The smell of so many pages (a hundred thousand? a million?) was narcotic. He sucked it into himself greedily, then turned and put out a hand—meaning just to touch the books—but then he remembered that his hands were wet, so he tried to scrub his fingers dry first on his soaking shirt, then on his filthy pants, and finally, the carpet.

Only then did he dare touch the books, gingerly running his fingers along the spines. For a moment, he didn't even look at the titles. He just touched them blindly, overcome by such riches. But when he *did* look (almost accidentally, almost guiltily), he saw *Kinematic Optimization—Recent Advances in Theory and Applications.*

*Serial and Parallel Manipulators in Overview.*

*Control Architectures of Biological Interfacing Systems and Cellular Automata in Post-Enlargement Society.*

*Trends and Developments in TeleHaptic Anti-Localization.*

He was fascinated. He was overcome. He was terrified, more than a little. He walked around the perimeter of the room, letting his fingertips bump against the books with their rough covers and strange, intoxicating names that he did not understand: *Nano-electric Materials Development* and *Multivariate Analysis in Theory and Practice* and *Open Issues in Planetary Signal Theory.*

Milo had no way to describe what he was feeling. Ask him today and he still wouldn't be able to put into words the sickening swoop of the world upending with every breath, the slow-fast realization that some things (maybe no things) were what he had believed they were yesterday or last week, last month, last year, and the awful, wonderful understanding that he would never, ever be able to un-know any of it. The boy had dreamed a world around himself for twelve years. Now there was another one that he was only just noticing, because he'd only just opened his eyes.

So imagine his surprise when a toy soldier stepped up to him in the Toymaker's library, cleared its throat politely, looked up and asked him what in the thousand hells he thought he was doing there.

Milo screamed.

You would have, too.

It was maybe three feet tall, the toy soldier. Dressed in a miniature uniform of blue jacket and trousers, high black boots, white belts, and a tall black hat with a silver medallion on the front. It wore a saber on one hip and carried a rifle out in front of itself as though on parade, a gleaming bayonet the size of the tine of a fork sticking up straight as an exclamation point. Its face was stiff and waxy. The eyes dull as glass. Its mouth didn't move when it spoke.

"You're a . . ." Milo said.

"Lord's foot, I am, I am," said the little soldier. "One hundred and sixty-first division, fourth automatic infantry. But that's not the issue here."

"You're . . ."

"Asking you one more time what you're doing in the general's library, I am, I am. Which is where you don't belong. Truth. Answer or you'll feel the sticking end of my toothpick, you will, you will."

"I was . . ." said Milo. "I . . . Well, they left me. Standing in the doorway. And I was dripping, so I didn't know where else I ought to go."

"Who's that now?"

"Sanel. And Dagda. My friend Dagda. She came to see Sanel.

I brought her." Milo inched closer to the little soldier, peering at its stiff face. "How are you—"

"Hospitality!" the little soldier suddenly announced, then leaned forward slightly at the waist. "You're a mess. Have you fought in a battle?"

Milo stared. "I have, yes. In a way."

"Recently?"

"Tonight."

"Smell like it, you do, you do."

"I'm sorry, I—"

"Hospitality!" barked the toy soldier again, and then spun sharply on one heel. "Hospitality, that's the order. Follow me. Quick time. No dawdling."

And Milo wanted more than anything to take a book with him. Or two. Or ten. *Any* of the books, but as he was reaching, the toy soldier stopped in its tracks. Its head rotated all the way around until it was facing straight backward.

"Touch another thing and I'll leave you bloody, son. I will, I will."

Milo lowered his hand.

"Hospitality!" shouted the soldier again, then turned its head back around the right way and marched straight out of the library with Milo following close behind.

# HOSPITALITY

HOSPITALITY was a room on the second floor of Sanel's house. The boy's muddy footsteps tracked a path on the carpets leading all the way to it.

Hospitality was a bed that looked like it was made of clouds— all fluffy white and quilted comforters and pillows frosted with lace. It was a blue-tiled bathroom, brightly lit, with a spotless white sink and a looking glass above it, and a spray shower with hot running water. It was a towel softer than anything Milo had ever owned, and a bar of soap that smelled like cream and honey, and the toy soldier, standing at rigid attention, warning him that if he left the room, he would be immediately found and brought up on charges.

"Desertion!" barked the soldier. "Dereliction!"

Hospitality was the soldier asking Milo if he required anything further at all and Milo, confused, saying "No, thank you," because he couldn't think of a single other thing to say. Because at what other time in his life had anyone ever asked him that question?

Once the soldier had gone, Milo stood in the tiled bathroom and tried to carefully peel off his clothes without scattering clods of mud and rattling little pebbles everywhere. He left the clothes in a pile, stepped carefully into the shower, pulled the cord and held it down until the water ran off of him clear. It took a very long time.

When he was done, he washed his clothes that way, too—holding them under the spray with one hand and pulling the cord with the other and then wringing them out into the tub and doing it again. The water swirled away black, and then brown, and then gray.

After that, he hung his clothes over a bar where they would drip into the basin, then laid one of the soft white towels on the edge of the bed and sat on it. All of his clothes were wet. His hair was still wet. He looked around the room and listened to the house. He thought that maybe he would just rest for a few minutes. Just close his eyes and try to think about where he was, what he should be doing next, and what Jules might be doing now.

And then, quite without meaning to, Milo lay over and fell asleep, as quickly and completely as if someone had switched him off like a light.

# WHAT JULES WAS DOING

**AT HOME,** inside Fort Kick-Ass, Jules clucked like a mother hen and piled blankets on top of Sig, whom he'd already helped to strip and wash and dry himself, because someone had to and Sig couldn't do it without help.

Arun had done what he could, but that wasn't much. Keelan sat in the corner, sniffling. Tristan had laughed and poked at Sig with a stick he'd found somewhere, as if this was all a game and all he had to do was make Sig laugh, too—make him smile, even— and that this would be enough to evaporate the blood and unwind the bandages and make everything right again. Like it was all just pretend.

Llyr had gone straight to bed.

So Jules piled on the blankets, because Sig was shivering and he didn't know what else to do. He'd nearly had to carry him back from the Haunts. The streets had been almost empty and the rain had been pouring. Arun and Tristan had tried to help, but they'd also asked him a hundred questions each, and Jules had no answers.

The bandages on Sig's hand were filthy already, but Jules was afraid to touch them. The blankets were none too clean either, but they were warm, at least. And Sig would not stop shaking, so Jules sat beside him on the floor and laid what he hoped was a comforting hand on the side of his head and did nothing else, be- cause he was so afraid of doing something wrong. He figured that at least doing nothing couldn't make things worse.

Keelan came to sit beside Jules and asked, "How bad is he?"

"I don't know," Jules said quietly, not sure if Sig was sleeping or what. "I mean, he hurt his *hand*. How bad could he be?"

"He looks bad."

Jules sighed. "Someone doctored him some. Can't be that bad."

"I'm just saying . . ."

"Yeah, I know. He looks bad."

For a few minutes, everything was quiet. Then Keelan asked Jules where Milo was. Where Dagda was. But Jules wasn't in the mood for telling stories.

"They'll be back," Jules said. And he really hoped it was true. He sent Arun to check the door—to make sure it was locked, barred, and secure. When Keelan asked why, Jules said, "Because Milo said to."

"What happened up there, Jules?"

"I don't know," he said. "But it's all going to be okay." And he hoped that was true, too.

Eventually, Jules fell asleep beside Sig. He did it staring at the spider ring Milo had given him, playing with the legs and watching the glass eyes glint in the dark. Arun fell asleep on the other side of the room, watching Jules. Keelan fell asleep worrying about every- thing and everyone and had chewed the nails on one of his hands all the way down to the skin until they bled. Llyr had nightmares about ghosts and terrible things following them back home from the Haunts.

Tristan walked from room to room to room to room as quiet as a cat and did not sleep. He couldn't. He was scared but wasn't about to tell anyone about it because he thought he was too big for that.

So instead, he considered himself to be on guard duty. He checked the door and he checked the porthole window. He stood in front of the door with a stick in his hand, then sat with it across his knees. Then he lay down, because it was more comfortable if he was going to be waiting a long time.

Then he fell asleep, too, right there on the floor. Quiet and the soupy, spicy smell of sleep and unwashed children overtook the rooms.

And so ended the first day of summer in Highgate, the Flying City.

# THE SECOND DAY
# OF SUMMER

✦

## HIGHGATE, THE FLYING CITY

# LLYR

**LLYR WOKE** from a dream of ghosts, pushing tears from her eyes with her small, hot fists. She walked from room to room to room, looking at all the sleeping boys and saying goodbye to them one after the other, because she'd dreamed them all dead, and in the dream, they'd all been sad because none of them had known it was coming and none of them had been able to say goodbye.

When she was done, she went back out into the main room where Tristan lay sleeping, curled on the floor like a question mark. She lay down next to him, facing him, and scrunched her tiny body as close as she could, then took his hand in both of hers. He woke slightly, one eye peeling open to blink and focus, finally, on her.

"What are you doing?" he whispered.

"I'm going to miss you when we're dead," she said.

And without thinking, without understanding fully what Llyr was saying, he said, "I'm going to miss you, too."

And then he closed his eyes and, together, the two of them fell back into a perfect, black, and weightless sleep.

# MORIC SHAW

**AN OLD MAN** with shaking, spotted hands and a smell like spoiled milk had set the grinding, snapped bone in Moric Shaw's right arm, held two sticks of kindling wood in place, and then wrapped everything in plastered cloth. He'd told the boy to lie down on the creaking cot in the corner of the dark, musty room where he worked and then told him to open his mouth.

Shaw had just stared up at him, his mouth clamped shut vise-tight, and the old man screwed his wrinkled face into a pout.

"Don't care whether you do it or not, fool," he said. "But you's in pain and I can make it go away. I'm paid either way."

So Shaw had opened his mouth and the man had shoved in a spoon of something that tasted like poison. He made to hurl himself up, to spit and thrash and murder the old man where he stood, but thinking about it was as far as Shaw got. He suddenly felt like he had a hundred stones tied to him. That he'd grown, somehow, impossibly heavy. His eyes went wide, then fluttered shut, and then he'd slept for ten hours.

It was dark when he woke. The old man was still there. He handed Shaw a clay bowl filled with lukewarm water and held him upright while he drank. The water tasted like dust and iron, but Shaw licked his lips when he was done.

"My boys," he asked. "Where'd they go?"

"Been most of a day," said the man. "Gone to play or get killed or whatever boys do. Didn't none wait on you, that's sure."

Shaw thought for a minute. "Can I leave?"

"Sure. Or stay. Don't matter to me."

His arm ached. More with each beat of his heart, as though something inside it was wrapping tighter and tighter. There was sweat on his face. He spoke through his teeth. "More medicine," he said.

"Thought as much," said the old man. "Open."

This time Shaw didn't argue. By the time he woke again, it was already the second day of summer, and he knew exactly what he had to do.

# SANDMAN

**HIGHGATE AT DAWN WAS BEAUTIFUL.** The air was cool and crisp. Last night's rain had washed the stones and made everything shine. In the brilliant pink and soft blue light of the rising sun, the whole world seemed new again.

Ennis Arghdal hated the dawn.

He hated it because if he saw the dawn from either end—either still awake when it came or woken into it from a sound and pleasant sleep—it meant that something had turned sideways on him. Seeing dawn always meant something had gone wrong.

All night long, he couldn't sleep. There was too much happening in every corner of the Flying City, and he felt all of it like carbonation in a bottle. He kept a room close by the Blue Lights, and he'd gone there after seeing Jules, but couldn't relax. So he'd filled his pockets with money and cigarettes and brass knuckles and went out onto the streets looking for trouble.

He'd been close to the mail yards and heard the commotion. He'd known that it was Milo, and before the morning sun had even begun to pink the horizon, he'd gone to the lower control gate, pushed through the crowds already gathering there and shoved aside the first Transit Post agent who'd tried to stand in his way. The second had recognized him and backed away with his hands up. No one had bothered him after that.

In the guardhouse, he'd talked to everyone. He took a sausage roll from a box sitting on a table and ate it as he listened. The table was still stained with blood, which concerned him.

The men he spoke to said it'd been commandos, saboteurs sent from the Armada, assassins, wolfmen. Some said it was just dogs they'd been chasing in the rain. Some said children, but several of their fellow guards were dead, so children (or dogs) seemed unlikely.

He'd talked to the drunken doctor, Bay Cobbett, who'd stitched one boy back together (either Arun or Sig, Ennis guessed) and then gotten completely bamboozled by another who Ennis was absolutely sure had been Milo. The only other man who'd seen any of them and lived was Joff Legree, who'd been watch captain last night on the #9 Caisson. He had a broken jaw, a broken arm, and broken ribs, and was missing most of his teeth.

So he wasn't talking to anyone.

Useless, Ennis thought. All of them. So he took another of their sausage rolls and walked out. There was nothing for him here. The boy was already gone.

Which meant that all Ennis Arghdal had to do now was look everywhere else.

# DAGDA AND
# THE TOYMAKER

**IT WASN'T PAIN THAT DAGDA FELT,** necessarily, but wrongness. Fault. Her failing systems itched at her in a way that she couldn't scratch. Like ants crawling under her skin and walking on her bones. She knew the broken arm was bad because she could see that it was bad, but it didn't *hurt*. Like she'd told Milo, it was . . . different.

She'd killed five men. Milo had only seen one of them. Unless he'd seen the others while coming back up the hill into the mail station and not said anything to her about it, but she didn't think he had. Because Milo would've said something. He wouldn't have been able to help himself.

She didn't feel bad about the men. It'd been necessary. Not unavoidable, but necessary. And when the killing was done, she'd led Milo away and through parts of the Flying City he'd never seen before simply because she had never before shown them to him. Milo, Jules—idiot boys, both of them. Years, they'd been on these streets and had never strayed from the straight lines that measured the shortest routes between here and there. They could walk a mile and see nothing but their own feet. They understood nothing about the place they were from and even less about anything else.

Still, sitting in the dark thinking about them made her smile. She was pleased that they were safe.

*Oh, Toy. Oh, oh, Toy* . . . Sanel had answered the door, taken her in, left Milo standing in a puddle in the foyer like he wasn't even there.

"Don't call me that, Sanel," she'd said once they were safely behind doors, closed and locked. "I hate it when you call me that. I'm not . . . I'm not a *thing*."

"Yes you are."

"Shut up."

She'd been damaged worse than this before. Not lately, but it'd happened. Sanel was not the mechanic his father had been (and his father, Roal the Toymaker, had not been the mechanic that *his* father had been), but Sanel had done more intricate work than this, mostly when he was younger. His great-great-great-grandfather had once had to reattach her head (a story for another day), and his great-great-great-great-*great*-grandfather? Well, those had been difficult years. Complicated.

Putting herself in the chair in his workshop, she'd helped Sanel bolt her arm into place, lock down the clamps on the restrictor and attach the leads to the ancient diagnostic monitor. It hadn't booted up at first, so Sanel had cursed at it, switched it off and on again, jiggled the power cord, made tea, cursed some more, stared at it angrily for ten full minutes, removed the case and blown out the dust, then lifted the entire thing a couple of inches off the table and dropped it, which had finally done the trick.

"Motion?" he'd asked her.

"None," she'd said. "But there's the conservancy systems still in place. Critical shutdown to preserve the damaged—"

"Bah, bah, bah . . ." Sanel had waved a hand at her. "Like I don't know. Who wrote your conservancy programs, Toy?"

"Your grandfather, Sanel."

"No, my *great*-grandfather."

"And don't call me Toy."

He'd puttered around his workshop gathering hemostats and curettes, forceps of varying sizes, two different elevators, a nerve hook, a handful of retractors and probes. He had six bone rasps in a leather case, all grained so fine that they'd barely grate hard cheese but were perfect for working on her latticed internal structure. The cauterizing laser suture would take forever to plot and scan the ripped edges of her skin. So to pin it temporarily, Sanel would use chained six-millimeter needle drivers that looked like millipedes crawling on her arm, gathering up the tatters of her, and squeezing them tight with their sharp little legs. The scars they left were fine and pale, the edges ridged where they were finally melted together by the laser. Sanel smoked the entire time, filling the air of the workshop with clouds that hung thick as milk around the banked surgical lamps.

"I call you that out of love, Toy. It's a . . . whatdoyoucallit. An *endearment*."

"They call me Mouse," she'd said, smiling.

"Who?"

"The boys."

Sanel huffed. "Boys," he'd said, and dumped his instruments out on a steel prep table, spreading them around with his fingers. "Well, let's see how bad it is. Did you tell . . ."

"Don't ask me that."

Sanel looked at her for a long moment. "I was going to ask how much fluid you lost before the pumps shut down. You have exposed vessels here. Shorted contact points. Carbon scarring.

The mechanical damage is not as bad as it looks. I was concerned about your fluid levels."

"You were not concerned about my fluid levels."

Sanel pursed his lips and pulled a magnifying visor over his head. He said, "No, I was not," and began setting the clamps and retractors without saying another word.

The work took hours. Sanel the Toymaker had missed Dagda, but he would not say so. And Dagda took a strange kind of pleasure in feeling him put the broken parts of her right again, but she would not say so either.

They sat together, occasionally speaking of trivial things, but mostly in silence. Every now and then Sanel would look up at her and smile as he patted the sweat from his face or drank from a plastic bottle of lukewarm tea through a long, stiff straw. And Dagda would smile back. Only one time did she say, "Thank you, Sanel. I'm sorry to have woken you."

"I don't sleep much anymore, Toy," he'd said. "The world has become altogether too interesting lately, and I don't want to miss anything."

# OSWALDO AND MEATSACK

**WHEN MILO WOKE UP,** the toy soldier was standing next to the bed and watching him with its dead doll eyes.

It said, "You're awake, you are, you are. It's about time. Shirking is what this looks like to me. Poor form. Embarrassing."

"What?"

"Slacking. Idleness. Torpescense. Shameful. Do you have any idea how long you've slept?"

"No," said Milo, rubbing his eyes and biting the tail off a yawn. "How long?"

"Don't know," said the soldier. "I don't have a watch."

Milo rose up in the bed. He was naked under the covers, between sheets clean and crisp with starch. He didn't recall climbing in.

"You're out of uniform. That won't do." The soldier turned stiffly and pointed with the bayonet on its rifle to a low bench on which Milo's clothes had been folded neatly. "Your nakedness is disgusting, it is, it is. Cover it up."

"How are you talking?" Milo asked.

"By thinking of words and saying them out loud."

"No, I mean—"

"Get dressed. Muster in five minutes. I'm to bring you, I am, I am. Orders."

"Can I open you up and see what's—"

The toy soldier bent its knees and lowered its rifle to its hip, the bayonet pointing at Milo. "Not unless I can do you first."

Milo raised his hands. "Okay. I was just asking."

"Orders!" barked the soldier. "Four and a half minutes."

"Dagda," said Milo.

"No," said the soldier. "My name is Oswaldo. And I'm going to call you Meatsack."

"I mean, is Dagda okay?"

"Four minutes."

Milo climbed down from the bed and padded over to the bench where his clothes were waiting. His things. He had a black-and-purple bruise covering one hip. Another already yellowing across his back. Everywhere else, cuts and scrapes and scratches, but Milo felt none of them. Not now, with the comfort and warmth of a shower and a proper bed and hours of smothering sleep still blurring the borders of him. "I'm just asking," he said while he stepped into his pants. "She's my friend. Is she awake?"

"Orders," said the soldier. "Can't be late."

"Is she downstairs?"

"Orders! Follow me."

"Wait," said Milo. "I need . . ." He pulled his shirt over his head, wrapped his scarf around his neck, shoveled treasures into his pockets. "Wait . . ."

But Oswaldo was already stomping out into the hallway. The little soldier turned sharply and then marched clumsily down the stairs, stepping two feet on each step before moving to the next one.

Milo caught up before the toy soldier was halfway down, but was still mashing his feet into his shoes and tucking in his shirt when they reached the ground floor. His hip hurt him again and he was hobbling a bit, favoring his good side as he came galumphing down the steps.

"Library," Oswaldo said without looking back. "The general wants to have a word with you."

"You mean Sanel?"

The soldier said nothing. And when Milo asked yet again about Dagda—was she there, and was she okay, and how long had he been asleep anyway—the soldier still said nothing. Milo hesitated, then stopped walking. The soldier turned around.

"Words," it said. "Words, words, words. All these *questions*. But you have to ask yourself something, you do, you do."

"What's that?" asked Milo.

"What makes you think I have any of the answers? I'm just a toy."

Milo tilted his head and looked at the soldier's tattered uniform, its waxy skin and unblinking eyes. With a whirring of gears, it leaned a little bit forward and stuck out its chin. "Or am I?"

"Oswaldo!" came Sanel's voice from the library. "Is that you? Bring the boy in here."

The toy soldier turned at the waist, then rotated its hips and legs into alignment. Stiffly, it marched down the hallway, then went stomping through the door into the library, rifle held out vertically in front of it, arms locked.

Milo scurried forward. He stood just outside the door. He heard Oswaldo addressing Sanel inside.

"Meatsack is here, boss," it said. "I had to see it naked, I did, I did. It seems in functional condition."

"Milo?" asked Sanel. "Are you out there? Come in."

And Milo stepped out to stand in the doorway, to look into the room filled with books and chairs and books and books. Sanel the Toymaker sat leaning back in one of the leather armchairs. He was wearing a pale blue shirt now, threadbare and soft. There was a china cup on the table beside him. A saucer and a gold spoon. Milo could smell coffee, but all he had eyes for was the half-a-woman ticking around the perimeter of the room on eight mechanical spider legs, picking up stacks of books and papers and quietly trying to find places for them on the shelves.

Sanel rubbed his face. The spider woman was dressed (or half dressed) like a maid, in a black blouse and white bib apron, a white kerchief holding back the matted mess of her curly black hair. Her face, he thought, was more natural than Oswaldo's. Until she turned her head directly toward him and he could see the glinting, dark pits where her eyes should be. When she blinked, Milo could hear a scrape and click. Mechanical. But the eyes were like black oil. Like something shiny and liquid at the same time. She ended at the waist in a kind of socket, where she screwed like a light bulb into a scuffed pink plastic egg with eight beautifully articulated and powerful jointed legs that rose and fell in a horrible, quick rhythm as she mounted the shelves, dragged herself straight up the wall, and stretched to put back two thick books with blue cloth covers.

When she paused to look at him, Milo tried not to scream. When she smiled, it was hungry and cold and the teeth in her mouth were too big and too white, and Milo covered his own mouth with both hands and felt nothing but the urge to run away from here. Like a hole had opened where Sanel's front door was and he was fighting against falling into it.

"Milo," said Sanel.

The boy's eyes snapped to meet the toymaker's, which were red-rimmed and tired, his whole face sagging with exhaustion. "I'm sorry, do you not want to come in?"

Milo did not move. The line between wanting to run and wanting to stay was thin as a razor blade. The tiniest shock could set him off.

Sanel frowned. "She shouldn't ever have brought you here," he said, then pinched the bridge of his nose between two fingers. "Dagda. I don't . . . She thought you might be ready for this. I can see she was wrong. This isn't something you should've ever seen." He raised a hand and fluttered it around. "Any of it."

The boy made a noise in his throat. He was trying to make words, but couldn't. He had to pee, and maybe throw up, too. On the shelves, the spider maid ticked her way sideways, ten feet off the ground, watching him. Her legs gouged scars in the wood shelves wherever they touched. Chips and splinters rained down onto the floor. When he looked at her, she clacked her teeth together like biting off mouthfuls of air.

"He's going to make a mess, boss," said Oswaldo. "He is, he is."

"Milo!" Sanel snapped, his voice like a sudden lash, demanding attention. "Get out of this house. Forget where it is. Don't ever come back. Do you understand?"

Milo nodded frantically. The spider maid snapped her teeth together again. Oswaldo rocked side to side beside Sanel's chair, which Milo immediately understood as laughter. Mimed, silent, mocking laughter.

"Go, then." Sanel waved a hand. "I had things I could've told you, but I don't want to now. Maybe some other day. Maybe not . . ." His voice trailed off. "I'm tired." He laid his head back again, his eyes closed. "Who ever expected to get this old so soon," he said quietly, mostly to himself.

The boy stood his ground, though, holding his hands over his mouth, panting through the gaps in his fingers. He swallowed and, quickly, before he couldn't anymore, barked just one word.

"Dagda!"

Sanel raised his head. He started to say something cruel, but then didn't. He wasn't a cruel man. Just very, very tired.

"She's fine," he sighed. "Just go. I'm sure she'll find you soon enough. When she's finished. She can't help herself, can she? She doesn't have any choice."

And then Milo turned and ran out the door and into the yard. He didn't scream and he didn't cry and he didn't throw up, but he'd come close to doing all three. Potentially all at once.

At the gate, he pushed and pulled, but it wouldn't budge. Pointlessly, he slapped his hands on the bars. All black metal. Didn't even rattle. There was a small post beside the gate with a single, round light that Milo thought was a button until he mashed his hand on it and found that it was not. In something very close to desperation, he looked back at the house and saw Oswaldo's face in one of the windows, heavy curtains rustling behind him. The toy soldier stared with its dead eyes. It reached up slowly with both hands and, with pointed fingers, pushed up the corners of its waxy mouth until they formed a frozen smile. And then it sank down out of sight, below the window's sill.

The gate unlocked with a snap.

# MORIC SHAW
# AND THE MILKMAN

**TWICE NOW** Moric had slept on the dirty cot in this dark room, under the weight of the medicine given him by this milk-smelling old man. The first time it'd been like falling into a deep black hole into which no light leaked. The second time, he'd dreamed.

He dreamed of Milo Quick and the bird. In his dream, Milo Quick was running from him, down twisting alleys in the heart of the Marche, and the bird—the carrier bird, in all its hugeness and ugly, squawking whiteness—was sitting on top of Quick's head, looking back at Shaw and mocking him for never being able to catch up.

In his dream, they stood together in the court of the Total King, and Cuthbert was there, looking sweetly down on Quick and asking him all these questions about the white bird on his head. Cuthbert was fascinated. He heaped praise on the stupid boy. But when Shaw opened his mouth and tried to say something (he didn't know what, his tongue was like mush in his mouth), the Total King had laughed at him. Quick had laughed at him. The bird, in its squarking way, had laughed at him. And when Shaw, in a pounding rage, had turned and raised a hand to Quick—meaning only to hit him just enough to make him stop laughing—the Total

King had reached out and broken off both of his arms at the elbows like snapping sticks off a branch.

Shaw had tried to scream, but no sound came out. The bird on Milo's head had laughed and laughed. The Total King Forever of the Marche and Everything in It had bent down and asked, "What good are you to me now, Shaw? What good is my right-hand man if he has no hands at all?" And Milo Quick had just stood there, towering over Shaw as he rolled, writhing, on the floor.

That was when he'd woken up.

The medicine made Shaw sleep, but the old man—Shaw had decided to call him the Milkman because of the way he smelled up close—said that was because he was giving him a lot of it.

"Don't like you nor no others of the boys that get sent my way," the Milkman said. "Last thing I want is to have to hear you all's whining and moaning in my sitting room, so I gives you all just a touch too much and it makes you sleep like you alls was dead."

"But if I swallowed less . . ." said Shaw.

"Sleeping boys is quiet boys," said the Milkman, and then went off to grab the little bottle and his spoon.

Moric Shaw was not one for thoughtfulness or for planning, so he was out of his element somewhat when he opened his mouth and allowed the Milkman to spoon in a third dose of medicine. He tasted the bitterness of it, the shocking sense of poison acting quickly on his brain and limbs, and he spat as soon as the old man turned away to cork the bottle and set it carefully back on a shelf.

He felt the pain in his arm like a hot wire, pulsing, and he felt the medicine muffling it like the pain itself was a thing being wrapped in layers upon layers of cotton before being placed back inside him. A sleepy, creaky smile drifted across his face as he felt his eyes sliding closed.

He bit down hard on the inside of his cheek and spat again and forced himself to move. Forced his legs off the side of the cot and his feet (stonelike, heavy as boulders) onto the warped wooden floor. If he made a fist with his right hand, he could make the swaddled bundle of pain in his arm flare up, bright red and fiery. He did that, and it focused him. He did it again, and it squeezed a whimper from his throat but burned through the fog in his head.

"Milkman," he slurred, and the old man turned back toward him.

"Oh, what's this now . . . ?" he said.

"Milkman," said Shaw again, and he made a fist and he gritted his teeth. "Milkman, Milkman, Milkman . . ."

"Lie over now, boy," said the old man. "No sense in fighting feeling better."

"Leaving," said Shaw. "Now. I want . . ." His eyes drifted, his head swimming in a clear, thick syrup until he made a fist and everything snapped back into focus again. "I want that bottle. The medicine."

The old man chuckled. He said no.

"The Total King will pay you," Shaw said. "I need it. Got things to do."

"He pays me to fix his broken things," said the old man. "Now lie over and shut up." And then he turned his back.

Shaw made a fist with his right hand. He stood up shakily. The sticks and the plaster made his arm heavy, but he was still young and strong, and when he swung it and hit the old man in the side of the head, the pain was ferocious but also clarifying.

Shaw shouted, "Don't turn your back on me!"

The pain burst in him like a red fire every time he raised his arm and brought it down again on the old man. It came and faded in brilliant explosions. And when he was done, Moric Shaw took the small bottle from the shelf and put it in his pocket. He turned in a circle and took the clay water bowl and drained it and then smashed it. He kicked over the table that it had been sitting on, and the Milkman's instruments clattered to the floor. Shaw bent down (almost falling, having to hold his breath against the vertigo that threatened to drop him, right there, on top of the bleeding old man) and took a knife from the pile. It was long and thin, ground down to almost nothing over years of use, but sharp enough to cut a dream.

He made a fist and stood up again. He staggered clumsily for the door and pushed his way through it and out into the glaring sunlight of the second day of summer in the Flying City.

Moric Shaw had things to do. And among those things was killing Milo Quick.

# MILO

**MILO SHOULD'VE GONE HOME.** We can all agree on that, right? But just because a boy knows that he *should* do something doesn't always mean that he'll do it. As a matter of fact, it usually means he'll do exactly the opposite.

So the boy should've gone home. At the very least, he should've gone *straight* home, wiped his feet, washed his hands, poured himself a nice glass of milk and told everyone everything that'd happened to him since yesterday morning. At the very, very, *very* least, he should've told Jules.

But think for a minute. If Milo *did* go home, Jules (and everyone else) would ask him where he'd been and where Dagda was. And what would he say then? How would he explain to everyone else what'd happened and what he'd seen? Particularly since *he* wasn't even sure what he'd seen.

No, that wasn't true. He knew what he'd seen (a talking toy soldier, a spider maid, a library unlike anything he'd seen before, Dagda's arm sparking in the dark). But how could he explain it? He'd promised Dagda he wouldn't say anything to anyone. And maybe he could just say that she was gone. Maybe he could say that she'd left him at some point and gone off on her own and he simply didn't know where she was.

But if he said that, Jules would do something stupid. It was likely that Jules was going to do something stupid anyway. He would insist on finding Dagda and rescuing her, and what would Milo say then? He wouldn't be able to stop it. But if Milo wasn't there, the stupidity of what Jules might do would be limited simply by the fact that he didn't know much of anything.

The boy's chest hurt. He'd run like a rabbit from Sanel's house the minute the gate had opened, and he'd kept going until he couldn't run anymore. Now he was leaning against a wall just trying to catch his breath.

Nothing in the city was the same anymore. It was like none of the things he'd known for all of his life matched his memories of them, like everything—every house, every pipe and every person— had grown or shrunk to some infinitesimal degree. It was nothing you'd notice unless you were really looking for it. Until, suddenly, you *had* to look, because every arm could have beautiful, delicate chrome pistons and pushrods moving beneath its skin. Any door could have a spider lady behind it.

And once you knew something like that, how could you not spend every instant of every day for the rest of your life wondering what was next, or what other secrets there were in the world, kept hidden only because you'd never bothered to look?

So Milo should've gone home, but he didn't. He stood with his back pressed up against a wall on the Street of Sighs in the Machinists Quarter and tried to breathe even though it felt like there wasn't enough air left in all of the Flying City. He just stood there—one surprisingly clean and well-scrubbed boy being slowly suffocated by his entire world turning upside down.

# CAPTAIN KLIM

**WHEN MILO QUICK SUDDENLY APPEARED** in front of him on the Street of Sighs that morning, Captain Klim's first thought was that he was seeing a ghost. That the boy, somehow, had died in the night and his spirit had come back to mock him for the previous day's failings.

What confused the Captain was that the boy he saw on the morning of the second day of summer seemed *insubstantial*. Cleaner than he had the day before. Washed out and faded, as though losing his varnish of dirt and scabs had scrubbed him of some essential connection to this place.

Quick had come bolting out of a road lined with tall, rounded houses and gone careening into the thin morning traffic, his chest heaving. The Captain saw him, grabbed Reyn's wrist and pointed.

Said, "Look there! Tell me you see him, too."

Said, "I can't believe it."

And Reyn didn't like being grabbed, but he nodded anyway. "That's the boy," he said, then leaned forward, squinting and looking closer, his top lip peeling back from his teeth. "What d'you think he's running from?"

It didn't much matter, because Milo Quick didn't run far. Almost as soon as the Captain and Reyn set off following him, the boy stopped to lean against a rutted plaster wall with his eyes closed, his hands on his knees, gasping for breath.

For a moment, the Captain didn't know what to do. And it should say something about the existence of his heart that he was momentarily flummoxed by the sight of a child in obvious distress. His instinct was not immediately to help, but neither was it to immediately reach out and stuff Milo into a sack. In any event, Captain Rodion Klim saw more than dollar signs as the boy stood, pale and shaking, in the morning light.

"Boy," he said finally, because he couldn't think of anything else to say. He reached a hand out slowly, not entirely sure what he intended to do with it.

# MILO

**WHEN MILO OPENED HIS EYES** and saw the airship captain and his engineer standing near him, he opened his mouth as if to scream, but then didn't.

The Captain took a step back. He'd stretched out a hand and now opened it to show his empty palm, waved it, and then slowly lowered it.

Milo should've run away, but he didn't do that either. The sudden appearance of the man who'd grabbed him yesterday in broad daylight in the middle of Oldedge Market, and the coincidence of him being here, at this moment, on the Street of Sighs, should've rung nine different kinds of alarms in the boy's head. But because he'd stepped back, because Milo believed he heard actual concern in the Captain's voice, and mostly because he was just happy to see any familiar face attached to a body with the normal number of legs, Milo did nothing at all.

"You all right, boy?" the Captain asked him.

"Yup," said Milo. "Course I am."

"Saw you running back there."

The boy shook himself a little, gulped air. He tried to stand straighter. "That's why they call me Quick."

"Is it," said the Captain. "You look like you're running *from* something is all I'm saying. And I wouldn't think there's anything in this city that would spook you."

"You should look behind you, then," Milo said, and forced a crooked, toothy grin onto his face.

"That's funny," the Captain said, remembering the panicked look in the boy's eyes the last time he'd said those words—yesterday, in the market—and the pain of him sinking those teeth into his fingers. "That's a joke from where you're standing?"

"I think it's a joke from anywhere, sir. Doesn't much matter who's standing where."

# CAPTAIN KLIM

**LAST NIGHT,** the crew had been in a fury when Reyn let slip that the Captain had actually had his hands on the boy and let him go. There'd been accusations, complaints, threats—all unwise things to make in the presence of Captain Klim.

So the Captain had thrown his arms out wide and asked them what he should've done. "Should I have punched the boy in the teeth? Put him over my shoulder? Carried him, screaming and kicking through the streets and up here to the ship? Tell me, *what should I have done?*"

They were all together on the *Halcyon*'s berth deck, Semyon and Vaclav, Laila and the Captain, and Reyn crowded together into the single small room where they'd all lived and eaten and sometimes slept for months and months, breathing each other's breath and suffering each other's moods and snoring. The rain had been pounding and the lightning crashing and the Captain had brought his hands down hard on the single too-small table they all shared, making the dirty glasses and silverware jump.

"And even if I'd gotten him here," he continued, "what then? We're grounded until we finish making repairs. The canvas, cordage? Ruined. Both motors are done in. The compressor, too. We did not land here so much as we fell, and there's not one of you doesn't know that in your better moments. Which, by the way, this is not one of."

He'd looked around the table, meeting each set of eyes and seeing the fractures in them. In the guttering light of the lamps they'd lit to drive back the dark and the wet and the awful anxiety of the thousand lies they traveled under, he'd seen the places where each one of his crew was breaking under the strain of knowing how close every moment they spent here was to their last.

He said, "Even if we had the boy in hand right now, what would we do? You all know what the Armada is doing out there. We will have one opportunity to leave this place without probably dying of it. And I promise you, *all* of you, that there will be one moment when we can take the boy. One perfect moment. I don't know when it will be or how it will come, but we'll have to be ready. The boy will come to us. And no matter what anyone else thinks, we will be his rescuers then. Not his kidnappers, but his *salvation*. Are we agreed?"

There'd been a raw moment then, for sure. The Captain's hand had drifted slowly to the butt of the pistol he carried even when among his own people.

But then Semyon had applauded and Vaclav had laughed and Lalia had asked him how long he'd been saving up that speech, and the Captain had said quite a long time, actually. And then all of them had laughed even harder and cursed the rain and the dark and boys of all shapes and descriptions. Only Reyn Farrago had remained quiet, because only Reyn really understood how much damage the *Halcyon* had suffered during its final, plunging run under the guns of the Highgate aerie. And how much work it was going to take to get her flying again at all.

But the Captain had breathed out anyway and tapped the butt

of his pistol with a thumbnail for luck when no one was looking. They'd been together a long time, the five of them. They'd done some terrible things. All of them knew there was a clock ticking on their job here. And that if they were still here when it reached the appointed hour, they'd all probably be too dead to hear the chime.

Anyway, now that the boy was right here in front of him again, Captain Klim had no intention of repeating the same mistake he'd made yesterday in the market. This time, he tried to appear casual, good-humored, slightly concerned but not at all *interested* in the boy. Coincidence was all this was.

Nothing more.

# MILO

**THE CAPTAIN DIDN'T LAUGH** when Milo made his joke, but he did smile. He rocked back on his heels and said, "All right, boy. You just looked a little bit out of sorts is all." And Milo said no, he was fine, thanks. Just catching his breath.

The Captain said, "All right."

Milo said, "Okay."

The Captain said, "So we'll be on our way, then."

And Milo asked, "What are you doing?" a bit too quickly. A bit too *hungrily*. "Where are you going?"

"Ain't any of your business, is it?" said Reyn.

"Reyn," said the Captain. "Don't be rude." Then, to Milo, "We're just shopping." He dug his hands into his pockets and shrugged. "We'll be leaving here soon, so Reyn and I are looking for some spare parts. Though it seems like there isn't much of a market here at all. Everyone appears closed. Is it some sort of holiday I'm not aware of?"

Milo hadn't noticed all the lowered gates and closed shutters. All the yards and garages empty of people. But he said no. No holiday. He said that things had been strange in the city for the past few days.

"Well, we're looking for a man," said the Captain. "Unusual name. Deals in parts. What was he called, Reyn?"

"Judocus," said Reyn.

"That's right," said the Captain.

"The Fish?" asked Milo. "You're looking for the Fish?"

"Let me guess. You know him?"

"I do," said Milo. "I've known the Fish most of my life!"

"Well, isn't this just our lucky day." The Captain squeezed his lips into a thin, doubtful line. "You know anything about motors, Milo?"

"I might," said the boy.

"You know anything about airships?"

"More than anyone you'll ever meet."

"Do you, now."

"I do," said the boy proudly. He said that he certainly knew enough to know that their ship must be having serious problems if they were shopping for parts in the Machinists Quarter rather than just getting repairs done in the aerie. And when Reyn started listing off the dozens of parts he required, Milo waved a hand at him. "Stator coils, housings, brushes, commutator arms and heads. Sure. What you want is two brand-new attack motors that'll work at the flip of a switch, right? But what you *need* is working motors you can take to pieces. You need parts, and the Fish has parts. The Fish will have whatever you need."

Which the boy would know since, over the years, he'd stolen most of what the Fish kept in his shop.

"What we need," said the Captain, "is to find this Judocus person and have a little conversation with him. But we don't exactly know where his shop is."

"It's not really a shop so much as . . . Well, that doesn't matter. I can show you."

"You?"

"It's not even far. Follow me."

Milo took a couple of steps, then turned back. "Trust me, sir. I know the Fish. And he can get you exactly what you need at half the price you'd pay at the fitting yards, if they were open. Which I guess they aren't anyway. So come on."

# CAPTAIN KLIM

**ONCE UPON A TIME,** Captain Klim had been an excellent fisherman. It was years ago. Long before he'd become what he was now.

Most people think that fishing is about patience. About dropping your hook in the water and just waiting for a fish to bite. Those people don't understand fishing at all.

Being a good fisherman requires trickery, deceit, concentration. It requires knowing where the fish are before you ever pick up the pole. It requires knowing exactly what they want. Being a *great* fisherman demands all of that, plus knowing what to do once the fish has taken the bait. How not to lose it once it is almost yours.

Captain Klim knew what to do when he had a fish on the line, when to reel in and when to let him run a little just to tire himself out.

# DAGDA

**DAGDA DID NOT DREAM.** She did not, technically, even sleep. What she could do was sit very still and very quietly for as long as was necessary and think about things.

Because she had no other language for it (because hers was now a language of one, spoken only by her), she called this state "deep processing," and over time, it had become important to her. She would begin by trying not to think of anything at all, by making her mind blank and quiet and smooth as a ball of glass. One by one, she would extinguish the day's concerns, then the week's concerns, then the year's, then the century's. She imagined them like match heads burning, snuffed by a soft breath, until her brain was dark and cool. And then, slowly, she would allow things to disturb this peace. Whatever thought came to her, glowing like a light in the glass. This was how Dagda dreamed.

And so she dreamed while sitting in Sanel the Toymaker's locked workshop with the pinch of the needle drivers pulling at the skin on her arm and the gentle *pop pop pop pop* of the cauterizing laser fusing her back together, leaving scars that would never fade. The thoughts that came to her were the smell of fresh cinnamon, the thatch of white hair on a black cat she'd befriended once and named Vasco, her father shouting her name from upstairs in their old house and the sound of panic in his voice that had given every letter a serrated edge. She thought of the view of stars from the sea—so cold and true and thick in the sky, they look like clouds spread thin and distant—and the bloom of artillery strikes from a distance, watching fire gush and spray like all the world was liquid, just waiting to be shaken apart by violence.

Time passed. She felt the vibrations of bodies moving about the house, and sensed the creak of stairs being descended and the scrape of doors against their brass footplates, but now, in deep processing, her memories were realer to her than the real world. Everything that had ever happened to her had happened in a perpetual yesterday, never further from her than that. Vasco's purr at 23 hertz (ingressive). The scrim of stars (each one a named object). Her father, shouting her name.

Now, Dagda's eyes opened slowly. It took a moment for her to separate the real thing from her memories of other real things. That her name was actually being shouted—and not by her father, of course.

It was Milo's voice, saw-edged in panic. And when it came to her that this was true and now, her awareness arrowed toward him. She heard footsteps, the click-slam of Sanel's big front door closing. She knew where Milo was even after he'd left the house, because she was, above all other things now, a compass needle pointed always in the direction of Milo Quick.

The stitchers and laser had stopped. Dagda carefully pulled the millipede from her arm and set it on a tray. She pushed at the newly scarred skin with a finger and watched it spring back. Unbolted her arm from the restraints and tested its motion. It was stiff, but operable. There was a tick in the wrist joint—some imperfect burr on the metal inside her—and the feeling of the repaired systems moving under her skin was strange because they were ever so slightly different from the old systems. Sanel had needed to shave the latticite bone by hand. Stent and graft ruptured vessels by eye. Lathe new fittings, replace shock mounts and lead assemblies. Nothing was ever perfect, but the arm functioned. It was an arm again, for which she was very grateful.

Dagda knew every lock in Sanel's house and had become friendly with each of them over time. None impeded her anymore. She could still feel Milo as a distant and receding point in her mind and experienced the track of his fleeing like a string that she could follow if she chose. It had been this way since the day they'd met, chained together on the street with Jules Cael between them. At that time, it'd been more than a hundred years since she'd found someone like Milo with her family's blood and unique pheromone signature. Since she'd been close to someone who felt like home.

The door to the library was open. She saw Oswaldo—who was the embodiment of Sanel's household security apparatus, confined forever to this house, never able to leave—marching stiffly from the front room. She stopped. Never sure of what the little toy soldier would do when it saw her, she chose not to antagonize it. Though Oswaldo (like everything else in the house) was programmed to protect her, the little soldier's captive intelligence was conflicted when it came to her because Dagda had smashed Sanel's stupid toy so many times when she was newer. She'd always felt bad afterward. Out of guilt, she would scavenge parts to fix it from places only she knew, bringing things home to Sanel that no one else in Highgate even recognized as valuable anymore. Those who lived now in the Flying City had lost nearly all memory of how the world had been before, even though they lived every day in the shadow of the miraculous, in the graveyard of history.

Oswaldo looked at her, clicked its miniature heels, saluted, and said, "Ada-4382, welcome home."

Dagda dipped her head in reply. "Pleasure to see you again, Oswaldo."

"You look terrible. Have you been in a battle?"

"I have."

"Recently?"

"Yes."

The little soldier regarded her for a moment, then said, "Lucky you," and stalked off.

From the library, Dagda heard Sanel call her name and she went in. On the walls, her sister climbed and clattered and fit thick books back into their proper places and looked down at Dagda with nothing but an icy, starving hatred.

"Finished?" Sanel asked.

"It is," said Dagda. "Internal diagnostics are still running, but the arm is operational. Thank you again, Sanel. Your work was exquisite."

The Toymaker huffed and waved a hand dismissively from his chair.

"Did Milo leave without me?" she asked, already knowing the answer.

Sanel looked away, disgust written in the slope of his shoulders and tilt of his head. "He seemed . . . *uncomfortable* here," he said, then, "Don't stand in the doorway. Come in. Sit."

So Dagda did, keeping one eye on the Marie-12 (Philomena) who crawled along the tall bookshelves. She settled onto the edge of an ottoman that was elaborately embroidered with a DNA sequence. "What did you do to him, Sanel?" she asked.

And Sanel insisted he'd done nothing. Dagda asked again and he shrugged, said that he'd given the boy a room and a bed and soap and water and offered him anything in the world that his tiny little boy's heart desired, but that, in the face of all this hospitality, the boy had bolted as soon as he'd come downstairs.

Dagda put her elbows on her knees and her face in her hands. "Philomena," she said. "And Oswaldo. He saw them? What else?"

"He saw my books. Seemed quite taken with them. He saw . . . I don't know, Toy. I was busy putting your arm back on."

"You scared him."

"He scared himself. Stupid boy."

"A child," said Dagda. "Who has never known anything but the worst parts of this world. Who is fascinated by airships and birds and the mail and machines. Who knows *nothing* about *anything*, Sanel! And you let him see the spider lady?"

From the shelves, Philomena made a spitting noise and showed her furious teeth, her lips making silent curses. Sanel said, "Don't call your sister that." And Dagda said, "Don't call her my sister." And Sanel said, "So what is she?" And Dagda said, "A terrible, broken *thing* that should've been put down and stripped for parts a hundred years ago!" And Sanel said, "Aww . . ." and waved his hands, and Dagda looked up at the shelves where Philomena clung, waving her front legs angrily and making a face like someone'd just fed her a live squirrel, so she said, "Come down here, then, Phi. I'll take you apart myself."

Sanel told her to stop it. The spider lady in the maid costume shook with rage and retreated farther up the wall.

"I'll take your head right off," Dagda continued. "Boot it straight over the edge of the city and into the sea."

"Dagda!" Sanel snapped.

She hung her head and hissed curses under her breath, then said, "I have to go."

"But we're still—"

Dagda stood up. "I have to go," she repeated.

"How long has it been since I had the whole family together here, Toy?"

"I have to find him, Sanel. I have to explain."

"You can't."

"He must be terrified. Milo, he's . . ."

"Simple?"

"Confused. He has no idea what's happening right now."

"They all are, these . . . people." Sanel spat the word out like it was something nasty he'd found stuck in his teeth. "None of them have the least idea. But you can't say anything to him. You know that. He's a boy, and boys . . ."

"Boys what?"

"Boys talk. Boys *pry*. It's not safe, and you know that."

"I have never felt safer than when I'm with him."

"Bah. That's just your core program executions talking. Signaler pheromone receptors and hybridized Nasonov reaction. DNA trace analytics in your bonding protocol. You were *built* to feel that way."

"I am not my protocols, Sanel."

"It's just programming, Toy. It's not *you*. And you've already spent too much time—"

"I am *not* my protocols."

The Toymaker sniffed. "Did he give you the ring yet?"

Dagda raised an eyebrow. "What ring?"

For an instant, the old man looked surprised, but then said, "No . . ." and grinned cruelly. "Have I ruined the surprise? Shame."

"Do you mean the spider ring?" She'd seen Jules wearing a new ring last night in the shape of a metal spider, and had wondered about it, but hadn't had the chance to ask him.

"Of course. The boy came to see me yesterday in the market. Traded for it. Said it was perfect for someone he knew, and I assumed . . ."

"Jules," said Dagda. She smiled. "He gave it to Jules."

Up on the bookshelves, Philomena crashed a leg against the wall over and over as if to say *Look at me, look at me, look at me!* Sanel and Dagda both looked.

"She hates it when she thinks she's being ignored," Sanel said.

Dagda huffed out a single laugh. "That sentence could've just ended with *hates*. That all she does now. She hates."

"Ah. Because you've spent so much time with her lately?"

Dagda looked up at her. At her face, her empty black eyes, her teeth, the rage and wrath etched into every inch of her. And Dagda pitied her with a depthless sorrow. Like Oswaldo, Phi could not leave Sanel's house. She couldn't speak anymore. She lived in a prison of walls and the prison of her failing, hodgepodge body, and had for a long time. Dagda felt the unfairness of the Marie-12's fate and sadness. Softly and slowly, she mouthed the words *I'm sorry* to her, but was met with only redoubled fury. Anger so hot and complete that silvery-white tears stood out in her sister's blank eyes.

"I've known her for almost four hundred years, Sanel," Dagda said. "Since before your grandfather's grandfather knew her. And she has never been any different."

# SANDMAN

**ENNIS ARGHDAL** spent most of the second day of summer trying to pick up Milo's trail. He didn't have to look everywhere himself. The Sandman had people who did that for him—who bought rum and bowls of cold noodles with money that had passed first through Ennis's hands.

So he talked to a man here and whispered in the ear of a woman there, and before long, word had begun to spread that the Sandman had gotten loose with his wallet and was buying eyes all over the Quarters, looking for a boy.

It took time, but not much of it. Most of those who came to him were liars, for which Ennis had no patience. They'd tell their lies and then ask for their money, and when the Sandman refused, they'd get angry. They'd claim that they were owed.

"No," the Sandman would say. "Liars owe *me*." And then he'd ask them how they'd like to pay. One eye? Both? Or maybe their tongue?

A girl with her feet wrapped in rags told him that Milo was dead, killed in the mail yards last night. Or maybe taken by Transit Post men. An old man said that he'd seen the boy in Oldedge talking to some soldiers. There was a woman who swore to gods whose names the Sandman didn't recognize that she'd seen the Quick boy staggering like he was drunk, running out of the Machinists

Quarter and across the Street of Sighs not long ago. When Ennis asked her to tell him about the boy she'd seen, she described a clean and shiny one, which, for better or worse, were two words no one who actually knew him would use to describe Milo Quick.

But then, later, a boy looking to squeal came to the Sandman on High Street, sliding up beside him with his eyes on his shoes and his shoulders hunched like he was waiting for a punch. His name was Luka Ajith. The Sandman knew him a little.

"Little Luka," said Ennis. "You here to snitch?"

And Luka Ajith said no. Except, maybe, yes. He said, "You're paying, ain't you?"

"That depends a great deal on what you have to tell me."

So Luka told the Sandman that he'd seen Milo in Oldedge yesterday. "He was trying to rob an airship pilot and another man that was with him. Got caught doing it, too. And the pilot didn't seem happy with him."

Ennis said, "Yesterday doesn't help me, Mr. Ajith."

"I know. But then I just seen him again this morning, too. Up near the Machinists Quarter. And he was running from them same men."

Now *we* know that's not precisely how things happened. But Ennis Arghdal didn't. So the Sandman stopped walking and stood very still. Behind his blue glasses, his eyes didn't even blink. He stared down at Luka Ajith long enough that Luka started to ease back away from him.

"You know," Ennis finally said, speaking slowly, and so softly that Luka could barely hear, "a woman just told me that she saw Milo this morning in the Machinists Quarter. She thought he was running from something, too. Now, this was a woman I *know*, Mr. Ajith. Someone who has provided me with good information in the past. And I threatened to feed her left eye to her for lying to me. But you, I hardly know at all. You've never been any use to me before. Just imagine what I will do to you if you are making up stories for a dollar."

Ennis leaned closer to him and sucked at his teeth.

"So tell me, Little Luka, is there something you want to say about Milo Quick?"

The Sandman expected Luka Ajith to run. That was mostly what liars did. But instead, Luka Ajith started to speak. He told Officer Arghdal everything he remembered about Milo, the engineer, and the airship captain, the words spilling out of him in a torrent. He told Ennis about the way Milo had spoken to them, how the man had grabbed him and not let go. "I was right there," he said. "Just on the other side of the noodle lady's stand. I seen the whole thing."

And then, this morning, Luka had been on the Street of Sighs. Everyone in the Marche had heard that there'd been trouble in the mail yard last night, and people were telling every kind of story, about spies and saboteurs and monsters.

Not having anything better to do and hoping for some free entertainment, Luka had been headed up there to see for himself. He said he'd seen Milo Quick come running out of the Machinists Quarter like he was being chased—barreling out of Tereshkova Road and onto the Street of Sighs. He said the same airship man and the same engineer were there, too. Following right behind him.

"That it?" asked Ennis.

"That's all I know," said Luka.

So that was two people now who put Milo in the Machinists Quarter this morning. Two people who said he'd been running from something. There'd been the one-eyed woman yesterday who said she was a mailman, now an engineer and an airship captain who'd laid hands on his boy. Possibly chased him, as far as

Ennis knew. Who had certainly been *near* him twice in as many days, which was exactly twice too often for the Sandman's liking.

He paid Luka, then turned and walked away.

Ennis needed more information, so he found chandlers and coopers and pickpockets, longshoremen with secrets, Transit Post agents who owed him favors, riggers and sailmakers and Highgate gunners, away from their posts and drunk before noon. He would come up on them unexpectedly and throw an arm around them, pulling them close. He would see them sitting at a table in the sun and pull up a chair. He would take their hand to shake and then squeeze until he felt the bones rubbing together. The Sandman would hold them and lean in close and whisper to them all of their most terrible secrets, just to let them know that he knew them. And that, if properly motivated, he might be persuaded *not* to tell those awful secrets to everyone a person loved.

When they cursed him, he didn't care. When they threatened him, he laughed. When they looked into the blue lenses of his glasses and saw the hard eyes behind them, most spoke without being asked twice. Those who didn't, the Sandman convinced. No one had to be asked a third time.

In this way, he learned a hundred things. And in among those hundred things, he heard about an airship that had landed under fire several nights ago. A mail ship that had been carrying no mail. A blockade runner, some said, that'd come drifting down from frozen altitudes carrying a crew and nothing else.

A five-man crew, he heard. Or maybe seven. Or maybe three. If he squeezed hard enough, Ennis Arghdal got better answers. Five it was.

The captain of the ship had been cheered when he brought his ship in. He was a tall man. Or maybe short-ish. Little mustache. Or a beard possibly. Scar on his face that somehow made him look younger, not older. One of the crew had been an old man. One of them enormous. And one of them had been a woman. With a patch over one eye.

"Names," Ennis would say, his lips so close to a person's ear that they could feel the dampness of his breath, the awful warmth of the pleasure he took from all of this.

And no one had any names until someone did. A cooper who'd been up in the cradles that night taking water barrel orders from the provisioners. Who'd heard the commotion like everyone else. He'd watched the little airship fall like a stone from the sky, barely under control. ("Fast," he'd said, his knees buckling as Ennis Arghdal held him close and dug a thumb into a soft part between his neck and his shoulder. "Fast ship. So, so fast.") And he'd been among those cheering when the Captain had leapt down from her battered, shot-torn top deck and waved.

"*Halcyon*," said the man. "Please, that was the name of the ship. It was the *Halcyon*."

"Thank you," Ennis said, stepping back. "Thank you so much. That was just what I needed to know."

# IN THE WORKSHOP
# OF JUDOCUS THE FISH,
# PART ONE

**THE BOY KNEW EXACTLY WHAT HE WAS DOING.**
He told himself so, over and over again.

He'd led the Captain and Reyn out of the Machinists Quarter and down into the Blue Lights, the heart of the Marche, where the streets snaked and curved beneath fluttering, stained canvas, the way lit with lights burning behind blue glass, and so narrow that the boy could almost spread his arms and knock on doors on both sides.

He wasn't stupid. He didn't trust the Captain or Reyn at all. But they knew things about him, and Milo wanted to know what those things were, and how they knew them. He also knew that he didn't want to be anywhere near either of them without someone watching his back. Except Dagda was gone and Jules would ask too many questions. Sig was hurt. Tristan and Llyr were children. Keelan was Keelan.

But the Fish? The Fish was a friend.

Kind of.

He was someone Milo trusted.

Kind of.

The boy had no idea how he was going to make the Captain tell him what he wanted to know, or what he would do after. But he was pretty sure that the Fish wouldn't let these men hurt him. And almost completely sure that he wouldn't care about anything the Captain told him, if he told him anything at all, which was actually the *second*-most important part of Milo's plan: walking out again with his secrets more or less still secret. The Fish was good for that. He didn't talk to anyone he didn't have to. Most of the time, the Fish didn't talk to anyone at all.

So Milo led them on, down shaded, nameless streets, until he came to a door. A single huge slab of oakwood stained a dirty black with no glass in it, no knocker, no beautifying detail to suggest it was anything other than what it was: a massive barricade meant for keeping what was outside out. There wasn't even a knob. Just a small brass plaque, unpolished and greening, bolted directly into the stone beside the door. It read

JUDOCUS THE FISH
THINGS FOUND AND FIXED
GO AWAY

"It's okay," Milo said over his shoulder. "He's a little . . . strange. But the Fish knows me. We're friends."

So Milo stood in front of the solid slab of oak that Judocus the Fish used to keep the whole rest of the world at bay, and he kicked it as hard as he could. He called the Fish's name and told him to open up.

The first thing that went wrong with Milo's plan was that the Fish didn't open the door.

"This is perfect," the Captain muttered from behind him. "I actually can't believe the old man was right about this."

The second thing that went wrong was the Captain kicking

Milo in the back, sending him crashing straight into the door. Milo bounced off and saw stars, spun around, and the Captain was right there, waiting, smiling. He caught the boy by the throat with one hand, then punched him in the stomach hard enough to lift him up off his feet.

Milo couldn't make his eyes focus. His legs weren't working right.

"Hey," said the Captain. "Hey!" He lifted Milo up and shook him by the neck like a kitten. "Look at me."

Milo tried.

"If we'd had the time to get to know each other, Milo, I promise we would've liked each other. I really mean that."

Then the Captain turned away and shouted at the door. "Hey, Fish! We're back! And guess who came with us, just like you said?"

Milo heard the sound of gears grinding and wood scraping stone. He knew it was the sound of the Fish's big door splitting in the middle and opening like a mouth, waiting to swallow all of them whole.

And that was when everything else went wrong, too.

# IN THE WORKSHOP
# OF JUDOCUS THE FISH,
# PART TWO

**WHEN I TOLD YOU EARLIER** that Cuthbert DeGeorge had told the Captain and Lalia everything he knew about Milo Quick, I meant *everything*. The Total King knew all about Judocus the Fish. Milo made some decent money with the Fish, so of course Bert knew. And he'd told it all to the Captain, because that was just the kind of person he was: a coward who cared about no one but himself.

And because the Total King had told the Captain about the Fish, the Captain had paid the Fish a visit. He'd gone at night. He hadn't bothered with the door, figuring that knocking was going to get him nowhere, so had slipped in by other means, and he and Vaclav had surprised the Fish while he was having his supper.

The Fish was not a man who looked like any other man Captain Klim had ever seen. He was, to start, nearly eight feet tall. Even stooped, he towered over the Captain, and was even taller than Vaclav. He wore pieces of an old airman's uniform, cut off at the knees and the shoulders, and a disreputable beard that looked as though it'd been assembled from six or seven other beards he'd found just lying around. His arms were long and his legs were long and his fingers were long and black from grease. Altogether, he looked like some kind of giant, bearded insect just looking for trouble.

It hadn't been a pleasant conversation that they'd had. The Fish had taken some convincing before he would listen to reason. And that was why the Captain had brought Vaclav along—because Vaclav was very good at convincing. Although the Fish had held up better than the Captain ever guessed he would, eventually they'd sat down to talk.

"Machines," the Fish had finally said to him, spitting out blood and dabbing at a cut over his right eye with an oily rag. "Talk to Quick about machines and he will bring you here, probably. If he does, I will talk to him."

"You'll tell him to listen?"

"I will *talk*. Maybe he will listen, maybe not. But he is growing too big for this place anyway. I would like to see him live long enough to grow a bit larger. If you mean what you say, he might agree."

The Captain had said that he did. They'd even shaken hands when he left—not friends, but not exactly enemies, either.

And now, the Captain was back, with the boy in tow. It'd been luck, a little. Planning, a little. Saying the right things, a little. The Captain had done his best to nudge fate in his direction. Like so many things, maybe it'd been luck a lot.

But whatever it was, he was here now. With the boy, who he'd dragged in by the neck, then dropped on the floor.

"So he came," the Fish said from somewhere off in the dimness.

"Brought me straight here," said the Captain.

"You hit him," said the Fish.

"Barely touched him."

"Was not part of the arrangement."

"Couldn't have him running off. Not now. This is too impor- tant. We have too much to talk about."

The Fish stepped forward into the dim circle of light cast by an overhead lamp. He had a rifle in his hand—a short, mean-looking contraption with a barrel so big Milo could've fit his whole fist inside. In the Fish's huge, spindly hands, it looked ridiculous. Like a toy. But it was enough. The Captain froze. So did Reyn. From the floor where the Captain had dropped him, Milo coughed and gagged and hissed, "Kill him, Fish. Do it."

The Captain shoved at the boy with his foot, and the Fish twitched the rifle barrel up. "Stop," he said. "Touch him again and you will walk home on stumps."

Milo wheezed, "Shoot him, Fish! Please!"

Judocus the Fish blinked his puffy, blackened eyes once or twice. He tilted his head down to look at Milo without moving the gun an inch and pressed his thin lips together. "No," he said.

"Fish!"

"Idiot boy. You will run away. And the man is not wrong. We have things that need talking about. So get up out of the dirt al- ready and come. I have a table. We can talk at it."

Milo said a very bad word in response. The Fish shook his head and clucked his tongue. "Quick," he said, "that is bad man- ners. I have a table. Let us talk at it. All of us."

The Captain and Reyn went and sat at a battered and stained workbench mostly cleared of clutter. Milo slunk backward on his hands and knees.

"Boy!" the Captain yelled. "Come. Sit. Listen to what I have to tell you, and I won't touch you again. Promise."

Milo pushed himself up to his feet and squatted in the dark, hurting, a trickle of blood dripping from his forehead from where he'd hit the door. When the Fish came toward him, Milo shied away, looking afraid, then concerned when he saw the Fish's face—the purpled skin, the half-closed eye, the split lip beneath his whiskers. He said, "Fish, what happened to you?"

Long fingers went reflexively to the spot and touched the swollen skin there, the blackness under it. "Disagreement," the Fish said. "Over bad manners."

"Did he do that?" Milo asked, pointing at the Captain.

"No," said the Fish. "One of his friends did."

Milo stood and turned on the Captain, hate flaring hot in his face. "You hit him?"

"No," said the Captain, turning around in his chair to look at the boy. "Like he said, not me. But one of my crew did. They argued."

The Fish caught Milo as he roared and charged at the Captain. He grabbed him by the back of the shirt, then wrapped one long arm around the boy's chest.

"You hurt one of my friends!" Milo screamed. "You think I'm going to listen to anything you have to say?"

"Yes," said the Captain calmly.

"I'll kill you," the boy said, shaking. "I will."

"You can try," said the Captain, shrugging. "I don't envy your chances."

The Fish dragged Milo around, putting both hands on his shoulders, his fingers twitching and picking at the cloth of his shirt. He said, "Look at me now, Quick. Listen. You will not kill this man. Understand?" Then he looked over Milo's head at the Captain. "Quick will not kill you. He is only a boy. But hurt him again or lie to him at all and I will. And I like my chances quite fine."

The Captain stared at the Fish for a long minute and then he nodded in approximation of a bow. "Fair enough," he said. "Boy? Come sit."

"No," said Milo bitterly, folding his arms. "I'm fine standing, thanks."

The Fish said, "Quick, go sit. I already know this man's story, now you listen. I will make tea."

Milo looked up at Judocus. "He hurt you, Fish. Why would I listen to anything he has to say?"

"Because I am big and you are small and some things need to be settled by hitting. This was one of those things."

"You trust him?"

The Fish laughed a little, a sound like a woodpile coughing. "No. Of course not. But he knows some things that you need to hear. And if he lies, I will know it and then I will tell you and I will kill him. That is our deal. Just made. You know the name of his ship?"

Milo thought for a second. "No," he said.

"It is called *Halcyon*," the Fish said. "Docked upstairs, in the Spire. I know where she is. So if he lies, that ship is yours anyway."

"Crew might feel differently about that," Reyn muttered, but the Captain told him to shut up.

"Go listen to him, Quick," said the Fish. "That is all. Just listen. I will bring tea. Cookie if you are nice."

So Milo went—grudgingly and angrily, but he went. He sat down on a too-tall stool across from the Captain, and he said, "Okay, so talk."

"Your name is Alef Prowst," said the Captain. "And someone has offered me and my crew a very large amount of money to bring you home."

The Captain glanced at the Fish, who was across the room, rattling among tins and canisters looking for tea. He was worried because he was only two sentences into his story and he'd already lied once.

Needless to say, he wasn't planning to drink the tea.

# SHAW

**SHAW HATED LIKE A SLOW FIRE BURNING.**

Thanks to the medicine, his head seemed to float a few inches above his body. His legs felt only loosely attached to the rest of him. His arms—the good one and the bad one—were too long and as heavy as stone, exhausting just to carry around.

But his hate kept him knitted together and kept all the pieces of him from drifting apart as he staggered his way through the streets of the Marche, aiming his feet always toward the Summer Palace and somehow always missing. As he walked, he talked to himself, saying a list of names over and over again, and the names were Moric Shaw's friends. Allies. Those who might help him do what needed to be done. For sure those who'd at least listen to what he had to say.

The problem was, the medicine muddied Shaw's head so much that while he was thinking about the names, he couldn't focus on where he was going, and when he focused on where he was going, the names flitted out of his head like so many birds.

The Total King would understand what he had to do, Shaw thought. Bert owed him. He'd always been loyal. He never asked for anything, never *expected* anything in all the years they'd been together. They were friends.

He looked at his hands, but they were so heavy and far away.

There was blood spattered on the blunt tip of his cast, smeared on the plaster and on the ends of the sticks that stuck out on either side of his knuckles. The nails on his other hand were black with grime.

Cuthbert would let him kill Milo. He had to.

"Arik Joffa," he said. "Arik the Aces. Arik for sure."

It was deep into the afternoon by the time his head cleared enough to concentrate on both things at once, but by then his arm was aching as though a hot, iron band was wrapped around it. Outside the palace, the boys and girls were gathering in tight knots, organizing themselves for their night's work. Shaw was sweating. His feet dragged when he walked. He held his broken arm folded tight against his body, and with his other hand he played with the little bottle in his pocket, rolling it over and over in his fingers. He wanted the peace and the coolness of the medicine so badly. Wanted the muffling of pain that came with it.

But not yet. Right now, while his head seemed attached to his body by something other than a balloon string, Shaw had business to do. And he could see Arik Joffa sitting on a curb outside the front door of the Total King's Summer Palace, rasping the blade of a homemade knife against the crumbling stone.

Shaw had nothing in him that approached subtlety, but he understood the contours of resentment and bitter anger better than maybe anyone. Yesterday, Arik had been in the palace when the Total King had broken his arm for touching Milo Quick. Not even hurting him or knocking out a tooth, but just slapping some of the smart out of him. Arik the Aces, one of the Total King's coldest killers (or so he claimed), had been there and seen it all.

Arik had also been the one that Cuthbert had hit with a rock. One of the ones who'd rushed to carry Shaw when the Total King had stroked his hair and said that he was to be taken to the doctor.

Arik had pushed his way to Shaw's side. He'd been so furious that little bubbles of spit had formed in the corners of his mouth. *This ain't right*, Arik had said to him when they'd carried him clear of the palace's gloom and into the alleys. *This ain't the way no king should act.*

Now, Arik spat onto the concrete curb beside him and ran the iron knife over it and over it, holding the dirty, string-wrapped grip with one hand, pressing down on the flat of the blade with the fingers of his other and whisking it back and forth with a sound like *SHIKshik SHIKshik SHIKshik.*

"Arik," Shaw said when he was close, and Arik looked up.

"You're back."

"Need to talk to you."

"How's your arm?"

"We need to do something. You and me."

And Arik looked at Shaw and looked around him and looked back at Shaw again.

"Not here," he said. "But okay, yeah."

And this was another thing that Moric Shaw understood perfectly. That boys could be talked into anything without hardly even asking. That all boys had the same few thoughts, all the time, and that when two of them had the same one of these few thoughts at the *same* time, it always seemed like genius, or inspiration. It always seemed like the best idea ever, even when it was the worst.

Almost always when it was the worst.

# IN THE WORKSHOP
# OF JUDOCUS THE FISH,
# PART THREE

**MILO HAD A HUNDRED QUESTIONS** for the Captain and he asked all of them. The Captain answered when he could. When he couldn't, he said so. Most of the time.

The Fish brought tea in mismatched mugs with greasy fingerprints on them and a plate of cookies that were so old they might as well have been made of wood. In one corner of the warehouse Reyn was making a list of pieces and parts—all the things he needed to get the *Halcyon* flying again. He spent some time arguing with the Fish, then some time sulking, then some more time arguing. And through all of it, Milo and the Captain talked.

The boy didn't like Captain Klim. Didn't trust him. He'd come to hate the man quickly, completely, and for very good reasons. So at first, Milo was defensive, angry, sitting with his arms crossed and one foot tapping furiously against the leg of his chair. He wanted to be away from this place so he could hate the Captain alone and at a more comfortable distance.

But the Captain had . . . a way about him. He was an excellent storyteller. His voice was pleasant and soft (when he wanted it to be). He sat comfortably in his chair, leaning back and then forward, his hands always in front of him and always moving. He was expressive and focused, and he answered every question in a way that suggested another question, and then another waiting behind that one.

And in this way, the Captain slowly drew the boy in, watching every shift in his posture, reading every change in his expression the way he did the ship's barometer when he was looking for the wind. He knew the Fish was listening, so he was careful to make his story mostly the same one he'd told the Fish a few nights ago, but he polished and embellished it in ways he knew a boy—*this* boy—would like. That he wouldn't be able to resist.

And so, bit by bit, he spun a tale of fantastic, faraway places, of pirates, smugglers, chases, and escapes. He told Milo about a war being fought between good and evil, right and wrong, and how the right side winning required just one thing.

"What thing?" Milo asked.

The Captain smiled. He pointed at Milo and said, "You."

Now listen: Everything that the Captain said to Milo was a lie, but it was also entirely true. It was like saying the sky is blue. The sky isn't really blue, but it *appears* that way some of the time. So saying the sky is blue isn't a lie, but it isn't exactly true either. You might have noticed already that the Captain is very good at saying things that are both true and not true at the same time. And if you haven't, it's certainly worth pointing out now.

Be careful what you believe. That's all I'm saying.

Be sure you know what's blue and what's not.

# DAGDA AND PHILOMENA

**IT HAD TAKEN** Sanel nearly twenty minutes to coax the Marie-12 down off the wall. Twenty minutes of promises. Twenty minutes of sweet words. Dagda had watched, but said nothing.

And even when the spider lady finally came down, she crouched in a corner, furiously snapping her teeth and raking her legs along the floor until they made splintered gouges in the wood. Nothing Sanel did or said could calm her.

Dagda left the library. She went up the stairs and down the hall to a room all the way at the end that had been hers for all the years she'd lived with the Toymakers. It was a small room with a single round window, dusty carpets piled on top of each other, pale blue walls and a narrow bed dressed in sheets and covers as white as clouds. The ceiling had once been a holographic starfield—a map of every known place—and she used to lie on her back and let it take her on journeys that no one alive in Highgate could even imagine. When the projectors had stopped working two hundred years ago, she'd drawn her own maps from memory, then read every book and paper in the Toymaker's library. When she'd run out of books, she'd had to find more creative ways to amuse herself.

Smashing Oswaldo had been one. Torturing Phi, another. She'd haunted the Marie-12 for decades—breaking her articulated legs, scrawling curse words on her ridiculous egg body that

Sanel's grandfather's grandfather had to scrub off with turpentine, stealing and hiding her things. That last one was the meanest, because Phi had so little that made her happy and she clung fiercely to objects that reminded her of her life before. So, of course, that was the trick Dagda had played on Phi the most because she'd been newer then, furious and cruel.

Along one wall of the small room, beneath the round window, Dagda had a desk that she hardly ever used and a chair she hardly ever sat in. Both were stacked with books furred in dust, their spines dry and cracked. *Proceedings of the 112th Stellar Congress* and *A Child's History of the Contraction* and a dozen others. She set these aside as carefully as she could, moved the chair, shoved the desk a few inches until she could reach a certain section of wall where she pressed her thumb into a dent in the plaster, and held it there until she heard the whine of old electronics coming to life. It'd been half a hundred years at least, but the house still recognized her. It still knew what she wanted. And with a grinding buzz and a cough of old plaster dust, a small section of wall levered open, revealing treasures that a newer, meaner, angrier Dagda had hidden inside.

A pair of round black plastic sunglasses with gold frames.

A pink-and-green child's hairbrush shaped like a turtle.

A silver hand mirror with a broken handle.

These she took, and then went back downstairs to the library, where Sanel now crouched, shouting at Phi, and Oswaldo lay on the floor, torn in half at the waist, moaning, "Mortally wounded, I am, I am."

Dagda said Sanel's name and the old man looked at her over his shoulder, frustration etched into every line of his face. "Look what she did!" Sanel shouted. "Look what you made your sister do!"

"It's okay," she said. "Take Oswaldo downstairs." And then she looked at the Marie-12, shaking with rage, and said, "Phi. Stop. I have something for you."

She showed Philomena the sunglasses first—opening the arms, putting them on her own face and smiling, then taking them off and holding them out to her.

Sanel ducked down, grabbed the two halves of Oswaldo and pulled him out of the Marie-12's reach.

"My only regret is that I did not live long enough to see the deaths of my enemies," said the top half of the little soldier.

"It's okay, Phi. Take them," said Dagda, and the Marie-12 did, snatching them from Dagda's hand with inhuman speed and sliding them onto her face, covering the awful black pits where her eyes should've been.

Behind her, Dagda could hear Sanel carrying Oswaldo out of the room, but she continued to watch the Marie-12 like it was a cornered animal. She held out the mirror next and Phi grabbed it, hugging it to her chest and rocking back and forth, then holding it out and looking at herself. With the glasses on, she looked almost human. Almost beautiful. She puckered her lips and kissed the air. She smiled the way someone might if feeling sudden relief after decades of pain. She looked at Dagda and shaped words with her mouth that Dagda couldn't read, but she understood the smile and the sudden, almost-alien softness in Philomena's face.

Finally, she held out the brush.

"I found it," Dagda said. "I'm sorry. Can I?"

And Phi reared back for a second, shouting wordlessly, reaching for the brush with starving fingers, then jerking her hands back and patting at her wild shock of dark curls. She settled, pulled at her hair and then lowered her head.

So Dagda went—carefully and slowly, because she knew how dangerous the Marie-12 could be. But Phi didn't move, except to lower herself down a little more on her spider legs so Dagda could reach her head without stretching.

Phi's hair was a mess of knots and tangles, but Dagda was gentle and patient. She brushed and brushed, and sometimes Phi watched herself in the mirror and sometimes she sat with her head down and her body pressed against Dagda, leaning into the brush like a cat.

Dagda heard Sanel come back up the stairs, heard him stop and stand in the door to the library as she pulled the brush through Phi's hair over and over, the *shushing* sound of it hypnotic, the scratch of the bristles like static in her hand. She dug her fingers into the dark hair and lifted it, pulling the tangles out of the ends, and said, "Phi, I need you to listen to me. I need to tell you something."

And then Dagda explained to Philomena about the Armada, about the men who would be coming for her, looking to capture and keep her.

"But you're strong, Phi. If the worst happens, protect the house. If you can't protect the house, protect Sanel. If you can't protect Sanel, protect yourself, you understand? Stay safe and find me if you can." She looked up and met Sanel's eyes. "These men have no idea what we are, but we've survived worse. And we can survive this."

# IN THE WORKSHOP
# OF JUDOCUS THE FISH,
# PART FOUR

**THE BOY ASKED,** "Why me?" and the Captain said he didn't know. Didn't really care, either.

"That's their business," he said. "Getting you to them is mine."

The boy asked, "Well, why do they want me?" and the Captain said, again, that he didn't know. And again, that he also didn't care.

The boy asked, "But what can I do?" and the Captain shrugged.

"I really don't know," he said. "What can you do?"

Milo hadn't touched his tea, but now he reached out, picked up a bearing cap from the table, and lifted off the cover. There was sugar inside and he dumped some into his cup, used the blade of a flathead screwdriver to stir, then the butt of it to break one of the cookies into pieces that he could dip into the tea until they were soft enough to eat.

"No," said the boy with his mouth full of cookies and tea. "No, no, no. This is all ridiculous. I don't believe you."

But the Captain knew the boy was thinking just the opposite, so he said nothing at all.

"Okay, so where is it, then?"

"Where is what?"

"This place. These people. Where are they?"

"Valonde," said the Captain, because Valonde was the closest place of any substance to the Flying City and happened to be in the opposite direction from where they would actually be going.

The truth was, he was taking the boy to Arcpoint, but the Fish didn't know that. Most of the crew didn't even know that.

The only other person who knew was Semyon Beli, and Semyon *had* to know, because he was the Captain's navigator and would have to get them there when this was all done. He'd had to promise Semyon an extra share, in secret, out of his own pocket, just to make sure the old man kept his mouth shut about it, because if the rest of the crew knew where they were really going, none of them would ever have come.

Why? Because Valonde was maybe six days away from the Flying City if the wind was kind, and Arcpoint was a hundred days' hard travel, clear on the other side of the world. Because Valonde was warm and sunny, full of charming cobbled streets and blue-tiled roofs, long beaches, cheerful fishermen and a thousand places for a smuggler to hide, and Arcpoint was a teeming, crowded, seething ruin. Because Valonde existed on the barest edges of the war that the Captain had gotten them all involved in, and Arcpoint was just about as close to the middle of it as someone could get without joining up. But the boy, whole and alive and delivered there, was the deal he'd made with the woman in the basement of Sea & Fortune. And Captain Klim didn't mean to fail.

"Valonde," said the boy. "That's far."

"Not too far," said the Captain.

"So if we went . . ." Milo hesitated. "*If* we went, when would we go? Would we go right now?"

"That depends."

"Depends on what?" Milo snapped. "You have your own ship, don't you? Which means we can go whenever you want. As soon as you make your repairs? And if we go now, we could meet your friends and be back soon, right? Before anyone hardly even knows we're gone."

And the Captain said, "No."

He tilted his head and looked at the boy named Alef Prowst. The boy who called himself Milo Quick and thought that he knew so much about so many things, and he said, "That's not how this is going to work."

He said, "I don't want to lie to you, Milo" (even though he already had, and very much intended to lie more), and then he told the boy that the war he was talking about was being fought in many places. In Ofrad and Obrya Station, in the Khalef Highs and at the Koerwe Docks. It was being fought by men and ships and machines just about everywhere that there were men and ships and machines, and very, *very* soon, it was going to be fought here, in the Flying City.

"This is a one-way trip," he said. "No one will be coming back to this place."

The boy, meanwhile, had stopped moving completely. He sat frozen with a shard of cookie in his fingers, dripping tea onto the table. He eyed the Captain for a long moment, then said, "No. I can't."

"What?"

"I'm sorry. I don't want to go. No."

Slowly, the boy put the cookie down on the table. He wiped his hands on his pants and looked over to where the Fish and Reyn were arguing. He called out, "Fish? I can't. I've listened to him and I can't go. Tell him I can't go with him."

The Fish looked up. "Why not?"

When he started to say it, the answer sounded stupid to Milo. So he closed his mouth. Opened it again. Closed it again. He looked back and forth between the Captain and the Fish, his eyes going wider and wider until finally, he just said, "This is my home. I live *here*," and then stabbed one small finger down onto the table to make his point and mark the place he was and had always been.

"That's the thing, Milo," said the Captain. "Pretty soon, *here* isn't going to be a place anyone can live. The Armada out there? My crew and I have chased them for thousands of miles, and they're not just here to take in the sights. They're after something, too, and they're going to burn this place to the stones to get it."

The Fish had come drifting over to the table and he *tsk*'d the Captain. The Flying City had seen battles before, he said. It had been attacked from the sea and the sky by those who wanted it for their own purposes, and not once had it ever been taken.

"Idiot man," said the Fish. "Do you forget that you are on a flying island? Do you think that maybe we have a few surprises here, huh?"

The Captain turned to speak to the Fish. "We have a deal. I promised I wouldn't lie to the boy. And I think you're under-estimating just how determined the Armada is to get what they want."

The Fish considered this a moment, then flicked his long fingers in the Captain's direction like he was shooing a fly. "Bah! I think you are trying to scare the boy into agreeing with you. Careful. Truths only. I have to go yell at your engineer some more now."

The Captain waited until the Fish was gone and then leaned in closer to the boy. "It's okay if you're scared," he said. "Trust me. I understand."

"I'm not scared."

"Really?"

"Of course not."

The Captain blew out a sigh and said, "Well, that's a relief. Because I certainly am. My crew is, too. So it might be nice to have someone aboard who's *not* scared for a change." Then he stopped and looked around the room—at the Fish and Reyn and over both shoulders. He inched closer and gestured for Milo to lean in, too. "Listen, Alef," he said, then stopped, correcting himself. "Sorry. *Milo*. Can I tell you something? Something even the Fish doesn't know?"

And Milo said, "Sure."

"I don't really know what I'm doing here," said the Captain. He spoke softly. The boy had to stretch across the table a little just to hear. "I mean, I'm a smuggler. A blockade runner. I've got a fast ship and a good crew and we're very good at what we do. But *this*? All this sneaking around and talking and convincing? I don't really know what I'm doing at all. So I need you to help me. I don't know if you've ever seen an actual war from up close, but I have. My crew has. And I can tell you for sure that we're all scared. Reyn was right. Our ship is a wreck. I don't know how long we have left to make repairs. A day, maybe? Because if we're not ready to leave here when the shooting starts, we know we're probably not leaving at all. We came here for you. All of us. We're your only way out and none of us want to leave without you. But none of us want to die here, either. No matter what the Fish says, please believe me when I tell you that what's waiting out there? When it comes, it's going to be worse than you can possibly imagine."

"Then what about my friends?"

"Bring them."

"All of them?"

"All of them who will come."

"What should I tell them?"

And then the Captain whispered to Milo about a world he'd only dreamed of. A world beyond the edges of the Flying City. He told the boy about cities made of glass and mountains wreathed in clouds, about pockets ripe for picking, ports full of plunder, lands where the sun shone day and night, and ancient bridges that ran from horizon to horizon. He told him about places where the walls spoke and sea monsters breached, where ghost ships floated on a sea flat as glass, and markets where anything a man or boy could ever want was for sale. He said, "If you think you've seen some-thing, living here, then you won't believe the things I can show you. And I promise you, Alef, however many of your friends you can get to come with you, you'll be saving them. You'll be a hero. You'll be saving their lives."

Then the Captain gave his bait one last tug. "And honestly," he said, "you'll be saving mine, too. Your father would kill me if I made it all the way back home again without you."

Milo said, "My what?"

"Your father," said the Captain. "Dragan Prowst. Who do you think sent me all this way?"

Be careful. Be sure you know what's blue and what's not.

# THE BOY, THE CAPTAIN,
# THE ENGINEER AND
# THE FISH

**THE BOY AND THE CAPTAIN** came to an agreement. Milo would think about what Captain Klim had said and what he was offering. He'd talk to his friends. And tomorrow morning, they would meet on Front Street, as early as both of them could get there.

When the Captain reached out to shake on it, Milo jerked back and stuck his hands in his armpits.

"Not promising anything," he said. "And don't ever touch me again."

"Drink your tea," said the Captain. "It's getting cold."

Eventually, Reyn made a deal with the Fish for parts. Milo helped the engineer load the smaller things into a cart. He avoided the Captain.

"Is he your friend?" Milo asked Reyn.

And the engineer thought about that for a minute, but then said, "No. He's the Cap'n, isn't he? He don't have friends."

✦

The Captain said he would need extra help dragging the cart up to High Street where two of the *Halcyon*'s crew would be waiting. The Fish said Milo would go.

"No, I won't," said Milo.

But the Fish said yes, he would. "Go with him, Quick. Meet his people. The world is big. You will need people." And when Milo looked like he was going to argue, the Fish sent him out into the street to hail down a truckman to carry the bigger parts up to the *Halcyon*'s cradle in the aerie.

Once Milo was outside, the Fish went to stand beside the Captain—towering over him, his busy fingers plucking at dangling strings and touching this and that. After a minute, he asked, "Are you really going to take Quick's friends with you?"

The Captain sniffed. "Does our deal cover me lying to you?"

The Fish smiled thinly from behind his beard, his eyes as sad as anything. "No," he said. "But say the truth to me anyway."

So the Captain dug his hands into his jacket pockets and said no. "One of them, maybe. But there's no profit for me in the others."

A moment passed. The Captain wasn't sure what was going to happen next. But finally, the Fish clicked his tongue against his teeth and pulled at his whiskers. "You will take the boy, though? Away from this place?"

"I'm certainly going to try."

"Okay, then."

"Okay?"

"Yes." The Fish nodded. "Okay."

And then the Captain looked up at the strange man the boy had chosen to be his friend. He asked, "What are you going to do when—"

"*Pssht*," said the Fish, and waved a hand at him. "Look at Quick."

And the two men did, standing beside each other in the Fish's dim, greasy kingdom, watching the boy leap and wave his arms in the afternoon sun as a truckman pulled up in front of the workshop's open door.

# SEMYON AND LALIA

**SEMYON BELI AND LALIA IVONA VICARIO** had spent most of the afternoon waiting for the Captain and Reyn to finish their shopping. To pass the time without murdering each other, they'd come to an arrangement: Semyon got to pick the place they would wait, and Lalia would choose how they spent the time.

So Semyon chose a delightful little tea shop with shaded tables on a patio raised above the traffic of the Flying City's High Street. Lalia agreed, and made only one rule: Semyon was not allowed to speak.

They were there for three hours. Semyon drank seven cups of tea and ate an entire plate full of lemon cakes. He purchased a newspaper and read it, front to back, twice. He watched the scudding clouds above and the people below, and when that became too dull for him, he got up and paced the length of the patio, back and forth, over and over and over again.

Lalia enjoyed every minute of watching him suffer.

Finally, though, they saw the Captain coming. It was Lalia who spotted him first, whistled through her teeth to get Semyon's attention, and pointed down below, where Captain Klim stood tall, trying to make a path for the cart coming along behind him.

"Oh, thank the many and merciful gods," said Semyon, all in a rush. "I thought he was never going to—"

"Hey!" Lalia snapped. She looked at Semyon and dragged a thumb across her throat. "We had a deal."

"Only for so long as we were waiting, my dear," said Semyon. "And seeing as we are no longer waiting but, rather, actively *finding* the Captain and Reyn and all their various encumbrances, your rule, I think, no longer applies."

For a second, it looked like Lalia was going to come straight across the table to strangle Semyon Beli with her bare hands. But then she stopped, looked past him, and asked, "Is that the *boy*?"

Which, of course, it was. And when Semyon twisted around and saw Milo Quick down on the street below, walking beside the Captain and his cart, he grinned wide enough that the two gold teeth he had far back in his mouth glinted in the fading sunlight.

"Yes," he said. "Yes, it is. It seems the Captain has been true to his word and fetched Milo Quick back to us after all."

# SANDMAN

**THE SANDMAN HAD BEEN BUSY.**

Once he'd learned the name of the ship that'd run the Armada blockade and brought the Captain and the one-eyed woman to his city, he went looking for the *Halcyon* up in the cradles. His plan was to light it on fire just to make sure no one went anywhere until he was ready to let them, but when he'd finally found it, he'd realized that wouldn't be necessary. It was a wreck—shot-holed, splintered, and ragged. And besides that, it wasn't empty. A very large man had been on the top deck, stitching sails and quietly singing to himself, so Ennis had passed on by. No sense in wasting his time on unnecessary things, he thought. Not right now.

After that, he'd headed back down into the Quarters to see again about picking up Milo's trail. The boy had to be somewhere, he told himself. They were, after all, on a floating island. There was only so far he could go.

Ennis had taken the fastest lift down off the Spire. At the lower control gate, he had to wait in line. There were crowds mobbing both sides, shouting angrily, and the Transit Post agents had their sticks out.

Ennis Arghdal thought about names for boats.

"*Halcyon*," he said to himself. "That's a terrible name. Now, if I had a ship . . ."

And as he'd waited, Ennis Arghdal imagined what he would name a ship if he had one. He came up with women's names and clever names and fearsome names and funny names, and he wasn't sure, but doing this—dreaming about having a ship of his own and the name he would give it once it was his—was maybe the best twenty minutes of his life.

His good mood lasted until he made it out through the gate, through the crowds and down onto High Street.

It lasted right up until he spotted the boy.

# ON HIGH STREET

**WE'RE NEARLY THERE NOW.** This isn't the beginning of the end of things, I promise. But it certainly is getting close to the ends of their beginnings.

Milo had done like the Fish had asked. He'd stuck by the Captain and Reyn, helping push their cart all the way from the Fish's door to High Street, where traffic suddenly stopped them. It seemed, for some reason, that every man, woman, child, dog, cat, cart, truck, and bicycle in the entire city was trying to squeeze its way up toward the Spire, but Milo couldn't figure out why.

"Where's everyone going?" the boy asked, standing up straight and wiping his face with his scarf.

"Up," said the Captain.

But Milo wasn't really listening. He pulled at his shirt where it was sticking to him, then put a foot into the spokes of the cart's wheel to give himself an extra inch or two of height and scanned the sweating, hot, anxious faces of the crowd. "They look scared."

The Captain said, "They're all trying to run, Milo. To leave." But the boy barely heard him. Milo reached up, found handholds and dragged himself to the top of the cart, where he knelt, wobblingly, on a jelly roll of sail canvas to have a better look around. Below him, Reyn complained the way he'd been complaining more or less nonstop since they'd begun dragging the cart upward.

He shook the yoke bar and shouted for everyone to get out of his way. But the boy was looking at the people crowding onto High Street—more, it seemed, every minute—and that was how he saw, coming straight toward him, the old man he'd seen yesterday morning boxing the carrier bird.

"Hey," he said. "I know that man!"

The Captain stood up on his toes and looked where Milo was looking.

"Oh," he said, seeing Semyon and Lalia pushing through the crowd. "You met my navigator? How unlikely."

And the boy said yes, he had. "I saw him fighting a bird."

"A bird?" asked the Captain.

"A bird!" the boy insisted. "No one would believe me when I told them, but that's what he was doing." Milo grinned and waved to Semyon, and for just a moment, he felt like the Flying City was full of wonders.

Down on the street, Semyon Beli waved back to the boy because he couldn't think of anything else to do.

Reyn jerked at the cart.

Semyon stepped around a putt-putt smoking and idling at the curb with bundles piled so high on its narrow seat that it looked like the driver was hauling a mountain. Lalia moved behind Semyon, her eyes on the boy. She'd never been so close to him before and was surprised by how much she could hate something so small.

The Captain put one hand to his mouth and called out, "About time! Look what I found down in the market!"

And the boy, from the top of the cart, shouted down to Semyon, "What happened with the bird?"

And then the putt-putt in front of Reyn ground its gears, lurching forward two feet, the bundles swaying atop it.

And then Reyn, seeing his opportunity, leaned hard into the

yoke bar and yanked the cart forward to make up the space between it and the putt-putt.

And then Milo, momentarily distracted, lost his balance atop
the cart's load. He waved his arms and fell.

The Sandman's gaze unerringly picked Milo Quick's face from
the mass of faces spread out below him. He saw the boy yell, saw
him leap from the top of an overloaded cart caught in the snarl
of traffic pushing up toward the control gates, saw the boy's arms
flail and a youngish, blond-haired man dressed like an airship captain reach for him, grab him, hold him by one arm and the back
of his neck.

They were a distance away, but the Sandman was already running, bulling heedlessly through the crowd, knocking bodies out
of his way. He was already leaping onto a pile of crates abandoned
by the side of the road, scrambling to the top, dragging himself
upright. He was opening his mouth before he knew what he was
doing. He was cupping his hands to either side. He was sucking
in a huge breath. And before he had any idea what he was going
to say, he was already shouting as loudly as he could, "MILO
QUICK!"

The Captain saw Milo fall. He lunged for the boy—catching him
by one arm and the back of his neck before Milo could split his
head open on the curb.

"Careful!" the Captain snapped. "You okay?"

But before the boy could answer—before anyone could say
anything else at all—there came a man's voice, shouting above the
noise of all the motors and all the traffic and all the other voices on
High Street. Just two words—"MILO QUICK!"—bellowed with
a force that made everyone stand up straight and look at the man

with the terrible fire in his eyes, standing on the pile of boxes on the other side of the street.

For an instant, no one moved.

No one but the boy, who hissed, "Sandman!" and twisted himself free from Captain Klim's hands for the second time in as many days.

Suddenly, all Milo could think about was last night. The rain and the guards in the pneumatic forest, the blood and the noise. If they knew it was him who had been there, the Sandman would be who they'd send. To hunt him in the streets for a thief and maybe a murderer as well. To catch him and put him to sleep for good.

The boy hesitated for only a second. "Tomorrow," he said to the Captain. "Front Street."

And the Captain opened his mouth to say something, any-thing. He reached out a hand for the boy, but it closed only on air. Milo Quick was gone. Vanished completely like he'd never even been.

And in his place came Ennis Arghdal, striding through the clamorous crowds.

# SANDMAN

**ONCE HE WAS SURE** that he had everyone's attention, Ennis jumped down from the stack of crates. He walked, and the crowds of people parted around him. He lost sight of Milo, but when he got to the airship captain with the scar and the missing bit of ear, he just lifted a hand up and punched him directly in the face without even breaking stride.

He did it because he hadn't slept in a day, a night, and a day. Because he was worried and ravenously hungry and annoyed at having already hurt some uncountable number of people in his search for the boy or information on the boy, only to see, finally, *the actual boy* right there with this man's hands on him in a way that, from Ennis Arghdal's view, had appeared less than friendly.

He did it mostly because he wanted to. But Ennis Arghdal hit the Captain and then he *kept walking*, because even though she was trying to hide herself, Ennis could see Ligeia Lindsay, the one-eyed woman from the Beautiful Stranger, and he wanted to have a word with her as well.

Ligeia, though, did not want to speak with him at all—or so it seemed, because she ducked down behind some old man with an impressive mustache and arms like knotted rope, shoved the man at him, and then came for Ennis's kidneys with a long-bladed knife.

The Sandman lowered his shoulder into the old man, heard

the breath woof out of him, caught the woman's knife hand as she snaked it past him, and twisted. The knife fell from her fingers as Ennis knew it would (she was hardly the first person who'd ever tried to stab him). What was funny, though, was that *she* seemed completely surprised by how ready he'd been. And was even more surprised when Ennis reached out, took her by the throat and lifted her until her toes were barely scraping the road.

"Why, Ligeia Lindsay!" he shouted into her face, watching the fear suddenly light in her eyes. "What a pleasure to see you again!"

And then he whipped her around to put her body between himself and the airship captain, who'd scrambled back to his feet and drawn a pistol from inside his long coat.

The man was fast. Ennis had to give him that. He already had the gun out and extended by the time the Sandman got turned around. So Ennis did the only thing he could think of to do. In the middle of High Street, in the waning moments of the second day of summer in the Flying City, the Sandman stepped forward into the barrel of Captain Rodion Klim's pistol. And then, with Ligeia Lindsay still struggling in one of his hands and the gun pressed against his smoke-colored shirt, he looked Captain Klim in his blackening eye and said, "Pull the trigger, Captain. I promise it's the only chance you're ever going to get."

"Who *are* you?" asked the Captain.

"Tell me what you want with the boy."

"The boy? Milo?"

"You know his name?"

"Of course," said the Captain. "I hired him. To help me find and haul some parts."

"Parts for your ship?"

"Yes."

"The *Halcyon*?"

"Yes. How do you—"

"Where did he go?"

"I don't know. How do you know the name of my ship?"

Ennis pushed himself against the barrel. "Pull the trigger," he said. "You're going to regret it if you don't."

But the Captain—who, let's remember, had no idea whatsoever who Ennis Arghdal was or what he was doing here punching and strangling people in the middle of a busy street—was completely flabbergasted by all of this. With wide eyes and a disbelieving tone, he asked the Sandman, "What are you *talking* about?"

"Where did he go!" the Sandman snapped. "The boy. Make me ask you a third time and I'm going to feed you that pistol."

"I don't know where he went. He saw you and ran like a rabbit. Who *are* you?"

And Ennis (who, honestly, was getting tired of holding her anyway) opened his hand and let Ligeia Lindsay fall to the ground. Then he extended that same hand to the Captain.

"Silvano Yoon," said Ennis Arghdal. He tilted his head toward the woman on the ground, lying on her back and coughing with her hands over her face. "She and I met yesterday while she was watching Milo Quick's front door. She said she was the mailman."

All around them, the High Street crowd was pulling in tighter. Reyn had left his cart and stood now beside the Captain, a heavy wrench in one hand. The old man had gotten to his feet and was crouched down beside the woman on the ground, but he'd picked up her knife from the street and his eyes were on Ennis.

"We're a mail ship, yes. She's my first mate. We ran the Armada blockade a few days ago. If she did something to offend you, Mr. Yoon . . ."

"What's your interest in the boy?"

"Milo?"

"Yes."

And here, Captain Klim's eyes went ever so slightly dead. He smiled a cold, thin smile and said what Ennis guessed (not incorrectly) were probably the first entirely true words to ever come out of his mouth.

"I like him. He reminds me of me."

Ennis Arghdal looked around. He understood that he was outnumbered. The High Street crowds pulled tighter around them, wanting to see blood. But right now it was wrenches, knives, and pistols against the Sandman's empty hands and rightness. And Ennis knew that rightness offered a man no special protection in a street fight.

"Hmm," he said, and "Okay, then." He forced his fists to unknot and his shoulders to relax. He stepped back and slowly raised a hand and tapped a finger on the top of the Captain's two-barrel pistol. "It's a nice piece," he said, and stepped back again. "Not much good at range, though, is it?"

He stepped back a third time, until he felt the combined breath of the rabble on his neck. He said, "I'll be seeing you around, Captain." And then he turned sharply on his heel and shoved his way out of the circle.

It wasn't easy going. The people of Highgate had their blood up and were disappointed that no one had been killed.

# A BOY PURSUED
# BY GHOSTS

**MILO RAN** while the streets went dark around him.

He was angry at himself for wasting time with the Fish, for wasting time arguing with the Captain and pushing his cart all over the city, for wasting any time at all while Dagda was missing and his friends were hurt and Jules was probably out of his mind worrying. He didn't know what he'd been thinking.

But now he knew what he had to do. He had to talk to his friends. He had to tell them everything. *Everything* everything. He had to tell them what the Captain was offering and what the Armada was threatening. About the Total King and Shaw. About Sanel. About his name.

They wouldn't want to come, his friends. They had no reason to leave. They weren't afraid of men or ships or wars. There was nothing for them anywhere else in the world that the Marche and the breaking yards didn't already offer. And the boy hadn't thought there was anything else for him either, until today. Until someone had told him that maybe there was.

Adventure. Cities of glass.

His father.

He would convince them. He would try. Because right now, he

had a chance—one chance to leave here that might never come again. One chance to fly.

And so the boy who called himself Milo Quick ran as hard and as fast as he could. He ran as though pursued by ghosts. He ran until he reached Oldedge. And there, by the crumbling wall where they always met, was Dagda.

Waiting for him.

# DAGDA AND HER FATHER

**DAGDA COULD FEEL HER FATHER** most strongly when she sat by the remains of the columns that bordered Oldedge. The wall where she and Jules and Milo would always meet.

That was where she'd gone to wait for Milo. Because she knew he was out there somewhere in the city. She could feel him moving through it as the day gave way to evening.

She'd gone home first, after leaving Sanel's. Back to the ship, to Fort Kick-Ass, to find the rest of them all present and accounted for—Arun and Jules and Keelan in the main room. Tristan fiercely guarding the door. Sig in the bedroom, broken and stitched back together and in pain. Llyr hiding in a cabinet. Everyone was waiting. For her, for Milo who wasn't there and hadn't been all day. Jules was furious. Scared, really, but he wore it like fury—righteous and blazing.

"I had no idea!" he said. "No idea what happened! Or where you were. Nothing!"

And so she'd explained it to him, using her softest voice. She'd told him only the things that she could tell him without really telling him anything at all and made up everything in between. They'd been chased, she and Milo. Had hidden. He'd saved her because that was what Milo did. He was the hero, always. And then, when everything was safe and all the danger was over, he'd gone off to work because that was *also* what Milo did. Something that Jules could understand. And in the meantime, she'd come here where it was safe. Simple.

Jules believed her because he had no reason not to. And because he really wanted to. He folded his arms scoldingly and told her never to ever, ever, *ever* do that again. To be gone so long. To make him worry like that.

"You're a girl, Mouse. And you don't know this city like Milo and me do."

Five years, and Jules had never noticed that she hadn't aged. Not a day. That she'd never eaten more than a bite in front of him. No more than she could spit back out again. That she'd never gotten sick, hungry, tired. But that was okay. Dagda understood. Jules, like Milo, was only a boy.

She'd sent Jules to the doctor—the Total King's doctor, who patched up all the Total King's broken things—to get medicine for Sig, who was awake now and shivering with pain. She'd told him exactly what to ask for, and said she would go to the wall—their place—to wait.

"Milo will turn up eventually," she'd said. "He always does."

The wall had its own unusual gravity. It drew people to it now the way it had once drawn eyes when it was new—when it was all smooth white composite pillars, their tops splitting and branching to form a lattice of geometrically perfect arches, a roof over a lovely, shaded, curving path that ran around the upper edge of the gentle bowl of the land. Back then—before Oldedge, before anything—the bowl had been a grassy park where her father would come to hear the music and watch the people and, if he was feeling particularly expansive or happy or calm, sketch them.

*This, Dagda*, he would say to her. *This is what they pay for. A* man and his eyes and his hand. *No machines. No computers.* And with his finger, he'd draw a frame in the air before him; would isolate a scene, render it, allow him to pixelate, shift, blur, texturize, add and subtract. He was an artist and very proud of it. And Dagda— which was his name for her, the name of his human daughter, still months away aboard the torchship *Persephone*—never reminded him of the incredibly complex machines and computers that made all that possible, because he knew that, and that wasn't what he meant anyway. Only later would he pull the images he'd stored out of thin air and use them as reference for his light sculptures or abstracts, for the occasional old-fashioned painting, oil on canvas.

At the time, Dagda didn't understand how famous he was. Be- cause what little girl ever does when it's her own father? She never understood that he was Yuri Prowst, the Eyes of the Common- wealth, whose images of ordinary life among the far-flung human colonies were so prized and so beloved that they hung in the homes of celebrities and industrialists. Whose eye became the eye of trillions. Whose images of a summer concert on the lawn of a floating city, of solar gliders ducking around the peak of a recovery spindle, of harvesters breaching the rings of Cheolara, or the wash of stars on a clear night over a sea of liquid helium that ran to the horizon in every direction, became the images that defined worlds other than their own for everyone, everywhere.

And Dagda's father wasn't even the *most* famous one in the family. That was Dagda's mother. A star, hot, white, and lumi- nous. But also like a star, distant, cold, and unknowable. She was both of those things at once. Two things in one person. And any- way, mostly what she was, was gone.

All of these memories, collapsed by the weight of time. They were all there for her as she sat looking out over the ragpickers and junk-sellers now clustered where, once, music had played and Yuri

Prowst had seen the future's most joyous, quiet, familiar simplicity with his daughter's surrogate by his side—an Ada-series artificial body, model 4382, carrying within it the mind of twelve-year-old Dagda Prowst, who, at the moment that Yuri was sketching the summer concert in the air, was asleep aboard the *Persephone* with her mother, coming to Tellus from their home on Ermidae.

By uploading Dagda's consciousness and memories and everything that was *her*, transmitting that data to Tellus, and then downloading it—downloading all that was Dagda Prowst—into this rented body, she could live months on Tellus with her father while her human body (and her mother's body) was in transit. She would lose nothing. All of the duplicate Dagda's memories would be available to her when she finally arrived. All of the days and nights of being twelve years old, free and adventurous, the daughter of one of the most famous artists in the many worlds, in one of the most beautiful, magical places there was. Highgate, Tellus. The Flying City.

The real Dagda and Yu Li Prowst slept aboard the *Persephone* while duplicate Dagda and Yuri Prowst sat against the colonnade and listened to the music. The trip would take their bodies eleven months. Yu Li had not arranged a dupe for herself and Yuri had not insisted. They'd lived most of their lives apart. They were accustomed to it. But they agreed that for Dagda to lose a year—her twelfth year—was unthinkable. Because that was not the kind of thing she could ever get back.

They slept while Yuri made the initial sketch of what would become his most famous image. They slept while the music played and Yuri watched Dagda's Ada-4382 surrogate body dance on the green grass and, with a few quick, confident motions, added her to the scene—a beautiful, young girl with pale skin and dark hair, seeming to almost take flight in her joy, her feet barely touching the ground. Yu Li and human Dagda slept while night fell on Tellus and Yuri and machine Dagda went home to the house they kept on Apollo Avenue with its tiled floors and crystal chandelier and, each in their own way, also slept.

And sometime in that span of hours, the *Persephone* was lost—exploded in a bright hail of tiny, jagged pieces—with 2,344 people aboard. Two of them were Yu Li and Dagda Prowst. This was the beginning of the end of everything.

And sometime in that span of hours, Yuri had woken, heard the news, and gone back to that rendering. He'd added the roses. Red ones, dotting the grass and one more in Dagda's hand, petals dropping from it almost like beads of blood. They hadn't ever really been there, those roses. But Yuri felt like they ought to be.

Some days, when she sat by the broken wall on the outskirts of Oldedge, Dagda could still hear the music that'd been playing while her father sketched. It would come to her unbidden—a bleed in her memory, some data sector overrun, incurable—and she would listen with her eyes open, feeling the sun on her face or the cold weight of starlight. She'd seen the world fall entirely to pieces. Seen her mother and her father and herself and everything they'd ever done, everything they'd ever known, be forgotten. Lost to fire and fury and time. For 398 years, she'd been listening to the music, waiting for herself to arrive, to become whole, to turn thirteen.

And she knew it was never going to happen, but she came to the wall anyway because she'd learned over all those years that certain places held tight to their ghosts. That some things carried the weight of their history with them. She was closest to her father when she sat here, her back against the wall that they'd sat against together almost four hundred years ago. Time and distance meant nothing. The stones didn't ever forget.

And neither did Dagda Prowst.

# MILO AND DAGDA
# AND JULES

**FROM AROUND THE GRAY AND CRUMBLING EDGE** of the market, Dagda saw Milo coming to her along the forgotten path of the wall.

"Your arm!" he said. Exclaiming. Stunned.

"It's better," she said, and flapped it around, rotated her wrist, to show him that this was true. "Milo, what did—"

"How are you?" he asked, interrupting her, throwing himself down to sit beside her, reaching out as if to touch her, the threaded, pale scars on her arm, and then stopping, pulling his hands back. "I mean . . . Does it hurt? I was there. At Sanel's house. And it was . . . Well, I left. But I didn't know if you were—"

"I was there," she said. "I heard you."

"But you're okay now? You're . . . fixed? Or whatever?"

"I'm okay."

Milo leaned in as though, again, he meant to reach for her. Like there was something in him that needed to touch her to make sure she was real and whole, but again he pulled back. And Dagda thought maybe he was just being a boy, just being Milo, but she worried it was more than that. That now, every time Milo got close to her, he'd think of Phi with her tangled hair and empty eyes, crawling the shelves in Sanel's library. That he couldn't stand even the idea of her now that he knew what pumped and ticked just beneath her skin.

And the worst thing was, she wasn't completely wrong.

"We should go back," Milo said. "Home, I mean. I haven't seen Jules since last night and he's gotta be worried."

"He is."

"You saw him already?"

And Dagda explained. Then she asked where he'd been, and Milo told her everything that had happened since leaving the Toymaker's house—about the Captain and Judocus and the Sandman showing up on the street. He told her what the Captain had said: that people from the Armada were going to burn down the Flying City because there was something here they wanted. Something they couldn't have. And Dagda knew exactly what it was they wanted, because what they wanted was her. Because these men weren't the first to come to the Flying City looking to find the magical girl who never got older, who never died. She'd spent lifetimes hiding from men who wanted to find her, capture her, cut her to pieces and see how she worked. The ocean beneath Highgate was full of their bones.

This time was different, but also the same. The Armada meant more men, but they were still only men. Only meat. None of them understood what she was or *why* she was. This world had forgotten everything, and Dagda Prowst had forgotten nothing. She would outlast them. She would survive, like she always had.

The only new variable was Milo. Milo Quick, who was really a Prowst, whether he knew it or not. Who smelled like a Prowst and felt like a Prowst and who still carried with him, four hundred years after she'd first opened her eyes, the tatters of Yuri Prowst's unique genetic signature.

✦

Dagda remembered the voice of the instructional terminal in Highgate 398 years, nine months, and eleven days ago. The voice was silky, soft, and smooth as honey pouring from hidden speakers in a pink room with no corners.

*Step Nine of the enlivening process will involve an experienced Manifest Technologies associate taking a simple cheek swab and saliva sample from you. This minimally invasive procedure will be used both as a DNA security lock, engaging the family-only, Trusted User status of your Ada-series companion system, and to initiate the surrogate's bonding protocols.*

She remembered sitting on the street outside the police station in the Marche next to Milo, four years, eleven months, and eighteen days ago. The way he'd reached for her shackles, spit into his hands, and touched her skin.

*Like waking Snow White from her enchanted slumber, this final step in the process of enlivening your loved one's surrogate can be an emotional moment. At Manifest Technologies, we call it "the kiss."*

Milo was still talking. Something about an angry little engineer and a ship called the *Halcyon*. How someone was coming to take them all away. And Dagda was listening. She couldn't *not* listen. But she was also lying on a table at the Manifest Technologies shop on Jules Verne Avenue four hundred years ago, coming alive for the first time as Dagda Prowst and seeing her father, his back turned, talking to a saleswoman and asking her if anyone had ever painted her portrait before.

She was sitting on the sidewalk with her wrists chained, every system in her body telling her that this filthy, skinny, strange, quiet boy was the most important thing in the world.

She was holding her father's hand and walking out of Manifest Technologies and listening to the door sing her a song: *Home, home, time to go home.*

She was in her room at the Toymaker's house, where a man who looked like an older, shorter, fatter version of Sanel was shouting at her, telling her that she would be safer if she just stayed where he put her. If she would just do the least little thing to preserve her systems. If she would just stay hidden. He washed the blood off of her with cold water from a bucket. None of it was hers.

Meanwhile, the boy just talked and talked. He couldn't stop himself. What he really wanted to know was what Dagda thought about all of it, and what had happened to her and, really, what she *was* (like *inside*), and how that was even possible, and why she'd never told him, but the words just wouldn't come. So he talked, hoping that his mouth would find its own way to the right thing to say, even if it seemed like he was only getting further and further away.

And then, all of a sudden, Jules was there, too—walking up along the curve of the wall—and Milo leapt up and grabbed him and hugged him (awkwardly) and pounded him on the back with a fierce energy and wondered (briefly) what Jules's insides were made of, but he didn't ask. He just said it was good to see him and, without thinking, started all over at the beginning and told all the stories a second time. He was so busy talking, he didn't notice the way Jules stood and shook and held his hands in front of himself, kneading them like they were made of dough.

Dagda noticed. She watched Milo as the words poured out of him like water, like he was trying to fill the entire night with his own voice. And she watched Jules stand and blink and wait for the torrent to end before he said the one important thing he had to say.

"The doctor was dead."

Then it was his turn to tell a story—to explain how he'd gone to see the Total King's doctor to get medicine for Sig's hand and had found the doctor's body instead, inside his little house on Clops Hill, cold and dead and smelling like . . .

"Like nothing I've ever smelled. Like nothing I could ever imagine."

But he was dead was the point. Beaten. Jules had gathered up some things that he thought might be useful, and then he'd held his breath and covered the doctor's body with a blanket, because the doctor had been a smart man who'd known how to fix things that were broken, and he'd deserved better than what he'd gotten.

Dagda asked Jules if he was okay.

And Jules said, "This day . . ." He shook his head. "Something about this day just feels like it's been wrong from the start."

And Milo bobbed his head up and down. He smiled because he thought Jules would've wanted him to. "It just feels that way, Jules," he said. "It's nothing." Then he reached out and took him by the shoulder, shaking him a little, his smile getting wider and crazier until it became that bright, blazing look the boy wore when he wanted to say (to *insist*) that life was all just a crooked game where winning was only a matter of deciding not to lose.

"And we can leave now if we want to," he said. "All of us. I found us a way out. We can be pirates, just like we said."

"We're going to be pirates?" Dagda asked. "When did we decide this?"

"Air pirates," said Jules.

"And we can just fly away from here. No more Cuthbert. No more tithe. No more worrying. The Captain said—"

"Wait," said Dagda, her voice full of suspicion, because at no point during either telling of his story had Milo said he was planning to *actually leave*. With this stranger. On his airship full of strangers. "You're not actually . . ."

"Let's go home," Milo said. "Tell everyone else."

And that's what they did, the two boys walking with Milo's arm draped over Jules's shoulders, telling him again and again about the ship and how he bet that if they asked, the Captain would let them steer it.

Dagda walked behind, saying nothing at all.

# ARIK THE ACES

**ARIK THE ACES** took Moric Shaw down around the corner. In an alley that smelled of lye and burning garbage he looked closely at Shaw and asked him, "So you want to be the new Total King, then?"

Shaw said, "No, Arik! No, that ain't what I'm thinking about at all!"

And that was true, because as much as Moric Shaw had thought about any of this (which was not that much), he hadn't thought at all about *that*. The Total King was the Total King. Was Cuthbert, who Shaw had stood by for almost all of his life. It was Bert who'd made him something, who'd told him he belonged somewhere and given Shaw's life a purpose. He'd risen with Cuthbert, through Total King after Total King until Bert had *become* the King. And Shaw was his right hand. He was Cuthbert's friend.

"He won't never let you kill Quick," said Arik. "*Never.*"

"Will," said Shaw. "Has to."

"Won't. Quick's an earner. Dependable."

Shaw picked angrily at the plaster on his arm. The pain was like a burn that wouldn't go away. It was so bad it made him thirsty. "He will. I'll ask him as a favor."

"Total King needs the Quick kid, and his gang, too. Just does. And he ain't gonna let none go for no favors. Not even to you."

Shaw thought about this for a second, then shook his head. "No. He owes me."

"Bert's the King," said Arik. "He don't owe."

"He's my friend."

"If you think so. But what're you thinking to do when he says no?"

And finally, Shaw couldn't take it anymore, so he went into his pocket with his good hand and took out the little bottle and pulled off the cap with its dropper and touched just the tip of it to his tongue. Just the tiniest little bit. And then, for good measure, he did it again.

A cloud enveloped him. It was magic. He was warm and shivering at the same time. His arms were longer than they ought to be, stretchy. He looked at Arik the Aces, who stared at him, tilting his head one way and then the other, and it was like Shaw was seeing him through shimmering water.

"Do what I need to," he said. "But first we do the ask. You with me?"

"Course I am," said Arik, smiling. "Whatever happens. But we's gonna need some more friends for this business tonight."

# SANDMAN

**CLEAR OF THE JOSTLING MOB** on High Street, Ennis sat on a bench outside a hardware shop with a smashed front window and scrubbed at his hair with his nails. He cursed under his breath and thought again about going up into the aeries and burning the *Halcyon*. Or maybe he'd circle back and find that captain again, tail him up into the Spire and then, at just the right moment, set him flying. Accidents happened all the time up there in the high cradles. Things that could always be made to look like just missteps or bad luck.

He thought about the boy. Milo was alive, and that was a comfort. On his own two feet, which was good. He thought about just going to the wrecked ship where they all lived and taking the boy away, but it occurred to him that there was nowhere to go, really. For all the years that Ennis Arghdal had spent watching Milo Quick, he'd never really wondered why. Being the sort of man he was, the whys of things never much mattered to him, and he'd never asked. He'd been given a task and he meant to complete it. That's all there was.

But Ennis was also a smart man, and a cunning one, too. He knew that something was happening with Milo that he could only see the edges of. And this infuriated him.

(Furious people—even smart ones—often make bad choices.

They do things they would not normally do. And Ennis Arghdal is about to do exactly that. Just watch.)

The Sandman stood up suddenly, shooting to his feet so fast he nearly jumped. He looked off down High Street, making a face like he'd seen someone he recognized from very far away, and then he started walking quickly with his head down and his hands in his pockets, knowing exactly where he had to go.

It was nearly a half hour before he looked up again. And when he did, he was standing in front of a fancy house on Apollo Avenue with a heavy door and a knocker in the shape of a brass fist garlanded in roses.

# SHAW

**SIMO DAHL SAID YES** after Arik punched him in the stomach and held him by the neck and shook him and shouted, "Say yes! Say yes!" into his face over and over again. Winter Bartel was easier. She'd shrugged, wiped some snot from under her nose and said okay.

Vitek Harsha had been working a corner near Shippers Alley. Arik had called out to him and said, "Doing a killing, Vit. Milo Quick and all his little rats. My man Moric here is after some revengement and wants to make a sweep of it. You in?"

Vitek had looked Shaw slowly up and down. "The King . . ." he said.

"Not your concern, Vit," said Arik. "Not a bit. We need killers and Moric Shaw has chosen you. You gonna be our man? Swear it."

And Vitek Harsha had said okay because he wasn't really friends with Milo or Jules or any of the rest of them and didn't really have anything better to do anyway.

The gang grew. These boys and girls that Shaw had picked. Names he knew. Who'd taken his orders before. Most of them knew what they were really saying when they stood before Arik the Aces and held up a hand and spat and swore they'd be loyal

to Moric Shaw. Most of them knew a change was coming. Cuthbert DeGeorge had made few friends since taking the chair and
becoming Total King Forever.

But he'd made plenty of enemies.

# SANDMAN

**ENNIS ARGHDAL** banged with the knocker, and no one came to the door of the house on Apollo Avenue. He banged harder and kicked at the door for good measure, but still no one came. He shouted and cursed and kicked and then, as a last resort, he tried the knob.

The door was unlocked and it swung inward on silent, well-oiled hinges.

# SHAW

**SHAW KNEW** that Bert would be at the Summer Palace. He rarely left it anymore. A thousand nights they'd spent together on these streets—robbing and smashing and, most of the time, just walking like proud, hard soldiers, the arrogance of youth and belonging baking off them like heat, knowing that they owned every stone they stepped on because there wasn't anyone to tell them any different.

But since Bert had become Total King, it'd been different. Bert sat in his chair now, and he shouted and made demands. To Shaw, there was no feeling in the world like walking through the Marche with ten boys at his back and knowing that no man, mother, or law could tell him what to do. But most of what he'd done since Cuthbert DeGeorge had become Total King was stand beside Bert's stupid chair and pretend like that was just as good.

# MILO

**MILO AND DAGDA AND JULES** went home to Fort Kick-Ass. Inside, Keelan was pacing nervously up and down the floor of the main room and Llyr wasn't talking to anyone and Tristan (who'd decided that he was in charge since no one else wanted to be) was shouting at everyone and Arun sat with Sig, who was wide-eyed, pale, sweating, and holding his own hand in his lap like it was some kind of wounded animal.

"I leave home for a few hours and look what happens," Milo said, and then he laughed too loudly and with a sharpness that rang on the iron walls.

# ENNIS ARGHDAL IN
# THE HOUSE OF ROSES

**ENNIS HAD BEEN TO THE HOUSE** on Apollo Avenue only twice before. Once on the night he'd been hired to fetch the boy and watch over him, and again on the night he'd brought the boy back to the Flying City. He hadn't liked it then, all cramped and crowded with boxes and shelves full of things he had no names for—pieces of metal and plastic and glass, machines furred with dust, stacks of faded plastic toys, curved boxes with glass faces, lamps and clocks and books. But he liked it even less now because it was nearly empty.

He called into the echoing darkness of the house and heard nothing back but his own voice. He knew the names of a few of the men who'd employed him, so he tried shouting all of those as he stomped around, looking through dark rooms all stripped to the walls. He went through an empty kitchen, then a dining room and, still shouting, turned a corner and went into a kind of open space with a curving staircase and a scuffed, cracked, stained tile floor. An electrified chandelier hung down from the distant ceiling.

Here, mountains of sealed cases and luggage were laid out in piles on the floor. Someone, Ennis thought, had been in the process of leaving this place for a very long time and this was the end of it. Last things. Those most precious. He reached into his pocket and took out a box of matches, struck one and, in its glow, saw a lovely vase sitting atop a stack of cloth-draped boxes.

He knocked it to the floor and the smash of it was like music to him.

Ennis shook out the first match and lit a second. He snapped back the corner of a sheet and saw a wooden case filled with bottles and lifted one out and dropped it onto the tiles. It smashed, so he took a second, examined the faded label, nodded appreciatively, and then turned and hurled it as hard as he could up into the tinkling glass of the chandelier, making it rain crystal and fine gold loops. Then he shouted all the names he knew again, one after the other, shook out the match and started kicking holes in the soft plaster of the walls.

"I know you're here!" he shouted into the dark. "You left all your rich man's crap behind!"

He lifted up the whole wooden case of bottles and threw it to the ground. The smell of sweetness and alcohol was overwhelming now. He rattled the matchbox by his ear. He still had a couple left.

"Now either someone can come out here and talk to me or I can start lighting things on fire!" he yelled. "What's it going to be?"

When the lights blazed on—the electric chandelier flaring into a hot and gleaming brightness—Ennis refused to shade his eyes and he refused to duck his head. His hands were knotted into fists and his jaw ached from clenching his teeth, and even though he had the sudden, animal fear of something attacking him in his blindness, he was stubborn and did not move.

"Officer Arghdal," said a voice from above him. "Gods, you do know how to make a mess when you put your mind to it, don't you?"

# SHAW

**WORD SPREAD** that Moric Shaw was going to visit the king.

Boys and girls came up to him panting, out of breath, grinning crookedly around missing teeth. When they asked Shaw what he was doing, he would say, "Going to kill Milo Quick," because it made him feel good to say it out loud. When they asked him what the Total King was going to say, Shaw would say, "Gonna say yes," because he was so sure of it. And then he would laugh, because with his head set to drifting again by the medicine, his voice sounded strange and slow in his own ears.

Some of them carried sticks or bats or pipes or knives. Some of them tried to touch Shaw, because on a night like this, his confidence felt a little bit like magic. Some of them tried to bow but Arik would shove them, tell them to save it, to shut up and get in line.

Shaw didn't care. Shaw didn't even notice. His gaze would flicker upward to the darkening bands of sky visible between cargo lines or slumping roofs, and he would see the white bird again and again. The one from the market. The one that'd sat on Milo's head in his dream. He would smile at it. Wave. The white bird was showing him the way.

And so Moric Shaw crossed the Street of Sailmakers on his way to the Summer Palace with an army behind him.

Or anyway, enough of one to do what needed to be done.

# SANDMAN

**IN THE HOUSE OF ROSES** on Apollo Avenue, Ennis Arghdal stood under the punishing whiteness of the chandelier's flaring light. Above him, Callias Fusco waited with his hands on the staircase banister. He had three men with him, and as Ennis's eyes adjusted, he could see the hard faces, the uniforms, the rifles.

"Callias," he said. "Going somewhere?"

"As far from here as we can get and as quick as we can go."

"I have some questions. And I swear, if anyone else points a gun at me today, I am going to feed it to them with a delightful cream sauce and a nice bottle of wine. And I'm going to sit there until they swallow every piece."

Callias Fusco laughed. "Bit late for that, Ennis," he said. "You smashed the last of the wine. And as you probably noticed, the kitchen is closed."

# THE TOTAL KING FOREVER

**THE TOTAL KING FOREVER** of the Marche and Everything in It sat on his throne and chewed at his thumbnail, idly wondering why it was so quiet tonight and whether he ought to be doing something about that.

He looked out over the floor of the Summer Palace, where a couple dozen of his boys still lingered, either playing quietly or sleeping or just talking. After that thing with Arik and the rock the other day, it was like a new line had been drawn, and now everyone stayed farther away from the throne. They didn't look at him unless they had to.

"Why is everyone so quiet!" he suddenly bellowed from his chair. "Why isn't anyone *doing* anything!"

Eyes turned up toward him from the floor. They caught the light of burning lamps and seemed to glow. Animal eyes in the dark.

Cuthbert banged his cane on the boards and shouted, "I'm bored! It's too quiet here. What should we do?"

He missed Shaw. Whenever he'd been bored before, he would have Shaw go out on the floor and fight someone. They'd draw a circle and lay bets. Make rules like no kicking or everyone gets a stick except Shaw. And even if the Total King Forever didn't really understand how odds worked, he would always collect, because

Shaw always won. Shaw never disappointed him. Never questioned.

And then, as though thinking about him had summoned him, the door to the Summer Palace opened, and there was Shaw, back from the doctor with a plaster cast on his arm and a gang following behind him. Arik was there. Azhar Biel, Winter Bartel, Vitek Harsha, and some others, too.

"Shaw!" the Total King yelled, and clapped his hands together. "I was just thinking about you!"

# THE RICH MAN
# AND THE SANDMAN

**CALLIAS FUSCO DISMISSED HIS GUARDS.** They went and sat on the floor, rifles across their knees. Callias wore good shoes, glasses pushed up into his thatch of white hair. He rolled the sleeves of his white shirt to his elbows, came down the stairs and leaned against one of the stacks of boxes near Ennis Arghdal like he had all the time in the world.

"You are stubborn, Ennis," he said. "*Dedicated* might be a nicer word, but *stubborn* is more correct. I've never doubted that you were the right man for this job. Of all the things I've bought, I think you were the most useful."

"You didn't buy me, Callias."

"Fine. *Rented,* if that makes you feel better. But you have to find a way out now. You've done a good job, but it's over."

The Sandman growled. This was the same thing Callias had said to him a week ago, and that conversation had ended badly. Now he stalked back and forth on the bare floor under the bright white lights and said, "I've been watching this boy for most of his life. I'm not sure you get to tell me when it's over."

"But it is," said Callias. "Over. There's nothing more to be done. We're actually surprised the Armada has held off this long. They're determined. They know she's here. Have for a very long time. But now they see her as a threat. Or a treasure. Or both, maybe."

"She?"

"The girl, Ennis. Dagda Prowst. This is about the girl. Have you not figured that out yet? It has *always* been about the girl. The boy no longer matters, unless . . ." And Callias let that last word hang in the air, heavy and lazy. He let it hang so long that his guards looked up, blinking, feeling the weight of it like the drop at the tip of an icicle, quivering and waiting to fall.

Eventually, Ennis spoke. "You're waiting for me to say *unless what*, but I'm not playing games with you, Callias. Not tonight."

Callias shrugged and rolled his eyes. "Stubborn," he said. "Violent. Single-minded. But never too bright."

Ennis stared at the rich old man in his shirtsleeves, with his mussy white hair and sagging, tired face, and the rich old man looked back at him.

"I'm not afraid of you, Sandman. I mean, what are you going to do? Kill me?" Callias chuckled. "The Armada may do that for you anyway. Who knows? But in the meantime, you can stop posing. I know what you are. I know what you're capable of."

"You think so?"

Callias waved a hand at the Sandman, turned his back, and began to walk slowly, running his fingers across the things stacked in his fancy room. "They're very angry and very worried," he said. "The Armada, I mean. The men from the Ministries who are commanding it and paying for it. *Powerful* men, who are trying to shape the future. Their ships have come from . . . I don't even know how many places. How many ports. The Ministries are strong and they think they can get what they want with violence. That's the only way they think." He shrugged. "Though, to be fair, it's always worked for them before."

"She's one girl. That kind of violence? Should be more than enough."

Callias shook his head. "No. Because they don't understand her the way we do. *You* don't understand her. We've been watching her for a very long time, and I'm convinced that there is no number of guns or men or ships that will make a difference. She'll meet force with ten times greater force. And if that's not enough, she'll vanish. Hide. Sleep. It's what she has always done. Powerful as they are, the Ministries are relatively new to this game, and that's one of the things they've never understood, the way the girl experiences time. How little any of us matter to her. So, by tomorrow, a lot of people will be dead and the Flying City will be in ruin and none of it will mean anything, because Dagda Prowst will be gone. We may not see her again for another hundred years. But in a generation or two, things might be different. The Ministries might think they've beaten us, but we will wait and hide, just like the girl will. Conserve our energies. Like you should, Sandman."

"Don't call me that."

Callias Fusco folded his arms across his chest and considered Ennis down the bridge of his nose. "But isn't that what you are? The terrifying Sandman of Highgate? How many awful things have you done in defense of that boy?"

"For *you*," Ennis said.

"For me? No, not for me. He was just some boy."

"No," said Ennis.

"Worthless except for what he could bring to us. And the things you did, Sandman . . ."

"I protected him!" Ennis roared. "That was my job! And he's somewhere on the streets right now with no idea what's coming." He pointed a finger at the old man. "All these years, Callias. And now you're running away and leaving him here?"

"The boy drew her out. Kept her visible. He was *bait*, Ennis. That's all. Chum in the water to bring the shark. And we were able to observe so much. The plan worked, we just never had the chance to—"

"Bait? That's what Milo was to you?"

"Alef," Callias said slowly. "Not *Milo*, Alef. Alef Prowst. Or have you forgotten?"

Ennis threw up his hands in frustration and Callias glanced around at the cases and boxes and the guards behind him, then down at the watch on his wrist. "You have time for a story, Ennis? A quick one, I promise."

"Not really, no."

"It's something you should know. I mean, that's what you're here for, right? Information? Finally, now, just when it's exactly too late to matter? Or what? Did you just want money or thanks or—"

Ennis said something nasty to Callias about what he could do with his money and his thanks, and Callias smiled warmly and broadly. "Sit, then. Just for a minute."

Callias turned and told the men waiting to pick up some boxes and load them, to do *something* useful other than holding up that wall with their backs. Then he turned back to the Sandman, leaned comfortably against the bottom-most post of the banister, and said, "The boy, Alef, never really mattered at all except that he was related to Yuri Prowst. Because he was the son of a son of a son of a son of the man who was Dagda Prowst's father a long, long time ago. But since Alef was a direct descendant, he still had some drop of Yuri's blood in him. And the girl—the machine *pretending* to be Dagda Prowst—somehow knows that. We have no idea how. There's so little we understand about her." Callias paused, made a face. "Or *it*, I suppose?"

"Her," said the Sandman.

Callias shrugged. "As you wish. There's so little we understand about *her*, then. And bringing Alef Prowst here was an experiment, but it worked beautifully. We hoped he might draw her out into the open, and he did. So, *of course* the stupid boy was bait. But let's begin a bit further back."

Callias pointed up at the wall behind Ennis. At a painting hung there, framed, huge, taller than both of them standing on each other's shoulders. "See that?" he asked. "We've been studying Dagda Prowst for more than a hundred years now. We're getting better at it. But when this all started? That was all we had. *The Girl on the Grass* by Yuri Prowst. That's the original. His most famous painting. He did it after the death of his real daughter four hundred years ago. The last painting he ever made."

Ennis turned to look up at the canvas. He could recognize the shape of the bowl where Oldedge Market now sat. The low white walls and pillars where, now, there was just the tumbled ruin of a wall. And he could recognize Dagda, the girl, dancing on the grass, feet barely touching the ground, her face half turned over her shoulder, surrounded by red roses. Roses piled at her feet, stretching to the far edges of the painting and off into the distance until the smallest of them were just dots. Pinpricks of red in the grass.

"That's her," he said. "Dagda."

"It is."

"But how—"

"There are 2,343 roses," Callias said. "We've counted them. One for every passenger who died aboard the ship that his wife and daughter were traveling on. The *star*ship, Ennis. One that traveled through space, from planet to planet."

And Ennis Arghdal said a rude, disbelieving word. A *starship*? That was just nonsense. No one traveled through the stars.

"Not now, no. But then? Yes. That's what we believe. That people went from planet to planet in space the same way that we now go from city to city. That they had machines of inconceivable complexity—machines like the girl—and could do things that we can barely understand now. But something terrible happened. We don't know what, exactly, but we do know that there is a rose in Yuri Prowst's painting for every passenger aboard that starship except *one*. Yuri didn't paint a rose for his daughter. Because he still had her."

"How?"

"He had a *machine* version of her, Ennis. And what a machine! Exactly like his daughter in every way except that she would never grow up, never grow old. It was enough. And the painting was all we had for the longest time. Rumors. Legends. Fairy tales of a remarkable girl in the Flying City who never aged and could not die. And that painting. That's how this all began."

Callias sighed. "The mechanical Dagda had within her all the memories of the real Dagda Prowst. And we know . . ." He paused, corrected himself. "We're *fairly confident* that this was commonplace back then. These disposable, mechanical bodies. The way we believe it worked was that the machine would've lived Dagda's life here, in the Flying City. It would've *been* Dagda Prowst. And then, when the real Dagda Prowst arrived here from wherever she was coming from, the machine would've had all those memories inside it. Everything the machine had done in the time that it was living the real Dagda's life. The two of them, the real Dagda and the machine, would've lain down side by side in some kind of apparatus—we don't really understand how it worked then—and they would've slept and dreamed together. When it was done, the machine Dagda would be empty and the real Dagda would have all of its memories. Like a fairy spell. Like *magic*. And then the machine would be discarded. Destroyed. Forgotten like an empty bottle of wine."

"I don't believe in fairy spells, Callias."

"And neither do we. We know it was technology. That it was devices and boxes and wires. We just don't know how it worked. And that's the point, really. Because the real Dagda Prowst never came back to the Flying City—because she *died*—the machine was never switched off. Never emptied."

He looked past Ennis then, up to the painting hung high on the wall, and walked toward it slowly while he spoke. "Imagine what it knows, Ennis. What it has *seen*. Dagda Prowst was alive during the Enlargement, and the machine out there has all of her memories. Then four hundred more years of collapse and contraction. Can you imagine the things it could tell us? All of the things we've collected. The things that once filled this house. That filled entire *warehouses* in the Marche. All of the books, clocks that ran with no clockworks, boxes that broadcast the news, wires that carried people's voices, ships that could fly through the stars. She could explain it all. The Ministries, they see her as a threat. And she *is*. She absolutely is. But where they see her like a gun pointed at a rich man, relieving him of his wallet, and our compatriots overseas fighting against the Ministries see her as a bomb capable of bringing a whole rotted structure down, my associates and I here? We see her differently. To us, it has always seemed best that she be used like a slow poison. Lethal, but completely undetectable. She could tell us more in an hour about the world we lost than we've discovered in a hundred years. Just imagine what someone could do with that knowledge. That *power*."

Callias turned suddenly, standing beneath *The Girl on the Grass* and looking back at the Sandman. "Do you wonder why we've never just scooped her up and brought her here? Taken her apart piece by piece? Asked her all the questions we need answered? She's just a twelve-year-old girl, right?"

Ennis said nothing. He stood and stared.

"Because it's a machine that survived the end of the world. That survived the Great Silence. That survived *four centuries* of waiting. This has made her more dangerous than you can possibly imagine. The Ministries have sent men after her before—hunters and trackers. Dagda killed all of them. You have no idea what she is capable of. *We* have no idea. But we know that Alef Prowst—your boy, Milo—would've been our best chance to get some answers from her if only we'd had a little more time."

"And if the Armada finds her?" Ennis asked.

Callias shook his head. "You still don't understand. The Ministries organized the Armada and sent it here to find Dagda Prowst. To capture her if they can and destroy her if they can't. But no kidnapper will ever lay a hand on her. The Armada can shake the entire city to the stones and the girl will be fine. She has survived four hundred years. We're confident she can survive this."

"Then what about the others? These pirates from the *Halcyon* looking for the boy?"

Callias sighed. "Idiots," he said. "From Terminal, the City of Doors, where the fighting has been worst. Our . . ." —he hesitated a moment, searching for the right word— ". . . *organization*, for lack of a better word, is large. All these years. Generations of academics, researchers, scientists, teachers." He puffed up a bit, like a little lizard trying to make itself large. "A few wise patrons like myself. But we don't always agree on best practices. We don't agree on much of anything, really. Those who've been fighting the Ministries the longest—in Terminal, Ofrad, and Obrya—now believe that the world is best served by the girl being brought out into the light immediately. *Shared*"—he said like it was a dirty word—"with everyone."

The Sandman watched him carefully.

"They thought they could use the boy for this. Could steal him right out from under the Armada's nose in the hope that Dagda would follow. So they hired this airship pilot with whatever pocket change they could scrape together and hoped to lure the girl away from Highgate and those of us who've been studying her for so long. They believe that she will follow wherever the boy goes. That she won't be able to help herself. But it doesn't matter now. That ship was their last hope, but they came too late, took too long. They don't have the resources required to make it through the blockade. They'll die here, same as the boy will. And all that will be left is the girl."

"And that's all that matters? The girl."

"She is all that has *ever mattered*, Ennis. Alef Prowst was just a way to find her. To bring her out of hiding. Yuri remarried after his wife and real daughter were lost. At least twice. He had five more children. Five more branches on the family tree. We have records. And now that we know about the machine's bonding protocols— the girl's response to the family bloodline—we are confident it'll respond to any blood relative of Yuri Prowst. We don't know how, but if the boy has proved anything, it's that the machine's protocols are still intact. So we'll find her again. We've learned to look at time the way a machine does. Some of us have gotten very good at waiting. We can afford to be patient."

"And in the meantime . . ."

"In the meantime, what?" asked Callias. "None of us matter individually, Sandman. We never have. Our lives? They're just a sigh to the girl. A blink. She was alive when your grandfather's grandfather was. She'll still be alive when your children's children are. The only thing that matters is what kind of world they'll live in. This ruined one? Or the one that Dagda Prowst once knew?"

Callias turned and looked back up at the painting on the wall. "Think for a minute. How did this begin with us? With you and me? The girl had been missing for years. Decades. No one knew where she was. But then we found Dragan Prowst, the boy's father, in a gutter in Arcpoint. He was a drunk, Ennis. A criminal. You *met* him, so you know. The man was willing to *give up his own son* for . . . what? What did that cost us?"

"Six hundred dollars," Ennis said. He'd never forgotten the weight of the envelope in his hand.

"For six hundred dollars? Gods, you can't say we didn't give the boy a better life than he would've had. That we didn't *save* him, in a way. And if we had to trade six hundred dollars and the lives of Dragan and Alef to bring Dagda Prowst out of hiding for a little while? Then it was worth it. Absolutely worth—"

"He can't ever know," Ennis interrupted. "The boy. Not ever."

Callias shrugged. "He's going to be dead, Ennis. It won't matter. Unless . . ."

"Unless what?" asked Ennis.

And Callias Fusco smiled. "Got you," he said.

# MORIC SHAW AND
# THE TOTAL KING FOREVER

**AT THE TOTAL KING'S SUMMER PALACE,** Moric
Shaw stepped through the door at the head of his army to find
Cuthbert on his throne, applauding.

"Shaw!" barked the Total King. "Fight with Arik! I'll give you
a dollar if you win. Arik, you get two if you can beat Shaw."

"No," said Shaw.

"Come on, now. Everyone clear a space."

And Shaw, his head swimming and his mouth dry and his
heart as light as a balloon in his chest, said "No" again, and kept
approaching Cuthbert's throne, his gathered troops at his back.

The Total King leaned forward in his chair. "No?" he asked.
"Did you just say *'no'* to me, Shaw?"

Shaw's good hand went to his mouth, where he felt his numb
face with his fingers. The white bird stood behind Cuthbert's chair
now, huge and bright, watching him with its pebble eyes. It'd led
him all the way here, that bird. It would show him the way to Milo
Quick, too. "No," he said again.

The Total King's eyebrows squinched together. "Wait. Are you
saying 'no,' like you didn't just say no to me? Or just 'no' again,
like no, you're not going to do what I say?"

Shaw's steps faltered. All those words. And he didn't want to seem dumb in front of Arik and the others. Not now, when he'd come all this way. So he plowed on. He said "No" again because it seemed strong. Forceful. "No, I ain't gonna fight with Arik. I need—"

"No?" said Cuthbert.

"We're here because we're gonna—"

The Total King leapt up from his throne, whipped his cane around and pointed it at Shaw like a rapier. He said, "You don't get to say no to me, *Moric*."

Shaw flinched. He remembered the pain of that cane hitting his arm. He remembered the sickening crack. Of collapsing on the floor right here, where he stood right now. He said, "I'm gonna kill Milo Quick." Then he said it again, trying to keep the conversation focused. "We are. Gonna kill Milo and all his gang. Gonna do it tonight. Okay?"

Slowly, the Total King of the Marche and Everything in It stepped to the edge of the platform on which sat his scrap-wood throne. The boards sagged under his weight as he stood and leaned, glowering down at Moric Shaw. "Are you asking my permission, Moric?"

"Yeah, I—"

"Are you asking *permission* to murder a member of this gang? *My* gang? Several of them, actually? Are you asking me if you can kill one of my best earners for . . . Wait, why do you want to do this exactly?"

Shaw stood in silence for a long, terrible moment because he couldn't recall just then exactly why he'd wanted to kill Milo. He knew there were reasons. He hated the boy, but he couldn't get his tongue around the whys of it. Behind him, he could hear all of his army shifting nervously in place. Their confidence flaking away.

Shaw looked up at the Total King and whispered, "*You have to let me do this.*"

"Why, Shaw?" the Total King boomed. "*Why* would I let you do this?"

"Because I've been . . ."

"You've been what?"

"I've been good to you for—"

"Good to me? *Good* to me? You are a subject of the Total King of the Marche, Shaw! You do what you're told and then you tell me how great I am. That's how this works."

"But we've been . . ."

"What have we been?"

"We're . . ."

"What?"

"We're *friends*!" Shaw shouted.

"Friends?"

"We're friends and I ain't never asked you for nothing but this! Just this thing! And I'm gonna do it. Tonight. Whether you say—"

And then Cuthbert DeGeorge, the Total King Forever, leapt down from his throne and stood, furious, before Moric Shaw, the most loyal boy he'd ever known.

"You're giving me orders now, Moric?" he shouted, standing close enough that Shaw could feel Cuthbert's spittle on his face. "*You're* telling *me* how this is going to go?"

The white bird fluttered up into the air, and Shaw watched it as it circled once and landed on the head of the Total King Forever. It looked at him and Shaw looked back at it. He smiled. Then he looked down and met Cuthbert's eyes.

"I'm killing Milo Quick," he said.

"No, you're not," said Cuthbert. He spun up his cane and whipped it down toward Shaw in a blurring arc, but when Shaw saw it, it was moving so slowly. A beautiful, shining, bright line of pain that took days to descend. That gave him all the time in the world to raise his already-broken arm with its plaster and sticks and catch the cane about halfway down the shaft. It hurt, but not too much. There was a crack. This time, though, it was Cuthbert's cane that snapped.

And with his good hand, Moric Shaw had already drawn out the long, thin knife he'd taken from Dr. Milkman. When the cane broke, Cuthbert staggered forward right onto that knife. The blade slid easily through the cloth and leather he wore, sank into the meat of him. And Shaw caught his friend as he fell, wrapping the broken arm around him and holding him tight for just one last second before Cuthbert began to scream.

He jerked away from Shaw. He dropped the stump of his cane and clamped both hands over the hole in his belly and stared, eyes as big as saucers, mouth wide, at Shaw, who stood now with the bloodied knife in his hand, looking up toward the ceiling at something no one else could see.

The white bird, flapping away.

Cuthbert staggered and fell to one knee. He looked up and saw Arik, one of his best killers, and shrieked, "He killed me! Shaw killed me!"

"Ah, yes," said Arik, grinning and bending down to take something off the floor. "He did, didn't he. Ain't that some kind of shame?"

"Kill him, Arik! I'm your king! Kill him for me and you'll have . . ."

"I'll have what?" Arik said.

"Anything," said Cuthbert, but his eyes were on Arik's hand now. On what he'd picked up from the floor.

A rock.

"Arik?"

Arik the Aces bounced the rock once in his palm like he was

weighing it, then raised it and smashed it into the Total King's face. Then did it again. The rest of the boys and girls all had rocks, too. And Shaw watched as they closed in.

Cuthbert called Shaw's name once more. And then he was quiet.

And then he was dead.

And then Moric Shaw was Total King Forever.

"Now," he said to his panting, blood-spattered subjects. "Now we find Milo Quick."

And all of them poured, whooping and yelling, out into the night.

# UNTIL THE DAWN

**UNTIL THE DAWN,** nothing important happened. Nothing that anyone who lived would recall in a year or ten or a hundred.

Ennis Arghdal came limping out of the House of Roses with blood on his shirt and flames flickering in the windows behind him. He had a plan. Not a good one, but a better plan than no plan at all. Step one: Get the boy to safety. Step two: Don't die during step one. After that, things became less clear. Out on the dark streets, Ennis heard all kinds of whispers and terrible rumors of death and the murder of kings and he was worried—not least because it looked like he was going to be starting another day without any breakfast at all.

Cuthbert DeGeorge's body was never found. But then, by the time anyone thought about looking for it, it was just one of hundreds or thousands that couldn't be found. And after that, no one much cared.

Moric Shaw, freshly minted Total King Forever, led his army out into the Marche, where they gathered their numbers and spread the word. There was a new king. It was a new day. And in the meantime, Shaw sent the best of them out searching for Milo

Quick. It was nearly dawn by the time he got them organized and set to their tasks. Shaw looked and looked, but the white bird was nowhere to be found.

Up in the high cradles of the aerie, Reyn Farrago worked like a demon, lit by blazing lights, dripping sweat. The Captain had given him six hours to make the *Halcyon* ready for flight. Every inch of her. And Reyn had said that was impossible. That he had days of work left to do. And the Captain had replied, "Six hours or we die here," which, all things considered, was a motivating way to put it.

The Captain had already sent Semyon down to keep an eye on the boy. To stake out the place where he lived, get eyes on him, and to be ready, just after dawn, to take him and go.

"So we're back to being kidnappers?" Semyon had asked.

"Just tell him we can't wait any longer," Captain Klim had said, looking over the *Halcyon*'s chipped and splintered rail, down into the swirl of ships' lamps and running lights far below. All around them, small, fast ships were quietly filling their bags. Loading cargo under guard. Everyone was making ready to run. "The whole city knows what's going to happen come morning. So you find him, Semyon. You tell him. We'll bring the ship in low. Near Front Street. Tell him there's no more time. He won't say no."

"There's going to be trouble," said Semyon.

"Then we'll be in the middle of it, I guess," said the Captain. He pressed a couple of flares into Semyon's hand. "We'll be looking for you, old man. Light 'em up."

At Fort Kick-Ass, Milo edged his way into the bedroom and saw Sig lying there, asleep, his head pillowed on a tangle of blankets. Dagda had changed his bandages and given him some of the medicine that Jules had brought back from the doctor's wrecked house. Now she was brushing the sweat-stringy hair back from Sig's forehead, looking down at him with her bottle-green eyes, her skin a maze of pale, thin scars. And suddenly, the two Dagdas that had been battling in Milo's head since last night—the person and the machine—came together. They resolved like they were coming into focus, one existing inside the other or over the top of the other. And when Dagda looked up at him, the boy smiled at her and asked her how Sig was.

"He'll live," she said. "It's just some broken bones and some stitches. How are you?"

"I'll live," said Milo, and he came in and sat down on the other side of Sig. He touched Sig's forehead and his unbroken hand and said, "We're leaving here, Sig. All of us. We're going away."

And even though Sig was asleep and probably couldn't hear him, Milo sat there in the dark and told Sig all about the Captain and the *Halcyon*. How they were going to leave this place— fly away and never come back. That they'd start over somewhere where no one knew them, where they didn't owe anyone.

"Like air pirates," Jules said, coming to stand in the doorway, his arms folded across his chest. "Right, Milo?"

"Exactly."

He told Sig about what the Fish had said and what the Captain had said, about the Armada and the war. And even if he didn't entirely believe it himself, he told Sig that it was going to be dangerous here now—too dangerous for any of them to stay—but that they'd be going somewhere safe. Somewhere where no one wanted to hurt them.

Arun had slipped back into the room. And then Tristan, too, who stood beside Jules, his arms crossed the same way. And then Keelan, rubbing his eyes and looking groggy. And then Llyr, who sat in the door of her closet and listened to Milo with wide, sad eyes as he talked about mountains and seas and cities made of glass, about the Captain's ship and how fast it was. How it could take all of them far away from here, to places they couldn't even imagine, and how they'd never have to worry again.

"They're going to take me to my dad, Sig," Milo said, his voice cracking just a little when he said it out loud for the first time, like it was a real thing. "That's what the Captain said. That he'll take us all to go and see my dad."

Later, Milo Quick would look back on these hours—on his last full day in the Flying City—and think only of the mistakes he'd made. How everything had led to this moment and all the moments that would come afterward. He would think about the choices he had yet to make—ones that were coming, all of them bad—and he would hate the boy he'd been. Hate that he'd understood nothing and, in the end, sacrificed so much for so very little. He was twelve years old. Nearly thirteen. He should've known better. And the guilt he would feel would eat at him for years until, eventually, there were parts of him that were completely hollow. Growing up does that to nearly everyone. It is the price we pay.

But that would all come later. In the meantime, he filled up that long, last night with stories and promises that he would never be able to keep. And his friends believed him. Not because they were dumb or gullible, but because they were his friends. Keelan insisted that he would get airsick. Tristan said he would need to gather a few things first, meaning all of his best toys and treasures, which he would not leave without. And Arun said the same thing, though meaning gold stickpins and watches and wallets and coins that he and Sig had tucked away over the months, because he had no intention of leaving them behind for some other kid to find and get rich off of.

Llyr didn't say anything at all, but she did come and sit close up against Dagda, who braided her hair without really thinking about it, then took all the twists out and did it again.

After a while, Sig woke, and even though he was pale and dark under the eyes, he insisted that his hand was feeling better, and that, anyway, he was still a better thief with one hand than Arun was with two.

"We've got work to do," said Tristan. "Got a trip to plan for, don't we?"

"We do," said Milo, nodding and smiling.

"Think we were going to let you have all the fun?" asked Jules. "Been sitting around a whole day, most of us, while you and Mouse were out there having adventures. So where do we meet?"

"Front Street," Milo said. "At sunrise. Go gather up whatever you'll need or whatever you can't leave behind, then we'll meet up on Front Street and either find the Captain or make our way up to the aeries all together. And be careful. If anything goes wrong along the way, just head straight for Front Street. Somewhere with a view."

And so, just before dawn, they left Fort Kick-Ass together for the last time, scattering and fanning out through the Marche full of joy and excitement. Alef Prowst, the boy who called himself Milo Quick, stood in the rich, liquid shadows on the fringes of the breaking yard and watched his friends peel off into the dark, laughing and calling each other's names. It was already warm even though the sun was barely a promise on the distant horizon. The air was sticky and still. The last few minutes of darkness held on to their quiet like they knew how much loudness was coming next.

Later, Milo would weep and regret. But not today. Not now.

Later, when he was asked about this day, he would sigh and shake his head. "I would always be twelve years old if I could," Milo would say. "And every day would be the first day of summer and I would never, ever leave the Flying City."

# THE LAST DAY

✦

## HIGHGATE, THE FLYING CITY

# DAGDA, MILO, AND JULES

**KEELAN** went straight to Front Street with Tristan and Llyr, because Keelan knew a place they could get bread and candy for the trip without having to pay. Sig and Arun walked off toward the Blue Lights to gather their own kinds of supplies. And then it was just Milo and Jules and Dagda standing alone, at the edge of home. The three of them together, like it always had been.

"So Oldedge, then?" asked Milo.

"Last look around for old times' sake?" said Jules.

And Milo nodded, but Dagda said, "No," and took a step back from the boys, who both looked at her and asked what was wrong.

She couldn't explain. Not to Milo, and certainly not to Jules. But as the hours and minutes of dark had ticked away, she'd known she was going to have to make some decisions. Milo was hers. For years, he'd been a fixed point in her head, a dot marked *home* on a map of her world. The darkest, deepest parts of her protocols bound her to him the way they had to Yuri Prowst, her father, and even if the signals were confused now, the rules were the same. She couldn't leave him. Couldn't *lose* him after centuries of being alone.

But if he left the Flying City with this airship captain, what would she do? Sanel was here. His workshop in the basement. A hundred years of spare parts. For generations, the Toymakers had kept her operational, guarding her secret and allowing her to pass as a real twelve-year-old girl. Her mechanical sister Philomena, the Marie-12, was here. The only other thing like her that she'd ever met. Oldedge, the wall, most of the memories she had of her father. Those were all here and present. *Real* to her in the strange ways her mind worked. Four hundred years of life balanced against the ancient grinding needs of her bonding protocols. Her version of love.

"If we're going," she said slowly, "if we're leaving here, I'm going to need some things. I have to . . ."

"We've got time, Mouse," Jules said. He stretched and scratched and said that he had a few coins in his pocket and that a coffee might do them all wonders, what with it being earlier than even the birds were up.

"All of yesterday sitting around the house doing half of nothing, and still you're afraid of a little honest work, Jules?" said Milo.

"Ain't that I'm afraid of it," he replied. "Just that I'd like to take my time sneaking up on it."

They both laughed, and Dagda tried to laugh, too, even though she didn't feel like laughing at all.

# COFFEE WITH SABEEN

**SABEEN THE MACHINE** was clunking around the top of Oldedge. For a minute, Milo made nothing more of him than he ever did. Sabeen was as much of a fixture here as the stones. But then he saw Sabeen's leg—that rough, grinding conglomeration of iron and disc joints and lock bars—and he was reminded of the terrible, clicking legs of the spider maid in Sanel's library, and of the beautiful, gory, sparking mess he'd seen in his brief look at the inside of Dagda's broken arm.

The moment passed. He told himself that as soon as they were away from here, in the air, flying, safe, he would find a minute to talk to Dagda. He would ask her all the things he needed to ask and find out what she was and where she'd come from. He didn't know how long they'd be with the Captain exactly, but he thought there'd probably be time.

Meanwhile, Jules got the coffee. Milo told him they'd be free.

"Traded with Sabeen, day before yesterday," he said. "Our coffee is free all week."

"I almost feel like we should stay, then," Jules said, grinning. "Seems a shame to waste free coffee."

Sabeen smiled and waved and winked at Dagda and blew a kiss. "Slow business this morning," he shouted, his voice huge, and filling, it seemed, the whole world. "But I'm happy to see three kind faces!" He was wearing the coat Milo had stolen. It fit him like it was made for him.

Jules brought three cups, sweet with cream. Though they couldn't see it from Oldedge, on the far horizon the sky was just beginning to pink with daylight.

# DEAD BOY

**A MINUTE LATER,** Jules looked over the rim of his tin cup and said, "Hey. That's Arik and his boys, isn't it? What're they doing here?"

Milo looked and Jules was right. It was Arik the Aces, one of the Total King's lieutenants, walking under a thin scrim of electric light shining out of the mouth of some nameless alley. He had maybe a dozen of his soldiers with him—boys and girls that Milo knew, all trailing in his shadow. And coming right toward them, too.

"That's strange," said Milo, finishing his cup in a swallow and wiping his mouth. "Looks like he's got business, doesn't he?"

Jules finished his own cup, then hooked Milo's out of his hand and twirled them both on his fingers like a pistol fighter showing off.

"He's always strange," said Dagda.

Jules asked, "Done with that cup, Mouse?"

She drank off the last of the sweet coffee and handed the cup to Jules, who ran back to hand them off to Sabeen.

"You okay?" Milo asked her.

"What do you mean?"

He shrugged. "I don't know. I mean, are you, like, *okay*? You never really answered before."

She smiled. "I'm okay, Milo."

"Because you were—"

"Yes. And now I'm not."

"I mean, with everything . . ."

"I know."

Jules came back. Arik and his friends were close and not slowing.

"Milo," Jules said. "They're armed."

And he was right again. Arik carried something in his hand. A stick. The ones behind him had rocks in their fists. Or lengths of pipe. Black-bladed iron knives showing just a fingernail paring of silver where the cutting edges had been ground against stone.

"Something isn't right here," Milo said. He raised a hand to Arik and waved. Some of the younger ones following him twitched back like he'd thrown something at them. He called out, "Arik!" but the Aces didn't answer.

Milo turned aside to Jules and Dagda. "Get ready to run."

"I ain't running from Arik the Aces," Jules said. His hands were balled into fists, hanging loose at his sides. He breathed in great gusts, his nostrils flaring, his face bright and hot in the nearly dawn light.

"Gonna be upset if you don't follow me," Milo said, and nudged Jules with his shoulder, then focused again on Arik. He said loudly and clearly, "Pretty early, Arik. Shouldn't some of those small ones still be in bed?"

And Arik stopped, all the boys and girls behind him crowding up. One of them stumbled and dropped the club he was carrying. The sound of it clattering on the stones was very loud.

"Still in bed," said Arik. He stood straight, his hands behind his back, his lanky hair wet and sticky-looking in the dark. "That's funny. It is." He turned to the gang following him. "Isn't that funny?"

None of them said anything. Just stared. Shifted their weight.

"Just saying it's a little strange to see you in Oldedge so early."

"Says the dead boy standing in our house."

Beside him, Jules said his name in a warning kind of way. "Milo . . ."

"This is ours now, Milo," Arik said. "Oldedge. The Blue Lights. All of it. It's mine. My territory. My house."

"Says who?"

"Says the Total King Forever."

"Bert?" Milo asked, nearly laughing. "Is this about our tithe? It's been two days, Arik. Tell Bert—"

"Cuthbert DeGeorge is dead," said Arik. "Got hisself perished last night. And the new king don't care a bit for your tithing. He wants a different price."

"Milo," Jules said, louder.

"Bert's dead?" Milo said to Arik. "You sure?"

Arik took another step. He brought his hands out from behind his back and held up Cuthbert's cane. Half of it, anyway. The half with the dog's head.

"Pretty sure, yeah," Arik said. "I was there."

And then Milo looked closer at his face, his hair, and realized that Arik the Aces was covered in blood. His hands stained with it, drying and flaking on his skin. The dog's head sticky with it.

"Moric Shaw is Total King Forever now. And you're dead already, Milo. Or well on your way. All of you are."

Jules cursed at him, spat onto the stones, told him to take another step closer and say that. From behind him, Milo could feel Dagda shrinking away already, picking at the tail of his shirt.

"Run," Arik hissed. "It'll make it more fun for us."

"Run, Jules," Milo said quietly.

"I don't run from—"

"Jules," he said, his voice calm, measured. "The others. Llyr, Tristan, Arun. They don't know. They're out there."

"Run, Quick!" shouted Arik. He twirled the broken cane in his dirty fingers.

"Jules, run!"

And they ran. All three of them.

Arik the Aces watched them go. He tilted his head toward one of the littlest boys behind him, hanging tight to a stick bigger than he was. "Find the King," he said. "Tell him we've found his prize." To the rest, he said, "Let's go," then turned, watched Jules and Milo and Dagda the Mouse bolting in the direction of the Blue Lights, into the heart of the Marche, and took off running with his soldiers all crashing and tumbling behind.

# SEMYON BELI

**IN THE FADING SHADOWS** of an ancient wall and the stumps of once-grand columns, Semyon Beli clucked his tongue. He'd been following the boy since he'd left the breaking yards, all the way to Oldedge, and had seen everything that'd happened.

"This is trouble," he said to no one at all. "And to have to run at such an hour besides . . ."

# ARUN AND SIG

**SIG WAS FEELING BETTER,** but still wasn't entirely steady on his feet. He was slow and grumpy, and he carried his hurt hand tight against his chest, afraid of anything touching it.

"Don't say anything to Milo," he told Arun more than once. "Don't say anything at all. I don't want him telling me I can't come along."

Arun and Sig had stashes of treasure all over the Blue Lights that they'd kept from Milo, because keeping it from Milo meant keeping it from the Total King. Their plan had been to empty the best of their secret hiding places into their pockets before heading for Front Street, but somewhere along the way they'd gotten turned around, distracted. Now they were just talking—about picking pockets and rolling drunks, best scores ever and solid gold hands.

"Solid gold hands?" asked Sig.

And Arun said sure. Why not? "Like a rich man gets his hand chopped off and wants to replace it with something fancy? Solid gold hand."

"When have you ever seen a drunk with a solid gold hand?"

"I haven't. But that's what I'm saying, right? Like maybe he keeps it in a glove or something so not everyone knows? You could miss a solid gold hand *easy* if you weren't being careful. Going through the pockets, rushing like we do? Might not even—"

Arun stopped talking. He stood very still.

"What?" Sig asked. "What's wrong?"

"Shut up," Arun said, then looked back over his shoulder, tilting his head. "You hear that?"

"Hear what?"

Arun turned around, said "That," but Sig heard nothing and thought that Arun was just playing and started to say something sharp back to him, when suddenly, he heard it, too. Someone shouting, far off but getting closer. Which wasn't strange for the Marche at all, even at this kind of hour, except that whoever was shouting might've been shouting one of their names.

"Did that voice say my name?" Sig asked.

"No, it said *my* name," Arun replied. "Because even with ghosts, I'm more popular."

Again, they listened, and again, the sound came. Closer now. Laid over all the other sounds of the Marche waking. And it was definitely someone shouting their names.

"Is that Jules yelling?" Arun asked.

"How would I know?" said Sig. Then he listened again. Then he said, "Whistle."

"What?"

"Whistle. You whistle loud. If it's Jules or any of them, they'll hear you."

Arun said okay, put his fingers in his mouth and whistled loudly. They heard their names again. Closer still. Sig cursed, cupped his good hand around his mouth and bellowed, "Jules!" It was loud enough to rattle the dead.

"What are you doing?" Arun asked, and Sig waved a hand at

him, took a deep breath and yelled again, "Milo!" and then looked at Arun. "You think they heard us?"

"I think everyone in the Marche heard you. Let's go see what's happening."

And so they ran, Arun and Sig shouting, "Jules!" and "Milo!" and somewhere ahead of them, Jules and Milo shouting, "Arun!" and "Sig!" and for the longest time, they seemed to be getting no closer. Until suddenly, Arun and Sig heard their names again from behind them.

"Arun!"

"Sig!"

And again from their right, and close by.

"Arun!"

"Sig!"

But the voices were different now. Higher, lower, meaner, laughing. They singsonged down the crooked alleys and bounced around the stone walls.

Arun said, "Sig, what's happening?"

And Sig said he didn't know, but they both stopped running when they came to a place where three sloping, narrow lanes all came together in a small court with a pool in the middle, low-sided, filled with clear water. Above it stood a statue of a girl, reaching skyward, dancing, and seeming to soar without going anywhere. Around her neck, she wore a garland of stone roses.

Sig was dizzy. He bent over with his hands on his knees, panting. He could feel his pulse in his wounded hand. It throbbed in a sharp, pounding beat.

Arun hauled himself up, meaning to shout again, but stopped. His breath caught in his throat when he saw Winter Bartel and a handful of the Total King's boys coming out of the dark street behind them, blue-glass light from the lanterns hung over closed doorways catching on the knives and clubs in their hands. There were more coming the other way, with Arik the Aces and Simo Dahl leading them.

"Sig, stand up."

Winter Bartel carried a length of pipe with a knotty, rusted elbow screwed onto the end, and she scraped it back and forth, ticking the head of it against the cobbles while she licked her lips. Arik had a long black knife, the edge of its blade bright and gleaming.

Arun took a deep, shaking breath and blew it out. He took another and yelled as loud as he could, "Milo, help us!"

And the King's soldiers all shouted, "Milo, help us! Milo, help us!"

Winter Bartel shouted, "Milo, help us!"

Arik the Aces shouted, "Milo, help us!" in a high, screeching voice and raised his knife in front of him. He looked at Arun and Sig and said, "King's orders," then ran at them, the knife held low and off to his side like a broken wing.

# MILO, JULES, AND DAGDA

**ALL THREE OF THEM** ran as fast as they'd ever run. They shouted as loudly as they'd ever shouted. They called Arun's name and Sig's name, hoping to find them, to warn them about Bert and Arik and the new Total King, hoping for luck—that somehow, they would just stumble across Arun and Sig in the tangled streets of the Blue Lights, laughing and joking like this was any other morning.

But it didn't happen that way.

They ran and they shouted, and for a moment, Milo, Jules, and Dagda thought they heard Arun and Sig shouting back. They thought they heard Arun whistle. But soon enough there were other voices, too, all around them, all yelling "Arun!" and "Sig!" and then, from behind them, Arun's voice shouting, "Milo, help us!" echoed almost immediately by a dozen other voices, all laughing, all singsonging, "Milo, help us! Milo, help us!"

That was enough to stop all three of them short.

Jules was first to get turned around. He shoved Milo in the direction they'd been running. "Go," he barked. "Front Street. I'll meet you." And he was gone before Milo could argue.

The boy tried to turn and follow, but Dagda dragged at his sleeve. "Llyr," she said. "And Tristan and Keelan. He's right."

So Milo watched Jules vanish around a corner and heard all the voices yelling *Milo, help us! Milo, help us!* and he thought they were in his own head. He thought he was going mad.

Dawn was maybe ten minutes away now, and the light beginning to spill into the Flying City was pure and gold and brilliant.

# SEMYON BELI

**SEMYON BELI** was an old man. He felt every year in every bone. But he was wise and he was canny. Semyon Beli had not gotten to *be* an old man by being anything less than that. So when he'd followed the boy and his pursuers into this labyrinth, he knew he could not keep up with the energy and murderousness of their youth. He knew he could not run and leap and hate the way they did—with such recklessness and abandon—but that he *could* track them by the wreckage such childish enthusiasm always left in its wake.

"Come on, Semyon Beli," he said to himself, encouraging his legs to move him and his heart not to fail him now, so close to the end of his labors. "The young leave such messes. Hardly need to be a genius to follow along to the conclusion of this story."

So he puffed and he jogged and he kept pace with the narrative being written on the stones of this place. First, it was the voices and the footsteps and, soon enough, the screaming. Then it was the blood. And after that, the bodies.

He never saw the shadow of the Sandman following behind him, though—the swirl of him in shadows, the blue gleam of his glasses.

Sly as Semyon Beli was, he never even thought to look.

# KEELAN

**KEELAN** lost track of Tristan and Llyr for just a second.

They'd been chasing birds near the Front Street battlements. Keelan had looked away, watching a man with a long pole walking along the street snuffing all the oil lamps on their high posts. He shuffled along in shoes stuffed with rags, his long stick scraping the stones with every other step until he would stop, lift it, expertly bump the handle that lowered the wick, extinguish the light, then move on.

The thing about the man was that he wore a long wool coat even in the morning's warmth, and wore a grease-colored scarf that was wrapped under his chin and trailed down the front of him. He looked, Keelan thought, a whole lot like *he* did, only grown terribly old. And for some reason, Keelan found that very funny.

So he'd called out to Tristan and Llyr, meaning to point at the man and say, *Look at him! That'll be me when I grow up!* But the twins weren't there.

Keelan blinked and looked around because they'd just been *right here*, playing on the teeth of the battlements and making nuisances of themselves. And it wasn't like there was anyone else around at this hour. Just them, a few soldiers, the lamp man. He walked a little ways down the hill toward the shield wall and the battlements, peering into the retreating shadows of this strange, in-between moment that was both dawn and not quite dawn.

When he did spot them, far down along the Front Street wall, he saw Llyr first, in a bubble of lamplight not yet put out, standing atop the wall with her arms out and her head back like she was hugging all of the coming morning. Tristan was standing below her, pointing at something.

Keelan squinted and saw, farther down, a group of girls and boys passing in and out of the circles of light thrown by the lamps. He recognized Moric Shaw and a few others.

He started walking in their direction. The old man snuffed another lamp. Keelan stepped out of the way when two soldiers not much older than him ran by, panting and carrying a wooden case between them stamped with yellow warning labels. They were followed by three men in hastily thrown-on coastal artillery uniforms who rushed past, pushing Keelan out of the way.

Keelan sniffed and muttered under his breath, but didn't fall. He looked and saw Llyr on the wall and Moric Shaw and the rest stomping toward her and Tristan, shouting at them. Something caught his eye then, and he glanced out over the wall, where, in the brightening sky, a fresh, new morning star hung, quivering, high above the distant horizon. It burned red and tremulous, and as he watched it, it arced up and hung in the sky for an impossibly long moment, and then began to fall.

# TRISTAN AND LLYR

**"JUMP WITH ME, TRISTAN,"** Llyr said.

She stood with her eyes closed and her arms spread, facing out to sea, standing atop her eighth favorite of all the teeth on Front Street.

"Jump with me," she said. "We can fly. We can. We'll fly together, and it'll be better. We'll be together. We won't be lonely."

Somehow she knew it was too late. It'd been too late last night when Milo had been telling them made-up stories about leaving home. It'd been too late even before that. But she asked Tristan anyway because she didn't want him to be scared. He stood below her, calling her name, telling her there were boys coming and asking her to come down, but she didn't. She stood and stretched her arms wider and imagined flying away from the city like a huge bird, on wings the color of smoke. Of rising and rising and never coming down.

"It's not too late," she said to Tristan, and even though she knew that was a lie, maybe it was an okay lie if it could keep him from being sad. "We can go right now. Both of us. We'll fly home and be there before everyone else."

She heard other voices. Angry ones. A rumble like far-off thunder. Llyr squeezed her eyes tighter. It was going to be okay.

Everything was almost over now. "Come on, Tristan," she whispered, too quietly for anyone to hear her. "Time to go."

She felt the hands grab her by the ankles and pull. She hit the stones and that hurt and knocked her breath out, but she hardly felt the knife. That was like nothing. Just warmth. And she never opened her eyes, even when she felt the push, and then she was flying. And she was sad because Tristan wasn't with her, but that wouldn't last for long. She flew and she fell and everything was like fire and then she died.

It wasn't as bad as she thought it would be, right up until it was nothing at all.

# AT DAWN IN
# THE FLYING CITY

**UP IN THE HIGH CRADLES,** Captain Rodion Klim chopped free the *Halcyon*'s mooring lines with a hatchet.

Emerging from the twisting canyons of the Blue Lights, Semyon Beli was so startled by the sound of the first shells impacting along Front Street that he dropped one of his flares, ducked down to grab it and, in doing so, narrowly avoided having his head taken off by a spinning shard of metal, which embedded itself, smoking, in a wall just above him.

Ennis Arghdal, who'd been following the old man silently since before dawn, saw the red signal flare from the rooftops and closed his eyes only long enough to say a short prayer to any gods that might be listening. *Just let me find the boy and bring him to shelter,* he said. *Take me if you need another body today, but let me see the boy safe first.* Then he blinked, gave a fierce look to the clouds where everyone's silly little gods traditionally lived and added, *And if you can't do that, then just stay out of my way.*

In the violence of the first impacts, a boy named Orfeo Jaka died, one of Cuthbert's favorites. A girl named Liesl Fellin died. Another boy called Bob Bobtail died. He was friends with Orfeo. Ran a gang of coat-tailers in the market. Liked salty fried potatoes and could count to a hundred without using his fingers and thought he maybe loved a girl called Nylah who worked in a store that sold paper just outside Shippers Alley. But none of that mattered now, because he was dead in an instant, and everything about him and all his loves and all his hatreds died with him.

Keelan was blown right off his feet. He'd been running toward where he'd seen Moric Shaw kill Llyr, which was not like him at all. He was shouting, but no one ever heard him. And then he was just gone.

# JULES

**JULES FOUND ARUN AND SIG.**

He'd gone back, twisting through the alleys of the Blue Lights, and had found them thrown into a small pool in the center of a square where three roads came together. There was a statue there of a girl flying. The water that sloshed over the low stone lip of the pool was red.

He saw Simo Dahl there, and Winter Bartel and Arik the Aces and some others, too, all standing and panting. Simo was holding his ribs and there was one boy on the ground, not moving at all, and Winter Bartel was shouting curses and crying and bleeding down half of her face, yelling, "Why?" and slapping her hands at Arik, who said nothing and didn't move and didn't even seem to notice.

Simo Dahl sank down to one knee, breathing hard. One of Arun's legs hung over the edge of the pool. And Jules saw all of this and heard all of this and he walked right into the little court without counting numbers or caring, because he was braver than he was smart and stronger than he was reasonable and *This day*, he thought. *This day* . . .

Winter cried and begged when she saw Jules coming. She held up her hands and said it wasn't her and that she didn't want to play anymore. Jules ignored her and she dropped her pipe and ran. Simo had fallen over onto his side and lay there, not speaking, leaking red onto the cobbles. Some of Arik's soldiers ran. Others jumped and shouted and jeered, bared their teeth and shook their sticks and knives.

Jules never slowed. He came on, walking, inexorable, and he opened his mouth to tell Arik that he wasn't running anymore. That he was going to kill him where he stood. But then all of them heard the sound of crumpling, rumbling impacts in the distance, the whistle of missed shots passing overhead, the screams of the mortars descending, and for a second, Jules Cael and Arik the Aces stood there, mouths open, eyebrows raised, each looking at the other as if to silently ask, *Did you just hear that, too?*

And then the shattering blasts. A building behind Arik was struck and Jules watched the entire face of it slide away, collapsing into the street in a cloud of dust, leaving rooms cut in half and open to the world. Fire leapt from somewhere to his right—flaring hot and orange and black and then gone. Thick clouds of smoke rolled in from behind him like a wave, engulfing the narrow alleys of the Blue Lights, and the ground beneath his feet shivered like someone had gripped the entire Flying City by its edges and shaken it.

Jules staggered and went down on one knee. All around him, the *dun dun dun* of the Highgate coastal artillery firing gave the entire city a pulse, a stuttering heartbeat. But Jules didn't care. He reached forward, wrapped his fingers around the pipe that Winter Bartel had dropped when she ran, and got back to his feet.

He yelled, "Nothing saves you, Arik! Not now!" But he wasn't sure if Arik could hear him. He could barely hear himself. There was something wrong with his ears—like they were packed with cotton. He raised the pipe up and charged.

And Arik the Aces just waited. He let Jules Cael come close.

Let all that energy and all that rage carry him forward. And when he was almost on top of him, Arik shoved one of his own boys in the back, sending him sprawling right into Jules's feet, tripping him up.

As Jules fell, Arik leapt clean over him, meaning to run, back toward Front Street where Moric Shaw, the new Total King Forever, and all the rest would be waiting.

And that might've worked, but in the smoke and confusion, he'd forgotten about Simo Dahl, who lay near the pool, dead now. Arik came down almost on top of him, his feet catching on one of Simo's arms or legs. He stumbled when he landed, then sprawled, skinning his hands on the stones and sucking in a lungful of dust and banging his knee on the stone lip of the pool.

Jules, meanwhile, had tripped and fallen and gone down hard on the stones, but he recovered quickly, getting to his knees first, butting one boy with his head, biting another, swinging Winter's metal-capped pipe to scatter those of Arik's boys and girls who hadn't already started to run.

And Jules was strong. So strong. He could hear shouting and screaming as he swung, connected, swung again. He felt a splash of water as one of Arik's soldiers went into the pool where they'd dumped Arun's and Sig's bodies. He reached out and grabbed a boy by the shirt with one hand, lifted him up and threw him in the direction Arik had gone. He was small, that boy, but still. His feet barely touched the ground.

Arik was just heaving himself to his feet, but staggered when he put weight onto the knee he'd hit. And then he felt something heavy and squirming hit him in the back and it occurred to him (as he fell, again) that Jules Cael had *thrown* one of his own gang at him. Had picked one of them up like nothing and hurled him like a stone.

Arik rolled onto his back and held his knee with both hands. He saw his army scattering as fast as they could and Jules coming. Blood dripped from the heavy end of the pipe in his hands. Broken children lay on the ground at his feet.

"Let me get up," he said, and Jules said nothing.

Arik pushed with his feet and crabbed backward, hands on the cobbles, fingers searching for a weapon, for anything.

"Give me a chance!" he yelled as, around them, fresh fires blossomed and the ground shook. "You can't do this! You can't—"

Jules raised the pipe and swung. Once was all it took. And then he threw the pipe away and took off running into the smoke. Back toward Front Street to try to find Milo.

# DAGDA

**MILO AND DAGDA** had come bursting onto Front Street at the moment the first shells struck. Dagda was fast. She'd recognized the sound of the thudding guns and the noise (a kind of shuddering hiss) of cannonballs and shells in flight, and she'd grabbed Milo by the back of his shirt and pushed him down, his face against the powdery bricks of a wall, scraping his forehead against the rough stone. She'd draped herself over him and felt the small impacts of bits of metal and stone nipping at her skin, but nothing that did her any harm. That wasn't merely cosmetic. *More scars*, she thought. *More damage.*

She'd lived through wars before. She'd lived through shelling and bombings and siege. She'd seen Highgate burn before and she'd survived. She'd seen it torn apart from within and without. She knew places to hide. Places where she could sleep and dream for a hundred years if need be. Places that had been lost or forgotten by every single person alive now, and that would shelter her until it was safe to come out and be a twelve-year-old girl again on these streets that she'd known for four hundred years.

*But Milo*, she thought. *What about Milo?*

She felt the ground shake. When she looked up, she saw huge airships come drifting through the rising smoke like breaching whales, stopping the wind with their miles of sail as they drew themselves up broadside to the Flying City. She saw smaller ones boiling out from around them like flies.

Milo was a boy. A real boy. He couldn't sleep in the cold places beneath the city. Couldn't live in the tubes and maintenance tunnels. He would need to eat, to breathe. If she took him down with her, he would grow old in the darkness like some monster, getting pale, his eyes turning white and blind. But she couldn't leave him either. He was her family. They were bound.

So she held him, and Milo crouched in the shelter of her as the world crashed down around them, and Dagda thought, *What do I do now?*

# THE *HALCYON*

**CAPTAIN KLIM** cut through the last of the mooring lines and bellowed, "Ship light!" which meant that the *Halcyon* was holding its weight—remaining aloft under the lift from its own gasbags.

From the very front of the ship, Vaclav answered him, shouting, "Balance!" and standing with his arms out and feeling the roll of the *Halcyon* as she lifted free of the cradle, inch by inch.

Lalia was on her belly, yelling down the engineering hatch to Reyn, "We are *going*, Reyn! Right now!" And even as she was doing that, the Captain was already clawing his way up the short flight of steps from the ship's middle to the command deck, to the pilot's box, where he slung himself into the braces and started cranking madly at the winch handles that controlled the dragonfly sails and locking them when they'd been wound out to their catches.

"Wings out!" he shouted. Vaclav was at the capstan now, the big wheel at the ship's waist that lofted her other sails. Lalia joined him, both of them throwing themselves against the bars, digging in their feet and pushing, turning the wheel that wound the cables, their muscles straining and their breath coming in gasps as grapeshot and chain from a passing frigate chewed through the slips around them and the Highgate gunners fired back.

"Backing!" the Captain yelled.

"Backing aye!" said Vaclav.

"Go," the Captain whispered, his hands resting flat on the winches that controlled the three pairs of dragonfly sails that sprouted from either side of the *Halcyon*'s sleek wooden hull. "Come on, beautiful. Go, go, go, go, go . . ."

And slowly, the *Halcyon*'s smaller sails gathered in the breezes. Slowly, she moved, sliding backward out of her cradle. Slowly, she slipped out into the smoke and fire.

Lalia shouted, "Brace up to port!" and everyone had to duck down behind the thin protection of the *Halcyon*'s low deck rails as another gust of cannon fire barely missed them. A swooping gunship flying the Armada's black flags passed by, orbiting the Spire, spitting fire into the aerie's gun emplacements. The Captain yelled curses after the little gunship, then leaned into the speaking trumpet and shouted for Reyn to engage the starboard motor, backing one-quarter. Then he called for Lalia and she came at a dash.

"Eyes!" he shouted. "Behind me!" And Lalia stepped to the rail at the very back of the command deck to peer through the gaps in the canvas and lines and pulleys to tell the Captain where he was clear and what he might be about to drift into.

Twice more they had to duck down and take cover as small airships made strafing runs against the high cradles. The big capital airships were more concerned with pounding the city below them to splinters, and the naval ships were obviously far out of range of the top of the Spire. So for the moment, all the *Halcyon* had to contend with were the smaller frigates and gunships that swirled around them like furious sparrows, sniping at anything that moved.

But the Captain knew they were going to have to go low—to drop through all that fire and all that lead to haul up near Front Street, in the middle of the worst of it—to take the boy. The girl, possibly. Semyon, if he'd survived.

The Captain yelled Lalia's name, and Lalia said they were clear. A fast frigate dropped down from above them, the aerie gunners chasing her as she fell, and Vaclav called for everyone to brace as the frigate's gunners briefly had the *Halcyon* in their sights, but they chose not to fire. For just a moment the Captain could see the men on the frigate's deck, shining with sweat, blackened with powder, swabbing the smoking barrels of their guns and rolling them out on their carriages, readying another broadside for which the *Halcyon* was simply not a choice-enough target.

With aching slowness, the *Halcyon* backed out of her cradle, turned around on her tail, and got her nose pointed in a more useful direction. Again, the Captain called for Lalia. "We're clear," he said. "Now we have to find ourselves a hole to fall down. Take the box." He stepped aside and helped her clip her harness into the safety braces that would hold her, standing upright in the pilot's box.

Vaclav yelled, "Brace!" and everyone ducked as shot rattled against the ship's port side, splintering chips from the rail and humming through the rigging.

The Captain felt something sting him and reached up to pull a splinter of wood from above his right eye, smeared blood back into his hair, and said to Lalia, "We have to get low and we have to do it fast. Follow my hands. You understand?"

Lalia nodded.

"Do this wrong and we die."

"We're not dying today," she said.

"It's early yet," said the Captain, smiling fiercely. "Time will tell."

And then he went forward into the *Halcyon*'s bow, shoving Vaclav out of his way, and looked down and down for hundreds of feet at the war being waged all the way from the sky down to the sea. He saw smoke and fire and ships, the twisted fingers of broken cranes, the splintering, crashing wrecks lashed to the edges of the city like armor, and the white sweep of Front Street far below. The long guns of the Highgate coastal artillery were exacting a terrible cost from the Armada. The sea was on fire. The big capital airships all gaped with holes in their hulls, raining men and broken pieces of themselves like dandruff down over the water. But the city itself was dying. From this height, the Captain could hardly see an inch of it that wasn't in flames. And all he had to do now was fly down into it.

The *Halcyon* had nothing. No guns, patches on its hull, only half its cordage. Even after a long, hard, desperate night's work, it was a broken machine.

But it had its sails and it had its motors. With no weight on her save crew weight, she was light and trim as a falcon. The *Halcyon* would move when Captain Klim asked her to. She would be faster than anything any of them had ever seen.

Right up until the point that she started shaking to pieces, of course. At which point all they would be doing was falling, down and down to the sea below.

But before that? The *Halcyon* was going to be *fast*. So the Captain held out his hands and directed Lalia to take them this way, then that way. They moved slowly, flubbed around in the sky like a ship already dead in the air. But all the time, the Captain was looking for his opening. One clear path down through all the layers of fire and dying that would leave them, for just a moment, broadside to Front Street where, he hoped, Semyon Beli and the boy would be waiting.

# MILO

**MILO HAD DUST IN HIS EYES.** He felt Dagda's weight on his back, her hands pushing down his head. He couldn't think clearly. He'd scraped his forehead against the bricks when Dagda had pushed him, and he could feel the blood beading up and leaking down either side of his nose. The air felt too thick to breathe.

"This is a war," he said. His tone was conversational. He didn't scream or bellow or cry, even though the words seemed to echo inside his head. "I had no idea."

"This is a war," Dagda echoed. He could feel her lips moving in his hair, but the words sounded like they were coming through water. "Get up now. We need to move."

# SHAW

**SHAW COULDN'T HEAR.** He pawed at his eyes, trying to
clear them of grit and dust. Wobbling to his feet, he rose to look
around at a world transformed by violence that he had not antici-
pated and didn't understand.

The little girl was dead. He'd seen her standing on the wall
overlooking the sea and said to no one, "What, is she going to
jump?" He'd called out to her as he approached, but she didn't
seem to hear him, so he'd reached out and pulled her by the ankles. She fell against the rocks and Shaw had stabbed her in the
back and thrown her over, all in the space of a second.

The boy, then, had rushed at him, yelling and screaming and
with his hands out, so Shaw had hit him, hard, with his cast-
wrapped fist, and then kicked him when he fell. But he was still
shouting and trying to get back up, so Shaw had knelt and run
the knife into the boy's side. It was more to make him be quiet
than anything else. More to stop the noise and shouting. But then,
while he was ducked down killing the boy, something had happened, and it seemed like the whole world had exploded.

And now he couldn't hear and his eyes were all blurry and
his head was ringing like a bell. He opened his mouth and rolled
his head on his neck and looked and saw that Orfeo Jaka was
dead, and some of the others, too. Everyone else was scattered

and covered in stone and dust and splinters of wood, bloody from cuts and scrapes and leaking from ears and eyes, but stirring. They were rising, those who weren't dead, like monsters clawing their way up from the dirt, with debris raining from them and their mouths open, howling in pain or shock or surprise.

The world went dark as a massive ship with black flags and pennants drifted in above them, casting them into its shadow. Shaw watched, mouth hanging open, as the guns of Highgate tore into it, blowing holes through its body and ripping into sails big enough to drape a building. It was called the *Lord of Storms* and when it settled itself into position and fired its hundred-gun broadside into the heart of the Flying City, Shaw was driven back down to his knees, screaming, at the sound of its roaring guns. Even in his deafness, he could feel it—like hot nails driven into his ears—and he shook his knife at it and yelled up at the ship to stop, to leave, to fly away.

But for just a moment, in the churn of its motors and the wind spilling from its canvas, some breeze whipped in, clearing away the rolling, choking haze and dust that hung over Front Street. In that instant, Moric Shaw saw Milo Quick standing, staring up at the *Lord of Storms* with his own mouth agape. The girl, Dagda, was beside him, pulling at his arm. And in the swirling wind, Shaw saw brick dust and gun smoke all twisting above Milo's head, and it looked to him like the wings of a bird. Like the white bird, squawking at him. Laughing.

Shaw pushed himself back up to his feet. His boys, his *army*, were all shouting up at the massive airship. Shaking their fists and stones and knives and clubs. But when Shaw shouted Milo's name (his own voice sounding flat in his head amid the bell-ringing chime that drowned out nearly everything else), they all turned. They looked at Shaw and then they looked where Shaw was looking, and they, too, saw Milo and the girl standing on the other side of Front Street. And then they, too, all shouted his name.

"Milo Quick!"

Milo seemed not to hear them at all, but Shaw knew they'd been loud enough, because the girl stopped what she was doing. She stood up straight. She turned away from Milo and the *Lord of Storms* and lowered her eyes until she found Shaw, standing in the rack and ruin of Front Street. And as he watched, her lips moved. She said something to Milo Quick, but she never looked away from Shaw's eyes. She shook her arms. She rolled her small hands into fists. And then she started to run.

But not away.

She ran *at* them.

# THE *LORD OF STORMS*

**SEMYON BELI** sat with his back to a stone wall that was crumbling to pieces. He held a sheet of tin above his head, and the gravel and rocks rang against it like hail. He had one flare in his hand and another tucked into his pants, and he looked down Front Street to where Milo Quick stood, staring up at one of the Armada's capital ships pouring fire into the city.

He'd served aboard one of those once. Not this one in particular, but one like it, flying out of Port Alpha in the City of Doors, far away from here. He felt for the men aboard as he saw the Highgate gunners find their range and fire into her from above and below, gouging pieces from her, holing her again and again.

"Keep your heads down, boys," he said to the poor gun crews and powder boys and shot carriers. To those who hung from her lines and spars trying to hold her in place while the broadside was reloaded. "It'll all be over and done with soon." And then he stuck his head out from around the corner, dropped his tin umbrella, cupped his hands around his mouth and shouted, "Boy! Over here, boy! Milo Quick!"

Ennis had lost sight of the old man when the firing began. He'd scrambled out through a narrow swath of the city that burst and burned behind him, then pounded out onto Front Street just as some fool of an admiral laid his big, ugly toy of a ship up alongside Ennis's beautiful city and tried to impress everyone with how big he was and how many guns he had.

And Ennis Arghdal had laughed. He'd shouted up toward the Spire and the gun emplacements, "There she is, boys! Teach her a lesson now!" Because although he knew the gunners of Highgate were all lazy, plump, and dim, probably nearsighted, certainly slow-witted, and absolutely too complacent by half (because who else would let an entire army descend on them before firing a shot?), they were still men and women of the Flying City. And when presented with a target so close and so fat and so arrogantly standing still right there in front of them, they were going to have their way with it. They were going to teach that crew, that ship, and especially the admiral aboard her what it meant to act big in a very bad place, and exactly what that would cost you.

The big ship roared, her guns all firing blind into the smoke. The Flying City answered with a brutal retort. And although Ennis would've gladly spent the day watching the coastal artillery take that big, dumb whale of a ship apart while sipping white coffee and cheering every hit from a comfortable chair, what he was even happier about was that with that stupid lummox hanging there, so close to the body of the city, the naval ships below couldn't fire for fear of hitting the *Lord of Storms* from the *other* side and catching one of their own capital ships in a crossfire.

For just a moment, Front Street was safe. And Ennis didn't mean to waste the moment he'd been given.

All he had to do now was find the boy.

✦

"There!" shouted the Captain, pointing down and shouting back over his shoulder. "There! Right there!"

He'd watched the *Lord of Storms* lumber through the clouds. He'd watched her tack broadside under motors and lay herself almost right up against the city, so low that the entire Eastern Fleet of the Armada was prevented from firing for fear of hitting her. She hung almost directly over Front Street. And all along the side of her facing out to sea there was no fire. That was his hole. The chance he'd been waiting for.

"Lalia, right there! In the lees of the *Lord of Storms*! That big, dumb tub right there! Vaclav! Vent the bags. All forward! Dive!"

Vaclav pulled the vent lines, and the Captain watched as the front cells of the *Halcyon*'s mottled gray-and-white gasbags blew with a shuddering exhalation and fell almost slack in their netting. The ship lost half her buoyancy in the space of a heartbeat. Her nose bobbed, then dipped, then fell toward the sea. The motors thrummed to life. Lalia cranked back the dragonfly sails until they were tucked tight against the ship's body, and the *Halcyon* shuddered, came about to the proper heading, and then fell like a hawk diving.

Captain Klim bent his knees and held to the safety lines, standing as far forward on the bowsprit as he could go. He lost his hat. His hair streamed back behind him as they fell faster and faster, plunging through the fighting ships and cannon fire and flaming wreckage falling all around them. He felt the breath torn from his lips and tears streaming back from his eyes, and he didn't care. He opened his mouth and he laughed the whole way down.

Milo had never seen anything like the *Lord of Storms*. Miles of sail. Motors driving a dozen airscrews. So many guns that the sound of them firing in concert seemed to shake the sky. He was stunned by her. Overwhelmed. He stood, staring, and raised his hands to her floating above him as though begging her to lift him up and take him away.

Then he heard his name called and looked and saw the old man, Semyon Beli, crouching down at the corner of a wall shattered by cannon fire and still raining stone. Milo opened his mouth to say something, but then he felt Dagda stiffen beside him, and he heard her speak.

"Milo. It's Shaw. He killed Tristan."

"What?"

"Shaw," Dagda said, and pointed toward the wall at the edge of the city. "Look."

Milo looked. He saw Moric Shaw. He saw Tristan's body lying at Shaw's feet. He didn't see Llyr and he didn't see Keelan, but he did see Vitek Harsha and Azhar Biel and two dozen other dust-covered, bloody boys and girls from the Total King's court. He saw them all turn in his direction. He heard them shout his name.

He knew then that Shaw had come to kill him.

He knew that this was also a war.

And when Dagda started to run toward Shaw, Milo ran after her—charging across Front Street to meet Shaw and settle this. He was afraid and he was sad. He was hurt and tired and confused and didn't want to die, but he was angry, too. Full of pain and rage because Shaw had hurt his friends and he wasn't going to stand around crying while Dagda fought an army all on her own. She was his friend. Tristan was his friend. Llyr was his friend. Keelan was his friend. And since it seemed likely that all of them might die today anyway, he didn't intend to do it alone.

"Mouse!" he yelled after her. "Shaw is mine!"

"I'll race you for him," said a voice from behind him.

It was Jules. He wasn't smiling when he said it.

And so they ran together, Milo and Jules, chasing Dagda over the broken stones and ruin while all around them the Flying City burned.

# MORE DANGEROUS
# THAN YOU CAN POSSIBLY
# IMAGINE

**SEMYON BELI** saw the boy turn toward him, then turn away. He looked and he saw a bunch of other boys and girls, all rising from the dust and broken pieces of the city, shaking their fists and sticks and stones, and for reasons passing all understanding, the boy ran *toward* them instead of, you know, running very fast away.

Semyon Beli had not been a boy in a long time, but he had taken one vital lesson away from his own boyhood—that *surviving* it was what mattered. That was how you won your youth. By living through it. And one didn't survive by running *toward* a fight.

Ennis ran down the middle of Front Street, leaping piles of tumbled brick and dodging burning timbers. He'd come out onto Front Street lower than Semyon Beli had, and lower still than Milo, Jules, and Dagda, but he saw them all when the smoke blew clear. He saw Dagda running. He saw Milo and Jules behind her. He saw Moric Shaw and a bloody, filthy mess of the Total King's finest, most murderous idiots all organizing themselves to receive those three children. Children he cared about more than any other creatures living. And he knew what was going to happen next. He'd seen enough mornings in the Marche to know how these things ended. Seen enough dead children to last him a lifetime. And suddenly, he did not want to see even one more.

Ennis shouted Milo's name and ran as fast as he could, but he was just too far away. For want of a handful of seconds—a hundred yards of broken street—he was going to fail the boy in this last moment at the end of the world. All he could do was watch as Moric Shaw's troops drew up together to meet Dagda and Jules and Milo Quick. All he could do was shout, "No! No! No!" until the moment he saw Dagda Prowst reach the other side of Front Street.

Because that was when something incredible happened.

Dagda knew what came next. She'd been here a hundred times before.

A tall, thin girl with white-blond hair stood atop a broken chunk of concrete with rusted twines of metal sticking out. She wore a wide, crazy smile and waved a knife at Dagda as she shouted, "We killed the little one! We killed the little one!"

Dagda Prowst leapt high, seemed to hang for an impossible second above the girl, then struck her like a lightning bolt, barely seeming to touch her, except that the girl crumpled, screaming. She was thrown aside to break against the knotty stones.

Dagda barely even slowed down.

A boy with a rock was next. Then another who swung a pole that she ducked under, grabbed, and wrenched from his hands before smashing her own head into his face and punching him hard enough in the chest that he lifted off the ground and dropped, lifeless as a sack of flour.

Dagda was a whirlwind. In this moment, on this terrible

day—suddenly released of all restraint and all fear and all need to hide herself from the mortal things of this sad and faded world— she was a deadly, merciless storm that tore through Moric Shaw's army like he'd drawn them on paper.

There was a danger here. She knew that. Limits to her systems and thresholds that couldn't be crossed without consequences. She would have to stop soon.

But not yet.

Semyon saw the *Halcyon* coming. He saw it falling from the sky like a stone. He ran across Front Street, safely away from the fighting, picking his way over broken stones, and climbed up onto the battlements. The first flare crumbled when he tried to strike it alight. The second one—the *last* one—sputtered and spat, then finally caught, burning a purplish red. Semyon Beli waved it over his head. He bounced up and down on his toes.

And he watched as the ship fell and fell, nose down, tiny beneath her soft, crumpling gasbags, in a dive faster than anything he'd ever seen.

Ennis never stopped running. He saw Dagda kill Laryn Salvage and Siska Lem and Metro Voss and Deva Vestri, and he saw her hit Denver Ayuma so hard that he flew backward like a doll.

Callias Fusco's voice was in his head: *This has made her more dangerous than you can possibly imagine.* That was why they'd never tried to approach her, take her. This little girl. Dagda Prowst.

He ran and ran, and he was close when Jules Cael began to dance with Moric Shaw and when Milo hit Vitek Harsha with his full weight. And it was all a mess then, with boys and girls and a murderous four-hundred-year-old robot all rolling around and fighting and trying to kill each other in the ruin of his city. And Ennis Arghdal had had just about enough of it. He was going to put a stop to all this nonsense right now.

He was a grown-up, after all. And this was his job.

# CAPTAIN KLIM

**CAPTAIN KLIM** wasn't sure if they were going to make it.

The compressor was straining to fill the gasbags vented for the dive and the drag sail had been deployed to slow them and Lalia was yanking on the dragonfly winches with both hands, trying to crank out the ship's wings to bring up her nose. But he wasn't sure if they were going to make it.

"Up!" he shouted, as if anyone needed to be told that that was what needed to happen next. "Up *now*!"

For a fleeting instant, Captain Klim saw Semyon standing on the Front Street wall, waving a flare over his head. And Semyon saw the Captain, crouched in the ship's pulpit, screaming his head off.

And then the *Halcyon* plunged past the edge of the Flying City, falling down and down toward the waves below.

# THE WHITE BIRD

**MORIC SHAW HAD SEEN THE WHITE BIRD.** He saw it swooping from the sky, its wings tucked. And right where it had fallen behind the edge of the world, there was Milo Quick. He'd already knocked down Vit Harsha and was backing away from Azhar Biel, who had a chunk of stone in one hand and a knife in the other.

"Milo Quick!" Shaw screamed, his throat raw, tears in his eyes, his army breaking around him.

"No," said a voice very close to him. So close that he could hear it, even through the ringing in his ears. "You want Milo, you gotta go through me."

And Shaw whirled, his knife in his hand, to see Jules Cael standing and panting, his bloodied hands hanging by his sides.

Shaw didn't say a word. He just went right for Jules, the thin, sharp blade flashing as, above them, the *Lord of Storms* began to die in a flaming rain of debris.

He'd seen the white bird, so Shaw had no fear. The bird had brought him to Milo. Jules was just one more body in his way. Shaw lashed out and Jules danced back. He slashed again, and Jules darted forward to slam a hard fist into his ribs.

Shaw screamed in luminous fury and dropped his cast-wrapped arm to knock Jules away, then swung wildly, catching Jules in the shoulder with what was essentially a heavy plaster club. The pain popped like starbursts inside him, clearing his head. He went in again with the knife and opened a bright red line on Jules's leg.

He'd seen the white bird, so Shaw was going to follow it. He was going to kill Milo Quick. He was Total King Forever. He was going to command armies and own the Marche. It would be different now. He would walk the streets proudly, his boys at his back. Every block would be his. Every stone. And no one would ever hit him again or make him feel like he was less.

But first, this. Jules was limping now. Blood was darkening the leg of his pants. But he was smiling. Shaw couldn't understand it. Jules had a look like he was having the time of his life. Like this was all some kind of game.

"You're going to die!" Shaw shouted, and Jules actually moved in closer so he could say, "Might," and then leapt back, slapped one of Shaw's hands out of the way, and pulled in close again to say, "But I bet you go first," then slid a fast punch in over Shaw's knife hand that caught him in the cheek and stung more than it should have. Shaw could feel blood.

But when Jules danced back again, he stumbled, tripping on some bit of this or that, and Shaw didn't hesitate. He charged.

Dagda ran to Milo's side. He'd lost his knife—the little hook-bladed one he used for cutting pockets and slices of apple. He'd left it in Azhar Biel's leg. Now Milo had a rock. His face was a mask of dirt and grit. A monster. Dagda put her hand over Milo's hand, Milo's rock, and held it. "We have to run, Milo," she said. "We have to . . ."

Milo looked around. There were too many. Azhar was crying. He saw Jules fighting with Shaw. There were bodies everywhere. Milo backed toward the shattered battlements at the edge of the Flying City. Dagda stood with him.

Milo yelled, "Jules!" and Jules ignored him, circling back out of Shaw's reach.

"We could jump!" Dagda shouted over the thunder of cannons and the sky falling.

"*You* could," Milo yelled back. "I can't swim!"

And then he looked up and saw Ennis Arghdal standing atop the tumbled stones. The Sandman looked at him. He pointed. He said something Milo couldn't hear, but Milo was pretty sure it was his name.

And Milo shouted, "Sandman!" as loud as he could, which, on any day, is still a more frightening word to the runaway children of the Flying City than any other. Those advancing on Milo and Dagda stopped and looked. The wounded did the same.

"He never stops," Milo gasped. "The Sandman."

"We have to run," Dagda said. "Milo, we have to run. We have to hide."

But then, rising up behind them, came the *Halcyon*, with Captain Klim standing on the deck, his hat missing, holding on to the rigging with one hand, the other one outstretched.

"Boy!" he yelled. "It looks like you could really use a ride!"

Shaw saw the white bird rise behind Milo.

Jules saw Shaw's eyes flick away and he shoved him before dancing back again. He glanced around and saw Milo standing with his back to the edge of the Flying City, and Jules kept moving in Milo's direction. Circling always, just out of Shaw's reach.

Ennis saw the *Halcyon* come bobbing up over the edge of the Front Street wall with that captain standing on her deck. He was missing his hat and bleeding from his head, but he had one hand outstretched and he was reaching for Milo Quick.

Dagda turned and saw the airship. She saw Milo climbing

onto the wall behind them, ready to leap. She shouted at him, but he didn't listen.

Captain Klim saw the madman from yesterday. The one who'd hit him. The one the boy had called Sandman. He grinned, stood up straight—taking back his hand even as the boy was reaching for it, and putting it inside his jacket while he shouted for Lalia to hold the ship steady.

A piece of the *Lord of Storms* crashed down onto Front Street in a shower of fire and sparks. She was slipping sideways—the whole massive ship falling tail-first, clear of the city. Burning sail-cloth, bits of spar, gun carriages and cleats and bodies rained from her. On the water, the Armada's Eastern Fleet trained their cold guns on the city and made ready for the order.

Ennis shouted Milo's name and held out his hands and ran for him.

Shaw shouted Milo's name and, ignoring Jules, bolted right past him, running for Milo.

Jules turned as Shaw ran past and saw Milo making to climb aboard an airship that'd just *appeared* out of nowhere.

Dagda saw Milo reaching a hand out to the airship Captain and tried to grab him, to pull him down, to keep him here, with her, where they could be together and safe, but her hands closed on nothing.

Captain Klim drew the pistol out of his jacket, sighted carefully over his arm and shot Ennis Arghdal with both barrels as he ran. He cheered when he saw the man drop, and yelled, "Ha! I guess I *did* get a second chance, didn't I?"

Shaw saw the white bird. He saw Milo climbing onto its back. He saw that girl, Dagda, trying to grab Milo. He saw his own army pulling back, not sure what to run from—the Sandman or the gunshots or the airship or the fire or the girl. All that was left now was Milo. So Shaw ran and he screamed and he waved his hands at the bird, trying to get it to fly away, to leave Milo for him. Because Milo was his. He'd caused all of this. This was all his fault. All of it. And he had to pay.

Lalia shouted from the pilot's box, "Captain, we have to go! *Now!*"

Down below, on the sea, the Eastern Fleet had restarted their bombardment as the *Lord of Storms* flailed and died. They were firing as their targets became clear, and the blasts of the shells hitting the city were slowly walking closer and closer to Front Street.

Milo stood on the wall overlooking nothing but the sky and the sea.

Captain Klim holstered his pistol. He knelt on the deck, held to the rail with one hand and reached for the boy with the other.

Shaw scrambled over a broken piece of the wall lying now in the street. He lunged forward, stretching his plaster-wrapped hand out toward Milo, fingertips brushing the boy's flapping pant leg. He still held the bloodied knife in the other.

Jules caught Shaw by the ankle as he was reaching for Milo. He tried to drag him back, but Shaw was strong. He was nothing but muscle and hate. So Jules climbed straight across his back and slammed both balled hands down on Shaw's broken arm.

Shaw howled and kicked and flailed his knife around and felt it bite into Jules Cael. He felt blood, hot on his fingers.

Jules felt the knife, but it didn't hurt. He hit Shaw as hard as he could, anywhere he could. The spider ring on his hand was bloody. He'd pulled the legs of it up, so that his right hand wore eight metal spikes. He caught Shaw by the shoulder with one hand and dragged the spider across one of his eyes, blinding him.

Shaw panicked. His broken arm hung dead. He couldn't even lift it. There was blood in one of his eyes and he couldn't see. Behind him, just on the other side of the wall, the white bird was leaving. Flying away and taking Milo from him. He howled and lashed out with the knife, but Jules seemed not to feel it. Seemed not to care that he was dying, right here, right now.

And so he kicked at Jules and hauled himself up to his feet. His dead arm hung useless and his knife hand was slick with blood, but he could see Milo with his one good eye. He was climbing onto a ship. A man was dragging him aboard. The bird was gone. It'd flown.

Moric Shaw made a last desperate lunge.

And Jules Cael pushed him off the edge of the world.

# THE *HALCYON*

**CAPTAIN KLIM GRABBED MILO** by the wrist and hauled him aboard the *Halcyon*. "Hold tight to something, boy," he said. "We have to move."

And then he stood, waved his hand at someone—a big man Milo hadn't seen before—and walked away, shouting, "Lalia, get us out of here!"

"Wait!" Milo said. "My friends!"

"No time," said the Captain over his shoulder. "Unless we all want to die here."

Milo felt the ship moving, turning with the wind and the push of its motors. He was on his hands and knees, and he scratched his fingers at the deck, tried to cling to it, feeling like he was going to slip right off. He scrambled to the edge and looked back at the ruin of Front Street. He clung to the rail and shouted Jules's name.

There was a thud, and Milo looked and saw Dagda dragging herself aboard, her fingers dug into the wood, then clawing at the rail as she pulled herself over.

"Captain," said the big man. "Another one is aboard."

The Captain turned and saw Dagda fall clumsily onto the deck.

"Get them below, Vaclav," he said. "Both of them. Stow them and let's see how fast we really are."

"What about Semyon?"

And the Captain stopped. He turned to look out over the wreckage of Front Street falling slowly away beside them, the explosions of the naval shells walking in their direction.

"You want to split the reward four ways or five, Vaclav? I'm pretty sure Semyon died flagging us in."

"You saw?" asked Vaclav.

"Sure," said the Captain. He turned to Milo on the deck and said, "Boy, you are going to make us all rich if we survive the next ten minutes."

And then he walked away, moving easily on the shifting, swaying deck, bouncing up a short flight of steps and taking over the pilot's box from an angry-looking woman.

Dagda said nothing. She just crawled over to where Milo lay on the deck and held on to him. She felt afraid for both of them. And that was not something she was accustomed to feeling.

# SEMYON BELI

**SEMYON BELI** squatted on a broken piece of the Front Street wall and watched the *Halcyon* fly away. He looked and he saw Lalia stepping to the railing along the back of the ship. Her eyes searched the wreckage of Front Street until she spotted Semyon. Their eyes met. And just as the ship's big, fluttering dragonfly wings went taut and caught the breath of air blowing away from the Flying City, she smiled cruelly, waved with her fingers and mouthed the word *Goodbye* . . .

He watched for a moment longer. And then, before the artillery fire reached the place where he was crouching, waiting for a ship that was never coming back for him, he slipped back into the alleys and headed in the direction of the ship-breaking yards. All this time, all this risk, all this loss. Semyon Beli was not going to be cheated out of his share of the reward. And if his crew—his *friends*—thought they were rid of him so easily, then they didn't know Semyon Beli.

"Surviving," he said to himself as he picked his way through the fire and the ruin of the Flying City like he was taking a walk in the park. "That's how you win."

# JULES

**ON THE FRONT STREET WALL,** Jules had watched Milo dragged by the wrist aboard an airship. He saw Dagda stand there watching, hesitating. And he'd called to her. He'd yelled her name just once—"Mouse!"—and she'd looked over her shoulder at him, and then she'd jumped, straight from the wall to the side of the departing ship, twenty feet if it was an inch, caught the wood with her fingertips and clung there for a terrible moment like a spider before dragging herself aboard.

He never heard Milo call his name.

Jules panted and bled and watched the airship turn toward open sky. All around him, pieces of the *Lord of Storms* came raining down. Explosions rocked the stones of the city. And Jules kept thinking that the ship was going to come back. That Milo and Mouse wouldn't possibly leave without him.

But it didn't.

So Jules did the only thing he could think of to do.

He went home.

# AFTER THE END
# OF EVERYTHING

**FRONT STREET WAS EMPTY THEN.** Anyone from the Total King's army who'd lived had scattered into the burning streets. The dead lay where they'd fallen, not lonely and not forgotten, because they were only a few of the thousand new ghosts who would be haunting this place come noon, when the firing from the Armada would stop and troops from the Ministries would land on the streets of the Flying City to hunt for a mechanical girl who was no longer there.

In the middle of the street, though, there was a dusty bit of stone and a smear of blood to mark where Ennis Arghdal had fallen, shot down by Captain Rodion Klim from the deck of the airship *Halcyon*. What *wasn't* there was Ennis Arghdal's body.

Ennis Arghdal wasn't dead. Because even after the end of everything, he knew Milo Quick was still alive.

Which meant he still had a job to do.

✦

# THREE ENEMIES

✦

**IT TOOK JULES MOST OF THE DAY** to make his way home through the streets of the Flying City. He saw things that no boy should see and that no man would forget. And none of it is worth talking about now, except to say that it was terrible and that there wasn't a single moment when Jules Cael didn't feel like he was about to die.

But he had been born to this place. He knew a hundred secret ways between here and there. So Jules bound his wounds as best he could and covered his mouth and nose with a scrap of fabric patterned with faded ducks and bears that he found fluttering from a fence. And in that way he went through the havoc and ruination of that terrible day toward Fort Kick-Ass. And when he got there—to the wreck of the old ship now even more wrecked—he found the Sandman, Ennis Arghdal, sitting in the dark, bleeding and smoking a cigarette.

"Hello, Jules," he said. "Been waiting for you."

He'd taken off his ruined jacket and hung it off the back of the chair on which he sat. His white shirt he'd torn to pieces to make compresses and bandages to plug up the two holes in his left shoulder, one an inch above the other. On the table beside him was a bloody fork, a sharp knife, a mirror, a pair of clamps from Milo's tool bag, and a glass of pink water with two flattened lead slugs resting at the bottom. He'd found coffee somewhere and was drinking it. And he sat in nothing but his pants and a white undershirt stained red, skin waxy and slick with sweat.

"Ennis, he's gone," Jules said. "Milo's gone."

And the Sandman shook his head, took a crackling drag and blew jets of smoke from his nose like a dragon. "Hey, so I hear you're the Total King now. Forever. Of the Marche and everything in it."

"No," Jules said.

"Killed Shaw, didn't you? That's how these things work." And then the Sandman chuckled a little, inclined his head in the barest sketch of a bow. "Your Majesty."

And Jules looked at the Sandman, his face collapsing, whatever hardness was left in him giving way like a landslide. "He left me. Milo. And Dagda. They got on that ship. And they left me."

"I know," said Ennis, wincing as he crushed out his cigarette amid the mess on the table beside him. "But it wasn't his fault. That man—that *captain*—took him. And now we have to go rescue him."

"Oh, delightful!" said a voice from the doorway. "And I was beginning to wonder where I'd find my next adventure."

Jules turned and saw a man standing just inside the door—an old man with white hair and a mustache. He was singed here and there and had a bleeding wound on one hand that he'd wrapped in a checkered cloth.

"You . . ." said Ennis from his chair.

"Semyon Beli," said Semyon Beli. "Formerly of the . . . Well, I guess you'd say *pirate* ship *Halcyon*? Though that makes us sound somewhat more swashbuckle-y than we were, I admit."

"The ones who took Milo."

"Well, I am certainly not one of the crew who snatched up the boy, because I am here now and they are gone. But yes. *Formerly* associated with them. Absolutely."

"Jules," Ennis said. "Kill him. I'd do it myself, but I'm tired."

"Ah-ah-ah," said Semyon, waving a finger. "Tut, now. I need you to think, gentlemen. We have all had a difficult day. And yes, we could stand here making threats back and forth and arguing over who is to blame—"

"Blame?" said Ennis from his chair. "You and your captain—"

"Rodion Klim."

"And that woman—"

"Lalia Ivona Vicario." Semyon sneered. "A *nasty* piece of work."

"You kidnapped Milo Quick."

"The Captain would say 'rescued,' but now's not the time to quibble over semantics."

"A boy who has been under my protection for eight years."

"And such a good job you've done of it, too!"

Ennis growled from deep in his chest and lurched up out of the chair, grabbing the knife from beside him with surprising speed. He staggered a step, then two, meaning to kill Semyon Beli and throw him out one of the many convenient holes that'd been opened in Fort Kick-Ass by the naval bombardment.

But Jules stopped him. He stepped between the Sandman and the old man in the door, and he asked Semyon, "What did they do with him?"

"With the boy? They have him." Semyon blinked and smoothed down his mustache with one thumb. "And the girl, too. But by now, if the Captain is up to the tricks for which the Captain is rightly famous, he'll have decked the ship out in Armada flags and Armada pennants—fancy dress that I went to a great deal of trouble to steal, I might add—and be making for open sky as fast as he can." Semyon paused, then added with sudden seriousness, "And right now, that is *very* fast."

"Where are they going?"

And Semyon smiled. "Ah . . . Now that, I think—"

Ennis sighed. He'd already sunk back down into his chair. "Is this the part of the story where you tell us that only you know where they're going, and that if we want to find them, we'll have to keep you alive and take you with us?"

"This is *exactly* that part, my friend!"

"Well, skip to the end, then. Time's wasting."

"Certainly!" exclaimed Semyon. "So . . . Uh, well, I guess just that then."

"Just what?"

"Just that I know where they're going. And if you want to find them . . ." Semyon rolled one hand around. "Et cetera, et cetera. They left me behind, Sandman. Cut me out of our deal. And Semyon Beli will not—"

"Don't care. You going to show us where they're going?"

Semyon Beli straightened himself up and pulled at the curls of his mustache. "I am," he said. "For no man should be forced—"

"Good. Then the first thing we need to do is steal ourselves an airship. Should be plenty lying around. Let's go."

"Go?" asked Jules.

The Sandman looked at the boy. "Go," he said. "To rescue your friends. Were you not paying attention?"

And then he stood up again, lurching to his feet and standing there, swaying in the dusty dark and shot-hole light of the ruins of

Fort Kick-Ass, as pale as a ghost and just as angry. "One thing," he said, breathing heavily and holding on to the edge of the table for support. "Once we find a ship and steal it, I get to name it."

"Why?" asked Jules.

"Yes," said Semyon. "Why? I would think that such a momentous and important bit of business at the start of an adventure ought to be decided democratically."

"No," Ennis said. "I pick. Because"—he pointed at Jules—"I'm bigger than you." He pointed at Semyon. "And because I don't like you. I've been thinking about it for a long time." Finally, he pointed at himself. "I pick the name."

Then Ennis Arghdal walked out of Fort Kick-Ass and into the ruin of the Flying City to steal an airship, with Jules Cael and Semyon Beli following closely behind.

# ACKNOWLEDGMENTS

This book—like all books—has a long, strange history. And like all books (though *particularly* books made during these unusual times), it was far from a solo effort.

First, a high five and an exhausted thank-you to my agent and friend, David Dunton. This book only exists at all because of him. Conceived partly as a dare and partly as a bet, Hawaii Dave believed in this book before it was a book at all—when it was just ten different ideas sharing an overcoat and pretending to be tall. Every big swing we took was your idea first, D. And you connected with every single one.

Simple thanks to my editor, Julie Strauss-Gabel, will never be sufficient. Y'all reading this will never understand the mess this book could've been (*would've* been) without her. She saw things in all these words that I never did—plots and schemes, strange histories, birds where I swore there were no birds. There is no one on earth who cares about Milo, Jules, and Dagda the way she does. She is their secret champion, occasionally their conscience, absolutely the voice in my head when I'm playing at being the voice in theirs. One of these days when the world rights itself again, we'll have a drink and laugh about all this, Julie. Gin and tonics are on me.

Thanks to artist Ian McQue for somehow reaching into my brain and pulling out the cover for the book I always wanted to read when I was a kid. I don't know how he did it. Magic, I guess. A talent I'll never understand. He doesn't know this, but his first sketches came through at a moment when I'd lost a lot of faith in anyone ever actually reading this thing, and to see a world that had only ever existed in my head through someone else's eyes for the first time? That was a day I'll never forget. So thank you, Ian. The Flying City never looked better.

Thanks to the team at Dutton and everyone who touched this project along the way. Everything smooth and pretty about this book is thanks to them.

Thanks to Andrew and Liz for the virtual cocktail hours and support. You've always believed I was better at this than I do, Andrew. Here's hoping you're right.

To Maile for reading an early version, and for the picture of Philomena (I still have it on my desktop). To Conner and Jocelyn, Jack and Julian and Amelie for keeping my kids occupied and giving me the time I needed to make up stories. Someday, when you're all grown, you'll understand what a gift that was.

Speaking of my own kids, you guys are my amazing weirdos and more responsible for all this than you'll ever know. Parker, thank you for the ruthless criticism and the occasional smile. Maddox, thanks for reminding me how huge and bewildering and joyous the universe can be. Every strength of the children in this book lived in you two first. And the robots are mostly thanks to Mad.

Finally (and most importantly), thanks to my wife, Laura. You know what you did. You know what you fixed. You know what parts of you live in every line and on every page. Like Marion and Indy, you're my goddamn partner. Always have been. Always will be. And none of this would've been possible without you.

I'll take out the trash when I'm done with this chapter. Promise.